I0824048

Dollface

Also by Lindy Ryan

THE BLESS YOUR HEART SERIES

Bless Your Heart

Another Fine Mess

A NOVEL

LINDY RYAN

MINOTAUR BOOKS
NEW YORK

This is a work of fiction. All of the names, characters, organizations, places, and events portrayed in this work are either products of the author's imagination or used fictitiously.

First published in the United States by Minotaur Books, an imprint of St. Martin's Publishing Group

EU Representative: Macmillan Publishers Ireland Ltd, 1st Floor, The Liffey Trust Centre, 117–126 Sheriff Street Upper, Dublin 1, D01 YC43

Printed in the United States of America. For information, address St. Martin's Publishing Group, 120 Broadway, New York, NY 10271.

www.minotaurbooks.com

Designed by Meryl Sussman Levavi

Library of Congress Cataloging-in-Publication Data

Names: Ryan, Lindy author
Title: Dollface : a novel / Lindy Ryan.
Description: First edition. | New York : Minotaur Books, 2026.
Identifiers: LCCN 2025041033 | ISBN 9781250888914 hardcover |
ISBN 9781250888921 ebook
Subjects: LCGFT: Horror fiction | Humorous fiction | Novels | Fiction
Classification: LCC PS3618.Y3356 D65 2026
LC record available at https://lccn.loc.gov/2025041033

First Edition: 2026

10 9 8 7 6 5 4 3 2 1

For M.

Dollface

CHAPTER ZERO

SUMMER 1998

My little sister collides with the open doorway of the master bedroom, skidding to a halt at the foot of the bed in a gust of chlorine and sunscreen and girl sweat. Remnants of last night's homemade makeover from our slumber party for two still cling to the round curves of Kitty's face—mascara smudged in purple-black bruises around her eyes, lip-liner residue crusted in damp red grit along the edges of her mouth. Hours of late-night Blockbuster New Releases and Girl Scout Thin Mints have thinned the stain on my little sister's lips from Fairuza Balk red to Alicia Silverstone pink, but even the chemically treated water from our backyard pool isn't strong enough to wash the color away completely.

The air-conditioning clicks on, and Kitty's teeth chatter when the blast of too-high cold cuts through her black one-piece. She hugs her arms across her chest, eclipsing pinprick nipples that stab out against the faded white and yellow daisies on the hand-me-down swimsuit. Dolphins coil around my sister's legs in sun-bleached shades of neon pink, blue, yellow. Longleaf-pine needles stick to her wet forearm.

She didn't bother to clean the pool before jumping in.

Adrift on my back in the center of the waterbed, I wait for Mom to say something maternal—*Kitty, go dry off*, or *Katherine, you're tracking pool water into the house.* But seated on the floor of the walk-in closet on the other side of the bedroom, her uncombed hair a wasp's nest around her as she studies her reflection in a cosmetic compact mirror, Mom doesn't say anything. She doesn't even look up.

"You're dripping all over the carpet," I tell my sister.

Breathless, Kitty's voice comes out shrill enough to shatter the tiny mirrors in our mother's compacts, send them glittering onto the closet floor. "Norman is dead!" She shivers again, and her wet feet stamp damp splotches on the carpet when she tightens the towel around her legs.

"Jill, come see, in the pool," Kitty says. "Norman is dead."

Water drips from the ends of my sister's hair, trickles onto her cheeks, and leaks down her chin. Even when they're plastered against her forehead, you can tell Kitty's bangs are crooked, chopped into erratic points when she'd used the kitchen scissors to barber free a stray splat of bubble gum, then snipped short the hair around her forehead so she could look like Drew Barrymore or Claire Danes. It might have worked, except Drew and Claire are both blond and skinny, and Kitty brunette and still growing out of her baby fat.

"You're lying." I use my Big Sister Voice. Norman is fine. Why wouldn't he be fine?

Kitty rolls her eyes as she pulls the towel tight over her chest. "Why would I lie about your stupid bird?"

"Because you lie about everything."

My sister staggers backward. Her lower lip trembles. Kitty's stunned by my cruelty. So am I.

We wait for Mom to intervene. *Girls, be nice,* she should say. *Jilly Bean, be nice to your sister,* or *Kitty Kat, don't antagonize Jill about her pet.* But other than the rain of Kitty's pool water onto the master-bedroom carpet, the slosh of the waterbed beneath me, the stifled, violent drumbeats of music somewhere beyond the patio doors: nothing.

I flop my head onto its side, so I face the walk-in closet where my mother hunches over a ring of pink plastic squares, each open to reveal colorful palettes of blushers and eye shadows. Capped pink lipstick tubes lay scattered around bare toes tipped in chipped nail polish as Mom uses a greasy white sponge to pat foundation across her cheeks, over her forehead, down the bridge of her nose. When she's finished, my mother's face glows too white against the crepey tan of her neck. She sets down the sponge without blending the foundation line at her chin, then reaches for a pink square and drags two fingers across a circle of blue.

Mom rubs oceans around each eye, her fingertips smudging bruisy blue on the stubby pink lipstick cylinder clenched in her first. Then, she pops the cap, twists out the stick, and traces red wax over her mouth from muscle memory: two quick dabs on the cupid's bow of the upper lip, a thick smear along the bottom.

She looks up and stares blankly in my direction. Then she rolls her lips together to spread the color even.

Again.

Again.

Color stains the skin around my mother's mouth. Her entire jaw is bleeding.

Mirror glass glints from the carpet as Mom trades one lipstick for another. She uses the waxy stick to scratch short dashes around her ankles, across her throat, up her arms, leaving behind lines of red thread that stitch my mother's extremities to the rest of her body. She presses her wrists together, spreading red over her skin. Her ocean eyes roll up to lock onto mine as she bends her head and drags a wet tongue up the seam on one forearm.

"Did you hear me?" Kitty's voice cuts me from the foot of the bed.

Mom's head lifts to reveal a liquid red streak down the center of her fat pink tongue.

"Kitty, seriously," I say as I look away. "Stop."

My sister vibrates at my feet. "I am *serious*! Norman is floating in the pool, I swear." Kitty's whine is helium and her face flushes. "Face down, one glassy little eye staring at me. It's creepy—like in *Psycho*."

"That's a shower, not a pool." The famous scene is even more harrowing in the book than it is in the movie, but this I don't tell my sister. In the book, Norman Bates doesn't stab Marion Crane to death; he decapitates her. "And Norman isn't the victim, he's the bad guy. So it's not like the movie at all."

Last Halloween, after Kitty went to bed, Mom and I stayed up late to watch the old Hitchcock film *The Birds*. Then we burned through my trick-or-treat candy, trading Almond Joys for Milk Duds in a double feature with *Psycho*. The next day I offered to babysit Kitty when Mom went to the grocery store, and we watched the movie again. My sister sat as upright as a headstone, silent and unblinking, when Norman and Marion debated sending his mother to the madhouse. "We all go a little mad sometimes," he'd said, and soon after that, Mom stopped talking, and everything changed.

When the cockatiel arrived on Christmas morning, the first name I thought of was Norman's. Now, when Kitty shivers, I think maybe it's not because she's cold.

Her next stomp sprays me with either pool water or spittle. "*Jill*, come see. Maybe he's still alive."

I fix my eyes on the underside of the popcorn ceiling. I don't want to look at my mother, the red lines beading on her skin. I don't want to look at my sister. I don't want to think about my cockatiel, or Marion Crane.

"Go away, Kitty."

"What is your problem?" My sister's shriek is lightning. "Your stupid bird is dead in our pool!"

I give the mattress another jerk then lie stiff, arching my back as the waterbed rises and falls beneath me. Kitty growls, then slinks away. When the glass door to the patio slides open, faraway guitar riffs spirit me downstream. When the door slides closed, the room falls back to silence, punctuated by the sound of my mother's paint-chipped fingernails tapping on shiny pink plastic compacts.

"Mom?" I direct the word to the ceiling, the single syllable heavy with my entire heart.

The waterbed waves go flat, and I twist to look at my mother, stitched together on the closet carpet. The tip of red wax slips between her lips. Her white teeth bite down. Red bubbles form in the corners of her mouth, then begin to run down her chin.

I climb off the bed, my bare feet following Kitty's cool footprints down the hallway, through the sliding doors that lead to our patio and the pool. Guitar and drums blend with male falsetto as music floats across the backyard from the boom box she's lugged outside from our shared bedroom.

My eyes slide to Norman's tall, wrought-iron birdcage.

It's empty.

Frost prickles through my chest despite the intense summer heat. The bird's perches are there, his toys and millet, but the yellow-face cockatiel is gone. The cage door is propped open with a clothespin bleached white by the constant summer sun. Before she'd gone into the master-bedroom closet, Mom had stood on the patio and stared into the surface of the pine-needle-strewn pool.

I drag my eyes to the water.

Wings splayed out on either side of his body, Norman floats face down. His small form lists lifelessly in the deep end of our pool, gray feathers and curly yellow crest waterlogged and dull in the filthy chlorinated soup. Longleaf-pine needles, like the ones slicked to Kitty's forearm, drift around him. A funeral pyre, unburned.

My feet sink into the water as I sit at the edge of the pool. Liquid laps over the tile, as warm as what slips from the tip of my cheeks and leaves tiny wet dots on my T-shirt. I hadn't realized that I'm crying.

Kitty's feet patter across the concrete and her damp thigh settles against mine. Her feet slide into the water, too, smaller than my own but just as blue.

"I'm sorry about Norman," she whispers, then takes a deep breath. "Is Mom going to be okay?"

"No."

Kitty's hand clenches in mine. "Who is going to take care of us?"

"I'll take care of you," I promise my sister. "And you'll take care of me."

"Always?"

"Always."

I hold her while the man in the boom box sings about karma and police and other things Kitty isn't old enough to understand and I pretend that I am. When the song ends, I push myself to my feet and fetch the leaf skimmer to spoon Norman from the pool. Water drips from his wings, his life turned to liquid that escapes through my fingers when I lift him from the net. Kitty hands over her dolphin towel and I fold the cockatiel's body inside the damp cloth, careful to wrap him without wringing him.

Kitty is already in the pool before I get back inside the house.

The boom box clicks to a new track as I slide the patio doors closed behind me.

The air feels different inside now. Norman's bundle sucks heat from my chest as my sister's damp footprints turn cold under my feet. Muffled bass notes from the backyard thrum beneath my skin as I retrace my steps down the hallway.

I walk until the carpet turns dry, then wet again. Cold, then warm, when my bare feet squelch into the fibers of the master-bedroom carpet.

The waterbed is still. The closet, silent.

Pine-scented water drips between my fingers as Norman's fragile bones snap under my grip.

Hunched over a glittering red pool in her bedroom closet, Mom's wasp's nest hair is a shroud over her shoulders. Broken free from the shiny plastic compacts, cosmetic mirrors lie in shards around her, their surfaces stained red like the discarded pink lipstick tubes at her feet. Crimson ribbons run from the dashes on her arms, her ankles, her neck.

My mother's stitches cut open, her entire body bleeds.

CHAPTER ONE

NOW

Someone once said that a mirror is a girl's best friend.

Someone lied.

Fourteen wrinkles. Sixteen, if I count the creases where my dimples used to be, the cute, pinprick divots now reduced to thin cracks running in parallel lines on either side of my mouth. I count them, of course, because what fun would criticizing my flaws be if I didn't throw in some math, too?

My stomach clenches. Even when I pick myself apart, I can't help but go the extra mile. Two birds, one stone—or whatever that saying is. My darling husband glares at me every time I use it. It's been nearly twenty years since Rob and I met while interning at PETA, but we still do our best to avoid meat, dairy, and cruel animal idioms.

Maybe *that's* the problem. The caverns under my eyes, the dark half-moons, persist whether I sleep four hours or eight. Maybe I need more collagen in my diet.

A voice buzzes against my ear as the phone grows warm in my hand. I set it on the soapstone countertop and push in AirPods. Half a second later, Bluetooth resumes. "And then somewhere in the northern Mojave," the voice in my ears says, "we came across these *incredible* hot springs. I just stripped down naked and—"

My body pressed against the edge of the vanity, my breath fogs the mirror as I lean in to scrutinize my former dimples under the bathroom microscope. Bathrooms: a nicer way of saying private, personal hells. Who needs fire and brimstone when you have recessed fluorescents and a full-length mirror? This might be the master bathroom, but we both know who is in charge.

"You should have seen it," her voice goes on, "an oasis in the middle of the desert. It was the perfect setting for inspiration—like, it's perfectly safe and beautiful, but could turn spooky in a heartbeat. That's the best kind of scary, right? Like, when it's *not* supposed to be?"

The voice becomes tinnitus as I wipe my breath-fog away.

It's not just the dimples.

My lips aren't totally recognizable anymore either. These, too, have begun to wilt, the slabs pale and ringed with withered edges, like peach skin sucking itself dry around uneaten fruit. My nose seems steeper. Eyelashes, thinner. My skin appears ashen under the bright lights, and a concerning amount of what I hope is not jowl trims the underside of my jaw. A fold runs diagonally down the length of my cheek from where flesh pressed against bedsheets all night.

Heeere's Johnny! My reflection flinches when Jack Torrance's maniacal grin shines back at me in the bathroom mirror. Forget Shelley Duvall. In the oversize horror-movie T-shirt and sleep-swept inkblot hair, I look like the Bride of freakin' Frankenstein.

A yawn slips out and my reflection grimaces at the quick peek of double chin. I *feel* like the Bride of freakin' Frankenstein.

I want to scream with her, rage against this monstrous shell I find myself looking out of. But if I do, Tanner will wake and come running, Lugosi hot on his heels. The retriever I wouldn't mind, but the few moments of quiet I get in the morning before my eight-year-old erupts from his bed?

Those are precious.

"And then we rappelled down this limestone—" The words pinch off when the bud ejects itself from my ear. I push it back and screw it against the side of my face like a bolt on a monster's neck. I miss the rest of her sentence, but that's okay.

Downstairs, among a sea of moving boxes I've yet to unpack, Tanner's third-grade school supplies lurk in disorganized piles—colored folders with pockets (no brads), No. 2 pencils (pre-sharpened), glossy yellow card-stock packages with rainbows of crayons, colored pencils, and markers (washable *and* nontoxic). Spirals (wide ruled). Glue sticks (four). I managed to find my laptop charger and a box of hardcovers I'm supposed to sign for some bookstore in the Midwest, but I still haven't unearthed the box that contains my son's lucky green vinyl lunch box with the broken zipper. Stacks of New Student paperwork await completion on the kitchen countertop, and our dog smells like road trip.

I think my husband got misplaced in the move.

I haven't touched my manuscript in over a week.

The details change but the headache doesn't. We've done this exact same thing twice in the past ten years. Doesn't matter that Rob's command in the Coast Guard is Department of Homeland Security and not Defense, there'll be no permanent home base for this military family. It gets harder, not easier, the effort of uprooting and reestablishing our household tangled with both the constant ache in my upper back and the road map winding across my forehead.

And that's probably why I became an author. A girl needs more than her child and partner. Books make it easier not to feel lonely, even if all your closest girlfriends are fictional.

I close my eyes and scream on the inside, long and hard and raspy just like the poor Bride. Then I let out a deep sigh and blink my eyes open.

So, sixteen wrinkles then. Sixteen seams weave across my face, like if I shake too hard, my skin might split apart. One thick, wet *schlorp* and all my stuffing spills out.

Bride of Frankenstein, I can handle, just please, *please,* don't let me turn into my mother.

"Hello? Earth to Jill!" Kitty shrieks in my ear so loud the AirPods rattle.

My sister's voice shifts into the infuriatingly adorable pitch she's used since birth. "The call is coming from inside the house," she purrs.

"You gotta get some new material, Kitty Kat." I can feel my sister's grin on the other end of my earbuds as I pull my house robe over Jack Torrance's face. It's too warm for the fluffy heart-print microfleece, but too public for the shirt alone. I leave the robe. Tanner shouldn't see his mommy in a shirt short enough he could make out her religion, and Lugosi's snout is on overdrive, investigating every nook and cranny of his new territory. It's best not to take risks.

"But you're *not* listening, Jilly Bean," Kitty says. "I can tell."

My insides curl. "I'm listening."

I am, in fact, not listening. I'm certainly *trying* to listen. There's just only so many times one can listen to her little sister ramble on about her glamorous, carefree social media influencer life while she—*I*—am ninety degrees over the counter in a bathroom crammed with boxes I'm too tired to unpack, watching my face mutate into someone else's in the mirror. "You're freshly rehabilitated," I say, "after spending half the summer running feral—"

"You mean living the van life."

"From somewhere in California to somewhere else in California," I go on, recalling the visual documentary on my sister's social media feed—her naked shoulders above a steaming hot spring, glamping in the converted space of her rented Sprinter, hair and makeup picture-perfect in every shot. "During the course of which you consumed approximately seven hundred thousand calories worth of Snickers and took three million nature selfies and didn't break a single nail."

But wait, there's more.

"And something about a guy named Leith—Keith?" My forehead puckers. My sister's flavor of the month is less country singer, more *my parents were hippies*. "Leaf!"

"That is correct." Kitty doesn't tell me which name I got right. "But you still weren't listening."

That's because my face is melting off. I shake my head and rake my fingers through my hair in a half-hearted attempt to comb out the tangles. Angry frizz hisses into the air. New Jersey humidity is not like Texas humidity.

This time when my exhale fogs the mirror, I leave it.

"I can't believe you're in New York." Kitty is five years, three months, and six days younger than me, but her sigh is the kind of bitter you have to grow into. She's in Portland—Oregon, not Maine.

"New Jersey," I remind her. Rob's new duty station is in New York, but we're in a suburb on the other side of the Hudson River.

"Why'd you have to move, like, a million miles away?" Her question is followed by a beat of quiet, but then my sister laughs and the moment's passed. Kitty can't be anything other than Kitty for long, even at the crack of dawn on her side of the country. "New York is somewhere *I* would go," she teases. "Not you."

"New Jersey," I say, again. We're here because when Rob's transfer list came out in January, it was already summer in hot, horrible Houston. He said, *Where you wanna go, babe: New York or Florida?* and—

Still combing, my fingers hit a snag. I work out a knot, then shield my eyes with one hand before reviving my limp hair with half a can of dry shampoo. Eight months ago, sweating out New Year's, New York had seemed less miserable than Florida.

New Jersey. Now I'm correcting myself.

"Florida would have been worse," I tell my sister for the zillionth time. "From your doorstep to mine is about a hundred miles closer here than if we'd gone to St. Petersburg."

She snarls. "It's a whole extra time zone away, Jillian."

"So is Florida, Katherine. East Coast runs all the way down."

We're both on edge—me from the cross-country move, her from

the recent return to captivity—but this is the farthest apart we've ever been. *Too far,* as Kitty whined when I told her about the move. A literal line crossed. Then, my sister pouted south to lick her wounds for the camera, and I hauled my family East.

I wrestle my hair into a high bun, then twist on the faucet, dampen a washcloth with cool water, and press life back into my face. Each inhale sucks the cloth tight against my flesh. Each exhale lifts it free. I shed a layer of skin every time I breathe.

"Nothing's changed," I remind Kitty. "We still have our chats every morning, just like always."

The line stays quiet.

I don't want to fight with my sister.

"So, how do you like your new house?" she asks, finally. "Tell me everything."

The wet washcloth makes a *thunk* when I drop it in the sink. "The house is beautiful, just like in the pictures, but it's so beige and *so* big. I'm never going to be able to keep it clean." Maybe we should have leased. "There's two ovens for some reason, and everything is creaky."

"Every good horror story starts with a creepy house," Kitty says, helpfully. "*Psycho, Amityville, The Shining . . .*"

"*Creaky,* not *creepy*—and *The Shining* is set in a hotel, not a house." I push away from the vanity, catch another glimpse of Jack Torrance's lunatic sneer peeking out from beneath my robe, and a certain hotel boiler comes to mind. "Though this house and the Overlook *do* both have creepy heating appliances in their basements."

"You have a *furnace*?" Kitty's voice deepens for emphasis, but I can hear her light up on the other end of the line. "Like, one of those big, octopus-armed things in *Home Alone*?"

Worse. "At least the McCallisters' gravity furnace had a cute smile." The shiny metal contraption in my basement is long and narrow, with two large panels stacked atop each other, like one of those metal boxes that magicians use to pretend to saw pretty women in half, flipped upright on its end. "This one looks like it belongs in a seventies sci-fi film."

"Send me a picture," she demands.

"Not a chance."

Kitty laughs. "My big, bad horror-writer sister, scared of a household heating device."

"I prefer *author.*" My editor always says it's best to be precise. "And I'm not scared *of* the furnace, I'm scared *for* the furnace. Because I am definitely going to do some damage the first time I have to go down there and turn it on."

This is a lie. I will not be going anywhere near the furnace.

"Okay, then, speaking of scary science fiction," Kitty says, moving on, "where'd you put your new laboratory, Mary Shelley?"

I want to tell my sister the difference between Mary Shelley's experiment and James Whale's, but instead I pluck my phone from the bathroom countertop, drop it into my robe pocket, and flip off the lights to scour the bedroom floor for slippers. Even on carpet I can still feel the cool chill of tile against my soles. In my extremely limited experience thus far, new-build colonials are just as drafty as their predecessors, but at least they reserve the cool naming conventions associated with the architecture: powder rooms, parlors, foyers.

"I have commandeered the conservatory on the first floor," I tell her.

Kitty snorts. "You bought the whole house for those French doors, huh?"

The little windowed room off the main floor won me over the first time I'd seen the house on the real estate website, before I ever shared the link with my sister. My Realtor had been so pleased to have an easy client. Or maybe she'd just been eager to get rid of the buyer who'd shown up in skull-print tights.

The slippers are nowhere to be seen, so I pull on a discarded pair of my husband's grungy socks and fill my sister in on the rest of the floor plan as I shuffle toward the bedroom doors. "Tanner's got his own suite and playroom upstairs, and Rob's setting up his drum kit in the basement."

"Throb's playing drums in the scary basement? *That's* creepy."

Aside from the furnace, it's not so bad—or it won't be, once he soundproofs the space directly below my new office. "Anyway," I say to get back to my sister's original question, "I'm going to enjoy looking out through all those dark glass panes while I write, but right now it's just a room full of boxes giving me dirty looks every time I walk by."

Kitty clears her throat, and her voice climbs to a Disney-princess lilt. "How *is* the new book coming along?"

I'm about to tell her that it's not *coming along*. In fact, much to my editor's mounting frustration, my poor manuscript hasn't moved beyond the title page, much less gone anywhere, what with the move and getting Tanner registered at his new school and sorting out the timelines of Rob's ridiculously long commute from our New Jersey suburb to his Staten Island office—and did I tell her Lugosi needs to go on a special diet?—when a noise sounds from somewhere else in the house.

I unscrew one AirPod in time to hear the last few notes of the Westminster Chimes.

"Is that the doorbell?" my sister's voice asks in one ear.

I shield myself behind the bedroom's double doors and attempt to peer through the crack. Downstairs, on the other side of the etched-glass panes that outline the front door, moves a woman's shape. She's holding a package with a tall, arched handle. The morning sun glints off shrink-wrap.

Not a package, then. A gift basket.

"Oh, sweet Tim Curry." I cup my hand over my mouth and whisper-yell into the earbud's mic, "I think there's a neighbor at my front door."

"I thought no one in New York knew their neighbors?"

"New Jersey." My sister is a riot.

The doorbell rings again, and the woman shifts in front of the windowpane, visoring one hand over her eyes as she leans forward to peer through the glass. Suddenly I'm very aware of my husband's socks on my feet, the toe poking through the hole. My lack of pants.

"I gotta go." I'm already fishing in my house-robe pocket for the phone to end the call. "I've been spotted."

"'Little pig, little pig, let me in!" Kitty mewls, then breaks into a laugh. "I gotta run anyway. Leaf is meeting me for sunrise caprine vinyasa, and I still need to do my morning skin-care routine before I drink my kombucha."

The trench between my eyebrows deepens. "Literally nothing you just said made sense."

Kitty grunts like she's already explained the finer points of baby-goat yoga. "You'd know if you'd been listening."

I can't decide what's worse: my younger sister's morning plans or the stranger standing on my porch. "Gross."

"Oh, go make some new friends, Jilly Bean," my sister titters. "Just don't invite any crazy, knife-wielding lunatics into your house," she adds, *shing-shing-shinging* in my ear as, downstairs, my new neighbor taps her fingernail on the front-door glass.

CHAPTER TWO

The woman standing on the other side of my open front door wears a shy smile and a crunchy mom-perm that contrasts with the blaring crimson of her bedazzled Brunswick PTA shirt. The top might once have been standard school-spirit attire, but the sequins glued around its letters are as homemade as the gift basket clutched in her arms. She is pretty and plump, and her cheeks remind me of powdered doughnuts. She wears Keds.

I did not know they still made Keds.

"Good morning!" The woman beams over her basket, and the wattage of these two words alone could illuminate half of the Garden State.

Nervous goose bumps prickle along my calves. Why hadn't I put on pants, any pants—anything more substantial than the ridiculous heart-print robe pulled tight from my chest to my calves? Kubrick probably hadn't orchestrated the shot of Jack Nicholson chopping through Shelley Duvall's bathroom door just so future fans of the film could welcome guests into their homes while Winnie-the-Poohing *The Shining* T-shirts. Doubtful this is the scare he was going for.

And yet, here we are.

"Good morning." I wince as my voice booms up the high foyer ceiling to the second story and knocks on Tanner's bedroom door.

Please let the kid stay asleep until I get a cup of coffee down. I'm not ashamed to admit that I'm a better mom when caffeinated.

"I'm sorry to drop by so early," the woman on the porch says, her mist-green eyes too busy smiling to linger on my messy bun, holey sock, lack of pants. "But I was on my way out and I saw your car and I couldn't bear the thought of you waking up without a proper welcome to the neighborhood!"

What is this, Stepford? I have no idea how to respond.

"Oh" is all I manage.

Still smiling, the woman's eyes land on mine. The sparkly red headband tucked behind her teased bangs matches the oversize costume earrings studded into her earlobes. "I'm Darla Lashett. I live right down there—"

She points well-trimmed, natural fingernails tipped in ballet-slipper pink down the street, past the unfamiliar gleaming purple minivan parked behind my road-worn Honda in my driveway, toward the perfectly manicured lawn with the lacquered BRUNSWICK ELEMENTARY sign staked in the front yard. A blooming pot of leafy pansies anchors the sign at the end of a circular drive with a beige town car. "Number Thirty-Four," she says.

Behind the shrink-wrap cloud, the edges of her smile dip when I tell her I'm at Number Twenty-Seven.

"I mean, I'm Jill. Jill Marshall."

Darla's smile springs back up.

Meeting my new neighbor wasn't at the top of my to-do list this morning, but I would have preferred to make a better first impression. "I'm sorry, I'm in desperate need of a cup of coffee. It's nice to meet you, Marla."

"Darla," she says, again.

"I'm so sorry." I *really* need that cup of coffee. "It's nice to meet you, *Darla*."

"Don't worry, dear." Darla waves away my apology with the hand she used to identify her house down the street. "I get it." The gems in her ears are fake, but the rock on her ring finger is a supernova when she holds her hand against her cheek. "I'm a total scatterbrain sometimes," she whispers, like it's a secret.

It's impossible not to return the woman's smile, even if she did call me *dear.* My sweet new neighbor is coiffed and hand delivering welcome baskets at nine o'clock on a Tuesday morning. There is exactly zero chance that Darla Lashett is ever scatterbrained. She's just going out of her way to make me feel seen and unjudged, and it's working. For example, I've almost forgotten I'm not wearing pants.

Darla shifts and I realize she's passing me the basket.

"I wanted to bring you all a little something to help you get settled in," she says as our arms interlock under the wicker. Her candy-sweet perfume wafts off her in aromatic waves of brown sugar and pear as she points to various items in the basket cradled between us. "Takeout menus to a few of my favorite local restaurants—most deliver. A notepad and pen for anything you need to jot down. Some of my homemade snickerdoodle cookies."

Darla relinquishes the basket and her eyes crinkle like shrink-wrap. "Just a few goodies to help you all feel at home."

The basket is heavier than I expect when she pulls away. There's a small LEGO set and a men's grooming kit. Basic household necessities (dish soap, laundry detergent, toothpaste) crowd around a cellophane bag of artisanal dog treats. A bar of posh hotel soap props up a king-size Hershey's bar, and a bottle of rosé winks at me from the back. Between all this, bulbous sample-size cosmetics give the bounty Easter-basket vibes.

"You'll *love* the samples," Darla promises, when she catches me staring at the pink-and-teal pods of lip balm, face cream, eye shadow. "They're life-changing."

Lots of women swear by their beauty products, but ever since my mother's death, I don't wear makeup if I can help it. I'm older now than Mom was when she took her life that summer, surrounded by compacts in her walk-in closet, and yet watching age melt my face in the bathroom mirror is still slightly preferable to seeing it painted on.

The frilly Fabergé cosmetics look like the sort of products streaming over my sister's social media posts, though, so if I ever summon the will to pack another box, I'll mail the samples to Oregon. Kitty will like them. She'd like Darla, too, with their shared love of serums and beauty potions, just like Mom.

"When I saw the Realtor put up the SOLD sign, I popped right over and asked Patti all about my new neighbors." Darla's smile falters. "I hope it's not too much."

Patricia Townsend and I only corresponded through mutually civil messages relayed through our mutually civil Realtors, but of course she would have given the scoop on the family from Houston who'd bought her house, with the young son and dog who needed a fenced-in yard, to her neighbor.

Darla increases the wattage of her smile until the shine off her teeth matches the earrings flashing on either side of her cheeks, and I'm taking way too long to say anything.

"It's incredibly thoughtful," I say too late, about the welcome basket. "Thank you."

"Patti told me you and your husband have a son in elementary school and a . . ." Darla's fists clench and she shakes cannonballs over her chest. It's more matronly than it should be, coming from a woman maybe five years my senior. "A golden retriever?"

"Tanner and Lugosi." If I told the Realtor what breed of dog I have, I don't remember, but the retriever *is* the only thing aside from book promos on my social media feed, so it's not exactly classified information. My kid's face stays off-line for privacy, but even internet trolls have nothing ugly to say about an adorable 115-pound floof. "He's big—but he's sweet," I add, because sometimes people get nervous about large dogs. "Goofy goldies, you know."

We shuffle our feet in the open front doorway, Darla a step below me on the porch while I lord her offering over her. "I should set this down," I say, though it feels ungrateful to just take the basket and run. "Would you like to come in for a cup of coffee?"

"Oh, I've only got a minute." Darla pretends to hesitate as she nods toward her minivan, but her shifting Keds give her away. "But I'd love a cup of coffee, if you're sure you're up for company?"

I continue to regret my lack of pants, but what's a little glimpse of thigh between girlfriends? "I am if you are."

Jenga piles of cardboard boxes crowd the entry as Darla steps inside, and inspiration strikes as I lead the way. "Maybe you can give me some ideas on how to organize my kitchen?" My new neighbor probably knows the place better than I do. "I always wanted more counter space, but now I don't know where to put the Keurig."

All that empty counter space makes for an excellent spot to put the gift basket, though, which is exactly where I set it once we're both in the kitchen.

An opened box marked KITCHEN/COFFEEPOT waits on the granite-topped island in the room's center, the machine still packed snug inside. Darla points to a thin strip of counter between sink and cabinet. "Patti kept her pot right there," she says.

Right there works. Once the pot's in Patti's spot, I fill its tank with tap water, plug it in, and switch it on. The first pair of mugs I unwrap are not polite company mugs: one is black with Michael Myers's knife-wielding silhouette, the other white and bearing the line I RUN ON CAFFEINE AND HORROR MOVIES. The first *O* in *horror* is shaped like a skull. Maybe the mugs are too weird, but it'd look weirder to keep fishing for more, so I rinse them and root out a couple of stray K-Cups from the box, then pop one into the Keurig.

Darla wedges herself in a corner as I place the black mug—the less weird of the two, I think—under the coffee spigot and press the brew button.

"So, Patti said you're an author?"

"I am, yeah." I talk into the fridge, retrieving the half-and-half while the machine gurgles proof of life. "I only have cream, hope that's okay."

"That's perfect. I like my coffee to bite."

I set the filled mug on the counter for her and scold myself for finding this surprising. My sweet new neighbor just *looks* sweet—the eighties halo perm, the acid-washed mom jeans, the heavy-handed application of powdered eye shadow. The Keds. I'd peg her for a caramel macchiato girl any day, and yet, of all people, I should know better than to judge a book by its cover. Besides, I can't remember the last time I had a visitor in my kitchen. Other than my sister, the Marshalls don't get a lot of company.

It's kinda nice, weird mug worries aside.

Darla does a double take at Michael Myers as she sips, the stone on her wedding finger glittering light off the slasher silhouette. Those mist-green eyes of hers flit across the kitchen to land on Jack Torrance's face, peeking out from behind the folds of my heart-print robe.

"What kind of books do you write?" she asks.

Unease crawls up my throat. As sweet as my new neighbor seems, past experience has taught me that most suburban women don't get too friendly with us spooky types. There's a lot more to the genre than chain saws and gore, but that doesn't make it any easier to make friends—not when other women blame you for putting monsters under their children's beds.

"I write horror," I tell her, owning up while I brew a K-Cup for myself. "Hence the mugs."

And with perfect timing, a door peels open somewhere above, the rotation of its hinges faint but shrill, then followed by slow, stumbly footsteps. A low, rolling moan echoes down from the stairway balcony. It appears Tanner and Lugosi have arisen from their slumber.

Darla smirks behind her coffee mug. "Explains the T-shirt." She sets her mug on the counter while I fidget with my robe. "I don't get a lot of reading time these days, but I *love* horror movies—the scarier, the better."

"What's your favorite?" I dump two glugs of half-and-half in my coffee while I listen to the oncoming approach of boy and dog, wiggle my toe through the open hole of Rob's sock, and try not to let Darla see this is a test. Of the small percentage of other moms I've met around my age who claim to love horror, when pressed on their favorites most default to *The Craft* or *Practical Magic.* Both are great witchy movies, but neither is truly horror, strictly speaking.

"That's a hard one." Darla blows cool breath over the rim of her mug, and the metal of her wedding ring taps against the handle, turning the kitchen into a disco. she muses.

"What's the one with Nicole Kidman?" she asks, and my stomach drops as Tanner and Lugosi pad into the kitchen.

The retriever reaches me first. His rear half wiggles, tongue and tail wagging, before he launches himself onto his hind legs. At his full height, Lugosi's snout is even with my shoulder. I hold my robe closed with one hand and hoist the coffee mug in the other while the dog gets a good lick along the bottom of my chin. Half of my face is wet with drool before he's satisfied, but there's nothing for it when he's almost as tall as I am.

"Not the best manners," I tell Darla, patting the retriever's soft golden fur when he drops back onto four paws. "But he gives great hugs."

The other woman laughs into her coffee, and if she's judging me about my overly affectionate, too-big-to-be-cute-when-it-jumps dog while I use the robe's fluffy collar to dry my face, I can't tell.

Darla crosses her arms over her ample chest. "I read somewhere that women sleep better with a dog in their bed than a man."

"I believe it." I scratch behind Lugosi's ear, marveling at how so much tongue can fit into such a small mouth. "This guy snores, but Rob could saw down trees in his sleep."

"To getting our beauty rest." Darla lifts her mug, and we mock salute. Nothing makes for easier girl talk between married women than complaining about their spouses' bad habits.

Darla snaps her fingers. "*The Others*!"

At first, I think she's referring to my son and dog, but then the cogs click into place, and I remember we were talking about her favorite horror movie. *The Others* she's chosen, in which Nicole Kidman indeed also stars, based loosely on a nineteenth-century novella by Henry James. Dreary, Gothic, and emotive, the 2001 adaptation isn't a bad pick, honestly. The film deviates greatly from the source material, but it works.

Chalk this one up as another surprise from the world's sweetest neighbor. Maybe I can make a new friend in the New Jersey suburbs after all. My sister might be proud—if she weren't so jealous.

Before I can share my thoughts on Darla's underappreciated film, Tanner wraps himself around my side. The movement shoves my heartbeat into my throat. Not too long ago I could carry my son around on my hip but, like Lugosi, the kid's head reaches higher than that now. Raising children is weird. You focus so much on making sure they survive that you barely have time to mourn the versions of themselves they outgrow. I've promised myself I won't become one of those cheek-pincher moms, but already I can feel my willpower waning.

"Tanner, this is Darla." Tanner's hug inches the robe's soft material above the fingertip rule. I pat his downy chestnut hair and twist so he can show his shy smile to the woman in the corner. I twist a bit more so he can see the welcome basket. Probably I should have introduced our new neighbor as *Mrs. Lashett* instead of putting them on a first-name basis, but it's too late now. "She lives on our street and brought some goodies to help us settle in."

Tanner's gaze wanders over the basket. He beams when he spots the LEGOs, mumbles something that passes for a thank-you, and buries his face in my robe. Around other adults, my son is shy to a fault: one more squeeze and he'll expose the hem of my T-shirt.

Halfway across the kitchen, Lugosi's tail picks up speed. He swivels his head toward Darla, then pads over to lick her denim-clad knee while Tanner detaches himself to give the dog his breakfast. This reminds me that we have dog kibble and kid cereal, but no milk. No fruit. No bread. By the time I'd panic-loaded my shopping cart with every art supply, notebook, and assorted oddity on the third-grade school supply list (potting soil, Q-tips, and a mandatory fidget spinner, which I guess makes sense), there hadn't been any room left for groceries. I'd picked up the half-and-half at Wawa.

"What grade is Tanner going into?" Darla asks me. "My daughter, Daphne, will be in fifth. Dylan, my son, is going into sixth."

I don't want to think about Tanner starting middle school. "Third," I say, spotting the snickerdoodles in Darla's basket when my son's gaze meanders toward the shrink-wrap. On a scale of *Give her a break, she just moved in* to *Call the authorities, she's a sugary breakfast mom*, exactly how terrible would it look if I offered my third grader cookies for breakfast?

Darla drains the rest of her coffee. "Speaking of school starting, I'm the president of the Brunswick Elementary PTA—which explains *my* T-shirt." She winks. "We need a new Cultural Arts person on the board this year."

Her hint is not subtle. "Oh, I'm—"

"Perfect for the job." Darla's eyes gleam. "The Cultural Arts chair handles all the author visits, and the assemblies, *and* they help plan our school events. Our Halloween Boogie Bash would be amazing with a real horror author's help," she says with a meaningful wiggle of her eyebrows.

"I'm already overdue on a new book," I try, but that gleam in Darla's eyes is as big as her earrings now.

Crap.

"You could help me end my last year as president with a bang!" she says. "I promise to make it worth your while."

Tanner tugs on my robe, jumbling the half-formed *No thank you*s and *I'd rather die*s piling up in my mouth. It's not that I don't want to help; it's that, so far, I haven't had much to offer the elementary-school mommy crowd—and I'm not lying about being behind in my writing schedule. Not only has my cursor not moved beyond the title page, it still has yet to type out a title.

"Mom, can you make me some eggs?" My son's squishable cheeks and sleep-puffed eyes stare up at me before I can find a way to politely pass on being enlisted into the PTA.

"That's where I'm headed right now, in fact, to a board meeting," Darla barrels on. "School starts Tuesday, and the back-to-school Ice Cream Social comes up fast. We're meeting at Dream Bean for brunch, and you two should join us!" She winks at Tanner. "The café has all sorts of scrummy breakfast options."

Even at eight years old, my kid's quick enough to do that math.

"I'm starving to death," Tanner whines, hands on his belly and all.

I am not prepared for this ambush. I gesture at myself—the sock, the robe, the melting face, and monstress hair—to tell Darla that I'm in no condition for brunch.

"Oh, just throw on some yoga pants and come on, we don't mind." Morning sunlight streams through the kitchen window, lighting on the shiny petals of Darla's unopened welcome basket, the sparkling sequins in her headband. "And no obligation. Come, meet the girls, have a bite to eat. It'll be fun!"

Like my sister and me, it seems my new neighbor and I do not share the same definition of fun.

Regardless, Tanner's hungry eyes turn hopeful. Visions of croissants and frosted Danishes dance in his head as my maternal instinct to nourish my offspring wins out over my ability to decline a brunch invite from a woman who just brought me a welcome basket—even if it does come with indentured servitude.

There are worse things than the PTA, right? She did say no obligation.

"Okay," I relent, and both Darla and Tanner clap their hands. Lugosi perks his ears at the sudden noise, but the dog is otherwise occupied with sniffing the baseboards, tail waving goodbye behind him like a long golden feather. "Let's go."

First, a surprise visit. Then a brunch invite—and not just any brunch, but with my new PTA-president neighbor, who has essentially just told me that I will now be helping to plan the school's Halloween Boogie Bash, whatever that is.

I am going to regret this.

CHAPTER THREE

Darla remote starts the purple minivan while I lock the front door. We'll take hers, my new neighbor insists, when I've managed to shuck the silly heart-print robe and pull on a pair of jeans and a hoodie. The Dream Bean is close, she says, and she's parked behind me anyway.

The woman hummingbirds around the minivan—relocating a Brunswick PTA canvas tote from the passenger-side floorboard to the back seat, pushing aside an open bankers box lined with shiny red pocket folders all pointing in the same direction, sweeping away invisible dust from the cushion. She hoists herself onto the driver's seat and waves Tanner and me inside.

As much as I'd prefer to take separate cars, I take one look at Darla's ear-to-ear grin, the sequins on her Brunswick PTA shirt, and shove my keys in my bag. I did just drive fifteen hundred miles behind a U-Haul? It might be nice to be a passenger for a change.

The automated seat belt slithers over Tanner the second I get him situated in the back seat, the tablet-size screen on the headrest back already flickering with silent cartoons. My toe scratches against the sole of my Converse through the hole in Rob's sock as I slide into the passenger seat. Even with her two young kids and welcome-basket side hustle, Darla still manages to maintain a spotless vehicle. Meanwhile there sits my dented, single-child Honda, one junk-food wrapper away from being declared a biohazard.

Darla clicks a button on the steering wheel. The minivan's door magics itself shut and I inhale Armor All New Car as pop radio filters at low volume through the speakers. Seriously, there isn't a stray french fry *anywhere.*

"Patti and I used to carpool together," Darla tells me as we buckle up. "All the time."

She leans forward to puff away nonexistent dust on the air vents. "I hope the car's clean enough for you. Hubby's a doctor, so he's a bit of a germophobe, but I don't mind." Darla's voice drops. "It's good to keep a tidy vehicle," she whispers, like it's another secret.

My phone dings in my jeans pocket. When I dig it out, a social media notification from my sister waits on the screen. I switch the phone to silent without swiping. Whatever baby-goat yoga pose has made it to Kitty's feed will be cute, well staged, and completely adorable, but it'll have to wait. How does one manage a selfie during caprine vinyasa anyway? Poor Leaf probably didn't realize he'd signed up for cameraman duty when he decided to date my sister.

Darla backs the minivan down the driveway, and I've got a clear view of Lugosi's snout pressed against the house's front windowpanes as the tires change direction. Tanner waves to the dog through the back-seat window and a cold spot blossoms between my shoulder blades. Is it cruel to leave the poor pup home alone in an empty house this soon? Hopefully the retriever makes another run around the perimeter, sniffs himself sleepy, and catches a nap by the door until we're back.

"Ready?" Darla asks, all rosy cheeks and crinkly perm in the driver's seat as her hand lifts to shift into drive, and even though there's only a sliver of a chance I'll fit in with these PTA moms and it'll probably end in a complete disaster, suddenly brunch doesn't sound *that* bad. Besides, even if it's a total nightmare, at least it'll give me some inspiration. Mustn't forget that new book I'm supposed to be working on.

And people think horror people are pessimists, I'll tell Kitty later. How's that for a glass half full?

We zip past Number Thirty-Four's lawn, with its BRUNSWICK ELEMENTARY sign and potted pink pansies, crescent-moon driveway, and boring beige four-door. The neighborhood streaks by in a colorful blur as Darla sails us through a sea of green lights. Three turns later, she pulls into a strip-mall parking lot.

The minivan comes to a complete stop at the end of a chain of familiar retail storefronts that begins with Trader Joe's and ends in Dream Bean Café. With its kitschy sign, mismatched paint, and wide picture windows, the corner café oozes afterthought—like a harried developer had worked his way down the line, realized he'd forgotten a coffee shop, and tacked one on before someone noticed.

Darla flips down the driver's-side visor mirror and applies a thick coat of ballet-slipper pink to her lips with a tube from the center console. "Isn't this place just *darling*?" She tips her chin toward the Dream Bean logo. "Is it just me, or does that mug look suspiciously like a stemless wineglass with a handle?"

She's not wrong. "Maybe this spot was supposed to be a Painting with a Twist?"

"Oh, wouldn't that be fun." Darla pulls a canvas tote over her shoulder. "I do love a good twist." She pushes through the driver's side and we both chuff at the misshapen coffee shop logo as we cross through the Dream Bean's threshold.

It *does* look like a wineglass with a mug handle.

Inside, soft rock pumps at low volume from a hidden stereo. Tanner's palm goes slick in mine the second he spots the glass pastry case at the front of the café. He wriggles free of my grasp and scoots across the faux-hardwood floor, eager to prepare his case for a sugary treat before he's doomed to steel-cut oats.

"Everything's delicious," Darla says, but her pretty pink smile begins to flake when she spots the twentysomething behind the counter. Her Keds snag on the polished floor, her canvas tote bag melds into armor over her chest, and whatever Darla mumbles next is sucked up by Bono's voice as a new song funnels through the stereo. She bites her lip, smearing pink on her teeth, and hangs a left, heading for the group of women situated around a table in the back of the café.

Darla waves for me to follow.

"Be right there, Tanner." My son's head swivels as he evaluates the items lined behind the pastry-case glass. The barista on the other side hovers over him in a shadow of disapproval directly at odds with her jubilant multicolored hair, but at least the kid is only looking. So long as Darla's quick, I can get back to Tanner, peel him away from the glass before he goes full snozzberry.

Darla leads me past exposed-brick walls checkerboarded with canvases like they're competing for structural status. Half of the chairs look refurbished, the rest designer, or maybe IKEA. U2 clicks over and Paula Cole warbles through the speaker. I'm fairly certain the soft rock filtering overhead is from the *City of Angels* soundtrack. The Dream Bean might be aiming for nostalgic nineties coffee shop, but it's landing closer to kitschy corporate coffee café.

Seated at the head of the rectangular table, a dark-haired woman in a silk blouse stabs a manicured fingernail into an open binder the same shade of red as Darla's bedazzled T-shirt. The print is too small to read from where Darla and I stand, but that crease is deep enough to see from Mars.

"Each three-gallon tub yields about ninety-six scoops." The woman's silk top, sleek black hair, and high cheekbones say Manhattan, but her accent says Brooklyn. "At two scoops per person, we need ten tubs. Four vanilla, four chocolate, two strawberry, including dairy-free options, of course."

Darla lifts a hand. She opens her mouth in a big *O*, but the woman with the silk blouse and the cheekbones powers right through it.

"At about eighty dollars a tub, that's eight hundred dollars. Plus, we need fixings and cups—"

"Paper this year, Maribel. Not styrofoam." A blonde in the seat nearest me tugs on a tea string, pours some Splenda into her mug, and sets the empty packet on a saucer. Her long ponytail whips behind her to reveal a neon-pink scrunchie that matches the pattern in her designer workout attire. My sister is the authority on viral trends, but nothing says *suburban supermom* like perfectly coordinated athleisure.

"*Even* if they cost more," the blonde adds.

Darla tries to jump in again, but Maribel is faster. "Of course we'll use paper cups, *Kellen,*" her cheekbones fire back, "but that's not the point."

Trapped between Maribel and Kellen, a mousy brunette scribbles furiously in a composition notebook, while a fourth woman with a puckered lemon face makes a show of glancing at the silver watchband on her wrist. We're a group of women staring down our forties, but this feels a lot like how I remember high school.

That warm fuzzy feeling that had started with Darla in my driveway? *Poof,* gone.

And yet my sweet new neighbor smiles harder, adjusts her tote, and cannonballs into the deep end. "Good morning, ladies!"

For a beat, silence so thick it's hard to breathe as everyone waits for the splash.

"You're late. We started without you." The lemon-faced woman speaks with a heavy Slavic accent that crackles along the lengths of her wavy dishwater hair. She twists her watch's face into view, holds up her forearm, and puckers harder. "Four minutes ago."

Precise. My editor would be proud.

Darla's canvas tote might now be fused to her squared shoulders. Her eye twitches but her smile sticks. "I'm sorry, Sasha, but it's for a good reason." She gives me a look I'm not sure I like. "I've brought our new Cultural Arts person."

My stomach hits my feet. So much for no obligation. The other women size me up like last season's sweater at Nordstrom Rack. The mousy one only gives me a passing glance before her eyes flick back to her notes, but Kellen's false eyelashes thin into bottlebrushes when she catches a glimpse of Jack Torrance sneering above my hoodie's zipper. Maribel's inspection of my luggage-wrinkled clothes and monstress hair pushes a lump into my throat. Sasha manages to pucker even harder.

Yeah, this is *exactly* like high school.

I sneak a peek at Tanner, still fawning over pastry at the counter. Next up on the café's playlist is Goo Goo Dolls. This is definitely the *City of Angels* soundtrack, which is right on time because it's 1998 and I'm a deer caught in the headlights of the popular girls' table.

Darla's hand lands on my shoulder. "This is Jill Marshall. She and her family just moved to Brunswick." Her fingers squeeze against my collarbone. "Isn't she just a doll?"

Never, not once in my life, has anyone called me a doll.

"Nice to meet you" is the best I can do.

Darla introduces each woman and their PTA Board position in turn: Kellen with the high pony and designer workout threads (fundraising); Sasha of the sour lemon face (treasurer, and sometime seamstress for the school's fifth-grade play); the mousy one with the wide rule notebook is Beth (secretary); and last is Maribel and her silk and cheekbones (VP). "Rosa is our Events chair, but her husband has a badge-pinning ceremony this morning so she couldn't make it," Darla explains proudly. "Officer Hudson just became *Detective* Hudson."

"Big day for Steve." Sasha's clipped tone dances between sincere and sarcastic, or maybe that's just her accent.

"For *both* of them," says Kellen, tightening her ponytail.

Beth marks the occasion in her notebook. "Being married to a cop must be so stressful."

"You said something about Cultural Arts?" Maribel snaps at Darla, and glares at my wrinkled self, until I feel about as confident as the lipstick still smeared across my poor neighbor's front teeth.

Darla's tight perm bobs and her hand slides to my elbow. "Jill is an author," she says, and I tense under her grip, scratching my toe against rubber through my husband's holey sock. "Her son, Tanner, is going into third grade."

She gives my forearm a quick squeeze before her hand drops away without pointing out the specific genre of my incriminating job title.

Kellen's lips twist to one side, puckering like Sasha's. "Is yours the family that just moved into Patti Townsend's old house?"

I don't miss the look she shoots at Sasha when I nod, but Darla's hand is back on my arm, tugging me away from the table before I can say anything. "We need to get ourselves a cup of coffee, but I wanted to let you know we're here first," Darla calls over her shoulder as she drops the tote into an empty chair and steers me toward the pastry counter. "We'll be right back."

Sasha tsks at her watch. Maribel and Kellen resume bickering. Beth shakes out her wrist and resumes scribbling. No one else has brought their kids to the PTA brunch, I notice.

Darla points at the autumnal tree painted on the large window we pass on our way to the counter. "Isn't that pretty?"

The display is pretty—prettier than the scene at the table, that's for sure. I've developed a tough skin to deal with book reviewers, but they have nothing on the Brunswick PTA.

I sneak my phone out of my pocket and snap a photo of the tempera masterpiece in the window, tapping out a quick text to my sister as we make our way to the counter. My new neighbor invited me to Mean Girl Brunch, I tell Kitty. If I go missing, show this to the police so they know where to find my body.

I add a zany face emoji at the end, so she'll know I'm kidding. Mostly kidding.

Three dots blip in response, but Tanner pulls my attention away before a return message pops on-screen. "Mom, the blueberry muffins here are *this* big." He holds his hands out in front of him, fingers splayed wide enough to clasp a basketball, when Darla and I arrive at the pastry case.

"I hope they're not *that* big." Tanner's grin doesn't dim when I ruffle his fuzzy-duckling hair, but his hands shrink back to a more manageable softball size.

A giant chalkboard menu consumes the café's back wall. I try to read my way through the bake shoppe font, but the barista raps her knuckles on the counter and the only word that's legible is the name spelled out in four black letters across Barb's name badge.

"The cream-cheese croissants are my favorite." Darla presses a hand against her stomach just like my son had, back in our kitchen. "But I promised Dave I'd be good."

I assume Dave is Mr. Lashett. The hubby who likes a clean car.

The barista huffs. "Are you ready to order yet?"

Probably there aren't many women bold enough to tattoo a wedge of Neapolitan cake onto their throat and still act so salty, but Barb is.

I'd kill for a bitter cup of diner drip with a couple caps of single-serve half-and-half, maybe a slice of reheated cherry pie, but neither of these appear to be on the menu.

Barb huffs louder. I'm out of time.

"He'll have a blueberry muffin and a small hot cocoa," I say, and Tanner claps his hands together, victorious, at my side. "I'll have a cream-cheese croissant and a medium coffee, extra room."

"Blond, medium, or dark roast?" Barb already has the muffin on a plate.

At a diner, it's simply the pot with the black handle. "Medium?"

Barb sloshes dark liquid to the brim of the to-go cup and I gesture to include Darla in the order. Springing for breakfast is the least I can do, after her overstuffed gift basket. "Actually, make that two cream-cheese croissants, and—" I glance to my side and watch Darla chew off her remaining lipstick. "Coffee, black?"

"You want *two* croissants?" Barb's acidic voice cuts through the first notes of Sarah McLachlan's "Angel" as her mascara-rimmed eyes stake into Darla's waistline. "That's a *lot* of calories," Barb says to the woman beside me. "Maybe you should try something less fattening?"

Touching beneath thin layers of denim, my upper thighs burn. Not very sweet, coming from a woman with a slab of pastry inked on her neck.

Only the sparkly red headband tucked into Darla's perm smiles now, though her cheeks have turned just as red. Half a dozen retorts pile up in my mind, none of them appropriate for Tanner's delicate sensibilities, still dangling from the umbilical cord at my hip. "Actually, I'll take three croissants," I say, because the only thing less appetizing than uninvited commentary on a woman's body is leaving a bakery counter with bran.

"Two for here, and one to share later while we feast on carbs and our enemies," I tell Darla by way of Barb, and my sweet new neighbor's lips twitch in my peripheral vision.

The barista sneers, but she serves the pastries, makes a mug of cocoa, and pours another to-go cup of coffee too high. We finish the transaction in silence. The cardboard cups in lieu of ceramic mugs are a middle finger, and she returns Tanner's "Thank you" with a snarl, but I rise above.

Karma's a bitch, Barb.

Kitty's return text buzzes the phone still in my hand. I've goat your back against those biatches, she captions a selfie of her snuggling a black-and-white baby goat, the pair in matching lavender T-shirts. Baaaa-maste!

Baa is a sheep sound, not a goat's, but I let it slide on account of the pun. My phone is halfway to my pocket when an incoming call flashes my editor's name.

On the second buzz, Darla's coffee breath fogs too close over my shoulder. "Do you need to take that?"

"It's just my editor." Charlene's call slides into voicemail and I stuff the phone back into my jeans, then pick up the white pastry sack with the funky wineglass/coffee-mug logo. "She's calling to remind me that we're talking about my new book tonight."

Darla perks her head to the side the same way Lugosi does when he hears a strange noise. "Oh, are you working on a new book?"

That *is* the problem, isn't it? Balancing the to-go cup and bag in one hand and a pastry plate in the other, I herd Tanner toward the back table. "I'm still figuring out a concept." I shrug to make it look like it's no big deal that I've got nothing but a blank manuscript, a blinking cursor, and indecision. "Probably just writer's block from the move."

"You never know where inspiration will strike. Sometimes in the most ordinary of places—like at brunch." Darla's tongue rolls thoughtfully inside her lower lip as we near the back table. "And if not, there's always feasting on your enemies." She tips her smile toward the pastry counter.

I can't tell if she's making a joke about Barb or the women at the back table. Maybe it's a general observation, like Kitty's comment about the hot springs on her summer glamp-about, finding inspiration in safe spaces turned spooky? Whichever it is, Kellen and Maribel are still going on about the stupid ice cream when Tanner, Darla, and I finally settle into our chairs.

The seat of the high-backed wooden frame bites into my left cheek, shooting a sciatic squirm all the way down my thighs while my fingers twiddle along the edges of my cardboard cup. I inhale coffee bean, exhale baked sugar, and Tanner nose-dives into his muffin like he hasn't eaten in weeks. The kid manages to get most of his breakfast down his shirt while Beth summarizes what we missed—something about the cost-savings benefits of single-serving cups versus big tubs: waste elimination, ease for the volunteers, blah blah blah. None of it tempers the fire raging between Maribel and Kellen, still staring daggers at each other from opposite ends of the table.

I slide a bite of cream-cheese croissant between my lips and push a stack of napkins in Tanner's direction while Darla taps into her phone under the table.

"Who are you texting?" Sasha's tone says she's the kind of mom who puts out a phone box at dinner.

I leave my phone pinned between my jeans and the butt-chewing high-back. Neither my sister nor my editor like to be left on read, but neither of them would have to endure the spotlight of Sasha's glower if I am caught texting at brunch.

Darla bristles and sets her phone on the table. "Just making myself a note."

The argument resumes, but by the time Kellen's voice reaches my end of the table, I've lost the entire thread of the debate. "I just think it should be Rosa's call," she says. "*She's* in charge of Events this year."

Red blooms in Maribel's cheeks. She pinches her dark hair behind her ear and doubles down on the many advantages of single-serving ice cream cups. Her lips curl as she snaps the binder closed. "But what do I know."

Without Rosa present, the Ice Cream Social is officially tabled until the next Brunswick PTA meeting.

"Oh, before we go, one more thing." Darla's painted-on smile is back but the twitch in her nostril is new. "You're all coming to my Doll's Night party Friday, right?"

Kellen adds another packet of sugar substitute to her cup and sighs. "What's Doll's Night again?"

Darla perks. "It's just a little pampering with the girls—"

"It's for the new 'beauty' MLM she's been talking about for months." Maribel crooks her fingers into air quotes, then points a manicured fingernail in Darla's general direction and pokes invisible holes in the softer woman's decades-out-of-style perm, bold eye shadow, homemade shirt. "The kids are at their asshole dad's this weekend, and I've got an *actual* spa appointment, so, no, I won't be at your makeover party," she tells Darla. "I'll be at home getting my beauty rest."

Kellen's lip curls as she smooths her shiny crop top. Apparently, she and Maribel do agree on something, and it's shitting on poor Darla.

Sasha busies herself plucking trash off the table, and Beth double-checks her notes while the hope on Darla's face closes in on itself. I have no idea what Doll's Night is, exactly, but even I could see those declines coming from yesterday.

Darla rallies. "You're invited, too, Jill. This Friday night at my place at seven." She slides a business card the same pink as her former lipstick across the table. "It's just a little kickoff to my new position as a Dollface sales rep. I put some samples in your welcome basket."

She gives me time to remember the bulbous pastel eggs in her generous housewarming gift. "You'll come, won't you, dear?"

I slip the business card into my jeans front pocket and rub my toe against the inside of my shoe again, digging the skin harder for every scrape that goes by without a single word from any of the other four women at the table.

There's no way I can tell Darla no, even if a makeup party is *literally* my worst nightmare.

"Sure, a girl's night could be fun."

The smile on Darla's face makes the lie worth it.

I am officially in hell.

CHAPTER FOUR

My pocket buzzes the second I'm back in the kitchen of my new creaky-not-creepy home. Probably another social media alert from my sister or, worse, another passive-aggressive reminder from Charlene. My dog won't curdle if he doesn't get his bath today, but my editor will expect *some* progress when she calls, despite the cross-country move that's siphoned weeks off my life.

You're all settled now, she'll probably say. *Stop fiddle-farting around and get crackin'.*

If only. There are four thousand boxes still to unpack, never mind the lightbulb book-idea moment I'm still waiting for. I really should have declined brunch.

The take-home Dream Bean pastry sack hits the counter with a heavy *thump.* Buying two of the greasy cream cheese–filled croissants felt right in the moment; eating them will not. Sugar slicks the backside of my teeth, and Darla's shrink-wrapped welcome basket winks at me from the counter, right next to the shiny red PTA pocket folder she foisted into my hands when I heaved myself out of her purple minivan.

"A list of all the school-year events, contact info for all the board members," she'd said. "Everything you need for Cultural Arts."

Another buzz rumbles in my back pocket, but I resist the urge to look at my phone when I unzip my hoodie and toss it on top of the folder. Like my buzzing cell phone, elementary school extracurriculars I'd never *actually* agreed to can wait. No matter how behind on writing I am, there won't be a word typed until I get this house in some semblance of order. Only problem: I have no idea where to start.

Despite his softball-size breakfast, Tanner darts into the kitchen and goes for the fridge, grunting when he finds it just as empty now as it was when he'd checked before brunch. Lugosi pants by the door until I let him out, and when the dog bounds back inside the house, both his and Tanner's shaggy heads shoot up the stairs to the second floor.

"No running," I call up after them as I slide the kitchen door latch home, because part of becoming an old, boring mom is becoming an old, boring *mom*.

Another buzz from my back pocket. Two more.

Orange kitchen scissors lie by the sink from when I'd cut into KITCHEN/COFFEEPOT. My fingers wander in the direction of the bottle in Darla's gift basket, but Jack Torrance glares back at me from my horror-movie T-shirt when I catch a glimpse of my reflection in the window over the sink. I stuff the scissors into the waistband of my jeans and scoop the shrink-wrapped bundle into my arms on my way out of the kitchen.

All work and no play, as they say.

Stiffness sets into my shoulders when my back pocket buzzes again. Even Kitty doesn't post, but I've never been one for numbers. Social media is a delicate balance between useful tool and soul sucker. Aside from the occasional book promo, my online activity is limited to researching answers for writing questions that have definitely landed me on some sort of government watch list.

I shift the basket's weight so that the scissors handle digs into my hip and tweeze the phone out of my back pocket. There are the expected social media notifications, Charlene's voicemail, and a text from Rob in his office on the other side of the Hudson River, but none of this is what's buzzing my butt numb.

It's the stream of text messages from unknown numbers with 732 area codes, daisy-chained together by a cluster of green bubbles.

Thanks for brunch, girls!!!

Welcome to the neighborhood, Jill!

Excited to have you at Brunswick.

A short gap, then, Have a great back to school week, all! I sent an invite for the Ice Cream Social—be there early to set up!

A thumbs-up.

An ice cream cone emoji.

When I gave Darla my cell number on the drive home from the Dream Bean, I hadn't expected to get added to a group text. I should have known better.

Three dots flash on-screen. Hope Steve's badge pinning was great, Rosa, someone types. Missed you at brunch!

A photo of an attractive, square-jawed Black man with a military haircut slides through next. He's dropped onto one knee, and a little girl pins a new bar to his uniform breast pocket while a dark-haired woman in a tight dress stands behind him with an infant crooked in one arm. This must be Rosa and newly minted Detective Hudson, their kids. A picture-perfect memory for a picture-perfect family. The kind of social media–ready snap that would make my sister seethe with envy.

A string of tap backs attach themselves to the pic. Someone throws in a blue heart.

Don't forget Doll's Night! This green bubble includes a fingernail-painting emoji and a lipstick kiss. No tap backs now, so I'm going to assume that number belongs to Darla.

My thumb hovers over the screen, considering a response, then taps the toggle to mute the chat. I've already put names to faces with these women. Sorting out whose number belongs to whom is like finding Tanner's lucky lunch box and fixing that damn broken zipper, a problem for later.

I evacuate the group text and thumb open my husband's message next:

Thinking about you. Need me to pick up anything on my way home?

I glance inside the shrink-wrapped basket against my hip. Actually, no. Grocery shopping is first up on the agenda tomorrow, and between yesterday's raid on Wawa and Darla's intuition, I think we're covered for the night. I glance at Rob's contact photo: a candid snap of him at his drum set. A tall drifter, I text back. Salt and pepper hair, mouth that looks like he knows how to use it. Glasses.

Three dots. Rob shoots back an image of Jeff Goldblum and a question mark.

So close, I reply.

Rob drops a GIF of Gomez Addams kissing his way up Morticia's arm. Be home ASAP.

I fire off a kissy face and readjust, returning the phone to my back pocket. Marriage isn't for everyone, but Rob is a man who knows how to speak my language. When you reel in a catch like that, you can't let him get away.

Hard plastic crashes upstairs, followed by a rustle and a child's exaggerated roar. Even with a belly full of LEGOs and action figures, that tub of road-trip toys isn't going to last forever, and *Nat Geo* kids' books only dazzle for so long. There's four bedrooms, three baths, plus a kitchen, living room, dining room, and more to unpack, but I should start in Tanner's room first: shelve his clothes, constellate glow-in-the-dark stars across his ceiling, find that damn lunch box.

I bet that's what Darla would do.

I decide instead to start in my office, because if I don't, I am going to scream. Not one of those *Bride of Frankenstein* shrieks, either. A big, jaw-unhinged, hollow-your-gut Final Girl scream, like my soul is being ripped out of my body all the way from my toes.

Darla's gift basket gets plunked on the desktop, and I go for the nearest cardboard square. My back screams when I try to lift it. My knees protest when I squat. Regardless of which way I go, something is going to hurt later. But I persist. Box after box is sliced open, gutted, and emptied, until the stacks of cardboard building blocks are gone. The room is an explosion of books and Bubble Wrap and packing-paper coils like snakeskin halfway up the office wall, but at least the tickle in the back of my throat has subsided.

"Mom?" Tanner's voice squeaks ahead of him as he and Lugosi bound their way back down the stairs.

"I'm bored." The retriever deposits himself on a pile of packing paper and deflates like a punctured tire. A green figurine hangs limp from Tanner's hand. "So is Godzilla."

Technically, it's just a generic giant green Japanese monster. "Do you want to help me unpack?"

Tanner shakes his head.

"Do you want me to help *you* unpack?"

Another shake.

Kids.

Tanner lifts his free hand and points his index finger at a blue box in Darla's basket.

Winner, winner. "You want to check out the LEGOs from the basket?"

I have no idea how my new neighbor guessed the plastic blocks were Tanner's favorite, but I'm lucky she did.

Shrink-wrap tears under my teeth as easily as the flaky outer shell of the Dream Bean croissant. It takes a second to loosen the LEGOs from their place between the hoard of cosmetics samples, but I wriggle the box free and hand it to Tanner. Lugosi snores from his nest and Tanner squirrels his new treasure upstairs while I pick plastic out of my teeth, the scissors glaring forgotten at me from the desktop.

By the time Rob's Texas-plated pickup slides into the driveway, Lugosi has ventured out to complete a few more perimeter checks between naps and Tanner has been up and down the stairs at least thirty-four times. A trail of stray LEGOs marks a path from his bedroom to my office door like breadcrumbs left behind by fairy-tale children, but I've successfully emptied all the boxes in my office and bundled up the packing scraps.

My husband's hair is scrunched on one side, the aftermath of a long and frustrating commute, when he pokes his head inside the office door. He pushes his mouth into a smile that manages to crinkle the edges of his baby blues. "You're kicking unpacking's ass," Rob says, his body leaned against the doorway like the spare mark on a bowling scoreboard. One of his hands touches the row of buttons that line his uniform shirt, the other dangles the Dream Bean pastry bag. "This for me?"

"It is if you want it." As much as I typically enjoy feasting on my enemies, not even a tiny piece of me can stomach another bite of Dream Bean croissant.

Rob peeks inside the pastry bag while he unbuttons, wispy chest hair fluttering free over the collar of the fitted navy-blue tee he wears underneath his blue uniform shirt. He sniffs at the pastry, makes a face, and tosses the bag on top of an unopened box. "I picked up a pizza for dinner. Pepperoni and pineapple. Hungry?"

On my first breath, I'm not. Then I catch a whiff of melted cheese and marinara sauce, forbidden tropical fruit, and my stomach grumbles. "I'll eat in a bit." I gesture at the diminishing piles, the bundled trash. "Still trying to get things under control in here."

I watch as Rob's fingers continue their downward trek over the length of his chest, twisting free the line of buttons to reveal thin cotton that clings to all my favorite places. He shrugs his arms free of the uniform shirt, hangs it on the doorknob, and casts off his glasses. When he pulls his T-shirt out of his belt, I start to fantasize about the warmth of my husband's fingers.

Cross-country moves leave little time for romance.

"Pizza box is on the counter, but I can reheat a slice whenever you're ready to eat." Halfway to me, Rob's eyes clock Darla's welcome basket. He stays on course, but I sense his attention wander when his arms wrap behind my back. "What's this?"

God, he smells good, even with the stink of a full day on him. "Welcome gift basket," I mumble into his chest.

He takes me with him as he steps toward the desk. "From whom?"

"Darla."

Rob shuffles us to the basket. I hear the crackle of cellophane, then the pop of tin that means my sweet-toothed husband has zeroed in on the cookies. "Who's Darla?"

So many questions. "The president of the Brunswick Elementary PTA." I tilt my head to speak to the underside of his jaw. "Let me tell you about brunch."

Rob slot machines in a snickerdoodle, and his breath comes out in a puff of cinnamon sugar above my head. "You went to lunch with the PTA?"

"Brunch." It's hard to nod with my husband's biceps crooked around my neck. "I just became the new Cultural Arts chairperson. Those are the president's cookies you're eating. She's our new neighbor, by the way." I tell him the Lashetts are Number Thirty-Four. "The house with the yard sign and the minivan."

"Friendly neighbors who bake cookies *and* some new mommy friends?" His arms still around me, Rob's fingers rummage inside the tin. "Not bad for your first day in New Jersey."

Oh, silly man. If only female friendships were so simple.

"Darla is a supersweet capital-M Mom straight out of Stepford, but those other women are the worst." I stop short, because if you don't have anything nice to say and all that, and nuzzle deeper into Rob's chest. If the Brunswick Mean Girls treated their own so poorly, what kind of terror will they have in store for me, once they figure out that I don't fit the PTA mom mold? "And people think *I'm* the one putting monsters under their children's beds."

Rob's arms tighten. "Well, to be fair, they really shouldn't read their kids horror novels."

An edge of uncertainty salts the sweetness on his breath. "It could be worse?"

"Oh, it's about to be: I've got a call with Charlene in a few minutes, and guess what I've got for her?" I take another drag of Rob's cologne and pull away to curl both hands into zeros.

My darling husband eliminates another cookie and gathers me back in his arms. "A new book idea will hit you when you stop thinking so hard about it," he says. "It's impossible to think of anything scarier than moving when you're still in the midst of unpacking."

He's right, but I nip his chest with my teeth anyway. Rob laughs and palms my shoulders. "Okay, handle your call. Tanner and I will take Lugosi for a *w-a-l-k*." The dog perks his ears up from his perch on his bed in the corner. He can't spell, but he also can't ignore the sound of his name. "I'll get the kid fed and bathed and tucked in, and when you're done, I'll have a hot bath waiting." Rob's tenor drops into a growl against my ear that makes my knees go soft. "With whatever bubble bath I can scrounge up."

I know that voice, these knees. "You're just trying to seduce me."

"Yes," he says, "but you're still wearing the shirt you went to bed in, you haven't eaten, and I think your hair might be flammable." Rob makes his serious face. "Unpacking isn't a one-person job, babe, and you don't have to do this alone. Let's take the night off, lay in bed, and vent to each other about our mutually awful days." He fingers an escaped strand of my monstress hair. "Maybe make out a little?"

It's the way the last ends in a question that makes me fall in love all over again.

"Just what I said—seduction attempt!" I swat my husband away with a stray shred of packing paper, but already my thoughts run to the bottle of rosé in Darla's gift basket. Wine gives Rob a migraine, which means it goes to the tub with me. The chocolate we can share. "Get out of my office," I order, still brandishing the packing paper.

My phone rings right as I chase him out. Rob blows me a kiss, pats his thigh for Lugosi to follow, and the pair are swallowed up by the stairs.

I answer on the third ring. "Hey, Charlene."

"How are you, darlin'?" My editor lives among the New York publishing echelon, but her homegrown Appalachian accent sticks. "How's the new place?"

"Coming along." I thrust my hands into the open stomach of Darla's welcome basket to pluck out the useful items. "Hopefully I'll be able to get back to work by the end of the week."

"And what exactly is it we'll be working *on*?" Straight to the point, this one.

The room is suddenly much emptier without Rob in it, just me and a collection of wrapped parcels lining the perimeter like a row of unplanted gravestones. I snatch up the scissors and slice one open. "Hopefully that new novel you're waiting on."

My answer comes out as glib as it feels. "I'm still getting my thoughts together."

Charlene clears her throat. "Sophomore novels are always the toughest. Nature of the beast. It's a good thing."

The first parcel is a framed print of my debut book cover—not my first attempt at a novel, but my first to land a deal big enough that I could start writing full-time. I set it aside with a grunt and reach for the next wrapped rectangle. "It's like squeezing blood from a stone," I tell Charlene. "Except it's a bloodless stone."

"Look, Jill—" Charlene plows ahead, switching gears from pep talk to tough love in one smooth sip of coffee on the other end of the line. "Your debut was a hit, but you had years to get it perfect while you tinkered with short stories and hired out for ghostwriting. You don't get that luxury anymore."

A sweet talker, Charlene is, but she's not wrong.

I make listening noises while she reminds me, not for the first time, that I have to earn my keep on the bestseller list. "There's a reason you found your voice in horror. Let your own experiences inspire you. Write what you know."

The adage is common enough, but it hits differently when one parent abandoned ship while the other sank from undiagnosed mental illness.

"I'm not sure how my sister would feel about that." Almost thirty years later, and I'm not the only one slugging around the inherited trauma of our mother's suicide, surrounded by bloody cosmetics on her bedroom closet carpet.

Charlene tsks. "How *is* Kitty handling your move?"

"She says she came back from her van-about with a ton of inspiration, so good, I guess?"

Never can tell, with my sister.

My fingers press into the soft material of the next parcel, and I peel away packing paper to stroke the corkboard's spongy skin. If I ever *do* figure out the plot of my new novel, this is where it will grow—seeds planted in pictures, note scraps, and doodles, until ideas take root and weave together into a plot. Two pins wait in one corner of the corkboard, eager to begin their sewing.

Charlene sighs. "Well, I know you well enough to know you've got somethin' rattling around up there." She means my head, where I keep all my rattles. "Tell me what you've got so far."

What I've got so far is nothing, so I look around the room, patting my pants like I can scrounge a plotline from pocket lint and packing paper. Darla's business card slips into my palm. *Isn't she a doll?* she'd called me, my sweet new neighbor with her blue eye shadow, powdered-doughnut cheeks, pink lips. My fingers track the delicate DOLLFACE script as I pin the pink square to the corkboard's empty center. "Dolls, maybe?"

Charlene clears her throat. This is not a good sound. This is the sound of my editor warming up for a lecture on Bad Ideas.

My thoughts flash to the women seated around the table at the Dream Bean Café. The way they'd all sat, plastic smiles and crimson binders, gaping at Darla and me like whatever's watching behind those cold reptile eyes, it isn't entirely human. "Haunted dolls?" I dump the congealed croissant from the Dream Bean pastry sack into an empty box, then pin the bag beside the business card. "Not like actual dolls, but like women *as* dolls," I clarify before Charlene can clear her throat again. "Stepford wives as lizard people?"

She snorts. "No."

Silence hums across the line while my gaze drops from the corkboard to the gutted welcome basket, sad now that its belly is mostly empty, its contents scattered around the desktop. Only the cosmetics samples remain, the pastel-bulbs-less Easter basket more disemboweled piñata.

"You're not serious?" Charlene asks.

"I'm not *not* serious."

"Listen, Jill." Charlene clears her throat, and there's no holding off the impending lecture now. "It's hard to tell good shit from apple butter these days. If you're gonna go possessed dolls, you better find a way to flip the trope. Make it your own."

I lift a pink compact from the welcome basket and click it open to reveal a palette of floral eye-shadow tabs framed in miniature mirror shapes: mint green (oval), pale pink (scalloped), dusty rose (rectangle). The circular, ocean-blue pod sends a shiver down my spine, like wafting down a waterbed current, and I snap the compact closed.

"And do it in space," Charlene says, because when my editor says to flip a trope, she means to flip a trope.

"Like cosmic horror?" I've never been a huge fan of Lovecraft, but as a woman fast approaching middle age, existential dread sounds right up my alley.

"No, set *in* space." Charlene's voice takes on its thinking-out-loud tone. "There's such a shortage of good, feminist sci-fi horror. Think about something that's *Barbarella* meets *Event Horizon,* with some of that Sigourney Weaver 'Get away from her, you bitch' energy."

A sexy space odyssey, a demonic spaceship just returned from hell, and an *Alien* reference? Now I'm pretty sure Charlene is just naming space things she thinks might go together. "Barbarella wasn't a doll," I manage, glib again, though Jane Fonda's iconic space-adventurer costumes did give off a certain fem-bot vibe.

Charlene scoffs. "Remember the mechanical dolls with razor-sharp teeth?"

I'd forgotten the film's dolls, but its birds dredge up another childhood memory: a broken cockatiel, floating in dirty water. I suck it right back down, fix my eyes on the pink Dollface business card tacked to my otherwise barren corkboard, and tell Charlene sci-fi horror isn't really my thing.

"Then think of your lizard-people dolls as a metaphor—a containment unit."

My stomach hurts from staring at the stupid cosmetic samples in the eviscerated welcome basket. I pin the phone against my shoulder, grab up Darla's gift basket, and head for the basement. After I flick on the light switch and pass the wedding cake–stacked hatboxes (kick drum, floor tom, snare, wing tom) of Rob's drum kit, I come face-to-face with the house's furnace for the first time.

Charlene clicks her teeth, thinking. "If these women are dolls"—her voice brushes against my ear—"are they the victims or the villains?"

I size up the appliance. Tall, encased in shining silver, and hinged along one side, the furnace up close is less the stage magician's prop and more a modern iron maiden. I think of the Bride, resurrected on her metal altar, in my bathroom mirror. Ellen Ripley, space's Final Girl, who survived, then sacrificed herself, only to be cloned and sent to fight the same monster, over and over. My mother, boxed in by her misery in the master-bedroom closet, desperate to cut herself free.

There are many ways for a woman to be contained. To come unstitched.

A pink glimmer catches my eye when I reach for the switch to flip off the basement lights. Dusty-rose streaks down the length of my palm, a scar left behind by the eye-shadow palette in Darla's welcome basket, which sticks to my skin when I try to wipe it away.

Make the trope my own, Charlene says.

If all those childhood memories are going to live in my head forever, maybe they should start paying rent, right? It's the twenty-first century. Even space has an economy to think about.

"You know what," I tell my editor, and hit the lights, "I think I might be able to work with dolls in space."

CHAPTER FIVE

The neon OPEN sign in the Dream Bean Café window reflects red off the blade laid across the passenger seat of the idling car.

Knives don't gleam in real life, the woman in the driver's seat thinks as she considers the long silver instrument—the sharp edge and blunt tip, the crimson glow that bleeds across the metal and into the ornate mother-of-pearl handle. *Not like they do in the movies, anyway.*

This dull truth had first reared its ugly head on her wedding day. An odd thing for the woman to think as she'd stood dressed all in white, her brand-new husband tuxed beside her, the bridal-shower cake knife not gleaming in her hands as it slid between frosted layers of Chantilly lace. Girlhood daydreams and bridal magazines promised glitz and sparkle on her Big Day, but the whole event had turned out as dull as the blade's rounded end. The walk up the aisle, short. The kiss, quick and perfunctory. The frosting gummed along the elongated metal shaft, too sweet.

The cake, dry.

Even now the woman can taste the pastry, lodged against her uvula at the back of her throat. She's choked down so much since her wedding day, but never the single bite of that seven-hundred-dollar dessert. Still the aftertaste of raspberry filling clings to her soft palate, as thick and heady and floral as menstrual blood.

The woman's mouth waters, and she blinks away from the knife, careful to keep her face hidden in the approaching shadows as the evening's last customers straggle out of the quieting café, sugar-stained pastry bags like pendulums at their sides.

She reaches to the fuse box under the sedan's dashboard, pulls the plastic tooth, and drops it into the cupholder. Then she sits and waits as sunset broadsides into dusk.

The sky burns orange, the neon-red OPEN sign flicks off, and the Dream Bean goes dark. The woman watches the late-shift employees trickle out through the double doors, past the window painted with sprawling tempera foliage. A lone figure stays behind to close up, and the woman watches as the figure locks the door from inside and disappears within the empty café. When only two vehicles remain on the far edge of the lot, the woman twists the key in the ignition and the idling car shudders still.

Burning dusk bruises blue.

The crackle of the pink rain poncho over the woman's clothes breaks the thickening quiet when she shifts in the driver's seat to twist off her wedding ring. She deposits the diamonds in the car's cupholder alongside the plastic tooth, smooths flyaway hair beneath the poncho's plastic hood, and pinches the drawstring tight. Years of practice help her slide the long yellow dishwashing mitts up her arms as easy as opera gloves. The woman balls her fists to loosen the rubber. She rubs her feet together, listening for the sibilant whisper of the bootees covering her shoes.

The drawstring chews into the underside of the woman's chin when she smiles.

Time to put her face on.

Shadows crowd the car's interior as the woman lifts the mask from her lap. She slides the thin plastic sheath over her head, careful not to scratch it against the bridge of her nose. With her eyes closed, she twitches the mask into position, lifts a dish-gloved hand, and flips the visor.

The woman's new doll's face opens its eyes.

Had its fuse still been engaged, the sedan's bright vanity would illuminate the flawless skin, long lashes, and rosebud lips of her new doll face—the perfect arch of her sculpted brows, her sunshine-yellow locks curled under an angled jaw. Her brilliant smile, whiter even than the creamy frosting of that tiered Chantilly wedding cake.

A bead of sweat prickles on the doll's upper lip and she licks the salt away, tongue slithering along the smooth grooves of the mask's backside. She exhales a warm breath, and the plastic sucks against her skin, melding the layers together.

This face feels better than her other one.

The doll cracks open the driver's-side door, waits until the dome courtesy light goes dark, then reaches to the passenger seat. Her nylon dish gloves squelch as one palm wraps around the knife's handle, and she lifts the blade to eye level, squinting through the narrow slits of her new eyes.

Let them eat cake, she thinks. One of the most infamous things a woman probably never said.

The doll mouths the words again as she watches the overhead lights inside the Dream Bean flip off one by one, until the only bulb still burning is the one near the café's back exit.

A streetlamp at the far end of the parking lot statics on.

She slips the cake knife under the pink poncho and pushes her car door open. When she's free of the sedan, she presses her hip against the driver's-side door until it clicks closed.

It's late enough in the year that the weather turns cool after sunset, but not far enough into autumn to keep sweat from pooling in the hollows of the doll's body—under her arms, beneath her breasts, between her thighs. Muggy dark licks the backs of the doll's knees as she pads across the parking lot, sweat slicking the plastic poncho to her skin like a pink shell as she patters toward the closed Dream Bean Café. Few cameras wait in the small alley behind the café, but the doll is camera ready. Soon the dumpsters will be full of sugar-soaked trash and just deserts.

The doll slips around the side of the building, her poncho scratching across the wall as perspiration spreads under the mask. By the time she reaches the café's back door, sweat collects on her eyelids. A thin line trickles down the center of her back, too far to reach and too humid to try.

Nearly twenty years fill the space between the doll's wedding day and this night. The cake knife has long since been cleaned of its gobbed frosting and dusty pastry, put away and forgotten along with its serving bride. So has the doll, tucked inside the confines of marital bliss and domesticity, tethered to the expectations of wife, mother, homemaker.

She's had bloody, saccharine cake stuck at the back of her throat for years—but not after tonight.

Tonight, she's the knife, and for the first time, she'll cut her own damn cake.

The doll pulls the blade free of her sleeve as she arrives at the café's back door. She steps outside the wan streetlight glow, lifts onto her tiptoes, and jabs the pearl handle into the security motion bulb. Glass pops and shards sprinkle onto the pavement, glittering on the concrete in the low light like dozens of tiny mirrors. The doll nudges the fragments to the side with a bootee-clad sneaker, then presses her back against the brick wall. Blade clutched in one dish-gloved hand, she waits beside the door's hinges, swishing the bitter taste of decades-old Chantilly around in her mouth.

When the door opens, scents of dried sugar and stale coffee push into the nighttime air. Dark renders the barista's colorful hair monochromatic, but even the night isn't black enough to eclipse the false sweetness inked on her neck.

The doll's lunge is a firecracker in the Dream Bean dark.

The blade catches the barista below the ear and pulls a thin red smile across her throat. The barista twists, trying to break free, and the dish gloves shriek as the doll holds her tight. This pastry is denser, harder to cut, than she expected. She slashes again, teeth gritted with the effort of pushing the blade into the doughy throat, forcing it through the rubbery carotid artery, the gummy jugular vein.

The barista stiffens against the doll's chest. A shrill quarter note pinches through her severed trachea, flattening into quiet as the organ pulls wide. The doll tightens her grip and slices again, deeper. Heat bursts against the yellow dish gloves as the barista's life pours in a wet red rush over them.

The doll's fingers go slick inside the rubber as she completes her first full cut.

The barista's arms fling backward as she bleeds out. The doll swipes once more and then again, until the barista's hands fall away and her body sags. With each stroke the blade slides through the tattooed Neapolitan wedge as easily as it had the wedding-day Chantilly lace. Three layers, three cuts. Vanilla, classic but boring. Strawberry, sweet and acidic.

Last, chocolate. Malty. Meaty. Divine.

The doll's stomach rumbles.

Ruined cake slides clean off the knife's edge, and raspberry compote gurgles between pastry layers. The doll slices the blade free, and the barista's body drops onto the waiting bed of shattered glass. The red smile in her neck pulses viscous filling down her chest, over the four letters on the plastic name badge pinned to her shirt.

The doll swallows, and at long last the taste of soured wedding cake washes down her throat. She twists the knife in the moonlight.

How neat, she thinks, as pale amber streetlight catches the gooey filling where it pools on the blade.

It does gleam.

CHAPTER SIX

When my eyes scratch open, the inside of my mouth tastes like sour milk and rotten grapes.

Yuck.

The murky hue filtering through the bedroom blinds makes it impossible to know how late I've overslept, but the drilling in my skull is grateful for the low light. Leftover bubble-bath fumes radiate off my skin and nausea rolls in the pit of my stomach. I'm old enough to know better than to down half a king-size chocolate bar and a bottle of rosé on a stomach lined with greasy take-out pizza and dairy-filled pastry, but young enough in spirit still to hope my digestive system doesn't self-destruct.

Soft snores roll up from the furry lump by my feet, but Rob's side of the bed is cool when I wand my hand over. The wine-and-chocolate hangover is bad enough on its own, but I've slept right through my darling husband's goodbye kiss. Worse, there's sandpaper in my eyes. I fell asleep with my contacts in.

So, today is off to a great start.

I peel a layer of corneal tissue along with yesterday's lenses off my Sahara eyeballs and leave the used plastic to dry out on the nightstand. A buzz somewhere near my hips vibrates all the way in my teeth. My hand slaps around on the mattress until it lands on my phone under the sheets. The battery icon is already red when I wrestle it free, hopefully because I forgot to put the stupid thing on the charger and not because the muted group text is sucking my iPhone's soul as dry as my eyes.

When the phone blinks into focus, half a dozen missed calls from my sister wait on the screen. The phone buzzes again and Kitty's contact photo fills the frame, but my groggy fingers are too slow. Voicemail beats me to the call, which is probably for the best. Usually, I love starting my day with our morning chats, but today Tylenol comes before my sister. She'd probably just tell me to chug a liter of kombucha and join her for hot yoga.

Not even if I were on my deathbed, Kitty, thanks.

Lugosi snuffles and I toss the phone back into the sheets, close my eyes, and time my breathing to the retriever's until the room stops spinning. My stomach gurgles its demand for something bland and starchy to soak up the acid in my stomach. As much as I'd love to lie and wallow in the leftovers of my bad decisions, this house isn't going to unpack itself. It's a miracle Tanner is still asleep, and there are groceries to buy.

The phone buzzes another incoming call from my sister, but I hit the red circle to decline and punch out a quick text: Overslept. Call you later.

A pinched-face emoji arrives instantly on-screen in response, steam blowing from both nonexistent nostrils, but she'll be fine.

Carbonation bubbles into my head when my bare feet hit the carpet, and the aftertaste of cream-cheese croissant surges against the back of my mouth. I wait for the fizz to die down while Lugosi jumps off the bed, shakes himself awake, and stretches his rump to the sky. Downward dog is funny because it's true. If sunrise caprine vinyasa exists, then surely so does puppy yoga? I make a mental note to ask Kitty. My sister's social feed could use more fluffy critters to balance out the sponsored beauty products, smoothie mixes, and outfits of the day.

The first T-shirt my fingers grab from MASTER/CLOSET, sitting open on the bedroom carpet, goes over my head. On its front, a horribly made-up face with a great swoosh of red hair and a mouth full of fangs. The cheesy eighties killer-clown flick is more Rob's taste than mine, but I leave the shirt on anyway in honor of Charlene's newfound interest in dolls in space. Not all clowns are dolls, but some dolls *are* clowns, right?

This morning, I skip my inspection in the master-bathroom mirror and find a pair of pants before I leave the bedroom. Lugosi bounds ahead of me as I shuffle down the hall to wake the sleepyhead in the next room. The dog pauses at the doorway and waits, then shunts himself between my legs when I arrive in the threshold of Tanner's bedroom. The retriever might be brave enough to traverse on four paws carpet booby-trapped with plastic bricks, but my slippers and I wait from a safe distance while Lugosi pads to the bed and uses his wet nose to snout the kid awake.

"Good morning," I say when Tanner rolls over, rubbing his eyes open with the backs of his hands. "How was your second night in your new room?"

Tanner's eyebrows furl like he's forgotten we've just moved. His eyes flick to the ceiling, tracking the lack of glow-in-the-dark stars over his bed. He mumbles something that might be "fine" into a yawn and tugs the blankets back up over his head.

Hard same, kid.

Lightning cracks across my forehead, thunder rolling in right behind it, and its officially time for coffee. Sugary-alcohol hangovers aside, the Marshalls are not morning people. There's a reason I unpacked the Keurig first.

"Let's go get some breakfast," I say in an attempt to coax my son's turtled form out from under the blankets, with no response. "We'll put your stars up today."

Tanner wiggles encouragingly, but doesn't emerge.

"You want to go back to the Dream Bean?" Unlike grocery shopping, another trip to the café wasn't on today's agenda, but maybe Barb the friendly barista has the day off? Maybe the place isn't so bad when it doesn't come with PTA? Either way, there's a Trader Joe's at the other end of the strip mall. We can grab a bite of breakfast, stock up on some real food, and still have plenty of time left to put up Tanner's bedroom stars and make a dent in the sea of cardboard boxes before Rob arrives for his welcome-home kiss.

"How about a blueberry muffin?" I offer my son, who still hasn't come up for air.

Tanner's fuzzy-duckling head appears from under his comforter. "Can I get cocoa again, too?"

At the mention of warm dairy, thick froth sloshes inside my stomach. "Get dressed," I tell him before the maelstrom in my guts meets the storm in my brain. Honestly, I don't care what the kid orders, I just don't want to think about it.

Ten minutes later we're settled into the Honda amid the road-trip litter. I plug my phone into the dashboard charging cable and choke down three Tylenol from the stash in my glove box while Lugosi stares from his spot at the front-door windows. The retriever's breath fogs the glass as I back out of the driveway. Still, leaving him behind feels less terrible when I'm in control of my afternoon.

It's overcast, but I slip on my sunglasses anyway as we pass Number Thirty-Four. The purple minivan is missing, but the man busy vacuuming the beige town car in the driveway must be Darla's germophobe doctor husband who makes her promise to avoid pastry, Dave.

He doesn't wave.

The drive takes longer without my new neighbor's smooth navigation, and the parking lot that runs against the row of brand-name stores is suspiciously empty when my Honda swings into the strip mall. Even in the magic hour between when the commuters trickle into their offices and when the lunch tide breaks, the Trader Joe's bumper-car parking lot should be crawling with stay-at-home moms and night shifters, but there are barely any cars between mine and the clump of police cruisers parked outside the lines in front of the Dream Bean Café.

Even in a mostly vacant lot, one cruiser would go unnoticed. Two might warrant a second glance. But five, parked in a misshapen string that centipedes from the front doors around the side of the building, sirens off, lights flashing?

Five is odd.

And then there's the yellow caution tape.

"Why are there so many police cars?" Tanner yawns in the back seat, so the rest of his question comes out in a jumble only a mother could understand as I slip past Trader Joe's and creep the Honda closer to the Dream Bean.

"Are they having brunch, too?" he asks.

"Maybe." Cops are known to enjoy coffee and pastry, after all. I push my sunglasses up into my hair. "Hey, look who I found." For once, my messy car comes in handy. I toss Tanner a blue kaiju from the front passenger seat. Just because I'm nosy doesn't mean my eight-year-old needs to see whatever is going on at the Dream Bean.

My Honda inches near enough that I can make out the numbers on the bright yellow wedges scattered across the hot top, but not what they mark. A crowd of uniforms lingers around the café's perimeter, heads down, faces grim in front of the colorful tempera tree. Lights off and back doors open, an ambulance sits tucked out of view on the side of the café. One of the uniforms squats with his head between his knees by the open doors.

You don't have to be a horror author to know that if an ambulance at a crime scene isn't moving, it's because whomever they're transporting is beyond help. That, and if a paramedic is sucking in air on scene, it's an ugly one.

There's a body bag on the asphalt.

The black bag arches up at one end where toes press against the plastic. An officer steps into my path and points me away from the Dream Bean before I can make out the face staring up between the unzipped folds at the other end. *Closed,* the cop's mouth shapes, about the café, but not before I catch a glimpse of colorful hair dredged in the same bright red as the bulbous red nose, the exaggerated scarlet sneer, screen-printed on the T-shirt stretched across my chest, staring out from inside the body bag.

My foot jerks against the brake pedal, yanking the Honda into a quick stop and release as my eyes flick to the rearview, to make sure Tanner's attention is on the monster in his hand and not the horror show on the other side of his window.

Hot fizzle roils up my throat, pushing at the back of my lips when I rubberneck back to the scene. I know the owner of that red-drenched hair every bit as much as I know the sludge puddled on the concrete is blood. It's Barb's head sticking out of the body bag, a bright red clown's smile grinning from where her throat should be.

The kaiju's growl from the back seat fireworks in the back of my skull, and I spin the car back toward Trader Joe's.

What the hell happened at the Dream Bean?

"Let's skip the muffins this morning, huh, kid?" My foot presses the accelerator to put the scene firmly in my rearview, and I park as far away as possible from the café. "How about we get stuff to make pancakes instead?"

We're out of the car the second the Honda's engine stills. Tanner allows himself to be tugged along but shoots me a withering look.

"Cinnamon rolls," he demands, as retribution for the lost blueberry softball.

"Deal."

The familiar mayhem of the grocery store helps to tamp down the swirling in my guts. Tanner runs relay races up and down the narrow aisles, his sneakers squeaking skid marks in my hangover while I fill my cart with the essentials, then toss in a can of ready-to-heat cinnamon rolls for my eight-year-old's second date with a sugary breakfast. At the checkout, he sneaks a bag of gummy candies into the cart.

"Tanner, come on—" Forget it. A little hair-of-the-dog sugar rush never hurt anyone. I toss a pack of premade chocolate croissants into the cart for myself. We'll all get back on the wagon tomorrow.

The bearded hipster at the register smiles a mouth full of white as he swipes the groceries and tucks them into brown paper bags. The bright red name tag pinned to his shirt says his name is Cicada, which I have to believe isn't what's on his birth certificate.

Good for him.

"Find everything you need?" Cicada asks when he's holding the chocolate croissants, but there's not a shred of malice in the guy's grin. Tanner snatches the gummy candy after it's scanned, tears into the packaging, and stuffs a squishy handful down his gullet along with my Mother of the Year award.

Cicada looks too young to have kids, but he nods like he gets it.

"Hey, what happened at the Dream Bean?" Cicada's junk-food discretion marks him as the sort who overhears a lot of juicy secrets, and his sweet-tooth grin suggests he might be willing to share. Tanner orbiting around my hips, I keep my voice low and skimp on the details. "There's a ton of cops down there," I tell the clerk, in case he doesn't know. "And an ambulance."

Cicada leans in close enough that I can smell Speculoos on his breath. "Rumor is somebody bit it," he says, sliding one finger across his throat. Throngs of customers shove their way through the market's front doors, and he cuts his slice short, ringing his register bell to smother the second half of his sentence. "Sounds like it's a real mess."

Cicada says he doesn't know anything else, just that the uniforms requested copies of all the strip mall stores' security-camera footage. "Not that there will be much," he says. Apparently while most stores have cameras, the lack of sufficient exterior lightning means most of the footage amounts to gritty nothingness.

"Sick tee." Cicada points at my shirt as we leave. "*Killer Klowns from Outer Space*. Classic."

Outside, a dark blue van jostles eagerly over the curb at the café's end of the lot as I stuff Tanner and three paper sacks in the Honda's back seat. *ABC7 Eyewitness News* brakes in a diagonal through the parallel parking lines, a uniform already waving away the van before it ever opens its doors. A dressed-to-impress reporter slides out of the passenger side with a mic, and a guy with a humongous video camera explodes from the back seat. Must be one hell of a story to have a reporter flying in all Gale Weathers in a power suit and stilettos.

Sounds like it's a real mess, Cicada had said, slicing his own throat.

I pull my phone out of my bag and ignore the barrage of notifications as I thumb my way to ABC7's Facebook page and click to subscribe to alerts. When there's news to know, thanks to the instant gratification of social media, Power Suit will make sure I know first.

It's already noon by the time I pass Number Thirty-Four on my return trip. The town car is gone, but the purple minivan is back, its trunk open to expose pots of pretty fall-colored mums awaiting burial. Undigested pastry sits like a boulder in my belly, weighing down my desire to tackle the mountain range of moving boxes that awaits me inside the house as I pull into my creaky-not-creepy driveway.

Plus, Tanner's soft chewing noises turned to snuffles three turns before we got home. My son's unfinished nap and gummy-bear sugar crash means he'll be a live wire for the rest of the day. Still, even if I find the time to fire up my blank manuscript document, there's next to zero chance I'll have the quiet to get anything intelligible onto the page—not that I have any solid ideas yet about what to write about dolls in space.

Car in park, my index finger hovers over the keyless ignition, but my gaze slides to the house's exterior before I push the button.

Every good horror story starts with a creepy house, Kitty said yesterday morning. Normally a comment like that would get my creative motor running, but the cookie-cutter neocolonial has none of the hallmarks of horror architecture. Its multipaned windows, pitched shingles, and moss-green shutters are a far cry from the iconic mansard roofs, widow's walks, and prominent central towers depicted in classic horror homes. This inviting newish construction isn't silhouetted against the desert sky (*Psycho*), doesn't feature intimidating, templelike structures (*House on Haunted Hill*), isn't even affected by wanton deconstructivism (*Beetlejuice*).

This might be worse, actually.

Anyone could take one look at Norman Bates's crumbling Victorian, or Frederick Loren's rented Mayan palace, or the Maitlands' remodeled farmhouse, and know trouble brewed within the walls. It's the perfectly ordinary houses—the cute little redbricks with the picket fences and backyard pools—that play home to the true horrors.

Forget spaceships, the burbs offer a much more sinister form of containment.

My phone buzzes with an incoming notification, but it's not Power Suit sharing news about the gory crime scene at the Dream Bean Café.

Freeze-framed in a half smirk that curls my nerve endings, my sister glares back at me when my thumb swipes the phone screen. Kitty as a monstrous clown.

Not one of the space-dwelling characters on my T-shirt, not Barb's slashed throat grinning up from the Dream Bean pavement, but a familiar white-faced dancing clown—more Bill Skarsgård's version than Tim Curry's, with bloodred hair, crimson scratches, swirling ocean eyes. Tulle frills erupt from my sister's collar. She's painted the tip of her nose cherry red, but even her dusting her face in glitter has done little to soften the effect of the bloody tears dripping down her cheeks.

Seeing my little sister painted up as a murderous, child-eating clown is a specific, sibling type of nightmare, even without what I'd just witnessed on the strip-mall parking pavement. Gotta hand it to her on the timing, though.

I swallow the sludge rising in my throat back down where it belongs, then tap the screen so the image dissolves into replay.

Kitty waves barefaced at the camera. "I was thinking," she says as she pulls her light brown hair tight behind her ears. "Brat summer is winding down and Spooky Season is right around the corner—" My sister paints a streak of white greasepaint down her left cheek, followed by a bold red slash on the tip of her nose. "Why don't we do a series of attention-grabbing makeup tutorials to practice manifesting our inner villains right in time for Halloween?"

I thumb the video ahead, silencing Kitty's narration as I watch my little sister paint herself into a monstrous clown. Scary houses, furnaces, Stephen King, Pennywise. Kitty's train of thought is easy enough to follow, even if I have no idea where she's going.

I drop a red balloon emoji in the comments section and am rewarded with an alert from ABC7: LOCAL BARISTA FOUND MURDERED. Her hair is a simple, single shade of green and she's managed to pull off a surprisingly pleasant smile, but the face under the all-caps headline is definitely Barb, Barbara Shelton, previously of the Dream Bean Café.

Because Bluetooth doesn't always make sense, the car's stereo intercepts the phone's audio as the news story loads. Kitty's evil clown cackles through the speakers, and my phone *thunks* into my lap when something knocks against the driver's-side window glass.

My window is down before I feel the button under my finger. If this were a horror movie, I'd be the first to die.

But it's Darla.

Wearing a wide-brimmed straw gardening hat dyed a perfect pink to coordinate with her purple leggings, my new neighbor beams on the other side of the driver's-side window, her smile cheerful in the bright midday sun. Dirt streaks down her cheeks and her fingers bear grass stains where she's got a death grip on a three-ring binder clutched to her chest. The binder is red, the same color as the pot of seasonal mums stuffed worrisomely under her arm, tucked in against a BRUNSWICK ELEMENTARY sign, twin to the one that's planted in her front yard.

"I'm so sorry to drop by unannounced a second time in a row." Darla keeps her voice low, so as not to rouse the kid who valiantly slept through his aunt's cackling in the back seat. "But I saw you pull in and I rushed right down to drop this off."

I'd like to think Darla only means the binder, but I have a bad feeling about the yard sign and the flowers. Like so many couples, lawn care is Rob's domain, though neither of us identify as yard sign people.

She peels the binder from her chest and turns it around like it's a cherished artifact.

"Is everything okay, dear?" Darla asks when I stare too long at the Xerox paper stuffed inside the CULTURAL ARTS binder's clear front cover.

I retrieve the phone from my lap and turn it so she can see Barb's face on its screen.

Her smile stutters but she recovers quickly. "I heard," she whispers. "Rosa mentioned it on the group text. Her husband was on scene this morning."

The group text. Damn it.

"I haven't had a chance to catch up on this morning's messages." It's only a *partial* lie, so I don't feel too bad about not admitting I haven't so much as taken the group text off mute, much less opened the thread, since yesterday. "We just came from Trader Joe's and saw all the"—I check the rearview to make sure my son's eyes stay closed—"*activity* in the parking lot."

"It's just *so* horrible, isn't it?" Darla's smile doesn't falter when she asks, and I wonder if she's thinking what I was—that Barb probably had it coming, with that shitty attitude of hers. "It's hard to imagine that something so terrible could have happened right in our neighborhood, isn't it? What a bizarre coincidence." She shudders. "We might have been some of the last people to see her alive."

The Dream Bean pastry bag Barb sacked my passive-aggressive bonus cream cheese–filled croissant in is still tacked to the corkboard in my work-in-progress office. It seems unlikely that we might have been some of the *last* people to see the barista alive, considering we left the café before noon, but the sugar-stained pastry bag probably still has her fingerprints on it.

Seriously, what the *hell* happened at the Dream Bean?

"I know just what we need to get our minds off all that mess," Darla says on the other side of my rolled-down window. She does a little skitter that makes the mums bob in their pot. "Let's get dolled up!"

She means she wants to make me up. "Oh, I've got so much unpacking—"

Darla shunts the binder through my open window. She sets the flowerpot and yard sign down at the edge of the driveway, does her little cannonball-fisted jitter, and has already scuttled halfway back down the street before I can tell her I really, *really* don't want to play dress-up.

A woman *just* died, after all.

CHAPTER SEVEN

When Darla barrels through the front door twenty minutes later, she's traded her gardening clothes for another coordinated sweats-and-headband ensemble and scrubbed herself free of grass stains. No Westminster Chimes this time, just two quick raps and a turn of the knob. You'd think new neighbors, like vampires, would need to be invited in. Probably the familiar entry is an old habit from when Patti lived in my house, but, besides my sister, I've never had a friend close enough to bypass the whole knocking part of coming around.

Inviting oneself over to get dolled up is new, too.

In the foyer, Darla parks her spotless Keds by the front door, then straightens them on the mat next to my Converse, sets her purse on the hardwood, and joins me in the kitchen. Her shell-pink toenail polish matches the little flowers embroidered along her sweatshirt neckline, the blooms in her cheeks. She clutches a cosmetics case against her chest with the same level of possession that Tanner guards his kaiju.

"Ready, dear?" she asks, about this completely unwanted makeover.

Not even close, but I don't want to risk losing a new friend.

"Maybe we can do this another day?" I make a show of shelving groceries. "My hands are just so full trying to get this place unpacked."

Tanner's mess of school supplies is still in a jumble on the countertop, waiting to be labeled with his name and grade and stuffed into his new backpack. "Maybe after school starts?"

A mom of two herself, I hope Darla will show me mercy, but her pout looks a lot like my sister's. "It won't take long, I promise. And I could *really* use the practice before Doll's Night."

Tanner bounds into the kitchen, Lugosi hot on his heels, before I can come up with another excuse. My son's eyes fix through the window on the swing set Patti left behind in the backyard. "Can I play outside?"

My hand stalls with a jug of soy milk halfway to the fridge while I run through my mental checklist of backyard dangers. The yard is mowed and fenced, there are no obvious sink holes or trees with branches low enough he could hoist himself up, break his neck falling back down. We do not have a pool. But with Darla in my kitchen, I'm no longer confident that eight is old enough to allow my child to play unsupervised in his own backyard. Why does being a mother make every decision so difficult?

"Mom, can I?" Tanner begs.

Darla sets her case on the counter beside the Cultural Arts binder and the sweaty can of unopened cinnamon-roll dough while I deliberate. "Oh, I have just the thing!" she says, then jigs back to her purse in the entry and returns with a worn yellow ball cupped in her palm. "I found it on the street while I was gardening." She passes me the ball. "I'm sure Lugosi loves tennis balls."

Of course he does. Few dogs can resist the siren song of balding yellow fuzz?

"Actually, this is one of Lugosi's." I point to the small pair of crossed blue anchors, the gnawed-upon Coast Guard life-ring seal, in Darla's hand. Usually, the retriever's a stickler about his toys. I have no idea how his ball made it all the way down to Number Thirty-Four's end of the street.

"It must have escaped from my back seat and tried to roll its way to freedom." My best guess, considering the convenience store in my Honda.

Tanner whines my name a few decibels louder.

"Back where it belongs then," Darla says, referring, I think, to the half-chewed tennis ball and not the kid slowly going caveman on the other side of the kitchen.

My eight-year-old begins to vibrate.

I toss Tanner the tennis ball before he can banshee out my name again. "Go wild—but just for a little while. We're going to put your stars up in your room." I have to call the rest after him when he pivots on his sneaker hard enough to leave a mark on the ceramic.

Tanner and Lugosi barrel out the back door, letting it slam shut behind them, and Darla spots the Keurig on the opposite end of the countertop. Her eyebrows pinch together, but the lower half of her face deflates like a balloon. "You moved your coffeepot?"

I pretend that sentence ends in a period, not a question mark. "Oh, you know. Still trying to find the perfect spot for everything."

From the look on her face, Darla feels she's already showed me the perfect spot for the Keurig. But she's back to white-knuckling that cosmetics case of hers, so we may as well get this over with.

"Kitchen table or the living room sofa?" I assume makeovers are a downstairs activity, but Darla releases her case to one hand, grabs my hand with the other, and tugs me away from the refrigerator. My feet are on the stairs before I can protest, like we're girls racing barefoot to our bedroom to dish about boys or put hexes on our enemies, and not like she's funneling me to my doom one step at a time.

"This is going to be so much *fun*," Darla says.

Suddenly, I miss my sister. Spontaneous homemade makeovers were regular affairs in our girlhood bedroom. Kitty harvested trash-can cosmetics leftovers, pilfered samples torn from magazine pages and drugstore counters. She always wanted to look just like Mom.

Just like Mom.

We hit the half landing and Darla squeezes my hand. She stops long enough to say, "You're going to be such a *doll*," then tugs me up the second flight.

I was a doll yesterday, Darla said at Dream Bean, in my monstress hair and two-day-worn horror-movie T-shirt, but maybe she forgot.

Carpet warms the underside of my feet when the stairs end. Darla passes the guest bedroom, the hall bath, Tanner's room, beelining for the primary bedroom. Like I'd guessed before, she definitely knows the place better than I do.

As our toes cross the double-door finish line to the master suite, Darla comes up short.

She points to my bedroom's far corner, where clumps of disemboweled duffel bags hemorrhage cotton entrails at the threshold of the empty closet. "Patti had a lovely vanity right over there."

Darla flaps her wrist to take in the room, and she's lucky Lugosi's not here to see the light from her disco-ball wedding ring skitter along the wall. She marches to the largest window and pulls up the blinds. "The light in the bedroom is so much better than the bath," she says, looking down to wave at the boy and dog invisible from my line of sight. "Natural is always preferable to fluorescent."

"You want to do this in here?"

Silly question, I know, but I have to ask. This morning, I got fully dressed before I left my bedroom, but I didn't bother to make the bed. Rob's corner of the fitted sheet has come free, and the top sheet is loose skin peeling off a sunburned back. We're active sleepers, but the twisted comforter just makes a night of tossing and turning look like sex bed. The empty rosé bottle on the nightstand from Darla's welcome basket doesn't help.

Oh well. There are worse things than another woman thinking I had a great time last night with my husband, right?

I throw the comforter over the mangled sheets and situate myself on the edge of the mattress. Darla climbs on after me, crisscross-applesaucing so we face each other. Our knees bump as she pulls the colorful plastic makeup case from the bed's foot and settles it between us.

She's so close I can see the foundation line on her throat. "Nice Caboodles," I say.

Darla's lip gloss slicks the curve of her mouth into a shiny smile. "You've seen a showcase like this before?"

"Not since the nineties." My mother had a traveling cosmetics showcase, back when she sold beauty door to door. Mom's was calamine-lotion pink, more padded vinyl briefcase than plastic shoebox, but Darla's pink-and-teal makeup organizer might have come straight out of my girlhood bedroom—minus the BPA-FREE label and Dollface branding. "I had one just like that, but in a different color."

"Do you still have it?"

When I shake my head no, she tsks and clicks open the case's lid. "That's a shame."

My girlhood Caboodles came with a mirror mounted inside the top, but Darla's has a photo tacked under its hood. Teased hair, pink on top of more pink, lots of glitter, Darla's face smiles back from the picture. Her pose is somewhere between old-school senior photo and 1995 Glamour Shots, but the photo is recent enough it might have been taken yesterday.

"Did you know that Caboodles were inspired by Vanna White?" Darla asks.

I did not. "Like, *Wheel of Fortune* Vanna White?"

"She was photographed in the late eighties using a Plano tackle box to organize her makeup." Darla nods as she parts the twin trays that form the kit's top shelf, splitting open the neatly arranged level of brushes and applicators. Underneath, full-size Fabergé-egg cosmetics pods and girlish embossed compacts stuff the Caboodles' belly, just like the sample-size ones she put in my welcome basket. Her voice goes flat as she runs her fingertips over the bounty. "The next year, Plano launched On-the-Go Girl Caboodles to help ladies organize and contain all their facial beauty products." Darla looks at me. "Iconic, right?"

Rebranded tackle boxes to contain women's faces, not so much, but Vanna White? Always. "Totally."

This close, I can see where ballerina pink blends into fuchsia in the creases of Darla's eyelids, the places where concealer smooths over her skin's imperfections, where her lip gloss has slipped outside the lines. A red blush line travels down the length of her cheek to meet the not-quite-blended foundation line on her throat.

"Well, if you fall in love with Dollface as much I have," my sweet new neighbor says, "you can get one just like mine."

It's unclear whether she means the face or the Caboodles. Either way, I'm good.

"I don't wear a lot of makeup," I warn her, carefully choosing my words so I don't come off judgy about her MLM. "I just keep my skin-care stuff in the canvas pouch that came with the product. But I only have foundation and mascara, a couple of eyeliners. The basics."

Darla lifts out a small Dollface-pink hand towel and smooths it on the comforter. Her lips purse together as she selects an assortment of bits and bulbs from the Caboodles' belly and positions them on the cloth, fingernails tapping along the edges in a series of soft clicks. Brushes and sponges from the twin trays are lined in neat rows at one end of the cloth. Arranged like this, the setup looks worrisomely surgical.

"You'd be surprised what a tiny bit of makeup can do." Darla lifts her hands and vogues around her face. "It can literally change *everything.*"

She frowns when I do. "What's wrong, dear?"

Even to me trauma dumping seems the wrong way to go toward making new friends, and yet my mouth is open and I'm already unloading on Darla about my dead mother. "Mom spent her whole life trying to build this perfect little family, but one day everything just fell apart. I guess she decided if she couldn't have the perfect life, she didn't want one at all." I'd almost been a teenager when Mom came unstitched on the bedroom closet floor, my little sister younger then than Tanner is now. A lifetime ago, really, but I can still see those red lines on her skin like it was yesterday.

"My mother sold beauty products, too," I tell Darla, weakly. "She even won a car."

"It's a terrible thing when our insides change the way we feel on the outside." The other woman's usual smile flatlines into concern as she straightens her final brush. "That's why I signed up to sell Dollface." She pushes a smile back into place. "Sometimes we need to look our best to feel our best."

A makeover is hardly a cure-all for undiagnosed mental illness, but the intent is sweet. "Anyway, makeup is my sister Kitty's thing," I tell Darla as my cheeks get warm. "I'm more of a mascara-and-ChapStick kind of girl—but I think I've seen this brand on her feed before, actually." So many products go across Kitty's social feed that it's impossible to know for sure if Dollface has made the cut, but it seems likely enough to take a guess.

"Oh, you're going to love it." Darla holds a bundle of bobby pins upright. "Are you ready?" When I nod, she bats her eyes as she bites a pin apart, holds it open in her fingers, and fixes a stiff, practiced smile in place that says we are ready to begin. "Now, first, I'm going to pin your hair back, out of the way." She illustrates this by pulling her own hands backward to brush away imaginary hair. "That way you can see her whole face," she says, more to my face than to me.

Cool metal touches my forehead and the bobby pins glide into my hair, scraping lightly along my scalp as Darla drives them home. A few stray strands must flutter loose because she licks at her lip and smooths her fingertips against my hairline. "There," she says. "Perfect."

"Do you do a lot of these?" It's hard not to speak to someone when their mouth is one deep breath away from yours. "Makeovers, I mean."

When Darla pulls back, her face is a different shade of pink. "You're my first." Then, "Take a moment to look at her features," she instructs herself.

Her breath blows against my face like a lover's, and her fingertips blur the edges of my vision. Darla's fingers are lighter than Rob's, cooler than Tanner's. I can't remember the last time someone other than my husband or my son touched my face.

"Okay, then." Darla's hands hover over her palette. She plucks up a baby-blue bottle from the lineup, presses two pumps of cream onto a sponge, and flattens it with the end of a Q-tip. The spatter is even cooler than her fingers against my skin. "Now that we have our canvas, let's apply just a light coat of primer to prepare the skin for full coverage. There, that's right."

She carries on two conversations as she works—one with me, the other with the items she's laid out on her cloth. Darla talks herself through a series of foundations, concealers, contour creams. "So, tell me all about your new book." She pulls a wand from a tube of highlighter and taps cream onto a sponge. "I'd love to hear all about it."

It takes me a few tries to get any words out, each one patted into silence by Darla's sponges against my skin.

"It's still . . . a work in progress." The words fall out while she works on my eyebrows, quick flicks with a spiky wand and a touch of pencil. "I've got a couple of ideas percolating, I'm just not sure how they fit together yet. I'm still waiting for the right spark to light the whole idea up."

I close my eyes so Darla can brush color over the lids. "You'll find the perfect inspiration." Now she slides the creamy tip of an eyeliner pencil at the edges of my eyelids, then pauses to grin. "If not, there's always feasting on your enemies." She traces the line back and forth, stretching it beyond the corner of my eye. "In the meantime, I'm so excited you've joined the Brunswick PTA. Patti was on the board, too."

Her hands move away, and I open my eyes to her pink headband smile, still as perky as when we'd started. "Isn't that lovely?" Darla asks herself as she dabs a thick brush into a rose palette, pats away the excess blusher, and dusts the soft pouf against my cheekbones.

"So that's why there's an open seat for Cultural Arts," I say when she finishes with the brush and begins pumping a mascara tube.

Darla prompts me to blink so she can twirl the spindly tube between my lashes. "Patti was vice president. Maribel moved into her position this year. She used to be our Events chair."

Now the whole Ice Cream Debate makes more sense, though VP feels like an upgrade.

"Maribel can come on . . . strong," Darla says, reading my mind. She pulls the wand away, then leans in close to check for clumps. "She went through a rough divorce last year, poor dear. Such a shame."

Darla selects a lipstick from the cloth and gestures at her own smile until I pucker up. The scent of red wax unfurls under my nose. "That's horrible," I say after she smears my lips, "but it doesn't give her an excuse to be rude."

God don't like ugly, as my mother used to warn my sister and me, which had nothing to do with looks.

Darla caps the lipstick, blinks at me, and cocks her head. "Did you think Maribel was rude?"

Maybe this is a trick question. Or a test, like when I'd asked about her favorite horror movie. "She . . ." Not just Maribel, but Kellen, Sasha, even Beth. The way they dismissed Darla, turned their noses up at her. "They all kinda came off a little . . . unfriendly. It's no big deal," I add when her face goes department-store-mannequin hard. "Just, you know, your garden-variety stuff. I'm sure they'll be great once I get to know them."

Darla packs items away without a word. My sweet new neighbor may have plastered fifteen coats of paint on my face, but that's nothing compared to how many emotions flash across her features. She lands on a smirk that's cyanide sweet, all lips and no eyes. Kitty has a similar one. It means she's up to no good.

"You know, they're about the same." Darla stifles a giggle. "But we can all have a fresh start toward a more beautiful future. Now that you're here."

My face is so stiff it cracks when my eyebrows crunch together. What I have to do with other people's fresh starts, I have no idea, but Darla spritzes my face with finishing spray before I can ask.

"Oh shoot," she says. "I left my phone in my purse. I want to take a photo for you really quick."

God, no. I push my feet to the edge of the bed to stand up. "That's okay. I can look in the bathroom mirror."

"A picture will help you re-create the look." Darla pats me back down and heads for the door. "I'll be back in a jiff."

I could go into the bathroom while Darla is downstairs, but I don't, no matter how much the sludge on my skin begs to be scrubbed off. Pics can be deleted, but the stuff you see in the bathroom mirror will haunt you.

Darla's footsteps carry her down the stairs and back up. She jostles onto the bed, aims her phone at my face, and clicks. She moons over the picture before showing it to me. "What do you think?"

I think I look like an Andy Warhol painting—thick lines, bold colors, unnatural smile. Blue clouds my eyes, red smears outside the edges of my lips. The black eyeliner wings out like it might try to fly off my face. A foundation line rings my throat, like the one on Darla. Barb had a wedge of cake tattooed on her neck, I remember. My mother, a red collar, like that old ghost story about the little girl's green ribbon. If I unstitch the line around my throat, maybe my head will fall off, too.

Just like Mom.

Noise funnels up out of my mouth, something halfway between a gasp and a gag. I'd confided about my mother's suicide, though not how she'd made up her face before she cut herself to pieces on the bedroom closet floor.

Darla claps her hands and snaps her case shut, mistaking my shock for awe. "I knew you'd love it."

When the front door closes behind Darla, I grab my phone off the counter, check to make sure Tanner and Lugosi are still playing on the swing set, and open the PTA group text, scrolling through the dozens of new messages as I head back upstairs. Her throat was practically sawed in half, the most recent text reads, but they aren't sure by what yet.

Barb, sliced apart in the parking lot. Mom, cut open on the closet floor. And now me, with my dead mother's face in my new master bedroom.

I twist on the bathroom sink faucet and dunk my head under. Eyes closed, I fumble for face wash while I wait for the tap to turn warm, then I scrub my face, raking my fingers into my flesh until I've peeled off both my makeover and my first layer of skin. I don't stop scrubbing until my face burns and soap stings my eyes.

CHAPTER EIGHT

Hot water turns my fingers pink.

The water from the kitchen faucet scalds off another layer of skin as it burns around the dinner plate clutched in my hand. Soap runs off the dish and stings my scrub-sore fingers. Probably I should have worn gloves, but it's no matter. I've shed a few layers of skin today already, consequences of the post-makeover detox that peeled off half my face along with the layers of Darla's war paint. It'd required three rounds of exfoliant to wash my dead mother's face off my own. Now, my skin feels warm and smarting, like sunburn. A faint ring of raw cherry red still stains the corners of my mouth.

My hands had been wet, too, the day I found my mother dead on the floor of her bedroom closet, the soggy bundle of my drowned pet dripping sun-warmed pool water, the smell of copper and chlorine from his feathers onto the carpet.

Kitty called twice while I was scrubbing my face, but both times I let voicemail take the call. We rarely miss our daily chats, and though I want to tell her about the Dollface makeover, some topics are off-limits, even for sisters.

In this case, maybe *especially* for sisters.

A muffled drumbeat (kick, kick, snare, kick) rumbles beneath me, and the sudden noise slips the plate from my hand. Soapy water bites at my chapped lips when the dish splashes into the sink. The worst part about settling into a new place is getting back to the humdrum of regular chores. KITCHEN/DISHES sits still half unpacked in the corner, newspaper spilling among a jumble of junk that still needs to find a home in the cabinets. We should have ridden out a few more nights on paper plates.

Rob's footsteps pound up the basement stairs.

"Soundproofing is coming along." My husband's voice comes out breathy from the climb. "Let me take care of the dishes," he says from the doorway. "You've done enough work around here today."

He's not wrong. After the disastrous makeover, I'd traded the *Killer Klowns* T-shirt and jeans for a pair of joggers and a plain black tank, corralled my monstress hair, and attacked unpacking as viciously as I had my own face: slicing open boxes, gutting their insides, stuffing away their contents. Our creaky-not-creepy new house is messier than before—the kitchen looks like a frat-party aftermath with all the cups and utensils scattered—but the Marshalls have officially moved into Patti Townsend's old house.

"I got it." I rinse ceramic under warm water, careful not to drop the plate a third time. "Thanks for getting Tanner to bed."

Rob's voice pours over my shoulder like a glass of wine: "You're next."

"Oh, yeah?" I set the clean dish into the dry half of the sink and turn to see my darling husband poised against the kitchen threshold like a romance-novel leading man, with one arm at his side and hand tucked wrist-deep in his pocket, other arm crooked on its elbow against the frame, both forearms swollen from use. Rob drums barefoot, says it helps his tempo, and when he scratches one foot against the Achilles' heel of the other, the movement ripples up his pajama pant leg to the hem of his white cotton T-shirt.

The sudden warmth in the lower parts of my body has nothing to do with the hot water still scalding my hand, the steam fogging up the window over the kitchen sink. If Tanner's down for the night, we're alone, Rob and me. "In that case," I tell him, "maybe you *should* help me with the dishes."

Rob's long fingers rake through the five-o'clock shadow spreading across the lower half of his jaw, but the dimple in his cheek shows through when he quirks his lips to one side. "My pleasure."

He grabs a dishrag from the stack on the counter, whips it unfolded, and dries one of the plates in a way that makes my insides burn.

"Tanner's stars look great," Rob says while I try to focus on rinsing silverware and not the way my husband caresses our dishes. "Is that Orion I noticed over his bed?"

"And Cassiopeia and Ursa Major." Two forks and a spoon get deposited into Rob's half of the sink, and I'm on to the next plate. "The kid was very specific about his constellations after having his nose stuffed into space books the last two days of the drive. It took me four tries to line up Orion's Belt, so getting space math right is going to be hell."

"Oh?" Well aware of my disinterest in sci-fi, Rob waits patiently for me to elaborate.

"The other day Charlene and I brainstormed about dolls in space. Still rolling it around in my brain to see if a plot falls out."

"You ought to watch *Superstar.*" He catches the face I make as I try to imagine what made him think of Molly Shannon's *SNL* skit-cum-feature-film. "The Karen Carpenter movie."

Different *Superstar*, then. "The singer from the seventies duo?"

"John Bonham had a lot to say when she was voted best rock drummer in 1975." My seventies musical-trivia knowledge runs thin, but Led Zeppelin's drummer is a household name, thanks to my husband. "But when someone asked Buddy Rich if he liked any rock drummers, he named Karen."

Like my editor's *Event Horizon* meets *Barbarella* horror space-odyssey pitch and my sister's newfound love of scary-clown makeup tutorials, I'm having a hard time following Rob's train of thought. "And *Superstar* has to do with dolls in space how?"

Rob shakes his head as if I should know this already. "In the movie Barbie dolls play all the characters."

"Great. Drum Machine Barbie can lead the mission to Betelgeuse," I tell him. "Tanner gave that one prime billing in his ceiling sky."

"It *is* one of the brightest stars in the night sky." Rob rubs the silverware dry, his thumb curving the dishrag across the forks' thin tines in a way that does something to my knees. Technically, Betelgeuse is only the tenth-brightest star in the night sky, but since it's the second-brightest star in the Orion constellation, I let it go.

"Sounds like *National Geographic Kids* is doing something right," Rob says. "Or we just lucked into a smart kid."

"Maybe next they'll put out an issue on household organization so he can help me figure out where to put everything." The stacks of homeless wedding china we never use, the half-sorted collections of spices and dry goods we'd packed instead of throwing out, need to find someplace to go. "The rest of the house is coming along, but this kitchen is very much a work in progress."

Rob toes an empty box out of the way and relocates a butter dish that belongs in the fridge. "What are you talking about? It looks great."

My phone flashes Kitty's contact photo as it lights up with an incoming FaceTime call. After two rings through to voicemail, video is the next escalation in our communication protocol. After that comes a panicked message to Rob, his least favorite step.

He nods at the phone. "Want me to finish up so you can talk?"

"I'll call her back later." After Mom died, Kitty and I bounced from relative to relative to stay out of the foster system. It kept us together, but after high school graduation I went off to college, then met Rob, and . . . well, life happened. Kitty hadn't hit double digits that fateful summer, and I've spent the better part of three decades insulating her from reliving our shared trauma, though things got harder when I became a mom myself and had to pull back on parenting my little sister. Now, it's not that I *don't* want to talk to Kitty, it's that between Darla's makeover and the book idea, it's probably better if I keep my thoughts to myself.

In my limited peripheral vision, my husband's gaze wanders over the splotches across my cheeks (pink), the skin on my chin (flaky), the stain around my lips (faint but obvious). Rob makes it a point never to comment on a woman's appearance, but the tone of concern is evident in his voice. "You sure?"

"Yep." I make my response as light as possible and start in on the skillet like it's done something wrong.

Rob side-eyes me a beat longer, but lets it go. "So, other than going full planetarium in Tanner's room, how was the rest of your day?"

Just like I promised to always take care of my sister, I've vowed never to lie outright to my husband. "Weird," I confess as a first layer of yuck rinses out of the skillet.

"I like weird." He flips the rag over his shoulder, waiting while I double down on another round of scrubbing.

I seriously doubt my day is the kind of weird Rob enjoys, but Darla's visit had eaten up my afternoon, and until he got Tanner to bed and out of earshot, I haven't had a chance to tell my husband about the murder at the Dream Bean. "Remember yesterday I told you about going to the café?"

He nods. "Your exciting PTA brunch."

"There's a Trader Joe's in the same strip mall. I went back over there this morning to get some groceries, and someone had been killed—the barista from yesterday." It happened sometime last night, I tell him. "They were still loading the body up when I drove by."

Rob blinks as he digests the information. "How do you know it was the same barista?"

"She had this super-colorful-hair thing going on. It's hard to miss." The scene flashes through my memory. So much blood, dripping from the tips of Barb's hair, pooling on the concrete. Almost as much as when I'd found my mother bleeding out on the carpet. "And then I saw her face on the news," I add, before he can ask if I'm sure.

Rob's five-o'clock shadow forms a ring around parted lips that seem to struggle to form words. "Wow," he manages, finally. "And you were worried the suburbs would be boring."

Another rinse and the skillet is in satisfactory condition to hand off for drying. Rob palms the damp dishrag into the pan.

"A coffee-shop murder," he adds, still musing. "Sounds like a cozy mystery—Charlene would lay an egg."

The skillet was the last dish. "We said no animal metaphors," I remind him as I twist off the tap.

"Charlene would shit a brick," he amends.

Better for the chicken, but probably worse for Charlene. Rob's right, though. My editor has a palate for mysteries, which tend to be better sellers than straight horror. Just when I'm starting to get okay with the idea of bleeding my trauma onto the page in a haunted space romp, one comment about Barb's bloody demise and Charlene would forget all about cosmic dolls.

Rob surveys the kitchen like he can divine which cabinet I've unpacked the pots and pans into, then gives up and puts the skillet on the counter. *"Nightmare at the Dream Bean Café."* He snaps his fingers and his dimple deepens. "It could be a whole series—*A Terrifying Tale at the Library, Slaughter at the Slap-n-Go Grocery.* You'd be the next Agatha Christie."

I suppress a snort. Darla had mentioned inspiration right after Barb body-shamed her about cream cheese–filled croissants. If the idea of my sweet new neighbor returning to the café after dark to take a slice out of the barista weren't so absurd, a whodunit could be a fun premise for a new thriller. *Kismet,* Charlene would call it—one of those beautiful moments when truth really is stranger than fiction.

Barb, bless her heart, would likely disagree.

"A woman is dead, Marshall."

Rob grimaces and loses the grin. "Sorry for bright-siding murder. It's a coping mechanism."

"What is, murder?" I waggle my eyebrows. "Or torturing your wife with terrible dad jokes?"

The dimple reappears in Rob's cheek. "You want torture? I'll give you torture." He slides his body close enough to mine that I can feel its heat, then runs his thumb down my spine and bends so that his next words brush against my neck on the way out of his mouth. A warm sensation spreads under my joggers.

Something cool touches my forearm, and I look down to see the unwashed glass Rob holds against my skin.

"You forgot a glass," he whispers.

Rob dumps the glass into the soapy water and his warmth peels away as I twist the faucet back on with a groan, plunge the dish sponge into the glass.

The news hadn't mentioned the method of Barb's death, but someone on the group text—maybe Rosa, who probably shouldn't be divulging police pillow talk—confirmed Barb's throat had been slit. I'm not a detective, but even a lowly horror author can tell a crime that's personal from a random tragedy. Cutting through Barb meant the killer had gotten close.

Close enough, at least figuratively, to taste the slice of cake tattooed on the woman's neck.

Not very sweet, I'd thought of Barb yesterday, and goose bumps prickle up my forearms despite the soapy dishwater.

"What's weird about the whole thing is that barista was over-the-top rude when I saw her yesterday." I tell Rob how she'd snarled at Tanner, shamed Darla for her pastry order. Barb basically called Darla fat to her face—not that there's anything wrong with a larger frame, much less anything appropriate about commenting on someone else's body, but comments like that could push a girl over the edge in a beauty-obsessed culture where a person's value is measured by their appearance. "Who knows how many people she insulted while she was safe behind that pastry counter? Maybe all that ugliness caught up with her."

"Extremely rude," Rob agrees, "but probably not enough to justify murder."

"Says a white man who's never had to defend himself against the insidious perils of the patriarchy."

My husband gives me that look, the one that says he's starting to worry. "You're not implying that our new-neighbor-slash-PTA-president had something to do with the murder, are you?"

"Of course not." Sweet suburban PTA moms are one thing, but yesterday even I'd assumed that karma would eventually come calling for Barb.

Apparently, last night it had. Barb's murder has been an ongoing discussion on the Brunswick PTA Mean Girls group text ever since it broke on the news. I hadn't read much beyond the neck-sawing part, but all those unnamed green bubbles had had a lot of snarky opinions on what had happened to Barbara Shelton.

Hands still in the water, I turn on Rob. "Tell me, honestly: Would you prefer it if I were the kind of work-from-home mom who wrote cozy mysteries between yoga class and grocery shopping?"

Rob's shoulders square up. "Whoa, where's that coming from?"

"I just never feel like I fit in with the other moms," I say as he drops the dish towel, puts the glass down, and rearranges himself to rub my shoulders. As rude as that barista was to Darla, the rest of the women on the PTA Board were just as bad, with their better-than-you attitudes, punctual timepieces, and designer clothes. "Would you prefer a wife who gets her lashes done and buys her clothes at Nordstrom Rack instead of Spirit Halloween?"

I can't see him behind me, but Rob's strong drummer's fingers press into the achy spot in my upper back. "The most beautiful version of the woman I married is when she's happy—not cooking, not cleaning, not . . . stretching?" Rob's hands go still. "Okay, wait, maybe I *do* like it when you get all bendy." He pulls me backward by the hips and presses my body against his as he kisses the top of my head, the side of my neck. "I was kidding about the cozy mysteries," my darling husband says. "I love reading reviews where readers say you gave them nightmares. *That's* the woman I married."

Rob reaches around me and turns off the faucet, then stamps a kiss onto my temple. When his lips leave my skin, they take my stress along with them. The day isn't completely melted away, but it's close. He spins me around, so we face each other. Halfway up his forehead, Rob's eyebrows wait for me to tell him I'm okay.

Instead, I apologize for the dramatics and pull the drain plug. "After the whole Dream Bean thing this morning, Darla came over and gave me a makeover. When she finished, I looked exactly like my mom. It just . . . it brought everything back." The plumbing slurps up the last sip of dishwater with an unappetizing gurgle. "It took me longer to wash all that makeup off than to put an entire night sky on Tanner's ceiling."

Dawn, on Rob's face. "That explains the—" He stops, splays his palm in front of his face, waves it side to side. "The facial?"

"Yeah, it's gonna take a while to regrow all my skin."

He shrugs. "Tell everyone you got a chemical peel."

Leftover dishwater drips off my fingers into the empty sink as I curve my lips into a frown. "You don't know what a chemical peel is."

"I do not," Rob admits, "but I can ask Kitty when she activates emergency protocol and calls me next."

Right. I'd forgotten about my sister.

"Please call her back—preferably *before* I get myself stuck in a three-hour infomercial for men's products about the beard I don't have."

"She's not that bad." Really, she is, but it won't be long before the next hashtag comes along and my sister abandons her sudden interest in makeup tutorials and is on to the next fad that helps her make a living on social media.

Or so I can hope.

I cringe, remembering Kitty's scary-clown tutorial. Not that I don't love a Kittywise in theory, it's just the look won't let me forget that mental snapshot of Barb and the red line running across her throat.

The unblended foundation line on Darla's throat. On Mom's throat. On *mine.*

"Jill." Rob's voice rumbles against the back of my neck, over my shoulder.

Water drips from my fingertips as my husband's hand slips under my tank top and slides around my waist. His fingers splay against my stomach, his palm hot against my flesh, his thumb brushing the soft curve above my hip.

"Relax." Rob breathes against my neck, right at the end of where that line used to be. "It's been a rough couple of days, and you've got a lot on your mind, but everything is good, I promise. The house is coming along, you're closing in on a new book idea, and Tanner is tucked in for the night." His pinkie tickles along the jogger waistband. "Things are always strangest right before they get back to normal."

Rob's right. Of course, he's right.

Probably.

"I just feel like I've wandered inside some *Twilight Zone* episode that's half *Stepford Wives,* half slasher movie. Everything from the gift basket to Barb. It's *weird.*"

"Now *that* could be your next book." Rob pins my body between his hand and his chest while the other hand lands on the swell of my hip. "Charlene would love it," he says, tightening his hold on me as he draws out the last two words, then lets them fade like the steam vanishing off the kitchen-sink window. Rob's hands slide together at my waist and his mouth drifts closer to my neck as he speaks. "But this is nothing like a slasher movie," his lips say as they move down my shoulder, my arms, my ribs.

Rob's body lowers alongside mine, taking my joggers down with him, and stubble tickles my skin as he kisses the backs of my thighs.

"Sure, it is," I say as he drops onto one knee behind me to lift one ankle, then the other, freeing my feet. "We just finished act one. New girl in town meets a new group of people and one of them turns up dead."

My hands clench around the edge of the sink as Rob slips my underwear off, his mouth inching closer to secret places. "That makes you the Final Girl, then," he says, between kisses.

His breath is warm against my softest parts. "Fuck me, right?"

Rob growls when he stands and a warm current rolls up my spine as he tightens my half-naked body against his. The dampness blooming in my lower half is nothing like the water still trickling from my fingers.

"But isn't the Final Girl always a virgin?" Rob asks as one of his hands finds its place under my shirt again. His thumb tickles just under my breasts as his other hand curls gently around my throat. It's a threat and a tease at the same time, the kind that makes my skin flare hot and knees go weak. "I wouldn't want to ruin your big climax."

My breath catches in my throat as my husband's hand moves up from around my neck to palm my cheek, thumb tracing the tender skin at my jaw, the curve of my cheekbone. A spur of movement on the other side of the kitchen window catches my eye, but then his palm twists my head away from the glass.

"Final Girl purity is an outdated misogynist trope," I tell him. "I'm sure I can find a way to survive."

My husband cups my face with both hands while I kiss him like thunder: breath booming in my throat, fingers crackling like lightning. My hands reach back and my fingers curl into his hair before grasping the soft cotton of his T-shirt, pulling at the fabric around his neck.

Rob breaks his lips away from mine, but just barely. "Careful," he growls, yanking his T-shirt over his head, then tossing the shirt away. "It's usually the boyfriend."

I run my fingers through the Rorschach blotch of my husband's chest hair. "That's a risk I'm willing to take."

"Good."

Rob's kisses pull me away from the sink, toward the big island in the center of the kitchen. He keeps his lips on mine as he sweeps away packing-material litter and loose kitchen items, clearing space on the cluttered surface behind my back. Spice canisters crash onto their sides followed by the thump of cardboard hitting tile as Rob's palms slide down my back, around my waist, over my hips. His mouth follows his hands down the length of my body as he bends to squeeze the backs of my thighs. Cool granite chills my flesh when Rob lifts me onto the counter, gasping as he fumbles with the waistband of his pajama pants, now significantly tighter than when he'd come in to help with the dishes.

"Should we go to the bedroom?" he asks.

Flashbacks of my earlier makeover, the sensation of cosmetics smothering my skin, the image of my dead mother's made-up face, flash through my mind. "Let's stay here."

"You're sure?" Rob parts my legs, then slides his body between my knees and fingers the hem of my tank. "I don't want you to be uncomfortable."

I pull the tank top over my head, drop it so it lands on Rob's shoulder. "Do I look uncomfortable?"

My husband brushes the fabric from his shoulder as his eyes drop to my bared breasts, fingers rising to twist and pinch and stroke. He growls something unintelligible and grips the undersides of my knees, then yanks me closer to him, anchoring me in place with one hand behind my neck so I'm not flung backward onto the cold stone surface.

Rob's mouth is hot on my skin, and when his hands drop to curl around my waist, I let my head fall back, flooded by the sensations of my husband's tongue and lips. The kitchen is turned upside down, the messy countertops and open cabinet doors topsy-turvy as they're washed away in the current of my husband's body on mine.

My eyes close as pleasure rolls through me, but then something on the counter catches my attention.

Across the kitchen, on the other side of the sink, sits the Keurig. Someone has moved the coffeepot. But no one has been in the house besides my family and my neighbor. Had Darla moved it back to Patti's spot when she'd come down to get her phone? I can't remember another time when she'd been alone in my kitchen. I do remember the movement out the window moments ago, but then Rob pushes himself inside me, and I forget entirely about Darla.

CHAPTER NINE

Suddenly, it's Friday.

Rob mumbles a half joke about how he and Tanner won't wait up as he walks me to the front door. "Enjoy yourself tonight," he says between yawns. "You deserve a night out."

It's hard to crook my neck far enough back that I can glare all the way up at my darling husband while I squat to lace my Converse, but I manage. "I've thinned the sea of moving boxes from a river to a stream. Bathed the dog. Found Tanner's lunch box *and* fixed the zipper." The only other chore on my to-do list before I get back to my manuscript is to clean my car. "I think you mean I deserve a night *in*."

"But then you'd miss Doll's Night." Rob pulls the door open and swats me on the butt on my way through. "And I know how much you're looking forward to that."

About as much as a Pap smear, as I'd told Kitty earlier, but I promise Rob I won't be late and listen for the sound of the dead bolt behind me. I didn't tell Rob about the movement I saw outside the kitchen window two nights ago. Probably just a tree branch, maybe a critter. No need to make him worry.

No need to make *myself* worry.

Dusk air tickles along my cheeks as my rubber soles pad the pavement down the sidewalk toward Number Thirty-Four. Memory of the makeover is still tender on my scrub-sore skin—in the raw patches under my eyes, the thorny cracks that prickle against my lips. "Cool water and Vaseline," Kitty'd said when she'd finished fussing about ignored texts and unanswered calls. "Nothing fancy, you just want to stay moisturized." Her grin had taken up all the space between our phone lines when she'd told me not to scratch if I started to itch. "You'll scrape your skin right off," she'd said, in this condition, "and you wouldn't want that."

My sister hadn't mentioned her creepy-clown makeup tutorial, and I hadn't mentioned our dead mother's face staring back at me from my bathroom mirror. I told her about brunch, about Darla and the Brunswick PTA Board, not about Barb. I haven't yet told her about the new book idea that's rattling around in my brain because I won't be able to take it back once I do.

A gaggle of unfamiliar vehicles crowds the purple minivan and beige town car in the Number Thirty-Four driveway. For all the blank stares and eye rolls before, Darla's Doll's Night turnout doesn't look half bad. Maybe the other women had reconsidered? Maybe they'd realized what absolute twats they'd been at brunch? Or maybe Darla threatened to revoke their cherished PTA privileges if they didn't?

Whichever it is, I just hope that the cars don't belong to an entirely different group of women. I'm not sure which would be worse: facing down the Brunswick Mean Girls again or meeting a new batch.

I make my way past the potted mums and BRUNSWICK ELEMENTARY sign in Darla's front lawn, through the freshly retouched landscaping, to a front door almost identical to my own, before it dawns that my knee-patched jeans and Elvira long-sleeve might not be up to the Doll's Night dress code. At least I managed to wrangle my hair into something half presentable . . . if a messy ponytail is appropriate for a hostage situation.

My fist is midway to the door when I realize I've shown up empty-handed.

Should I have brought a gift for my first visit to my neighbor's house? Not a welcome basket, obviously, but a grocery store bouquet, a bottle of wine? Something.

Darla swings open the front door before my finger presses the bell. Her perm has loosened into gentle waves that tickle her shoulders, and she wears a sweater with kittens embroidered on its front. No Keds, but I already know she leaves her shoes at the door.

"Jill, I'm so happy you could make it!" An eggy silver-polish smell pulses between notes of brown sugar and pear as Darla reaches through the front door and reels me in across the threshold. The bubble-gum rosettes on her headband match the blush marks on her cheeks, the ball of yarn on the sweater's front. Darla's preppy pastels might come straight out of the eighties, but she's definitely got an eye for details.

She brandishes a bottle of the same rosé she'd put in my welcome basket in one hand, a corkscrew in the other, and my throat swallows on reflex, remembering the week's earlier hangover.

"I wasn't sure you'd be able to come," she says. "You've been so busy getting settled in."

It's only been two days, but other than a couple tap backs and one-liners, I've kept pretty quiet in the group chat.

"Your flower beds look incredible," I tell her as I shrug out of my jacket. The potted mums she'd left on my driveway only moved to the porch because Rob nearly ran them over, but so far, they're still doing fine. "School starts next week, and it still looks like spring out here."

The pride in Darla's voice is unmistakable. "The secret is to deadhead the old blooms to make room for new growth."

"Deadhead?" I'm an author, not a gardener.

"Snip the old head right off the stem." Darla scissors her fingers around the corkscrew. "If you get the timing just right, you can still get a few fresh blooms before the first real chill sets in. It's so much more fun to say than *pruning*," she whispers, so the women in the living room beyond won't overhear.

And here I thought the gardening term was a nod to Grateful Dead fans.

Darla waves me inside and I slip off my canvas sneakers by the collection of women's shoes at the doorway.

"I'm sorry I didn't know if I was supposed to bring anything," I say, about my empty hands, but she clicks her teeth like I'm being silly.

"I've got everything I need to take good care of you." It's not what Darla says but how she says it that makes me think of Bobbie Markowe, welcoming Joanna Eberhart into her home after she's been Stepford-ized. But maybe it's just nerves. Doll's Night is a big deal for Darla, she'd said so at brunch.

She pops the cork and ushers me out of the entry and into the large family room.

Potted silk plants lurk among wall-size mirrors mounted in thin frames (gold) and wallpaper (paisley). Centered on the square coffee table, the pink-and-teal cosmetics showcase is open to reveal pastel bulbs and compacts arranged like a sacrificial outpouring across the glass top. It's not just her outfits that are straight out of the eighties. The living room in my mother's house used to look a lot like Darla's.

"Ladies, you remember Jill," Darla says as she sashays me across eggshell low-pile carpet to one of two unoccupied seashell armchairs at the front of the room. I recognize Kellen's designer athleisure, Sasha's pucker, Beth fidgeting in the sectional's connective crook, but the leggy brunette with the mane of salon lookbook hair is new.

"This is Rosa, our Events chair." Darla gestures at the new woman. "You didn't get a chance to meet at brunch."

"No PTA talk tonight," Sasha grouses from behind her wineglass before I can introduce myself to Rosa. "I am here for wine and lotion only."

"Don't worry, Sasha. We couldn't talk about PTA business if we wanted to." Kellen rolls her eyes and salutes across the sectional, muttering into her wineglass before she pours the last swallow down her throat. "Maribel isn't here," she says when it's gone. "We couldn't *possibly* discuss anything without her approval."

The Ice Cream Social debate is still on, then.

Darla's grip tightens around the wine bottle neck. "I'm just making introductions, Sasha," she says, and refills Kellen's glass.

"Would you believe she told me to drop off the pricing list from Cold Stone at her house?" Kellen says. "'Use the spare key under the back doormat' like I work for her!"

Rosa flips her hair over her shoulder while Sasha sucks down what's left of her wine. "Maribel will calm down once school starts. Besides, Darla is PTA president," she says. "It's her job to deal with Maribel." Rosa shrugs. "If she can."

The way my new neighbor is squeezing that bottle neck, my odds are on Darla.

"This is Jill Marshall," she powers on, determined to finish her introductions. "She's our new Cultural Arts chair—"

"The writer who moved into *Patti's* old house," Kellen says, with a meaningful raise of her eyebrows. She shot the same look at Sasha when Darla first introduced me over brunch, but I'm still not sure whether it's got to do with Patti, or my new creaky-not-creepy neocolonial—or me.

Probably me.

Rosa flaps Kellen's eyebrows away. "Jill Marshall?" My name sounds exotic in Rosa's lilting accent. She squints at me, at my horror icon T-shirt, and when she snaps her fingers, I feel it between my eyes. "You're Jillian Marshall, the author," she says, like we've met before.

My skin is still too raw to know for sure if I've managed a smile or just split my face open. Rosa is one of those women who all other women are measured by. How does someone like her even know who I am?

"That's me," I say, like a total idiot.

"I knew I recognized you." Rosa's features all smile at the same time. "I never forget a face. Even if I've only seen it in a picture."

Darla backs me into the seashell chair before I can turn and run. "Rosa works at Brunswick County Library. She knows *every* new book that comes across her shelves."

Librarians are the most wonderful creatures on earth, I just hadn't expected to run into one at Doll's Night. Ever since my debut hit shelves, I've been recognized once or twice from the photo on my dust-jacket cover, but not so much that I'm accustomed to it, and never outside of a literary event. Authors' lives are spent behind keyboards, not on red carpets.

Horror authors, in particular. We're weird little cave people, usually unfit for public consumption.

And yet Rosa taps a fingernail against her wineglass, still aiming mascara-rimmed lashes in my direction. "What was your last book about again? I remember the cover but not the title." Her face says, *Silly old me,* but I've heard that tone before. "I just remember it involved children."

At the mention of precious offspring, Sasha's lips pucker and Beth blanches. Kellen digs a socked toe into Darla's living-room carpet like she's bearing down for the starting whistle. The other women gawk at me like I've sprouted an extra appendage, and this is it: the moment my cookie-cutter neocolonial becomes the street's newest haunted house. The expression on Rosa's face hovers somewhere closer to curiosity than disapproval, but she's not going to stop staring until I answer. None of them are.

"Changelings." It takes a couple of tries to get the word out. "They're fairies, technically. Not human children." My debut novel involved a group of children who go missing in a forest only to be stolen and replaced by something sinister. Really, the book's about the body horror of pregnancy, the out-of-body experience that had been until after Tanner hemorrhaged from my womb, but I have a feeling it won't hit the mark with this audience.

"It's based in Irish folklore," I add, so dumbly that poor Darla reaches over and pats my arm.

"My tastes run a little more literary," Rosa says, a diplomatic way of looking down her nose at my chosen genre. "But you hit the bestseller list, didn't you?"

"I did." Nice of her to notice. Really nice, for someone who doesn't read a lot of genre fiction.

"It's not every day that a horror novel makes the *Times* list," Rosa informs the group with a flick of her wrist. "You should be very proud of yourself, Jill."

My smile is definitely splitting my skin apart now. Horror may not be literary enough for Rosa's bestseller list, but tell that to Stephen King and Shirley Jackson. Still, I can feel my blush from the tips of my ears all the way down to my toes.

"Jill's just started on a new novel," Darla says, swooping in to save me. "Isn't that right, dear?"

"It's still just an idea." My editor is all for getting weird with a trope, but I can already imagine the looks on these women's faces if I start going on about dolls in space as a metaphor for suburban containment and gender roles. "Too early to talk about," I say, and hope there will be no follow-up questions.

Without Maribel to direct them, the other three mean girls look to Rosa as she sets her wineglass on a seashell-shaped coaster on Darla's glass coffee table. "Whatever it is, I'm sure it'll be fantastic," she says, and air rushes back into the room, though I catch Beth crossing herself on the other end of the couch.

Rosa reminds everyone that libraries and local authors go hand in hand. "Let's set something up. Maybe around Halloween? It's the season for horror, after all."

The librarian and I might not see eye to eye on year-round Spooky Season, but that's what's so magical about the book community: the love of the written word, regardless of genre.

I gladly accept.

"Well, let's not forget about Boogie Bash." Darla's tone is tight as she pours a splash of bubbly for herself and sets the bottle on the table. "Soon Jill will have her hands full with our *spookiest* event of the year."

"No PTA!" Sasha comes in hot. "No Ice Cream Social, no Boogie Bash." She leans forward to snatch a cosmetics pod off the coffee table, then clicks it open, gives it a sniff, and frowns. She drops it back on the table. "I didn't leave the twins home alone with the Old Goat so I could talk PTA."

"Sasha is absolutely right," Darla says, beaming. "Tonight is just about us girls." She readjusts the items scattered about her Caboodles on the glass coffee table, lips moving as she rehearses her spiel, then picks up a long narrow tube and squares her shoulders. She serves each woman a small white plastic dish shaped like a flower, with little hollow grooves for petals and a larger circular crevice in the center. A painter's palette, but for our own face canvases.

The raw spot under my eye tingles, but I rally and fix on a half smile.

"I'm so excited to share these incredible new products with my best girlfriends!" Darla's script may be rehearsed, but her smile is real enough that my chest hurts when the other women lock eyes behind her back as she moves around the sofa, squeezing bits of cream onto palettes. "From concealer to eye shadow, Dollface helps showcase your inner beauty on the outside."

Darla mimes as she talks, her voice taking on the same rehearsed tone she'd used in my bedroom makeover. "Tonight, we're going to discover exactly the right tool to eliminate your biggest flaws."

"Speaking of spookiest events of the year," Kellen cuts in just as Darla squeezes a bit of green-tinted cream onto her palette. "Rosa, has Steve said anything else about what happened at the Dream Bean?"

My horror author's ears perk despite my best attempt to remain focused on Darla's sales pitch. She flutters around the living room, squeezing bits of colorful creams onto each woman's palette, her face a mask of civility while the others lean forward to hear the latest gossip. When Darla stops in front of me, I dutifully serve up my palette and try not to flinch at the thick curl of pink she squirts into one of the petal grooves.

Rosa's low voice pulls the women into her orbit. "They haven't made any official statements yet, so this is off-the-record." She pushes her long dark tresses behind her ears, and now I'm leaning in, too. "But whoever did this planned it well. They smashed the lightbulb at the café's back door so the camera wouldn't see their face. Forensics found pieces of broken glass in the dead woman's hair."

"Do the police have any suspects?" It's the first time Beth has spoken all evening, and her voice cracks with disuse, or maybe nerves. "Why would anyone want to hurt that barista?"

"There's always a motive." Kellen speaks with the authority of someone who spends a lot of time with true-crime podcasts. They pair well with exercising, or so I've heard. "Jilted lover, disgruntled customer, opportunists. Maybe the question is, Why *not* her?"

"She was a barista at a trendy strip-mall coffee café." Sasha rolls her eyes just as Darla lifts a palm, opens her mouth to speak, and pauses. "What'd she do, forget to put cream in someone's coffee? Give them a stale pastry?" It's somehow possible for sarcasm to pucker her face even more.

"She wasn't very nice," Beth squeaks from the sofa cushions.

Darla presses her fingers and thumb together and passes around slivers of sponge before settling into the open armchair that matches mine. "I thought we'd start with skin care first," she says. "I've put just a tiny bit of some of our most popular products in each of your trays—"

"But to answer Beth's question, no leads yet," Rosa says, and shakes her head. "Apparently the killer was better at planning the kill than carrying it out. Steve mentioned something about they're still trying to figure out the murder weapon, but they think it was some kind of serrated blade, probably one with a blunt tip based on the angle of the cut."

Kellen pulls a face. "Like a bread knife?"

"More like steak." Sasha puckers when everyone looks at her. "What? Rosa said that the neck was sawed open." Sasha raises the cosmetics palette to her throat, jerks it across in a series of sharp back-and-forth movements hard enough that the plastic edge leaves a faint scratch, and shrugs.

Dark, but a fair point. It'd be ironic, wouldn't it, if the barista with the cake wedge tattooed on her neck indeed got cut down by a bread knife?

Beth chitters like a frightened squirrel and manages to shrink even farther into the couch cushion, and I keep my thoughts to myself.

Kellen takes another sip of wine, then looks at me and aims her glass at the thin pink stitch across Sasha's throat. "If you need ideas, Jill, you know who to ask."

Cute, if she thinks this is how I source my scariest ideas.

"I've put dots of three of our most popular products on each of your palettes," Darla tries again. Her smile tries to match her kitten-sweater energy as she holds her tray and points at each small dollop in turn. "Retinol-infused eye serum, to brighten while eliminating circles and puffiness." She runs fingertips under each eye. "Rejuvenation moisturizer, with collagen, to reduce wrinkles and fine lines overnight." She gently touches the corners of her eyes, followed by her lips. "And my personal favorite"—she traces the outline of her lips with her index finger—"the replenishing lip mask to moisturize and plump."

Sasha sniffs her palette, curls her nose, and fans the scent away. She sets her palette on the glass table. "Smells like a funeral home."

It's silver polish, I almost say, about the eggy scent I'd noted when I first arrived, but Darla doesn't flinch.

"Dollface products are all natural, with no added chemicals or fragrances, so what you smell are the floral and herbal ingredients."

Darla swivels in her seat. "Rosa, which of these three products speaks to you?"

Rosa sets her palette on the table beside Sasha's and pours herself a third refill. "I'm good on skin-care creams," she tells Darla, then, "but Sasha isn't wrong," she tells Kellen. "Whoever killed Barb either didn't have the strength to cut through her jugular on one go or didn't anticipate how difficult it would be."

Darla turns to the next woman on the couch. "Kellen, how about you?"

"So, they were smart enough not to leave any evidence behind but not enough to know how to perform a clean kill." Kellen clicks her teeth, adds her palette to the growing pile of discards on the coffee table, and polishes off the bottle. "Sounds like a disorganized killer."

Beth mutters something about hoping whatever happened at Dream Bean isn't the start of something worse. When her name is called, she fingers her palette, but then sets it untouched on the table with the rest.

A chill breathes in from the chair beside mine as Darla's forced smile locks into place. Maybe she's breathing, but her chest doesn't rise or fall any more than her eyelids blink. My poor, sweet new neighbor, edged out first by an Ice Cream Debate and now Barb.

It's hard to compete with the memory of a dead woman.

CHAPTER TEN

Under her doll's mask, the woman's breath beats warm against her face. She cuts the sedan's headlights before she turns off the street and pulls into the long driveway.

The sough of nighttime wind through the dense canopy of oak tree branches conceals the rumble of the engine as the car's tires slip off the main drive and onto the narrow stretch of concrete, rolling toward the garage tucked out of sight at the back of the stately house. A carriage drive, this once was called—a separate entrance for deliveries and other domestic servicers.

Times have changed, but the hidden driveway is still appropriate, since tonight the doll is here to help.

Tonight, she is here to prune back old growth. To make room for the new.

A security sign sits staked into the house's front flower beds at the edge of the bricked perimeter, but the blue-and-white octagon is a relic from before Wi-Fi-enabled gadgets disrupted the home-security market. Now, a ringed blue eye casts its vision out from the wide front stoop, its gaze focused over the front lawn. Homes like this like to remind visitors that the residents are always watching, but the camera, like the house's columned entrance and expensive landscaping, is for show, only interested in presiding over its manicured hedgerows and hollyhocks, not those who come to service it. It's an illusion, a reminder of the untouchable status housed within.

Out of the camera's view on the hidden drive, the doll's sedan slides past the darkened front windows, the tall columns that anchor double front doors, the gabled windows that line the upper levels. Electronic light flickers from a rear downstairs window as she curls the car around and aims dead headlights toward the street. The doll brings the wheels to a stop beneath the foliage at the edge of the drive, rolls the driver's-side window down, and lets the car idle in the thickening dark. She considers the boughs overhead, the intentional overgrowth, meant to guard the privacy between each home.

No ringed blue eye watches over the back door, visible in the sedan's rearview mirror, which opens into the kitchen she can glimpse through the curtains over its sink.

The doll twists off the engine, quieting the keys dangling from the ignition inside a gloved fist. Sprinklers spit onto the over-manicured lawn, and an owl hoots somewhere far away, but otherwise the night is still. The streets, the heavy autumn branches, quiet. Even the summer cicadas have retired their chirps for the season, bedded down like the street's other residents.

It's the perfect place for a fresh start.

Through the narrow eye slits of her beautiful face, the doll watches light flicker through the kitchen window. A single bulb flashes on, then off, and she times her breath to the rush of wind through the sedan's open driver's-side window. Ten minutes pass, then twenty, then thirty. When she's sure the house is still, the doll slides into the passenger seat.

Unlike at the Dream Bean, tonight the doll already has her face on.

Tonight, she's worn soft, noiseless black sweats instead of the crinkly pink poncho, cloth work gloves instead of rubber dish mitts, no shoes. She's left her wedding ring at home and found the fuse for the dome light.

The doll opens the glove compartment, removes the instrument, and runs her fingers over its edges. Just like the cake knife before, no red light reflects off the sharp, curved edges, the rubber grip, of this tool.

So many options had presented themselves in the gardening shed. Scythes, sickles, trowels, hatchets—all with sharp edges, with cutting curves. The doll flexes the shears in her hand, testing the tension as she feels for the telltale prick of the hooked blade against the cloth gardening mitts. She took care when she chose which tool to bring, selecting the pruning shears because she only needed to remove the spent flower.

The old must be pruned away, to make room for the new.

The doll pushes open the passenger-side door and rises out of the sedan. The ground is warm and damp from the evening sprinkler, as soft and yielding as the clothes that hang loose from her arms and legs, and her socked feet slip soundlessly into cool fall mud.

She moves slowly, each footfall deep and unhurried, warm earth pressing under her heels as she plods across the manicured lawn. A thick layer of wet ground cakes the bottoms of her socks, until her footsteps are earth upon earth.

A rubber welcome mat waits at the back door, a station for leaving outdoor shoes before stepping onto the home's pristine tiled floors. Three sets of discarded shoes sit beside the mat. Two are too small, children's shoes, but the pair of women's sneakers are nearly the same size as the doll's own. She peels off her muddy socks and steps into the sneakers, testing their sound as she lifts the mat to reveal a spare house key tucked underneath. The doll peers through the pane of glass centered on the door, into the living room inside. A crown of dark hair is just visible over the back of an oversize recliner that faces a flickering television.

The doll tightens her grip around the shears in her fist.

She keeps her eyes on the chair as she fits the key in the lock and twists. She presses her ear to the glass, listening to the disembodied voices and commercial jingles, and when the din is loud enough, she turns the knob and pushes the door open. The doll slides through and pulls the door closed behind her. When the knob's latch rests against the jamb, she lets go.

Since she's only here to visit, it's best to leave the exit open.

Light flickers from the living room, bold television hues casting brief flashes of color through the adjoining doorway. The thick rubber soles of the stolen sneakers are silent on the ceramic as the doll steps through the kitchen, into the living room. She pauses only once when the crown of dark hair shifts, but silk rustles against silk, and the woman in the chair snuffles. The doll sees the empty wineglass, the pill bottle, on the side table beside the recliner. She registers the deep pulls of slumbering breath, the slight forward bend of the sleeping head, and inches closer.

In the chair, the woman mumbles something unintelligible, and the sound of her voice prickles thornlike under the doll's skin. She positions herself behind the chair, adjusts her stance, and uses both hands to raise the gardening shears. The curved tip points down, directly over the crown of dark hair. The doll tightens her grasp, curls her gloved fists around the tool's rubber grips, and inhales strength into her lungs.

Before, she'd held the barista in her arms as she sliced through layers of throat. She'd had time, then, to get it right. Now, the doll has only one chance.

Blue light pops to darkness as the television set times out and turns off. From her position, the doll sees their reflections in the blackened screen: her own, glamorous and perfect, and the sleeping woman's, pale and severe between dark brunette curtains, cheekbones as sharp as the metal in the doll's hands.

Startled awake by the sudden silence, the woman's eyes flicker open just as the doll drives the gardening shears into her skull. The woman's gaze clocks in the darkened television the cherub cheeks and golden frame of the doll's beautiful face behind her. Her mouth widens into a scream, but the shears slide through the top layers of scalp and membrane, loosing a red waterfall that rushes over her forehead. The short blades stop suddenly when they reach the cranial bone, and the shock renders the woman unconscious before any sound escapes her lips.

Red drips down the woman's forehead, trickles through her eyelashes, and leaks down her cheekbones. Dark liquid pools over the silk in her lap. Word fragments slur from her throat, blood slipping between her lips to coat her too-white teeth in a slick red sheen. Her jaw hangs, tongue limp in her open mouth. Her chest rises, but her breath comes shallow now, no longer the deep pull of wine-and-pill sleep.

Bone is stronger than skin and cartilage and tissue; the shears sharp, but thin. The doll burrows the tool as deep as she can into the woman's skull, but she stops short just as the blades begin to dig into the fertile earth of brain matter. She has to work to wheedle the edge out. It will leave a scar, but the wound will heal.

With time, a new bloom will take root.

White matter winks through where the doll has bored a new hole as she treads back toward the kitchen's rear entry. She takes a moment to admire her work, and then she slides out of the woman's sneakers on the mat beside the back door and plods in mud-socked feet back the way she came.

CHAPTER ELEVEN

We make it to Brunswick Elementary a solid fifteen minutes before the bell rings for the first day of school. Tanner's new backpack is so stuffed full of paperwork (completed), school supplies (labeled), and his lucky green vinyl lunch box (repaired) that it sits like a shell against his back. The moment he spots other kids his age, he wrenches his hand from mine, squeezes me around the hips, and shoots off down the hallway. In a group of adults, my son's a wallflower like his mom, but in a room full of kids, there's no time for goodbyes.

Who could blame him, really? Poor guy has spent the better part of two months being schlepped across the country with Mom, Dad, and dog. It's a wonder he hasn't packed himself up and bolted already.

Tanner frisbees a wave over his shoulder as he disappears into the swarm of fellow shell-backed children while I trudge behind in his wake. Halfway down the third-grade corridor, an impossibly young teacher waves him into a classroom. The construction-paper tree taped on the door bears a striking resemblance to the Dream Bean's tempera window display, only instead of cupcakes and falling leaves, apples tattooed with student names in loopy Sharpie letters cling to twisted paper branches.

Fall into learning, the arch of bubble letters over the tree instructs, and no matter how old you get, doors like that still bring you back.

The teacher introduces herself as *Miss* Frost, thanks me for allowing her to teach my child, and says she's new to town, too, freshly transplanted from Nebraska, where they probably farm cute elementary school teachers alongside corn and beef. "I hope you're enjoying Brunswick so far," Miss Frost says. "I *love* living in the Garden State."

"We're getting settled," I tell her, instead of sharing about the recent murder at the café with a window display that matches her classroom door.

"Oh, and Mrs. Marshall"—Miss Frost bats big brown doe eyes as I turn to go, enunciating my name in a way that swishes against the marital status—"Principal Hart would like to see you in his office."

Spontaneous early-morning meetings with the principal were not at the top of my School Year Bingo Card any more than joining the PTA was, but life is full of surprises. "First day of school and I'm already being sent to the principal's office." I nod at the teacher, shoulder my bag, and wish I were better at jokes. "Can't be a good sign."

Miss Frost gives me a gold-star smile. "I think he's calling everyone on the PTA Board in."

The first sign this is more than a friendly first-day PTA group huddle is the burly school security officer with a pistol tucked into the holster on his hip, standing hands clasped stationed outside the door marked PRINCIPAL'S OFFICE. Across the hall, COUNSELOR'S OFFICE. I hope to God Tanner never winds up there, though they gotta be better now than back in my day. In the late 1990s, even a court-appointed child psychologist wasn't worth a damn.

Kellen, Rosa, Sasha, and Beth are already corralled around a circular table wedged into the corner of the room, all four of their freshly made-up morning faces blank, when I enter Hart's office. Cold stings inside my teeth like a cavity, and I regret my glib attempt at humor with Miss Frost. Schools aren't just schools anymore, I remember;

they're targets. I could write horror novels for the rest of my life and still never pen anything scarier than what parents, teachers, and children experience every day in one of the places they're supposed to feel the safest.

But this is Stepford, right? Nothing bad happens in Stepford.

Not to the kids, anyway.

A plainclothes cop with a steam-shovel jawline and lineup cups his hands around Rosa's shoulders. My interactions in the group text are still slim, but I recognize Detective Steve Hudson from his badge-pinning photo on the number I've programmed as Rosa's from the board directory in the PTA pocket folder. This means the balding man in khakis situated on the edge of the too-big desk keeping his hands to himself must be the principal. A small metal placard on the desk spells out FRED HART in small block letters. The A in his surname is shaped like one of the construction-paper apples taped to Miss Frost's classroom door, but I'm betting it's that first initial that gets the most laughs.

Surely some ten-year-old has already figured out Principal F. Hart is one easily removable space away from becoming Principal Fhart.

I flag that to share with Kitty later. Even grown women enjoy a dash of adolescent toilet humor now and then.

"Come in, Mrs. Marshall." The bags under the principal's eyes are more last-day-of-school than first as I settle myself into an empty chair between Kellen and Beth. "I'm sorry to call you all in like this on the first day of school, but it's best if we talk as a group." Hart palms at his slick forehead. "This won't take long, we're just waiting on Mrs. Lashett."

"And Maribel," Kellen says, and behind Rosa, the detective's lips go flat.

Beth raises her hand, which earns her a patient smile that sucks the rest of the life out of Hart's Vincent Price cheeks. "You don't need to raise your hand, Mrs. Martinez."

"Darla isn't here this morning." Beth's voice is tinny and thin, like she's not sure she's allowed to divulge this information. "I saw Daphne get off the school bus."

It's a minute before I remember that Daphne is Darla's daughter. Fifth grader, if memory serves.

Judging by the expressions around the table, I'm not the only one surprised to learn the Brunswick Elementary PTA president has missed the school year kickoff. "She must be at Vincent Middle, helping Dylan with his first day," Rosa suggests finally. It sounds logical—Darla *did* mention her son would start sixth grade this year—but not a single set of eyebrows unfurl around the table.

The woman wasn't wearing a bedazzled Vincent Middle School PTA T-shirt the first day I met her, after all.

Principal Hart claps his hands to his knees and unhinges himself from the desk. "In that case, let's get to it." He pulls the office door closed now that we're all here, except for Maribel. "I hate to be the bearer of such tragic news, but—"

A sharp chime, then two, then three. School has officially begun for the year, cutting the man off mid-sentence. When the bells fade, a woman's voice picks up over the PA system, and I hear the echo of the receptionist in the adjoining room. She recites the beginning-of-the-year greetings in a stilted tone that says someone handed this task off to her last minute. Hart, I'm guessing.

When she's finished, the principal palms his forehead again, but it's Detective Steve Hudson's voice that cuts the tension.

"As Principal Hart was about to tell you, there's been an incident." Steve adjusts his palms, still planted on his wife's shoulders, and clears his throat. "Maribel Wolff was attacked in her home Friday night. She's in stable condition," he adds, after a round of gasps from the table, "but she's suffered a terrible injury."

Sasha's tone is even more clipped than usual. "What kind of injury?"

Principal Hart glances at the detective and waits for a nod before answering. "Someone broke into her home—" He looks to Steve for another nod, and the rest tumbles out of his mouth like ice out of a cocktail shaker. "And stabbed her in the head with a pair of scissors."

The words clatter onto the table, inciting collective gasps and one literal pearl-clutch that's dramatic even for this group. Detective Steve Hudson blinks a few times extra. "For Christ's sake, Fred," he says, then to the table, "Ms. Wolff sustained a *head injury*"—the cop pauses to shoot an incredulous look at the other man, palms up in the air by his desk—"but is going to be okay."

The lower half of Principal Hart's face blanches an appropriately sheepish smile, and the room settles. I can appreciate the man's candor, but dang. Hopefully he adds more padding before breaking bad news to kindergartners.

So, a *head injury* then. Beth glances my way. This is not the first time I've gotten a look like that when something goes wrong. Guilt by association, I guess, like writing about horror conjures it into reality—or maybe I'm just projecting. Rob says I do that sometimes. Charlene says it's part of the writer's shtick. Life imitating art, or whatever.

The shock has subsided, though, and Kellen's ponytail whips through the air so fast it'll leave welts if it contacts skin.

"Wait, Friday? Oh my God!" She wrenches her cell phone free of her yoga pants side pocket and jabs at the screen. She checks the group thread, the ABC7 social media feed, but Power Suit offers no updates on this breaking news, so Kellen plunks her phone face down on the tabletop.

"When will information be released to the public?" Sasha demands to know.

Rosa shrugs under her husband's hands. "The police wanted to keep it quiet."

"*Want to,*" Steve clarifies. "Please treat this information as confidential, ladies. We don't want to incite speculation. For now, we're still trying to gather as much information as possible."

"Did *you* know about this, Rosa?" Kellen's tone leapfrogs from surprise to accusation, like she's more upset to be left out of the knowing than by the knowledge itself, but the other woman shakes her head.

"I just found out this morning, when Steve told me we'd be meeting. I can't believe it. It's too awful." Rosa shudders out a breath that's either genuine or well acted. "We were all just together Friday night."

All of us except Maribel. The only member of the Brunswick PTA not to attend Doll's Night. Because she'd had a spa appointment and wanted to get her beauty rest, or so she'd said at the Dream Bean.

"If she'd've come to Darla's party," Beth says, narrating the obvious, "this never would have happened."

Detective Hudson shakes his head. "Not necessarily." He's got a good bedside manner for a cop, probably earned from tucking his children into bed. "We believe the attack took place late in the evening, possibly after midnight."

My brain tracks Brunswick's recent violent crimes on my mental corkboard. Police keep things quiet for two reasons: Either they have zip, or they have something really good. If it'd been the former, they wouldn't have put us all in one room. They'd have called us in one at a time, asked us a dozen questions apiece. "You think this might be connected to what happened at the Dream Bean."

Beth isn't the only one giving me side-eye now.

Steve uses his palm to squeegee away the suggestion. "Absolutely not," he says, a touch too quickly. "These are different methods of attack, different weapons—"

"But the events *do* share a few commonalities," I say, because I can't help it. This is literally what I do for a living: line up the plot beats, figure out how they connect. I remember Maribel's red fingernail slicing down the plastic sheet protector in her binder the day Barb was killed, the red gash across the woman's throat the next morning as they'd zipped her into a body bag on the other side of the café's tempera-painted window. "The PTA brunched at the Dream Bean

Café the day of the barista's murder, and now one of its members has been attacked. That reads like a link to me."

"Or a coincidence." Steve gives me the kind of look one never wants to get from a cop. "Violent criminals escalate," he says, like I'm stealing his thunder. "They progress from assault to murder, not the other way around."

But still. "Isn't it possible the attacker tried to kill Maribel but failed? Or assumed she'd die from her injuries?"

Steve's expression gives him away. I'm not saying anything he hasn't already thought of and decided not to share with the group. The question is, Why not?

Kellen's palm flies to her chest. "Oh my God, you don't think *we* had something to do with this, do you?" Her gaze darts to Hart, to Steve, but Hart's head is already shaking.

"No, ma'am," Principal F. Hart says, like he's whom her question was intended for. "No, I do not."

Sasha mutters something under her breath—*lawyer,* I think—and crosses her arms over her chest. Rosa goes pale. Beth legit pulls a strand of rosary beads from under the collar of her blouse.

Were this a cozy mystery, this would be the moment they arrest Kellen for letting the ice cream feud with Maribel go too far. In the police procedural, where the plot twists and we learn pious Beth has a dark side. I'm the obvious red herring, with my scary books, melting face, monstress hair.

But this is not prime-time TV. One woman is dead. Another, stabbed in the skull.

The conversation I had a few days ago with my husband in our kitchen bloats into a painful bubble in my gut. Barb's murder, Maribel's attack, these are not plot points, I tell myself. Not the opening beats to a slasher movie. Its just truth being stranger than fiction.

"We are not investigating the Brunswick PTA," Steve says, patting the air for quiet. "But we need to know if you ladies have seen anything, heard anything, that might fill in any missing pieces to help us identify who attacked Ms. Wolff."

"We know nothing," Sasha snaps, emphasis on the *nothing*. She glowers at the detective. "You want something from us, then tell us what *you* know."

Gotta hand it to Sasha. She's KGB-level tough.

The principal's palms float back to his forehead while the detective gives the room time to speak, but when no one offers up anything, he relents. "The perpetrator didn't drive their weapon deep enough into the skull to cause serious injury to the brain, either because they could not or it was not long enough," he says, back to my earlier point, which means I was right, they *do* have something. "We have not yet identified the weapon, but scissors are our leading theory."

"Whoever killed Barb cut multiple times, too, right?" This from Kellen and her true-crime podcasts. We'd discussed the Dream Bean Killer's sloppy work at Darla's the same night Maribel was attacked, hypothesizing that maybe they didn't anticipate the difficulty of carving through human flesh. Barb's laceration suggests it took multiple attempts to sever her throat. Steve says there's no connection, but in both the Dream Bean murder and Maribel's attack, the attacker seemed to struggle.

Coincidence my big Goth butt. "So, it could be the same person."

The detective responds with some line about the attacks not fitting the same profile, no material connection between victims, blah blah blah. They're not treating this as a serial yet, but that doesn't mean they won't, and it's easy to anticipate the sort of binary list utilized by law enforcement to weed through a potential list of suspects for someone too weak or unprepared to cleanly carry out their kill. Someone young or old, not in their prime. Someone disabled.

A woman.

"Ms. Wolff was lucid enough to give a brief statement before undergoing surgery," Steve says. "She reports seeing a woman's reflection in her television right as she was attacked."

Door number three, then.

"A *woman*?" Around the table, the other four women's voices crash together like cymbals, and Hart scratches uncomfortably at the back of one heel with the toe of the other loafer.

"Pert nose, blond hair to the jawline, beauty mark," Steve lists. "Do any of you know of anyone who matches that description who may have an issue with Ms. Wolff?"

As with Barb, I could imagine a lot of women having a beef with Maribel. Neither of them would win the award for Nicest Gal in Brunswick. But now I know why local law enforcement doesn't have its eye on the Brunswick PTA Mean Girls: no one seated at this table fits that description.

"Beauty mark?" Rosa taps her index finger against her temple like she's scrolling through her mental mug-shot reel. "I can't think of anyone in Brunswick with a beauty mark, and I never forget a face."

Steve takes a deep breath. "Ms. Wolff has had a craniotomy to remove multiple bone fragments. Assuming her healing progresses as expected, her doctor says she should be released in two weeks—but that can be difficult to anticipate with an injury of this sort."

Yeah, I'd guess so. The woman didn't catch a cold; she was stabbed in the head with a pair of freaking scissors. That's not the sort of thing you just sleep off.

Principal Hart's hairline has receded another millimeter from all the forehead rubbing. "I know Mrs. Lashett isn't here to give her verdict as PTA president, but if anyone feels we should postpone the Ice Cream—"

"No." Rosa bristles enough under Steve's hands that he lets her loose. "We should continue as planned. No need to disrupt activities that our students are looking forward to."

Nobody challenges her, and it's enough that the motion is passed.

"Okay, then," Hart says. "The show will go on. Speaking of," the principal adds, taking another pass across his forehead with the handkerchief, "I know we still have to get through the Ice Cream

Social, but the kids won't be bobbing for apples at Boogie Bash this year, right? The cafeteria practically flooded last year."

Beth fidgets in her chair. "Darla's figured out a fix for that."

The ugly matter of briefing the rest of the PTA Board on Maribel's attack behind him, Hart is back to school business, and clearly unhappy about the apple bobbing. "Can one of you please pass the news about Ms. Wolff along to Mrs. Lashett? She can let myself or Detective Hudson know if she has any questions or needs anything."

No one volunteers, which isn't the surprise it should be.

"I'll let her know," I say. She is my neighbor.

CHAPTER TWELVE

Darla is on her hands and knees at the edge of her front flower beds when I pull into the driveway at Number Thirty-Four. She visors one cloth-gloved hand over her eyes when she twists to look over her shoulder, squinting through the sun as I park behind the purple minivan. She waves when she recognizes my road-worn Honda.

The drawback to the short commute from the elementary school is that the five-minute drive isn't nearly long enough to swallow the lump that had lodged itself in my throat back in the principal's office. The debrief with Detective Steve must have gone on longer than it felt for the mom of two to have had time to get her son situated at Vincent Middle and then back home to her gardening, but then I have no idea what the first day of middle school is like.

Sort of like how I have no idea how to tell my sweet new neighbor that one of the Brunswick PTA Mean Girls has been stabbed in the skull in her own living room.

Writing down bad news is so much easier than saying it out loud, but back in Hart's office, I'd volunteered for the job, and the rest of the women had agreed to keep things mum on the group text until the deed was done. So I cut the car's engine and push myself out from the Honda's driver's-side door. This is a rip off the Band-Aid moment, both for me and my neighbor.

"Good morning!" Darla calls over her shoulder as I trudge my way toward her blooming fall flower beds. She snips the bud off a mum with a pair of rust-tipped pruning shears. "How did everything go at drop-off for Tanner's first day?"

Better than mine, that's for sure, but pleasantries are a good way to pad the bad news bubbling on my tongue.

I recall the sight of my son's beetle back fleeing up the hallway toward the swarm of other kids. "He barely waved goodbye, and his teacher seems very sweet."

"Oh, that's fantastic!" Darla decapitates another flower. "I met Miss Frost at the back-to-school teachers' breakfast. She seems like such a doll."

Miss Frost seems like a shiny new first-year teacher who doesn't know what she's in for with a room full of rambunctious kiddos, but what do I know? I'm just a one-kid mom.

Darla rocks back on her heels then pushes herself to her feet. She stuffs the shears into her gardening apron and swipes a set of muddy handprints onto the cloth. The edges of her smile sink into a frown when she clocks the look on my face. "You look upset, dear." Her mist-green eyes crinkle at the edges. "What's wrong?"

Suddenly, I feel bad for passing premature judgment on Principal F. Hart, sweating his hair off in his office.

And here goes nothing.

"Mr. Hart called us all into his office this morning," I start, preparing for the *rrrpp*. "Rosa's husband was there—Detective Steve?" Darla nods at me to go on, and I pull the bandage. "Maribel was attacked the other night, Doll's Night. Someone broke into her home and stabbed her in the skull. She's alive, but bone fragments have been removed from her brain. She'll be back in a few weeks, I guess."

The other woman's eyes hold their position, but her lips pinch together. She blinks a few times, like she's digesting the information.

"I'm sorry to be the one to tell you, but you know . . ." I shrug and attempt to fill the awkward silence with a half-hearted smile. "We're neighbors?"

Darla makes a tsking sound and busies herself with peeling off her cloth gardening gloves, which are muddier than I'd expect, given the lack of rain, but I know even less about gardening than I do teaching third graders.

"That's just so awful about Maribel." Darla shudders. "Stabbed in the head with a pair of scissors—right in her own living room."

Shock, I'd been prepared for—a gasp of disbelief, a clutch of phantom pearls. These were the reactions of the women gathered around that circular table wedged in the corner of the principal's office, while the man himself rubbed off the rest of his hair. From Darla, I'd expected an immediate rush to planning get-well-soon baskets and casserole delivery schedules, the sorts of motherly, well-intentioned responses I'd assumed someone like my sweet new neighbor would know exactly how to do. Not a headshake and a tipsy smile.

That, and I never mentioned the weapon used in the attack.

Now I'm the one squinting through the sun at Darla, with her prim gardening clothes and rusted shears. "Did you already know about Maribel?"

"Oh!" Her cheeks go pink. "Yes, I did. Dave was the attending doctor when she was brought in."

Oh, right. I'd forgotten about Darla's doctor husband. She could have led with that—why didn't she lead with that? The weird lump in my throat would have been but a mere tickle if I'd known Darla already knew what had happened to Maribel, but whatever.

Germophobe Dave probably told his wife about what had stabbed into the woman's skull, but it's unlikely he'd known what she'd told the cops before she'd undergone surgery. "Detective Hudson said Maribel got a glimpse of her attacker before she blacked out."

My neighbor's smile drops, but her eyebrows shoot up. She stuffs the dirty gloves alongside the rusty shears in her apron pocket and waits for me to go on.

"'Pert nose, blond hair to the jawline, beauty mark.'" I don't specify that they're looking for a female attacker because Hudson's list gives it away. "He said you can reach out to him if you think of anything that could be useful."

"I'll be sure to do that." Darla's eyebrows settle into their usual position, but the hitch in her voice pangs in my chest. She's more shaken about Maribel than she'd like to let on. "Would you like to come in for a cup of tea?"

I actually do wish I could stay and visit with my neighbor. As bizarre as the past week has been, Darla's company has made it better. A spoonful of sugar, I guess.

"I wish I could, but my editor is becoming impatient." I mimic typing on my air keyboard. "It's time to start writing."

Darla's eyebrows shoot back up. "Oh, you've decided on a new direction, then?"

Not even close. "I'm circling something," I say with a self-deprecating sort of chuckle. When I'd told Rob that Barb's violent death at the Dream Bean felt like the end of the first act in a slasher movie, I'd only been half serious. Now, after Maribel's attack, life feels like it's taking a definite step toward act two.

When I explain this to Darla, her face breaks into the same mischievous smile I'd glimpsed back when we'd touched knees on my bed. "It's terrible what's happened to Maribel, but maybe you could use it as inspiration for your next book. You know, spin straw into gold?"

My eyebrows lift, but then I remember that my new neighbor loves horror movies. Despite our differences, that little dark streak is the glue that binds us together. The only problem is that every time I work through the plot beats it ends with me as the Final Girl. As much as I love my genre, I've already lived through my own horror story. Hard pass on the sequel.

"I suppose it depends on what happens next," I tell Darla, and she shakes her little cannonball fists in a way I choose to believe is excitement over the prospect of a new novel direction, and not whether there will be another attack.

She sheds her gardening apron on the grass and jerks her head toward Number Thirty-Four's front doors. "Before you go, I've got something for you." She beckons me to follow. "I'll just go grab it—back in a jiff."

Darla leaves the front door open when she bolts into her house, and I trail her to the porch to wait on the mat. The eggy silver-polish scent is gone, but I still wrinkle my nose when I see the novel sitting square on her glass coffee table.

Mine.

What's left of the lump in my throat turns to salt water. Sure, every author *wants* the public to read their work, it's just a special kind of agony when it's someone you know. Somehow their opinions matter. I like Darla, so hers matters more than most.

She returns to the door beaming through a fan of lime-green Xerox pages. The colored sheets flutter as she flips the pages around and holds them against her chest for display. "What do you think?"

Letters shaped like ice cream cones line the top half of the page.

> *Put the cherry on top of the new school year at the*
> *Brunswick Elementary PTA Back-to-School Ice Cream Social!!!*
> *Friday, September 15th, at 7:00 p.m. in the*
> *Brunswick Elementary gym*
> *Strawberry, vanilla, and chocolate! $2 a scoop!!*

With a price per scoop, it looks like Darla settled the Great Ice Cream Debate. Good for her for making an executive decision as president.

"It looks great," I say, and Darla thrusts a green sheet in my hand before I can stop her.

Her gaze peels away from me and back to the flyers in her hand. "I should have printed these on pink. That seems more appropriate, doesn't it?" She squints at the page. "I think I'll redo it."

Darla waits until I open the door to my Honda before calling out congratulations.

I put my palm over my eyes to shield the sun and squint through the glare. "For what?"

Still holding that fan of green pages, Darla waves them at me. "With Maribel indisposed, I need a new VP to take her place, and it's the president's job to nominate who," she says, like I'm so silly for not putting two and two together. "We're going to spend *so* much time together, just like me and Patti." My heart thumps. "How perfect since we're neighbors!"

The flyer crinkles under my grip. Everyone's got a coping mechanism, I guess. My sister's is to hide behind a wall of overly filtered selfies, mine to pour it out on the page. Darla's, apparently, is to focus on her PTA work.

Could be worse, I guess. She could have deadheaded *all* her new mums.

The Ice Cream Social flyer goes on top of the pile of unopened mail on the desktop when I finally get back into my new office. My phone lights up with texts from my sister, but I flip it face down. I've got six hours before I need to pick up Tanner, which gives me plenty of time to get some words onto the page, but time will dwindle quickly if I start gabbing with Kitty. My cursor blinks rudely at me from the blank manuscript page. If I don't get started now, I won't have time to idly scroll around and pretend to do research, regardless of how long I ignore my sister. But the orange kitchen scissors are still on my desk from when I'd finished unpacking my office, and no matter how much I try to think about dolls in space, the only thing on my mind is how much force it would take to drive those blades through a human skull.

So hard that scissors couldn't do it? Or just hard enough that they could? And assuming it could be done, why did whoever attacked Maribel stop before they could finish the job?

Over my shoulder, my corkboard winks at me in the dark space on my monitor. I still haven't managed to get anything up about either dolls or space, which means Darla's Dollface business card and the Dream Bean Café pastry sack are the only things still affixed to my corkboard, like they're the first beats of whatever it is I'm supposed to be writing.

Maybe you could use it as inspiration for your next book, Darla had said, about all this weird crap going on around town, and as amped up as my editor is about dolls in space, a suburban slasher *would* be right up Charlene's alley.

Screw it.

It's not the story I intend on writing, but the only way to get these beats out of my head is to poke holes in my own plot. Then atrophy will have its way, and I can finally get to work on my actual novel.

I abandon the word-processing software and type *ABC7* into my internet browser's search bar, screenshot Barbara Shelton's barely recognizable photo from her headline news story (no leads, the latest update says), and send it to the printer, then navigate to Brunswick Elementary's PTA page on the school website and do the same to Maribel's.

The group photo on the site is still last year's board. There's Maribel, Kellen, Beth, Rosa, and Sasha, which means the petite blonde standing beside Darla must be Patti. The woman wears the kind of strained, toothy smile you hope doesn't come back to haunt you in a missing person's photo, her knuckles gripped so hard against her crimson PTA binder it half looks like a row of teeth set inside gums. I can't help but notice Patti's pert nose and blond hair. No beauty mark that I can spot in the grainy photo, but Rosa would have known if Patti had one because she never forgets a face.

Or maybe she forgot that detail like she'd forgotten the title of my book.

Or maybe I'm projecting, *again.*

Before I close the browser, I send the group shot of last year's board to the printer, too. I rearrange the pinned items so that the Dream Bean sack comes before the Dollface card, then tack Barb's pleasant smile under the Dream Bean pastry sack and Maribel's cheekbone smirk under the pink business card.

Lugosi rolls liquid brown eyes up at me when I tack the green Ice Cream Social flyer next on my corkboard, directly over the PTA group photo, and my finger grazes Patti's jaw-length blond hair as my hand pulls away.

"Things are getting weird around here," I tell the retriever, but it's more than weird, really. The whole living-in-a-slasher-novel thing is not out of my head, now that I see it on my corkboard.

It's right in my face.

CHAPTER THIRTEEN

Rob's face is between my legs.

My darling husband's hands grip my hip bones while my thighs clamp around his ears, his five-o'clock shadow scuffing like warm sandpaper where my flesh anchors against his mouth. Soft lips suckle the warmest, most tender parts of my body. Rob's tongue is warm and slick, his fingers taut—and all I can think about is my neighbor's pink-not-green Ice Cream Social flyers and the slasher novel beating itself out on my office corkboard.

Come *on.*

I grip the bedsheets in my fists. Glare at the ceiling fan that whirls lazily overhead. Time my breathing to the rhythm of Lugosi's snuffles on the other side of the master-bedroom floor. Now is *not* the time for intrusive thoughts, and yet all I can think about is a pair of scissors crooked like rabbit-ear antennae out of the top of Maribel's head, Barb's life spilling over pavement in the brief swirl of color. Those nightmarish images helped me outline a few emerging beats on my corkboard not-outline, but they're not gonna get me over the blissful, climactic crest Rob's lips and tongue and fingers are pushing me toward.

And mama *needs* to cross that crest.

I arch my back against the mattress, force my exhale into a moan, and rake my fingers through the dark swatch atop my husband's head. Soft, Rob's hair is. Soft and dandruff-free and not even close to balding, and all from good genes and a two-in-one shampoo/conditioner. Funny how men seem to look better as they age, while my reflection melts in the bathroom mirror like someone tossed a bucket of water over my head. The older I get, the more sympathetic Margaret Hamilton's Wicked Witch of the West becomes. Only thing the woman wanted was revenge on the farm girl who'd dropped a house on her sister.

That, and a good pair of shoes.

Sweet suction tugs in my lower half, and my hips twist under Rob's mouth. His teeth are smooth and round as braille when he mistakes my wriggling for pleasure. "I love the way you taste," he mumbles into my skin, and I push my knees closer together. The man needs room to breathe, not speak.

Lugosi yips in his sleep and I curl my fingers into Rob's hair, close my eyes, and grind against his jaw hard enough that prickly facial hair chaps soft skin. He makes a noise that might be pleasure, might be suffocation, but he doesn't pull away. Instead, strong drummer fingers clench my hips, stubble tickles my thigh—and I barely feel any of it.

Come onnn, Jill. Focus.

Rob's grip tightens on my thighs, his fingers digging into flesh hard enough to promise bruises, and an electric tide pulls me back into my body. He flicks his tongue, flint against steel, and my toes curl. I close my eyes against the whirling ceiling fan and ride the current that sparks under my skin, sharp and metal and red.

Like the blade ripping across Barb's throat.

The shears biting down into Maribel's skull.

The made-up hinges in Kitty's clown-face jaw.

The mirror shards, dripping red as they rip through my mother's stitches in her bedroom closet.

Tangled thoughts wrench me free of Rob's electric tide, shoving me back in time through Hart's office, into my childhood. My toes unfurl and my eyes open to see the ceiling fan make another turn under the white popcorn sky. On the carpet, Lugosi chases something in his dreams.

Just because things seem the same doesn't mean they are, I remind myself. Not all threads connect, no matter what the items tacked to my corkboard insist.

And crossing that crest is, officially, not going to happen.

Rob's tongue winds a slow circle somewhere in my lower half, but I'm numb from the waist down. My fingers pull free from his hair to tap the poor guy out. "A for effort," I tell him, which is true, "but it's just not in the cards for me tonight" (which is, unfortunately, also true).

My husband wipes his lips on the inside of my thigh. He groans into my skin, then pushes himself up, flops onto his side of the bed, and talks to my profile. "Please tell me I'm doing a horrible job and you're not still fixating on this whole Dream Bean Killer thing."

Of course I'm *still fixating* on this whole Dream Bean Killer thing. It's been hours, not eons, since I heard the news about Maribel. "I was half kidding about the *Stepford–Twilight Zone*–slasher thing before," I admit, and roll onto my side. "But it *is* bizarre, don't you think? Two attacks within days of each other. The first one literally the day we moved in. I mean, what are the odds on something like that?"

Rob makes a valiant effort not to stare at my boobs when I don't pull up the covers, but at least he doesn't parrot the party line about coincidences. "We are not living in a slasher movie, Jilly Bean."

Nothing thrusts your brain back into your body like hearing your childhood nickname, the one your dead mother used to call you but now only your little sister does, which is exactly why Rob does it. He scoots closer and lifts an arm, catching me in the crook of his elbow as he tucks my body against his. "Besides, don't slasher villains always use the same murder weapon anyway?" he says, humoring me. "Michael Myers and his carving knife, Freddy Krueger and his finger knives—"

"Glove." I can't help myself. "Freddy made it based on a clawed weapon used by female ninjas." A gurgling animal sound, a huff, and our giant golden retriever redeposits himself along my side of the bed. "Wes Craven got the idea from his cat."

My darling husband squeezes me against him. "And Jason Voorhees and his chain saw," he finishes the list I interrupted. "Can't be a trope if you don't play by the rules, right?"

"Well, Freddy didn't use his glove to kill in *Freddy's Dead,* and about half the kills in *Friday the 13th* came from a hunting knife, but there was an axe to the face and a machete decapitation. Oh, and Kevin Bacon's character got impaled under a cot with an arrow—but Jason never used a chain saw." My husband's fingertips tickle out a patient tempo against my rib cage. "That's a Mandela Effect thing from mis-associations with generic hulking killers in hockey masks portrayed in cartoons and comics."

But none of that matters because Jason wasn't even the killer—at least not until Alice Hardy gave his mother a taste of her own medicine. "And it was Pamela Voorhees behind the kills in the first film, not Jason," I add, because sometimes I don't know when to quit.

"A woman." Rob knows where I'm going because I've already told him Hudson's possible-suspect profile. "Yeah, didn't see that one coming."

"No one saw it coming. That's why it was a twist." Women as monsters is a trope as old as time, but statistically female serial killers aren't as uncommon as people think, though they rarely make the cut in pop culture. "Everyone always expects the bad guy to be, well, a *guy.*"

Rob feigns offense. "Men can kill, too, Jill." He snaps his fingers. "Wait. Ghostface, in *Scream.* Multiple murder weapons."

Just because *Scream* revived the slasher genre that *Halloween* defined doesn't mean the two are cut from the same cloth. "Multiple Ghostfaces. Two killers." I can remember Billy Loomis's name, but not the other one. "Again, twist."

Rob yawns. He leans up onto his elbow to kiss the edge of my lips.

"Jill, what happened is horrible and frightening and I am not at all trying to dismiss your feelings." His lips paint the words against my cheek, but his voice is too reasonable. "But you're spinning out. This happens every time."

Suddenly chilled, I pull the sheets up to my shoulders. "Every time what?"

"Every time you—" Eggshells crack under Rob's feet as he reconsiders the rest of his sentence. Every time I start a new novel, he means. He's right, but it's like someone you love telling you that your butt does indeed look fat in a new pair of jeans—like, *Thanks for the heads-up, but screw you for noticing.*

"Look." Rob's hand moves under the blanket to find mine, then squeezes it. "You're an amazing author but you have this tendency to let the horror get under your skin—and I get why," he adds quickly, before I can shape my lips into rebuttal. "You write so well because you know what real horror is, but I also know that sometimes getting in the right headspace means kicking up dust in places even you are scared to go." Another squeeze and this time he holds it, like the pressure of his hand can force his words to take root. "Please be careful. Don't let this one get personal."

But it *is* personal, isn't it? "Why, because I've known both victims?" The words snap out before I can stop them, and my husband's beautiful mouth thins into a line.

Rob's blink runs a little too long. "Because you're stressed from the move," he says carefully, "and because Tanner *just* went back to school, *and* there's a mess going on around us—literally and figuratively. That's enough to overwhelm anyone, and now you've got both the neighbor and your sister pushing triggery makeup buttons. Add in the fact that you're actively *trying* to think up something scary, and of course you're going to—"

Rob's voice breaks off when his words butt up against a line he tries never to cross, his eyes scouring the freshly regrown skin of my over-scrubbed face, and he redirects. "Promise me you'll give yourself some space. The police say there's nothing for you to worry about, right? They have all the information, and we're only working with partial data—we're at a disadvantage." Rob's lips fill back out into their usual slope, his eyes so wide and blue they're oceans on my dead mother's face. "Besides, they know who they're looking for, right? A woman with short blond hair, a beauty mark, and a 'pert' nose, which seems very specific. Have you met anyone who even remotely meets that description?"

I don't mention Patti in last year's PTA group photo. "No."

"Okay," he says, like that's that. Rob's hand lets go of mine under the covers and lands on my cheek. "Tell me you promise."

Just because my darling husband is probably right doesn't mean I have to admit it. But he's giving me the kind of hopeful, tortured look a person never enjoys seeing on a loved one's face, and that means I have to agree to his terms. "I promise."

"Okay." A thick sheen of doubt coats Rob's baby blues, but he peels his palm away and gives me a kiss that holds on.

When the warm imprint of Rob's kiss cools, I fish my underwear from where they'd fallen off the bed, then push my legs into fluffy pajama bottoms, pull a fuzzy cardigan over my arms, and, because I've already shed my contacts, settle on thick-rimmed glasses so I'm not completely blind.

"I'm not quite ready to go to bed," I tell Rob, as I swirl my monstress hair into a messy bun and strap it down with a few twists of elastic. "I think I'll go downstairs and work a bit more." He rolls away with a sigh, and I plant a kiss into the wedge of his neck. "I'm sorry about—" I wiggle my legs so he doesn't have to guess what I'm apologizing for, and he grunts in response. "I love you, *Throb.*"

Two can play at terrible nicknames.

He groans half a laugh into his pillow. "I really hate that your sister gave me that name and not you."

I stamp a quick peck onto his cheek. "That's my favorite part."

"Of course it is." Rob reaches behind him until his hand lands on my arm. "Seriously, honey"—his look says he's still worried—"give yourself some space. Stay with me."

Downstairs, the windowpanes in the first-floor conservatory watch like a wall of empty eye sockets as I step inside my new office. The retriever curls under my desk while I close the double doors against the empty staircase, the silent kitchen, the darkened entryway and settle behind my keyboard. Enough light filters in through the windows that my reflection is a ghost on the blank monitor, features more blurred than melted, stray tendrils of monstress hair floating around my head, like I'm looking at myself underwater—a broken bird in a murky pool.

"Okay, I see what Rob is talking about," I mutter under my breath, loud enough that I can pretend I'm talking to the dog and push the image into the recesses of my brain. Bad memories aside, agreeing with yourself, out loud, alone, in the dark, makes it somehow worse to realize why your husband thinks you're losing it.

But I am *not* losing it.

The corkboard looms over my shoulder as I nudge the mouse to wake the monitor. A previous version of my son, barely bigger than a baked potato, beams at me from the desktop wallpaper. Tanner sits in Rob's lap behind his drum kit, my husband's face scrunched in a rock-'n'-roll grimace while our son's frenzied fuzzy-duckling hair statics away from the headphones clamped over his ears. The kid's toothless mouth hangs open in a delighted shriek, and the drumstick clutched in his chubby fist blurs where it bounces off the hi-hat.

A happy family. Everything I always wanted. Everything Kitty and I never had.

I should get back to my outline, to dolls in space, not the Dream Bean Killer, but instead of writing I track down the movie about Buddy Rich's favorite rock drummer.

I never make it as far as the Barbies. In the *Blair Witch*–style opening, Karen Carpenter's mother finds her collapsed in a closet.

Of course it's a closet.

A lot of articles place full blame for pop culture's most famous case of anorexia nervosa at the feet of the mother (they always blame the mom), while other articles accuse Karen's sibling of joining in on the abuse. Her brother should've been her biggest ally, but the apple of mother's eye got stuck playing second fiddle. So, the story goes, Richard needles at his sister, too.

Karen's own doctor, Steven Levenkron, explored the link between eating disorders and self-harm. Seems so obvious now. Some Italian doctor named the disease *dysmorphophobia* in 1886, but the term didn't catch on in the United States until shortly before Karen's 1983 death and wasn't recognized in the *DSM-III* until 1987. Levenkron literally wrote the book on it in 1998—then two novels adapted into films.

Maybe he was too busy writing books to save the young woman struggling in his care.

The chime of an incoming video call flings my pulse directly behind my ears, interrupting my internet rabbit-hole research. Deer-eyed and mouth agape, my face is a horror-movie poster in the pop-up window in the corner of my monitor. I missed my morning sister chat while I got Tanner off on his first day of school, but thanks to the news about Maribel and the goose trail winding across my corkboard, I accidentally ignored Kitty's texts all afternoon, too.

I twist a bit of crust from the corner of my eye, push flyaway hair behind my ears, and accept the call, ready to remind my sister that it's almost midnight on my side of the country—until I see her face.

"Holy shit, Katherine." Were it not for her brunette hair and trademark smirk, I wouldn't recognize the figure with buttons for eyes on the other end of the video feed, its face cracked like a china doll that's just taken a bad spill on a hard floor.

"What do you think?" Kitty blinks her button eyes open.

I think we should stick to audio only if she's going to keep up this makeup trend, but maybe that's my fault for leaving her on read.

"Another Halloween makeup tutorial?" I ask once I swallow down the swill of chlorine that rushes into my mouth.

"I'm a doll." My sister closes her eyes, so I get another look at her eyelids-turned-buttons, complete with white stitches through each set of four holes. "Get it?"

"It's terrifying, Kitty." But it does look like a doll.

She tsks approvingly. When she focuses back on me, my sister makes a point of sweeping her button eyes around the room. "You in your new office? I like the windows."

Movement flashes in my peripheral vision, but if something lurks outside those darkened panes, it's not enough to rouse Lugosi, whose hot breath forms condensation on the underside of my feet. The house is settling, probably. Hopefully.

Every good horror story starts with a creepy house.

"It's creepier at night than I expected," I confess, remembering the Keurig's mysterious self-relocation. When I'd asked, Rob had insisted he hadn't moved the pot. Probably I did, in all my unpacking craze, and just forgot.

My sister gives me the full weight of her buttons as she tilts her head to the side and channels her inner Boris Karloff. "Do you like scary movies?"

Right movie, wrong actor. Or, right actor, wrong movie, depending on your preference.

When I respond with an eye roll, Kitty strains her head to the other side, as if she thinks she can look over my shoulder in 2D. She can't, of course, but it's sort of fun to watch her try.

"That your new book?" she asks, about the corkboard over my shoulder.

"Worse." My chair wheels rattle over the hardwood as I scoot aside to give her a full view of the items tacked to the corkboard. "That's my week."

"More drama in PTA land?" Kitty's button eyes roll. "I wouldn't know, because you never talk to me anymore," she scoffs. "Not since you met *Darla.*"

We've missed *two* of our morning chats, and neither of them have been due to Darla, but it's not worth arguing the point with my sister, who'll insist missed is missed. Instead, I scoot my chair to the corkboard and tap the Dollface card, with its delicate script and bold pink background. "You've really never heard of this brand before? I could *swear* I've seen it on your socials."

One of Kitty's shoulders bumps up toward her ear. "MLMs don't bother with influencers. Kind of messes up the whole pyramid-scheme thing to bring in outside help."

Seems like MLMs, since they function by enlisting the most people possible to peddle their products, would be all over influencers, but whatever. "Anyway, the day I met Darla"—another eye roll from Kitty at the mention of my new neighbor, but I ignore it to tap the sugary, grease-stained Dream Bean sack, then the image of Barb from ABC7—"I went to that PTA brunch, right? The barista that served us was found murdered the next day."

"And?" Kitty makes a face. We haven't talked but we've texted, so she already knows this part.

My fingers crawl over the Dollface business card to the photo of Maribel. "Maribel, the only woman on the PTA who didn't show up at Doll's Night, was attacked in her home later the same night with a pair of scissors."

"Doll's Night?" Kitty's tone is heavy on the disdain for a girl literally dolled up. "Like, playing with dolls?"

"Remember those makeover parties Mom used to do?" We'd carry her padded pink briefcases, watch her twist and pinch samples of creams, pad dabs of blue, cream, yellow, green, on her clients' faces. "Anyway, it was like one of those," I say, because of course Kitty remembers, even if she hasn't said so.

"How did it go?" The corners of my sister's mouth are turned down when I glance at the screen. At least I think they are. It's impossible to read her expression through the layers of cream paint on her face. "The party, I mean. Did you have fun with all your new Mean Girl mommy friends?"

If memory serves, not only had the women completely railroaded Darla's sales pitch to talk about Barb's murder, but I don't think the PTA brood spent a penny. "Every woman ran out of there so fast, if they'd have been cartoon characters, they'd have left their skin."

Kitty's face shapes into a pout. "Poor Darla," she says, without a shred of sympathy.

"Otherwise, it was fine, I guess," I go on, ignoring my sister's sarcasm in an effort to get back to the point. "I met Rosa, the Events chair who missed brunch. She's a librarian—recognized me from my author photo. Said she never forgets a face but couldn't remember the name of my book."

"Weird flex for a librarian," Kitty grumbles.

"Her husband, the detective, was with her at school this morning. He was the cop who told us about the attack on Maribel."

Finally, I have my sister's interest. "Do the cops think the attacks are connected?"

"They are adamant that they're not."

Kitty yawns and stretches on the other side of the screen, suddenly bored when the juicy details run out. "I mean, it's a little weird, yeah. But if the cops aren't worried about it, then I wouldn't make a big deal, you know?" she says as soon as she's finished her exhale. "It's probably just coincidence, right? Everyone you ever hear about getting murdered on the news was somebody's friend. It's like six degrees of Kevin Bacon or something."

My sister doesn't know it, but she's just proved her own point, since I'd just reminded Rob about Kevin's impalement back at Camp Crystal Lake. If you look hard enough, even the most random of events can be tied back together. Butterfly effect or something.

"Don't get yourself all worked up over nothing, Jilly Bean. Focus on what's important—like me." The cracks in Kitty's doll's face widen when she attempts a smile that's probably meant to be reassuring but makes her look scary as hell. "You don't want to turn into Mom."

Rob danced around that cold truth earlier, which only makes it sting worse when my sister says it—sort of like how Karen Carpenter's doctor was too busy writing about her mental illness to help her survive it.

Other than my new neighbor, no one is interested in the slasher plotting itself out on my corkboard, which is probably for the best. I've got a book to write, after all, not a murder to solve, and Kitty and Rob are probably right: It's easy to get snared in the details of a crime that has absolutely nothing to do with you. Such is the siren call of the true-crime genre.

I flip the corkboard to face the wall while, on-screen, my sister gushes about her latest Halloween makeup tutorials and plans for her next social media campaign—and she hasn't told me about the new chanty Japa meditation she's just discovered, has she?—but my eyes linger on the corkboard's blank back. Maybe no one else is concerned about the week's strange occurrences, but if something happens after the Ice Cream Social—if another woman I'm on a first-name basis with ends up with her photo tacked to my corkboard—I'll know whatever is happening in my new neighborhood is not just a coincidence, like Detective Steve said.

It's a problem.

CHAPTER FOURTEEN

By the time the Ice Cream Social rolls around a week later, things almost feel normal. Most of the cardboard boxes in my new creaky-not-creepy house have been unpacked and most of the unpacked stuff has found places to go. I've only got half a plot and no title, but at least I've started adding words to my manuscript. Most important, there have been no further attacks: Maribel is recovering well and the Dream Bean Killer chatter in the group text has reduced itself from a boil to a simmer.

With my corkboard still facing the office wall, it's almost like nothing ever happened.

And yet, there's a weird taste in the back of my throat when I arrive at the elementary school that I tell myself is just first-PTA-event jitters and absolutely *not* a plot movement. Just because the first act started with Kellen and Maribel locked in debate about ice cream servings over brunch doesn't mean tonight's social is the story's natural midpoint. No highly dramatic moment here, just normal back-to-school happenings and a lot of dairy and sugar.

Like, a *lot* of dairy and sugar.

About ten tubs, just like Maribel had said back at the Dream Bean, and all the fixings Kellen's high-adrenaline little runner's heart could ever desire. All waiting to be scooped into paper (not styrofoam) cups.

The spoons, though, are as plastic as the pink, white, and brown sheets shellacked over every available surface. Students and their families won't arrive for another hour, but the room is midway through its transformation from elementary school cafeteria to Baskin-Robbins circa 1985.

"Isn't it coming together just perfectly?" Darla bounces on her heels at my side, the cherries on her dangly sundae earrings the same red shade as the one's that top the ice-cream-cone appliqués on her homemade pink Brunswick PTA shirt. "I just love the Neapolitan color scheme—it matches our outfits perfectly," she says loud enough for my jeans and staple black T-shirt to hear as she leads me toward a table where Beth and Kellen are busy fashioning ice cream cones out of construction paper and latex balloons.

"Pink for strawberry, white for vanilla, and brown for chocolate." Darla points to various articles of clothing as she names off flavors.

"It was on the group-text chain," says Beth, whose chocolate slacks and strawberry blouse clearly got the memo.

"I'm wearing the right colors." Kellen's expression dares Darla to say something about her pink camo athleisure as she tugs at her Stanley thermos. "I'll be running off ice cream calories later and don't feel like changing."

Well, crap. Not only did I miss Darla's text with the board-member-uniform instructions, but other than the fluffy heart-print robe I'd unfortunately worn the day we first met and an old *Carrie* T-shirt, casually specked with screen-print blood splatter, there's not a single article of pink clothing in my closet.

Darla waves away my apology, then plucks the sparkly red headband from behind her teased bangs and tucks it into my hair like a high school prom-queen crown. "I'll bring you a red apron and you'll be the cherry on top of the whole shebang."

This, I think, is a good thing, but I hold my breath for a beat anyway, just in case a bucket of pig's blood drops from the ceiling.

Darla flashes a bright smile, urges me toward a stack of unblown balloons, and scuttles off for the giant bags of ice waiting near a stack of single-use aluminum trays along the room's front wall. The malt-shoppe dress code is nauseatingly twee, but it *does* add a certain extra sweetness to the social. I'm woman enough to admit when I'm wrong.

Kellen, however, is less understanding.

She huffs into a ball of pink latex, then pinches off the tip and twists the rubbery neck into a knot. After I bop the balloon into a pile with the others, Kellen celebrates with another tug off her thermos. The hiccup that follows suggests there's something other than water in that Stanley.

"It feels weird, doesn't it?" Kellen says, notes of butter and vanilla beating off my shoulder when she leans in close enough to whisper-talk into my ear. "I mean, look at this." She wands her thermos at the room before I respond. "We're setting up for an Ice Cream Social. Meanwhile Maribel *just* got released from the hospital and is probably still jumping at every shadow in her house, and for what?" Kellen hiccups. "So we can stuff our children full of crap and pretend there isn't some lunatic running around attacking people with bread knives and scissors?"

This from the woman willing to go to war over the paper-cup budget. So much for pretending nothing happened. It feels a little odd to be on the same side as Kellen, but with my husband and sister both handling me with kid gloves, it's weirdly reassuring to know that I'm not the only one still holding my breath for the next attack.

Beth's voice rattles like a breakable thing as she leans in to trace lines of brown marker onto the giant wedge of Kraft construction paper. "The first documented ice cream social on American soil was in Maryland in 1744," she says, and Kellen groans before pumping another pink balloon full of wine breath while Beth lattices the brown triangle into a waffle cone, ribbing in shading along one side for a cute 3D effect. "The governor served it at a dinner party—for dessert," she adds, as if maybe I'd assumed the old colonizer would serve his guests frozen sugar during the salad course.

Wild, those early Americans were.

Kellen tugs at her Stanley, I bop balloons across the table, and Beth prattles on about George and Martha Washington's ice cream machine in Mount Vernon while she staples balloon butts onto the construction-paper cone. "In 1802, Thomas Jefferson was the first president to serve ice cream at the White House, but socials became even more popular when ice cream became available to the public and organizations like churches and schools started hosting them. Now they're common community events, especially for back-to-school."

By the time Beth is done beating her buried lead to death, Kellen is wine drunk, and I am out of balloons to bop—but it's fine because the DIY construction-paper ice cream cone is finished. Families are probably piling into their minivans and four-doors now, winding their way toward the school.

I hold the crafted cone to the wall while Beth peels off tape.

"Those early socials were sometimes called 'ice cream gardens' because the cones look like flowers on a warm summer day." She points at other paper-and-balloon cones strewn around the room, and I get it.

"Strawberry, vanilla, and chocolate flowers," I say. "Classic."

This is the first time I've seen a real smile on Beth's face. "Yes, but early Americans had a taste for more unusual flavors, too." Her eyebrows push up into her hairline. "Some of the most popular flavors in the 1800s were tea, Parmesan, and"—she cuts off long enough to tack on an impressively sly grin—"oyster."

"Sounds delicious."

"Maybe you can use it?" Beth's voice turns hopeful. "In a book?"

"Hey, you never know." Perhaps I've misjudged these women—ironic, since I'd been so preoccupied with their misjudging me.

Kellen snorts, and I sneak Beth a wink. No sense letting the little chardonnay cloud rain all over her ice-cream-social-trivia parade.

Before she can dish out another thrilling ice-cream-social factoid, there's a loud bang, a burst of harsh consonants, and Sasha barrels through the double doors ahead of a pair of matching miniature duplicates. I catch a glimpse of the parking lot before a man trundles in towing a child's red wagon loaded down with more toppings (chocolate-coated candies, sprinkles, gummy bears), jugs of syrups (strawberry, chocolate, caramel), and extra napkins (recyclable).

"The Old Goat moves too slow," Sasha says as she passes, as much of an excuse for her tardiness as we'll get, and marches her family toward the table designated for toppings.

The doors swing open again, and Detective Steve Hudson strolls in gripping dynamite. The little princess tethered to his palm has dirt caked onto the hem of her dress and a feral ponytail, but Rosa's daughter is every bit as glamorous as her mother. Steve holds the door open for his wife, and Rosa's petticoat poodle skirt might be a tad short for an elementary event, but I'd show off my legs, too, if I had gams like hers. The metal box in her hands is almost as big as the baby strapped to her hip, but nowhere near as cute.

"It's almost time to open the doors!" Darla is at my side in a rush of brown sugar and pear, handing me the red apron she promised. "This is going to be our best Ice Cream Social yet."

Kellen snorts and her Stanley makes slurpy noises, and Darla squints hard. "Don't *you* think so, Kellen?" she asks, too sweetly, like cyanide.

The other woman pulls a face, but a man's voice cuts her off.

"Darla!"

I never noticed the side door at the opposite end of the room, but it's unmissable now that someone is using their gut to shove a plastic tub through from the other side with all the finesse of childbirth.

"I've got your scoops." The guy's outside-voice holler is wholly unnecessary from less than fifty feet away.

Darla grabs my hand and tugs me along the same as she had the day she'd come over, lured me upstairs, and made me over just like my dead mother in my own bedroom. "Come with me, Jill. Let me introduce you to my husband."

So, the sweaty guy bellowing across the cafeteria is Dave Lashett, Darla's germophobe doctor husband, who has to stop short to wipe a sheet of sweat off his forehead and wheeze after moving a seventy-quart Sterilite, but makes his wife promise not to order a croissant for breakfast.

Oh, Darla. You deserve better.

Dave dumps the bin like a body on the rubber-tile floor, paws at the sweat under his hairline, then his hands take a quick trip to his pocket. The plastic bottle squirts into his palms as he grunts upright. "Don't know what in the hell you've packed in this," he grouches at Darla, "but it's heavy as a ton of bricks."

Darla tsks away her husband's grousing. "Dave, this is our new neighbor, Jill Marshall." She glances around the room, asks if Rob is bringing Tanner later, and I nod while Dave does a double take at my T-shirt and crinkles his nose. It's just a couple of cute little skull graphics, but I should put the apron on sooner rather than later.

"Yours the family that just moved into Patti Townsend's old house?" Dave says, probably because he's the sort of guy who likes being told he's right, even when he knows he is, since I haven't noticed any other U-Hauls on the street as of late.

Dave grumbles something under his breath that might be *Good to meet you* or *Go to hell.* Hard to be sure as he doesn't bother to make eye contact or shake my hand before he trudges off toward the other end of the room. "Hey, Hudson, you boys catch the guy who cut that girl's throat open over at the café yet?" he calls, voice booming through the acoustics, and I'm glad no one's let the kids in yet because this guy's bad-news-in-front-of-children filter is *way* busted.

There's some backslapping and bro-hugging among the men in the room. Even Sasha's Old Goat gets a shoulder squeeze before the small husband herd retires to the coach's office to let the girls handle the rest.

I'd murder Rob. But Rob wouldn't dare.

"This is the best part," Darla says, about the tub, as she pops the lid to expose a hodgepodge of cleaning supplies, stray plastic spoons, and leftover napkins from Ice Cream Socials past. "Donations, mostly, but it's always good to have extra supplies on hand." She winks at me over the impressive selection of ice cream scoopers. "Never know what you might need at an Ice Cream Social."

Agreed. "Like, seven hundred and twelve ice cream scoopers."

Darla roots around in the tub, careful not to chip her nail polish, and pulls out an old-fashioned scooper. The long metal tube fits snugly in her hand, though the bowl seems smaller than average. "This one was Patti's favorite," she says proudly. "It's a vintage gelato scoop, technically, but works like a dream."

"Cool." Having a favorite scooper seems odd at first, but this is one of aging's microaggressions: You stop caring about fancy restaurants and date nights and develop attachments to things like stovetop burners and decorative hand towels.

The metal scoop is smaller than modern versions, but it fits in Darla's palm like it'd been shaped for her grip. Or Patti's, I guess.

"You should use it tonight, Jill." Darla holds out the scoop. "After all, you're the new VP."

My fingers twitch toward the tool, but then I remember that Rosa assigned me to cashier duty, back on the parts of the group text I *did* read. Darla's smile melts like oyster-flavored ice cream under a nineteenth-century sun when I tell her I'm working the cashbox tonight. "You should use it," I say, about the vintage gelato scoop. "Patti would totally agree."

Across the room, Sasha snaps at her husband, or maybe her kids, and Rosa's baby starts to cry. Kellen fumbles her Stanley and Beth scuttles after it.

I lean closer to Darla and lower my voice. "Is it just me or does that mug look suspiciously like a wineglass with a handle?"

Darla gets the joke. She giggles and waves me away with Patti's scooper.

Someone pushes through the double doors and we both catch a sea of fuzzy-duckling heads as a gaggle of parent volunteers slip into the room to be appointed duties and assigned serving tables.

"Two dollars per scoop, and toppings are fifty cents, regardless of type or quantity," Darla reminds me as she waves me toward Rosa and the cash table.

I tie the apron on as I go, cut off midway across the room by a dark-haired man in a three-piece suit and a couple of snooty-looking kids I haven't seen before. The trio passes like I'm the hired help, the kids peeling off to join up with Sasha's twins while their father joins the husbands in the coach's office.

"That's Chad, Maribel's ex," Rosa says as I take my seat beside her at the cash table. "I'm honestly surprised he brought the kids, but they probably wanted to come, and he probably didn't have a good reason not to." More and more families have been admitted into the cafeteria. Rosa identifies a gorgeous Asian woman and a freckle-faced fourth grader among the crowd as Kellen's wife, Rena, and their son, Clay, then excuses herself to say hello.

I nearly jump out of my skin when a hand lands on my shoulder. "Whoa," Rob says, and pulls back. "Sorry to scare you." He leans down to deposit a kiss on top of my head and a couple of dollar bills in the till while Tanner ignores me completely. He tugs at his daddy's hand, begging him toward the tubs of ice cream, while I sit there like chopped liver.

Ice Cream—1, Mom—0.

"Can I have sprinkles *and* M&M's?" Tanner's voice shrills in the giant rubber room, but at least he's asking me now and not his dad—not because I wear the only pair of pants in the family, but because I'm the easiest to sucker. "And strawberry *and* vanilla scoops?"

Rob forks over another wad of bills. "What flavor scoop would you like?"

"Oyster."

My darling husband's eyebrows twist, but I shake my head. I'll educate him on early-American ice cream palates later. An especially tiny kindergartner tosses a pile of coins onto my table, and I swipe them into the cash box as Rob leans down to ear level. "Help me out before I face the PTA tribunal." His grin warns of an incoming dad joke. "Give me the scoop: names and faces."

"Darla, our neighbor, is at the strawberry station, Beth is at chocolate, Sasha at vanilla. The one slumping over the toppings table is Kellen." The husbands are in the coach's office, but Rena has posted up to help her wife with sprinkles. "The woman just here is Rosa. Her husband is Steve, the detective."

Rob's a good listener, but his eyes light up like Christmas morning when he hears that last. "He's investigating what happened at the Dream Bean Café?"

"And what happened to Maribel." I swear to all that is good, if my darling husband beelines to the cop just like Dave Lashett did . . .

But he doesn't. Instead, Rob blows me a goodbye kiss as he lets himself get hauled toward the ice cream tables.

Familiar faces begin to queue in my line—the principal, Miss Frost, the security guard—and Rosa reclaims her seat. When we clear the staff, she turns to face me. Beth's a sweetheart, but of all the Brunswick PTA Mean Girls, Rosa is probably the one who scares me least.

But that may be my book-buddy blinders talking.

"So, Jill, how are you settling into the neighborhood?" Her eyes are warm with what looks like genuine concern.

Part of me, that niggly horror-author part, is dying to ask if there's been any further development in identifying the blonde with the pert nose and beauty mark, but I force a smile and try to be a normal suburban mom and not a morbid weirdo, jonesing for fresh blood on the gory investigation. "It's been an adjustment," I start, but Kitty would say that's mid, whatever *mid* means, and Charlene would say its ambiguous at best, and so I try again. "Transfers always are"—I fumble with a handful of crumpled bills a harried father thrusts at me like I'm a teenager at a fast-food chain—"with the schools and new commutes and stuff. But Darla's been incredibly welcoming." Over at strawberry, Darla wields her vintage gelato scoop with the precision of a surgeon. "She's really gone out of her way to make us feel at home."

The other woman's perfectly sculpted brows furrow. "That's . . . nice. I'm glad you're finding your footing here in Brunswick. You know, Patti *loved* that house."

"It's just . . ." I pause to buy time straightening the stack of dollar bills in front of me. "As great as Darla's been, sometimes I can't help but feel like I'm living in her old neighbor's shadow. Darla talks about her so much, it's like she's still there, you know?"

Rosa's eyes go wide. "*Her* as in Patti—Patti Townsend?"

She leans in closer, but the cafeteria's double doors swing open, and a horde of elementary schoolers burst through, voices at full volume. Whatever Rosa says is lost to the ruckus, but even with the noise, I'm pretty sure I can read her lips.

"Patti *hated* Darla."

CHAPTER FIFTEEN

The steering wheel goes slick under the doll's hands as she watches the runner ignite in brief bursts of color under the streetlights. The doll keeps her speed low, the sedan held back at a far enough distance that the runner doesn't slow her pace as its tires crawl across the asphalt behind her. One footfall at a time, the runner passes quiet homes and closed storefronts, those brief flashes of color blinking in and out of sight as she makes her way into the shadows that stretch along the grassy boundaries of a community park.

The designer activewear hugs the hard angles of the runner's toned figure, but does nothing to hide her ugliness. The doll's milky breath buffets against her own nostrils as she watches the runner's pendulum ponytail swing behind her. The doll listens through the open driver's-side window to the soft thumps of rubber soles.

Mile after mile, the runner runs, unaware she is being followed.

Minutes tick by on the car's dashboard.

The tool is a pleasant pressure in the doll's lap. She cradles the instrument like a babe as she drives, its heartbeat pumping in the soft thuds of the runner's sneakers outside the car window. When the doll curls her fingers around the utensil, the metal kitchen tool fits inside her palm as if it were molded just for her—the aluminum barrel cool in the natural warmth of her hand, the tip smooth where her thumb rubs its bowled end. Shorter than the cake knife and the pruning shears, this tool is sturdy and durable, but rounded and slick, with no dead corners.

The doll tests its grip, its heft, its torque. Like before, she is not here to kill, but to prune. Tonight, to scoop.

The doll releases the tool in her lap, her vision narrowing through the thin slits of her beautiful face when the runner's feet tangle beneath her. One sneaker scuffs against a curb, a scratch of rubber against concrete that's audible through the open window. The hiccup sends the runner's stumble into a lurch, then into a stagger. Cold seizes the doll's chest when the runner swerves into the sedan's path. The doll's shoe lifts from the accelerator, hovers over the brake, and her smile goes rigid, knuckles white where they grip the steering wheel.

It won't do for the runner to have an accident. Not when the doll is so close.

One set of the doll's fingers unfurl from the wheel to grasp the tool in her lap, but the runner recovers. Her ponytail coils around her neck when she dips her head to peer over her shoulder into the sedan's headlights, and the doll smiles as she presses the accelerator. The runner's eyebrows pull together when the engine revs, and her pace quickens, veering off the road and into the parking lot of the community park.

The doll follows, slicking her fingers into sheer plastic food-worker gloves as the runner picks up speed, jogging toward the empty jungle gyms of the nighttime playground. When the runner sprints over the wheel stop at the top of a parking space, the doll pulls in quick behind her. The squeal of the brakes hides the crunch of the runner's sneaker as it's pinned between the sedan's grille and the parking block.

The runner screams as she pivots, palms splayed on either side of her thin frame. She uses one hand to shield herself from the car's headlights. The other, to send an obscene gesture to its driver. Her movements are loose from the run, from the pain in her broken ankle. "What the f—"

Behind the windshield, the doll's beautiful face smiles.

The doll raises her window against the runner's voice, her gestures. She shifts on the sedan's high beams, watching the runner's face flinch against the light. Her mouth opens, her lips and teeth cutting out unkind words, but whatever ugliness the runner yells, whatever her hands say, the doll can't hear on the quiet side of the glass.

She waits for the runner to go blind.

During daylight, flash blindness persists for seconds, maybe a minute, the retinal pigment bleached into whiteness by bright light. At night, when the pupil is dilated, the darkness is more absolute. The brighter the light, the more intense the stare, the longer the vision impairment. Partial recovery could take minutes, could take longer.

The doll counts to twenty while the runner rages into the headlights, pulling at her stuck leg like a mouse in a glue trap. Then, the doll twists off the lights, pushes open the driver's-side door, and steps out of the sedan without cutting the engine. Blinded in sudden darkness, the runner blanches. She lets go of her ankle and pushes herself to full height, still blinking as the doll approaches, the ice cream scoop clutched at her side.

Wedged between the car's front tire and the parking block, the runner's sneaker sticks at an unnatural angle, the rubber edge on the outside pinched and puckered. Tight enough that the foot won't come free until the sedan moves away. The ankle will need tending, but the doll prefers to take care of things at their root.

"What do y—" The runner rubs her eyes as the doll approaches, her vision returning, but her words fail when she sees the approaching form is female. Relief washes over her, but then recognition widens her features. The runner rears backward, stuttering as she takes in the doll's flawless skin, long lashes, sunshine bob, rosebud lips.

"No!" The runner screams when her gaze locks on the pinprick beauty mark in the doll's cheek.

How nice, the doll thinks. *It's so good to be recognized.* Even better that her beautiful face will be the last thing the runner ever sees.

The doll's fist curls around the metal instrument in her hand, gloves crinkling around the tool's shaft.

Guttural sounds mewl through the runner's lips as she wrenches with all her might, struggling to free her ankle. "Get away from me," the runner gasps.

The doll pads a step closer.

"Get away, get away, get away!" The runner's knees buckle. She falls backward, her free sneaker tangled inside a nest of twisted legs, and her head cracks against the pavement—a sharp sound, then a dull thud. The runner moans, stunned, as her eyes roll back in her head.

The doll curls her thumb inside the curve of the metal spoon as she anchors herself to the earth, straddles the woman beneath her, and plunges the scoop into the runner's eye.

The runner screams, writhing on the cooling pavement. She grasps at her face, her head, her ears, but the doll digs the tool in further, until smooth metal scrapes against the hard bone of the eye socket. She forces the aluminum lip inside the runner's eyelids, under the curve of the moist orb. This close, she can smell the acrid scent rising up off the woman's breath: butter and smoke and old fruit.

The doll's sheer plastic gloves are red, the ice cream scoop in her hand glistening with pink. She sets the instrument aside as the runner writhes on the pavement, still screaming. The orb is loose now, gouged, but still attached. Thumb, index, and middle, the doll forces her fingers into the warm cavity. She grips the glistening ball, twists, then plucks.

The eyeball pops from the socket and falls into the doll's hand, while the runner's head sags against the concrete. She whimpers and groans still, but shock has muted the screams. Now the doll can work in peace.

Goopy membranes still attach the wet lump to the optic nerve and vascular supply. The doll tugs the nerve taut but doesn't stretch the thick, tough dura around the sheath. The optic nerve stretches in her grip, but she's careful not to pull too hard. The doll doesn't want to sever the nerve's attachment at the back of the brain, cause trauma and damage. Neither does she want the runner to see.

She holds the eyeball in her plastic-gloved hand, wraps the cord through her fingers, and crushes the eyeball inside her fist.

Viscous jelly runs through the doll's fingers as she opens her palm under the moonlight. Beauty is in the eye of the beholder, and the glistening mass in her hand, the webby gel that sticks to the vinyl, stretching and reshaping as she bends her hand, is divine.

The runner comes to as the doll drops what's left of the eyeball, like half-melted cream, onto the ground near the crushed sneaker. Clutching at her face, the runner turns toward the splat and screams.

She's still screaming when the doll settles behind the wheel of her sedan and pulls away.

CHAPTER SIXTEEN

Few things are as sacred in the Marshall household as Saturday mornings.

Saturday mornings are pancake mornings, and after weeks of moving, unpacking, and getting settled, we are finally underway with our very first Saturday Pancake Morning in our new creaky-not-creepy home. The sizzle of batter on the hot griddle *should* be soothing, but set on the kitchen countertop, text notifications bloom on my phone's screen like contagion in a zombie franchise. This is not a good sign on any morning, but at nine AM on a Saturday?

Notifications glare up at me while I stand at the stove, spatula in hand, watching the edges of a pancake bubble and crisp. It's Boogie Bash, right? Has to be. With the Ice Cream Social now in our rearview, the Brunswick Elementary Mean Girls are probably pedal to the metal, full speed ahead for the biggest event of the school year.

But it's *Saturday* morning. Shouldn't the other moms be making their kids breakfast, too, instead of obsessing over an event a month away? I've heard the phrase *have it all*, but my version of work-life-PTA balance includes melted butter and maple syrup.

And coffee. My kingdom for a good cup of coffee.

The group-text bubble pings again, and I feel it prickle underneath my sleepy weekend-morning skin.

"Mom, can you make my pancakes look like ghosts?" Perched on a stool at the kitchen island, the downy quality of Tanner's chestnut hair is an eerie match to that of the Good Guy doll on his adult-size pajama shirt. It took me forever to convince the kid that *Child's Play* isn't a children's movie, but still he insisted on the T-shirt. Like mother like son, I guess, though Tanner is the spitting image of his father, right down to the way his fingers patter a mini-drumbeat against the countertop while he waits for an answer.

Another *bing*. My finger hovers over the little red dot in the upper-right corner of my messaging app, resisting the urge to tap.

"Mommm!" Tanner's voice climbs to a whine. *"Ghosts."*

"Sure, kid." The group text can wait. It's mid-September, after all. 'Tis the season for spooky breakfasts. "Pancake ghosts, heard," I tell him, playing at chef. "Coming right up."

The good thing about a pancake ghost is that so long as one end is curved and the other mostly flattish, all it takes is a little imagination and a couple of well-placed berries to pull it off. Easy-peasy, even for a distracted mom with twitchy text fingers. I spatula the burnt pancake onto a plate, pour a fresh spoonful of batter onto the griddle, and shape the sludge into a vaguely ghostly form as the batter starts to golden.

A text from Darla blinks across the top of the phone screen while Tanner chatters with Lugosi and a one-armed kaiju.

Did you hear about Kellen?

An emoji slides through next and I squint at the face on the screen. I'm not so well-versed in the emoji lexicon that I know *exactly* what the screaming yellow face with wide white eyes and a long, open mouth, hands to cheeks, is supposed to mean, but I gather it's not good.

I knew all those stupid messages on the stupid group text had nothing to do with the stupid Boogie Bash.

Rob arrives in the kitchen with the carton of fresh eggs I forgot on my last trip to Trader Joe's. As much as I enjoy my catch-ups with

Cicada, I need to find a grocery store that doesn't share a parking lot with a crime scene. Last time, I left without the half-and-half.

"Uh-oh, what's wrong with Kitty?" Rob asks, catching Darla's screamy emoji but not her contact name.

I set the spatula down and lift the screen so Rob can see. "She was chugging chardonnay out of a thermos at the social, but said she was going for a run after," I tell him, about Kellen, who hadn't wanted to change her outfit but at least wore the correct colors to burn off "ice cream" calories. "Surely she didn't drink and drive and cause an accident?"

Rob pulls a face, but really, is it *that* terrible to hope it's something as ordinary as a traffic violation, all things considered?

Another ping. "I can't take it anymore," I tell him. "I'm going in."

There are too many messages to read them all, so I scroll backward until I hit Darla's instructions for the Ice Cream Social dress code, then skim up, hit the key words. With each line, my pulse crawls higher in my chest—

Found screaming in the park. Blood everywhere.

Her entire eye, gouged out with a spoon!

Optic nerve completely stretched.

Ruined like a broken egg.

My pulse is in my throat. The ghost on the griddle begins to curl, but my eyes are locked on the tapestry of violence stitching itself across my phone screen.

"Jill?"

Whoever attacked Kellen, they mowed her down and enucleated one of her eyes, according to the text chain. To *enucleate* means the removal of an organ or tumor in such a way that it comes out clean and whole, like a nut from its shell. It's like gouging, but worse. A gouged eye is knocked loose in its socket. Enucleated, and it's out completely.

In my ears, my pulse sounds like my name.

The pancake on the griddle begins to smoke, and Rob bumps me aside to take over. Cast iron clangs as he slides the charred ghost into the trash, but his swear is creative enough that Tanner probably doesn't catch it.

My darling husband shoots me a concerned glance as he pours fresh batter onto the griddle, the familiar hiss momentarily drowning out Tanner's excited chatter.

"Everything okay?" Rob asks, his voice low and tinged with worry.

My throat is too tight to answer, so I shake my head and figure out how to break the news without ruining my son's breakfast. Just because Saturday Pancakes are over for me doesn't mean the kid has to lose out, too. My voice comes out barely audible over the griddle's sizzle. "She's been attacked."

Rob's eyebrows furrow as he flips the pancake with a practiced flick of his wrist. His baby blues slide to Tanner and back to me. They blink for more, ready, but my thumb is still scrolling through the group text.

Airlifted to Newark.

Cracked fibula and torn ligament in ankle from where she was pinned.

Eye socket cauterized.

Permanently blind.

Rob exorcises a ghost onto Tanner's plate, and I wait until the kid is two glugs of syrup deep before I give my husband the G-rated version. "She was found unconscious in the park . . . mangled ankle . . . minus an eye."

The last thing she saw was her attacker, Rosa's bubble says onscreen. It was a WOMAN!

Same woman? Sasha asks.

Dots flash while Rosa types. Same woman.

Pert nose, blond hair to the jawline, beauty mark.

That's two women on the Brunswick PTA down. The corkboard where I plan my horror novels is no longer a plot map. It's officially an evidence map.

Pancake batter drips from the spoon in my husband's hand as he summons another ghost on the griddle. Dark droplets stain the fabric of his socks from the batter drippage, and blood chills to ice water in my veins. My gaze rolls along the smooth length of the rounded tool in Rob's hand. The thin metal bowl at one end. The long torque of the handle.

This one was Patti's favorite, Darla had told me, back at the Ice Cream Social, about the vintage gelato scoop with the perfect grip and smooth end.

I blink, and suddenly the batter dripping off Rob's spatula looks a lot like what I imagine melty eyeball sludge might.

"Rob." My goal is for a whisper, but my voice comes out phone-sex-operator husky, like Jane Fonda's in *Barbarella*, that doll in space. "I think I know who the Dream Bean Killer is."

My darling husband raises an eyebrow that doesn't offset the skepticism etched across his face. "Jill, we've been over this." He shuts my office door behind him because there's not enough maple syrup in the world to sweeten up this conversation enough for eight-year-old ears. "The police are handling—"

"No, listen." I shove my chair aside so hard that it rolls back and bangs against the wall. "It's Patti. The woman who used to live in our house." My hands grip the corkboard. "She's the Dream Bean Killer."

Rob's expression shifts from skepticism to concern. "Jill, we've never met her, never even spoken with her directly. Patti moved out before we bought the place. Why would you think she has anything to do with this?"

Heart-print micro-fleece swishes around my calves as I whirl the board around over my pounding heart. There's Barb's photo, pinned below the Dream Bean pastry sack. Maribel's, beneath the Dollface business card. I relocate last year's PTA group photo and tack it beneath the Ice Cream Social flyer, then ring Kellen's face in red

Sharpie. It's the awkward angle, not my manic scribble, that makes for such a sloppy circle.

"Look, it all fits." It's hard to gesture wildly without dropping the board, but I manage. "Patti was the previous owner of this house, right? And she was deeply involved with the PTA before she left."

VP, just like I am now, since Maribel.

Rob's brought the spoon into the office with him, and batter still drips from its end, leaving a trail of pale dots on the hardwood floor. Both my husband and the ghosts are following me, but neither seem thrilled about where we're headed. "Yeah, but—"

"Darla is always talking about Patti, how they were best friends, how they used to carpool everywhere." My words tumble out in a frenzied rush over the corkboard clamped against my chest. "But at the Ice Cream Social, Rosa told me that Patti *hated* Darla."

Rob's eyebrows are confused.

That's fair. I'm not going in order. "The rest of those women are routinely terrible to Darla, right?" I try again, starting from the top. "That's why I call them the Brunswick PTA Mean Girls?" My husband nods, and I add the motive. "If Patti and Darla were besties, what if they were the same to her, and she's angry with them, and maybe jealous of me, and is taking her revenge?"

Rob's eyes go wide over the small puddle of pancake batter that has begun to form at his feet. "Jill, that's a stretch," he says carefully. "Even if Patti hated Darla, which we don't know that she did, why would she attack the *other* women?"

"Because it's formula. The villain is always someone that seems just too far out of reach to be obvious, someone the group at large never suspects," I remind him. "That's why you have to pay attention to the details."

He groans. "This is harder to follow than *Inception*."

"No, look." The timbre of my voice's frequency escalates as I seat the corkboard in my desk chair. "At the Ice Cream Social, Darla went out of her way to make sure I felt included, just like always." Upstairs, my neighbor's sparkly red hairband is still smiling on the master-bathroom soapstone. "She even showed me an old ice cream scoop that she said was *Patti's* favorite."

Rob's eyes follow me as I move, his expression a mix of concern and growing unease. "Okay, but how does that connect to the attacks? It's a random comment on a random object that, in context, is perfectly normal."

"Because Kellen's eye was enucleated—*scooped* right out of her face. I mean, think about it." I stab at the corkboard. My fingers trace the connections between the photos, the flyer, the scraps I've collected. "Darla's been grooming me to be the new Patti, right? But what if the real Patti isn't ready to let go? What if she *let* the other women think she hated Darla so no one would suspect her when she came back to take revenge?"

And what if she's working her way down the line to me, the woman who has literally taken over her old life?

I use the red marker to start circling items, stitching lines between them. "Barb. Remember how she insulted Darla at the Dream Bean that very first day? That night, her throat was slashed behind the Dream Bean, right where she had this piece of cake tattooed on her throat." The cops weren't able to get any decent camera footage, I remind him, but whoever killed Barb had a hard time cutting her open, like they were too weak or inexperienced to slit her throat on the first try.

Rob's face pales. "Jill, that's—"

"And Maribel." My voice rises, manic with insight. "At the Dream Bean, she refused to attend Darla's Doll's Night and mocked her for joining an MLM. She said she'd be at home resting, and someone snuck into her house and stabbed her in the head with a pair of scissors *that night.*" When Rob asks how Patti snuck in Maribel's house, I remind him about the PTA group info in the pocket folder. At Doll's Night, Kellen had commented that Maribel kept a key under her back porch mat. "She probably knew that, too." A gal like Maribel, surely this wasn't the first time she requested a hand delivery. "Patti was the PTA VP before Maribel."

And Kellen?

Kellen showed up to the Ice Cream Social with a thermos full of wine.

My voice drops to a whisper as I tap the Sharpie against the last photo. "Between drinking at the social and mocking Darla's efforts . . ." I trail off, unable to finish the sentence. The image of Kellen's enucleated eye is too horrific to voice aloud, even to me. Not only are my victims completely imaginary, they only bleed on paper.

Rob's face is a mask of concern. "Jill, honey, I think you need to take a step back from all this."

But I can't stop now. My mind is racing, connecting dots that have been there all along. "Don't you see, Rob? It all fits!" Thumbtacks scratch my palm when I lift the board, slap at each piece of evidence. "The motive, the pattern, the opportunity—they're all connected to the PTA and Darla's attempts to integrate me into the group."

Rob's skepticism is evident as he steps closer to examine the board. "Jill, honey, I understand you're worried, but this is a big leap. Like, *Murder, She Wrote* big."

That's exactly what I'm trying to make him understand. I think of all those women, perfectly sane and rational, institutionalized for speaking their truth. Is this what it feels like, those last few moments before someone shows up with a white johnny gown, tells me I'm being hysterical?

Crazy, just like Mom.

"Rob, look here." My finger stabs the last year's PTA group photo, to Patti. "Blond hair to the jawline, pert nose, beauty mark. Sounds familiar?"

Rob squints at the grainy inkjet photo, then looks back at me, his brow unconvinced. "If that description matched, wouldn't one of the women who actually knew her have said so?"

"If she was anything like Darla," I tell him, about how these things work, "it would never cross anyone's mind to think of the woman that didn't fit in who used to live here—she's as good as a ghost."

Trust me, the weird orphan with the mom dead by suicide and the needy little sister, bounced from house to house until I turned eighteen. All these years later and I'm still trying to find a place that'll remember me when I'm gone.

Rob's expression goes flat, the way it does before he toes the line about my mother.

"You have to admit that something strange is going on around here," I say. "*Two* women on the PTA board have been attacked." Not even just attacked, but personally hunted down and mutilated. "How can you think this isn't a big deal?"

"I never said it wasn't a big deal, but you're thinking like Jessica Fletcher, not a detective: building bias into a math problem." My husband scratches at his head with his scooper hand, so that he doesn't actually have to say how ridiculous he thinks I'm being. "Two women in a small group seems like a significant percentage, but push out. Two women, same race, same approximate age, both mothers of school-age children in a small township on the edge of one of the biggest cities in the world?"

"But they both saw the same person attack. And Barb—"

"Look, I'm not saying these things aren't connected, but I'm saying *you're* not connected, babe. You think whoever is targeting these women has some kind of personal vendetta, right, because they're connected—"

"Rob, I was *at* the Dream Bean with those women. I was *at* Doll's Night with those women. I am *on the PTA with those women.*" By the time I finish, my chest is so tight I can barely squeeze the words out. "I live in the woman's house. *I* am connected."

"So disconnect!" The spoon leaps into the air, propelled by the sheer brilliance of my husband's sudden idea. "Quit the PTA. Tanner can ride the bus. Stay home, work on your new book, and wait for this whole thing to be over. The cops'll catch this guy."

"Woman." *Patti*. "Maribel and Kellen both saw a woman," I tell him, again. "What if I'm next?" I keep sensing movement outside at night, feeling like I'm being watched through the windows. "*Someone* moved the coffeepot, and I'm certain it wasn't me."

Rob flinches. The corkboard speaks for itself, but I should not have mentioned the Keurig. Inanimate objects don't just grow legs and walk around.

"Jill." He flinches again. "All this on the corkboard, about being watched, you're—"

"Paranoid? Off my rocker? Turning into my mother?"

"That is not what I said."

"But it's what you're thinking."

Tension snaps between my darling husband and me, ripping like Kellen's optic nerve from the back of her skull. Rob pivots on his heel in the rebound. He wands the spoon in the corkboard's general direction, and a bit of batter splats against my cheek before he shucks the tool, sending it clattering over the hardwood.

Rob leans over the desk. "Damn it, Jill." The edges of his voice have rounded into a low growl that won't carry over to Tanner's ears in the next room. "You're not the only one who is worried."

He stares at the drop. He waits for me to reach up, wipe it away, but I don't.

The thing is, we're worried about two different things. Me about me losing my life, him about me losing my mind.

But I am not my mother.

I sink into my chair and stare, unblinking, while gravity forces the bit of batter down my cheek and my husband backs out of my office. Rob opens the basement door and disappears downstairs.

The batter makes its way to my chin by the time he sets in on the drums, smashing the hi-hat, stomping the kick drum. Drumsticks crack against the toms and sweep the cymbals, and even with the soundproofing, the violent crashes of wood on plastic and metal are loud enough to vibrate the entire house, send a shiver all the way up my spine.

It's only a few seconds of sound, but it's enough for me to recognize the drumbeat. I haven't heard this song since it played on the boom box my sister took outside to the pool, that summer day our mother cut her stitches open on her bedroom carpet. Finally, I think I understand what the singer means about karma and police.

I'd love to be wrong. But the thing is, I don't think that I am.

I think Patti is the Dream Bean Killer, the blonde with the pert nose and beauty mark that stabbed Maribel and enucleated Kellen.

And I think I might be next.

CHAPTER SEVENTEEN

While neither Maribel's nor Kellen's attack happened on the school grounds, and neither the school officials nor law enforcement see any threat to the students, Principal Hart has agreed to meet with Darla and me to lay out a plan for increased security at Boogie Bash. Detective Steve continues to insist that the investigation has no reason to believe the PTA is being targeted specifically, but is happy to load up a few off-duty cops with some overtime anyway, for the sake of school safety.

And his wife's, I presume.

Number Thirty-Four's beige town car rumbles in my driveway when I lock my front door and make my way across the lawn.

"Morning, neighbor," Darla calls out through the four-door's open driver's-side window. "Hop in!"

I wrap my cardigan tighter around me. We've agreed to a buddy system until the Dream Bean Killer is apprehended, but nobody said anything about switching vehicles. Should Rob have taken my Honda to his office? Are our vehicles, with their out-of-state Texas plates, too easy for a murderess to spot in suburban New Jersey?

"Is something wrong with your minivan?"

Darla waves the question away. "Just thought I'd give you the royal treatment. It's not every day a couple of girlfriends get to spend the day in a Benz, is it?"

All I know is the car is shiny and beige and very, very clean. Crazy clean. And I'd thought Darla's french fry–less minivan set the standard for cleanliness. The town car has never even seen a speck of dust, let alone dirt.

"I told you he's a neat freak," Darla says to the face I pull as I slide into the passenger seat.

We back out of the driveway and head for the school. When Darla hits the brakes at a stop sign, something bumps against my heel. The thick medical textbook must have been tucked under the seat.

"Dave's quite the bookworm." Darla's nails tap a rhythm against the steering wheel and she suggests I nudge the text back under. "He's constantly studying, even after all these years. As a surgeon, it's good to keep abreast of the latest research."

I feel my eyebrows jump. A doctor, I knew, but Darla never told me her husband is a surgeon. Dave definitely has good-ol'-boy doctor energy all over him, but I'd have pegged him more for the general-practice type, not the needles and scalpel sort. "That's impressive. Good for him."

"He's absolutely brilliant." Darla beams with pride. "Always has been, ever since high school—we were sweethearts."

"Aw." High school sweethearts are equal parts gross and cute.

"What about you and Rob?"

"We met in college. Not really the romance of the century, but definitely the love of my life."

Darla titters behind the steering wheel. "Happy is happy. What about your sister, is she married, too?"

The only thing Kitty is married to is her social media account. "She's not really the type." Too young when our dad split, our mom died, to remember things like Saturday Pancakes, my little sister always insists that I'm the only family she needs.

The commute to Brunswick Elementary is short, and my mind

races even faster than the town car. Finding out Dave is a surgeon adds another layer of texture to this story. I'd been so focused on the women of the PTA, I'd barely given a thought to their spouses. To dig deeper, I need to know all the characters. Right now, though, that starts with the woman at the top of my suspect list: Patti.

The elementary school comes into view, its redbrick exterior already festooned with colorful banners announcing the upcoming Boogie Bash. Darla parks the Benz farther away than is necessary just to put as much distance as she can between her husband's immaculate town car and the shedding fall trees.

It's now or never. "Hey, before we go in, I wanted to ask you about something."

Darla turns toward me with an encouraging smile that promises I can ask her anything. "Of course, dear." She pats my hand on the center console. "What's on your mind?"

This is delicate. How exactly does one ask their new friend if their former bestie might, in fact, be a crazed lunatic? "I've heard a little bit about Patti, the woman who used to live in my house before—you two were close, weren't you?"

A shadow flickers across Darla's face, or maybe it's just a falling leaf. "We were. Patti was something special: brilliant, driven, always full of ideas for the PTA. We became the best of friends the moment she moved in—just like us."

Us, she says, as in Darla and me.

"So why'd she move?" I'm careful to keep my tone casual as I redirect back to Patti. "I mean, Brunswick is such a wonderful township." Aside from the recent murder and string of violent attacks, anyway.

I think Darla's fingers tighten on the steering wheel. "Things changed," she says after a long pause. "Patti didn't get along with some of the women on the PTA, and things got intense toward the end." She crooks on a smile. "But that's all in the past now."

So far, this unfortunately tracks with my premise: Patti hasn't quietly let go of her past.

"It's kinda funny." The lightness in my voice definitely sounds fake now, but I throw on a smile and hope for the best. "But sometimes I feel like I'm being watched in that house—and I know how that sounds, trust me."

"Watched?" Darla's eyes widen, but not like my husband's. "How do you mean?"

My shrug aims for nonchalant girl talk, lands closer to awkward lying teenager. "Oh, you know, just little things. Like the other day, I could have sworn I left the coffeepot in one spot, but when I came back, it had moved. It's silly, I know," I say, before she can. "Sometimes, late at night, I hear creaks that don't make sense, feel like there's eyes looking in the windows." I tell Darla it's probably just my imagination. "Between working on a new book and what's been going on, my brain is probably just having a hard time parsing things out."

"Oh, you writers and your imaginations." Darla clucks as she unbuckles her seat belt. "I sure wish I had one like yours, but I'm sure it's nothing for you to worry about, dear. Houses settle, and as for the coffeepot, well, we all have those moments when we forget where we put things. All the rest, use it for your new book!"

She says this like it's the most normal thing in the world—but even Poe said words don't work without the "exquisite horror" of their reality, so, point for Darla.

"You're probably right. It's just every time I hear someone mention Patti, there's always these glances, like there's more to the story." Not to mention the blond woman with jaw-length hair and an angry, pinched expression in last year's PTA group photo. "Do you . . . Do you think she could somehow be involved in all this?"

Darla's smile tightens. "People love a good mystery, don't they? But really, Patti just needed a fresh start," she says tightly. "Nothing more dramatic than that."

"Like Maribel?" We'd talked about fresh starts the day Darla gave me a makeover in Patti's old bedroom. Now, when she goes quiet, I wonder if she's remembering that conversation, too.

Unspoken words hang heavy in the air between us, and Darla's face pales in the driver's seat. Her fingers grip the steering wheel so hard her knuckles turn white. Clearly, I have taken the wrong tack, going in this way to needle her about Patti.

Time to course correct, before Darla chews off her lipstick.

"Maybe I should change the locks, just as a precaution?" That's a perfectly reasonable thing for any new homeowner: scrub down the cabinets, shampoo the carpets, change the locks. Probably, it's the *first* thing I should have done when we moved into our new creaky-not-creepy home. For all I know, there could be a spare key to *my* house hidden under a mat somewhere.

But when I look toward the driver's seat, Darla is studying her reflection in the pull-down sun-visor mirror. "Oh, would you look at that? My lipstick's smudged. How embarrassing."

She fumbles with her purse, hands shaking as she retrieves a tube of lipstick, and Darla's fingers tremble as she touches up her makeup.

Good work, Jilly Bean, Kitty would say. *You've terrorized your sweet new neighbor.*

Okay, maybe the horror author in me shouldn't have voiced my Patti suspicions so bluntly to Darla. They were close, after all. With everything going on, the attacks on the other PTA women, I'm scared, but I am the new girl here. I just moved into this town, this life, but Brunswick is Darla's world. Here she'd been trying to make pleasant conversation about our significant others and *not* talk about the elephant in the room, and I'm the jerk who decided to interrogate her on the woman who used to live in my house.

Darla's suburban-PTA-mom facade cracks, revealing a woman with her own burdens. Maybe Darla and Patti *weren't* friends, just like Rosa said. Maybe Darla had only been pretending they were—to protect her own feelings, make herself more presentable to her second chance.

I get it.

My sweet new neighbor is many things, but she's not oblivious. Surely Darla sees how the Mean Girls treat her. Just because she's chosen to kill them with kindness doesn't mean their behavior doesn't still hurt.

"I'm sorry if I upset you, Darla." And I am. "I didn't mean to pick at old wounds. I know you miss Patti."

Darla's shoulders sag, but she twists the waxy pink stick home and snaps the lipstick tube shut. "Oh, it's all right, Jill, dear. It just . . . it isn't always easy, you know? Everyone expects so much. I do my best, but it never seems like it's good enough for some people."

"That's why they pay you the big bucks, right, Madam PTA President?" I'm trying for humor, but judging by Darla's distant gaze, I'm failing miserably.

"You have no idea." She sighs. "Sometimes I feel like I'm walking on eggshells, trying not to crack under the weight of everyone's expectations. The others—Maribel, Kellen, Sasha, even Beth and Rosa—they can be so . . . ugly sometimes."

And God don't like ugly, as my mother used to say.

But from her crinkly outdated perm to her powdered-doughnut cheeks, her Keds, Darla is as sweet as they come. It's not her fault the Mean Girl mommies are too blind to see that. As blind as Kellen.

"You're a really good friend, Darla. I'm lucky to have you—and so was Patti."

"Thank you, dear." The other woman's hand is cool when it takes mine. "You know, last year, Patti made a snide comment about my cupcakes for the Mother's Day bake sale. She said they looked 'store-bought,' can you believe it?"

"Not from a woman who owns her own heat gun." Anyone who spends that much time with shrink-wrap is not the type to cheat on homemade baked goods.

"I was up until two AM frosting those darn things by hand." Darla squeezes my hand. "I guess what I'm trying to say is that I'm lucky to have you, too."

Crisp autumn air nips at our cheeks as Darla and I make our way across the grounds to the elementary entrance. It's a different place during the school day, not the zippy movement of pickup and drop-off, but warm and bustling with activity as children stream through the hallways in orderly duckling lines.

Security lets us pass through the locked front entrance. Darla wiggles her fingers at the guard I'd met that day outside Hart's office, the one with the gun, but instead of the gruff greeting I'd expect, he waves back. Gotta hand it to my new neighbor. She might not fit in with the mean-mommy crowd, but Darla's smile could charm the venom out of a rattlesnake.

This place is a matrix. Not that I've been in the main part of the building much, but if I ever need to find my way to the principal's office without directions, maybe a guide, I'm screwed.

Darla leads the way and Hart waves us to the circular table wedged in the corner. The room looks more or less the same as it had the last time, emptier without the rest of the women around the table and Steve's hands clamped to his wife's shoulders, but at least this time Hart joins us at the table instead of perching on the edge of his desk to rub off what remains of his hair.

Darla might worry about not living up to the heavy expectations of being PTA president, but she outlines the PTA's security plan for Boogie Bash like a pro, without so much as a hint to what we're protecting against.

"We'll only use the cafeteria entrance," she says, "and we'll have a check-in station, with wristbands for all attendees to record everyone who enters the school."

My gaze wanders to the playground while Darla drones on about extra security and crowd control. Even at midday, the autumn sun casts long shadows across the equipment. The cafeteria itself will be divided into zones for Boogie Bash, Darla says, each monitored by a parent volunteer. A gentle breeze sends leaves skittering across the playground when Hart presses her about the apple-bobbing barrels, but Darla promises to oversee them herself.

"All the danger will be locked out, and everyone will be safe inside the school for Boogie Bash," Darla says. "Isn't that right, Jill?"

It takes me a minute to recognize my name, but my head nods to catch up. Sure, we'll all be safe, unless whoever the Dream Bean Killer is ends up locked inside the school with us.

CHAPTER EIGHTEEN

October arrives in a burst of color. Outside, cool wind blows through leaves burned brilliant shades of gold and carnelian, scarlet and brown, while what's left of the Brunswick PTA is trapped once more inside the sterile gray confines of the elementary school cafeteria. Halloween is still weeks away, but Boogie Bash is scheduled before the holiday, and according to the checklist pinned to the top of our group text, there's a lot of work still to do to ensure everything is ready for the school's biggest fall event.

With Maribel still at home recovering and Kellen out of commission, we're two ladies down already—and Darla has decreed that today is unpacking day.

"Boogie Bash is my *favorite* event of the school year," she tells me over the top of the unreasonably heavy plastic storage tub cradled between us, while I try my best to not let my knees buckle. "All the pumpkins and decorations and spooky skeletons. I just love it all, don't you?"

We're sharing the weight of this thing the same way we'd shared the heft of her shrink-wrapped welcome gift basket that day on my front porch, but whatever is loading down this tub, it's not basic household necessities and cosmetics samples. Bags of cement and bricks, maybe?

My grunt is supposed to signal agreement, but comes out more like agony, which is fair.

"It's a lot of work, but so worth it in the end," Darla says. "When everything comes together, and we get to finally sit back and enjoy the fruits of our labor."

She's telling me. Here it is only a couple of weeks before my favorite day of the year, and I haven't enjoyed so much as a single pumpkin-spice latte.

Not that a trip to the Dream Bean Café has been high on my to-do list these past few weeks, what with all the murder and mutilations, but I did just finish unpacking my entire household after hauling it halfway across the country. Another bout of manual labor so soon seems almost cruel, but at least the physical activity keeps my mind occupied. It's hard to fixate on rampaging ex-homeowners and stress about the book you're still not writing when you're knee-deep in plastic orange-and-black storage tubs.

"I just hope we've got enough Boogie to make this year's Bash perfect," Darla says, finally starting to wheeze. She pauses mid-step, hoists her knee, and shunts the tub into a tighter grasp. Her powdery makeup and homespun garments make her look soft, but I've learned not to underestimate my sweet new neighbor.

"We've just lugged six million pounds of party supplies from the PTA closet to the cafeteria." I do my best to jerk my head toward the Sterilite totes jigsawed together on the rubber-tile floor without knocking us both off-balance. "That's a *lot* of freaking boogie."

"Yes." Darla grins. "But is it *enough* boogie?"

"Over here, ladies!" Rosa's four-inch heels tap us toward the other side of the cafeteria. Sasha is busy tending to Kellen, whose bad leg is casted and propped up on a metal folding chair, and Beth has employed not one but two clipboards to catalog and organize the storage tubs on opposite sides of the room, which leaves the role of supervising the unpacking to Rosa.

One of the Event chair's manicured nails points us toward the plastic tubs clumped at one end of the cafeteria. We dump the deadweight and Beth checks her clipboard, then shoves the tub among its fellows while Darla and I shake the strain out of our arms.

I'd have joined the PTA sooner if I'd known I'd get such a good workout. At this rate, I'll have biceps by the holidays.

But Kellen glares at my two working legs from her chair, and, well, maybe not.

Rosa lifts her hair off the back of her neck with one hand and fans herself with the other, like she's just been the one hauling a dozen tubs of concrete across the cafeteria.

"Why in the world do we hold on to so much random stuff?" She drops her hair to fan with both hands. "That stack of tubs is taller than I am—and I'm wearing heels."

Four-inchers, and a formfitting, plum-red, wool-cashmere-blend sweater minidress. Rosa Hudson is not only one of the few women in the world who can pull off chunky cable-knit, but is possibly the only one to bend it to her will. Still, I doubt the outfit is what Darla meant when she'd suggested we all wear something "seasonally appropriate" to help get us into the Boogie Bash spirit. My THIS GIRL LOVES HORROR BOOKS hoodie may be childish with its swirling pink font and double thumbs-up—not to mention its golden glitter, because black clothing and a shedding retriever go so well together—but at least this time I paid attention to the instructions in the group text.

Darla's Keds chirp across the shiny rubber floor like cute little albino bats, but somewhere the old gods of Halloween are screaming at her patchwork candy-corn sweater vest.

"All right, ladies," she says, and I can *literally* feel Sasha's pucker, as she glowers beside Kellen's chair when Darla's skeleton earrings jangle from her lobes. "Let's get to work!"

Beth peels the lid off the nearest storage tub, exposing the world's largest Halloween-themed junk drawer of tableware (paper plates, plastic utensils, napkins), balloons (latex), and party favors (miniature cauldrons, spooky straws, temporary tattoos). A smattering of die-cut orange, black, and gold jack-o'-lantern confetti have collaged themselves to something that looks like it used to be a paper-towel tube before being DIY-ed into a taper candle. Wads of crepe paper are stuffed into every available space. Beth's fingers come away coated in sparkly purple when she pops the lid off a second bucket, and I stuff my hands in my hoodie's pouch.

Dog hair is one thing, but there is no greater evil than *actual* glitter.

"There's all sorts of things in the tubs." Darla gestures at the row of wooden shapes stacked against the wall on the other side of the storage containers. "Our biggest task is to get those scene flats in order so we can transform this plain ol' school cafeteria into a proper haunted house."

Enough painted plywood to stage a production of *The Phantom of the Opera* is lined along the far side of the room, but the wood flats are so warped and worn they might actually have been recovered from the charred remains of the Palais Garnier opera house.

Ten bucks says at least a handful of kids are going to leave with splinters if they get too close to those things. "Are you sure you want to use them?" I ask Darla, or Rosa, or whoever owns this decision, which is hopefully not under the purview of Cultural Arts.

"Oh, they just need a little pampering." Dara talks about the wooden flats like they're faces at a Doll's Night makeover. "A little TLC and they'll be good as new." Her eyes dart between the chipped wooden scenes and an assemblage of handheld construction tools scattered in heaps atop the nearest tabletop.

Sasha pats Kellen's good knee, hands over a water bottle, then makes her way to the tool table with both hands pinned to her hips. She raps one set of knuckles on what might be a battery-powered nail gun, might be a cordless hand sander, might be neither.

"I borrowed every tool I could from the church library," she says, and Rosa's nose curls at the appropriation of the word *library.* "We only have them for today." Sasha pulls her hand back and pats the pocket of a fleece zip-up the same watery yellow as her loose curls. "But I have a key, so I can drop them off as late as I need to."

"Don't forget about your buddy," Rosa tells Sasha, because until the woman with the beauty mark is caught, we're still traveling in pairs. Kellen is Rosa's buddy, since Rosa's SUV is high enough to step into with enough trunk space to store crutches. With Maribel still home recovering, that leaves Beth to buddy up with Sasha.

Sasha's pucker fits about as tight as Rosa's dress, but she thrusts her chin the way Tanner does when he ramps up for a fit. "I'm a grown woman, not a kindergartner. I don't need a buddy."

"It's for our safety, Sasha." Rosa's eyebrows shift in Kellen's direction, but she's trying to be sensitive. "Remember what happened to Kellen," she hisses under her breath.

Or Maribel, I want to add. *Or Barb.*

For the first time since I've met her, Kellen isn't shrink-wrapped in color-coordinated athleisure. The gauze wrapped around her casted leg is the same hot pink as her comfy sweats. Probably the wrinkled velour tracksuit had been stuffed in the back of her closet since the early aughts, but I'm guessing it's still more to her taste than the yellowing bandage taped over her missing eye.

Limp hair strings over Kellen's shoulders, and she's got a death grip on the water bottle Sasha thrust in her hands. Kellen hasn't spoken once in the entire two hours that we've been here, hasn't even made eye contact with anything other than the shiny confetti glinting on the rubber cafeteria floor. Rosa probably dragged the poor woman out of her house on the promise that a change of scenery would do her good. Rosa might be right, but a real buddy would have combed Kellen's hair first.

Tell me about the woman, I want to ask Kellen while Darla inspects the tool collection borrowed from Sasha's church. *Did she look familiar? Like someone who used to live here?*

I need to know.

Sasha clicks the conversation back into motion, reminding Rosa that not everyone else is married to a cop. "I have the Old Goat and the twins to worry about already," she says, as if she's the only woman in the Brunswick Elementary PTA with a family waiting for her at home. "Too much to do to babysit." She shrugs at Beth. "Nothing personal."

Beth squints a smile, then pops open another storage tub and exhumes yet more hodgepodged glitter from the tombs of Boogie Bashes past. A tangle of fake cobwebs spills over the tub's lip, followed by a parade of plastic spiders. The musty stench of old bake sales mingles with the funk of school cafeteria lunch.

My fingers twitch inside my hoodie pocket. Both Rob and Kitty have warned me to keep my suspicions about Patti to myself, but that doesn't mean I can't *ask* if the police have made any progress identifying the woman who attacked Maribel and Kellen, does it?

Like Rosa before, I keep my voice low enough that it doesn't wander all the way over to Kellen when I ask if she's heard any updates.

Rosa shakes her head. "They're going to release the description of the attacker to the public."

While what little Kellen remembered of her attacker matched what Maribel had seen of the woman with short blond hair, pert nose, and beauty mark, law enforcement's previous suspect profile had insisted that the attacker either could not or was not able to dispatch her victims. Barb's clumsy murder aside, while the attacks on both Maribel and Kellen had been vicious, it was pretty clear the Dream Bean Killer wanted to maim, not murder. Maybe rather than seeking revenge, Patti wanted to teach the other women a lesson?

Still, the only update worse than another attack is that there *could* be another one, and with no progress toward solving the case, all we can do is wait. If the description isn't enough to generate some leads, Steve will bring in a sketch artist next, per Rosa.

"Battle stations, everyone!" At the tool table, Darla tests the grip of a power tool that's something part nail gun, part hand sander, part torture device. "Let's divide and conquer. Rosa, you and Kellen help me with the flats. Jill, you, Beth, and Sasha tackle the rest of those tubs."

Technically, the painted plyboard pieces used to represent walls and backgrounds in onstage productions are called Hollywood flats, not scene flats, but I don't know the proper names for half the stuff Sasha pilfered from her church's tool library, so I keep my mouth shut, thankful I'm assigned to tubs and not arts and crafts.

"How is Maribel doing?" I ask my team as we corral the unopened storage tubs. It's been a month since she got a pair of scissors stabbed into her skull, but other than a few trite contributions to the group text: nothing.

Sasha puckers. "Her recovery is taking longer than they'd hoped." She peels the lid off a tub filled to overflowing with half-used spools of crepe paper. "She has headaches, problems concentrating, a sore incision—all things the doctor warned her about though, so at least it's normal. She'll be here for Boogie Bash. Hopefully."

The storage tub I open is full of faces. The plastic lid clatters against the rubber tile, screeches across the floor, before I realize it's slipped out of my grasp.

Staring up from between the folds of cheap nylon capes and costume accessories, dozens of shiny plastic faces glare at me with empty eye sockets. Curled eyebrows, rosebud lips, whiskers, snarls, these are the faces of monsters, princesses, animals, superheroes. Faces with no eyes, frozen lips, and holes where their nostrils should be.

"What's wrong, Jill?" Beth's voice sounds too far away.

I shove the tub toward her with the toe of my Converse. "It's full of masks."

Some of the costume masks are felt, a few are the rubber *Point Break* variety that pull down over the head. Most are molded plastic sheaths with elastic strings, reminiscent of the Ben Cooper masks of my childhood—the kind sold in thin cardboard boxes with window-screened fronts, plastic-smock costumes paired with plastic-skin faces.

Sasha looks into the tub and clicks her teeth. "These store-bought costumes are nothing but cheap crap. I can sew better ones myself." Nose curled in disgust, she tweezes a vampire's wrinkled nylon cape from the tub. "We should throw them out."

"That box is a treasure chest for children who forget to wear their costumes!" Darla brandishes a palm-size device, round with a flat handle, a little dust bag attached. The scene flat at her feet depicts a spooky graveyard scene, bats, and a full moon. "Or for those whose parents can't afford costumes, or when something breaks, or they want to try on different outfits for the photo booth. There are hundreds of new personas in that tub. With the right face on, our students can be anyone they want."

"Too bad they're all bald," Sasha mutters as Beth rifles through the tub, sorting through duplicates of various monsters and characters. She lifts out a cartoon rock-star face, trimmed in pink plastic hair and star-shaped earrings, and straps the mask around her head.

"We can't keep wigs," Beth explains through her rock-star mouth. "Because of lice."

Paint flecks from the edges of some of the melted string masks, but it's an impressive collection, the kind that takes years of haunting thrift shops and stalking eBay to build. "A few of these might be worth something," I say. "Some of the old Ben Cooper masks are collectibles."

Sasha puckers. "Who's Ben Cooper?"

Rosa wiggles a large wooden tombstone shape against a clearing in the wall space, then dusts her hands on her dress. "Some silly little costume company that went out of business because razor blades in candy made kids stop trick-or-treating in the 1980s," says the same librarian who said horror didn't make for *Times* bestsellers.

Ben and Nat Cooper founded Ben Cooper in 1937 as a vaudeville- and masquerade-costume company only to become one of the three largest Halloween-costume manufacturers in the United States from the 1950s through the mid-1980s, and the slowdown in Halloween costuming had nothing to do with razor blades—but I bite my tongue.

"You mean razor blades in *apples,*" Sasha counters, incorrectly.

"I thought it was Pixy Stix," Beth says, still holding her rock-star face. "Several children died after getting them trick-or-treating."

"Now, Beth," Darla coos before my head explodes. "No child has ever been killed by eating Halloween candy from a stranger."

Finally, someone else who's heard of Snopes. And I thought my sister was bad about passing social media rumors as empirical facts.

"The razor-blades incident was in the sixties," I can't help but chime in, now that Darla's paved the way, "and it was a hoax. Research in the eighties investigated all known Halloween candy-tampering claims between 1958 and 1983, something like one hundred cases." In the end, all were hoaxes, urban legends, and pranks, maybe someone trying to inspire a lawsuit or cause a media craze. "Medical records confirmed the few actual tragedies to be the result of heart defects, infections, and other explainable illnesses."

Rosa grunts as she wrestles another tombstone free. "But the Tylenol bottles—"

"—*were* tampered with," I finish for her. "Someone added in deadly doses of potassium cyanide." Seven people died in Chicago, including an infant and a twelve-year-old, prompting a massive recall right in time for Halloween. "But it wasn't targeted at children."

Just a coincidence as my darling husband, as Detective Steve Hudson, would say.

"Well, the Pixy Stix thing was real," Sasha insists. "That's what started the Candyman legends."

In the seventies, an eight-year-old boy died after eating a Pixy Stix his own dad laced with cyanide to cash out an insurance policy. "That kid's father got the death penalty," I feel it's important to note, "and Candyman is rooted in racism and gentrification."

Darla puts away her sander and joins us. "Now, one man did put needles in a Snickers bar in 2000. A child did bite in, but the poor dear didn't even require medical attention. Thank goodness."

The other women sympathize, and suddenly my little Grinch heart swells three sizes. Here I sit, clumped together on the school cafeteria floor, among this odd group of women I was sure would never accept someone like me, gossiping about morbid Halloween-candy hoaxes while we unpack spooky elementary-school carnival decorations.

And I thought I would never find my people in New Jersey.

"In any case, Ben Cooper dominated the Halloween-costume market until the Tylenol thing, but it wasn't candy that changed things." I pluck a plastic doll's bridal gown from the pile as I work the conversation back to Sasha's original question. The company's death blow had been less about hoaxes and more the result of the demand for higher-quality costumes at a price point too expensive for the company to survive. "Materials cost and greed for cheap consumables," I tell her, still sifting in the tub for the mask that goes with the flimsy costume wedding dress, "*that's* what wound up killing Ben Cooper."

The white veil crown is bent, sliced open on one side where someone must have taken a pair of scissors to it, but the bobbed yellow hair is perfect when I find the face that pairs with the costume. The bride has pink rosebud lips, blue-coated lids, and dimples. A classic beauty that never goes out of style.

The doll face fits cool against my skin when I slide the mask over my face—and then Kellen begins to scream.

She looks at me and she screams and screams.

CHAPTER NINETEEN

The doll cuts the sedan's engine at the edge of the parking lot.

She plucks the interior-light fuse from the panel beside the steering wheel, balls the plastic tooth in her fist, and pushes herself between the front seats. Cool evening breeze filters through the car's open windows, tickling the smooth edges of the doll's beautiful face as she lies supine across the back-seat cushion.

With its engine off and windows down, the sedan is as quiet and still as the church that looms outside its windows. With her toes the doll counts the wall of brown bricks on the other side of the window, *tap-tap-tapping* away seconds, minutes, an hour, until daylight dims and the streetlights standing sentinel around the hulking two-story building flicker on. The motion security bulb on its back door stays dark.

Soon, the doll thinks.

Dusk grows warm inside the sedan. The padded-leather armrest rubs static into the doll's blond hair. Strands of wiry gold crackle like lightning above her face as thin beads of sweat dribble down the back of her neck. Sweat drips between the layers of slouchy socks and disposable bootees on the doll's feet at the other end of the long bench, but her hands suck in oxygen like gills, her breath a warm current between the skins of her face.

The plastic tooth bites into her flesh as she curls her fist around the fuse. *Just a little bit longer.*

The doll rolls a swatch of sweat-suit cotton between the bare fingers of her free hand. Black thread sticks to her skin when she lets the black cotton slip away, a single stitch left in her palm.

The best remedy for a loose stitch is a quick snip. The doll knew this truth when she sliced open the barista's throat with her bridal-cake knife, when she pruned back the sleeping woman's old growth, when she helped the runner to see.

Sometimes, we must cut to stanch the unraveling.

The doll lifts her sweatshirt and runs the fingers of her empty hand along the curves of the scissors tucked into her waistband. Two long loops, like a bow in a beautiful doll's hair.

When her toes have tapped through another hour, headlights swing into the parking lot. The doll drops the fuse onto the floorboard, flattens herself against the soft back-seat leather, and listens to the soft crunch of rubber on cement. The high-pitched shrill of brakes. The thud of a car door opening and closing.

The doll tugs her sweatshirt over the looping handles and pulls its hood over the staticky strands crackling around her face.

A trundling sound accompanies footfalls, the sound of someone laboring under a heavy burden. The doll watches through the narrow slits of her beautiful face as a tide of curly dishwater waves rolls past the sedan's back seat.

The woman passes the open windows without looking.

The doll waits until the motion bulb flickers to life before she reaches behind her, curls her fingers under the lever on the passenger-side door, and pulls the handle. The doll watches upside down as the woman squats, plastic milk crates filled with tools crooked under each of her arms, sets one crate by the church's back door, then wrestles the remaining crate onto a bony hip. Her hand plunges into the pocket of her fleece jacket as she pushes back up, emerging with a small key that she thrusts into the door's lock. She twists the lock and wrenches the door wide, footing the grounded crate to wedge the door open while she slides inside.

Now, the doll thinks.

Pushing with socked feet, the doll delivers herself into the cool evening dark. She crouches by the passenger door and slips her fingers into a pair of woolen gloves, balling her fists to loosen the weave as she moves across the lot, toward the wedged-open door. Metal glints in the crate that still holds the door open, the eager shine of tools ready to slice, to drill, to hem. The doll's gloved fingers reach to stroke handle edges, but the woman's sneakers shriek against the linoleum as she makes her way back toward the open door, and the doll tucks herself into the shadows.

She watches through the sliver between door and frame as the woman stoops to retrieve the second crate, and when her sneakers' squeals reduce to a whimper on the other side of the door, the doll slips inside the receding space. Automatic locks slick into place when the door falls closed behind her.

The doll masks her footsteps inside the shrills of the woman's sneakers, stepping when she steps so they move in tandem down the hall. She studies the rolling waves that cascade over the woman's shoulders, between her shoulder blades.

The woman mutters as she unloads the crates with the quiet confidence of the unwatched. She hangs a nail gun on the pegboard but needs both hands to lift the sander. When she squats to grasp the tool, the doll pulls the scissors free of her waistband and inches closer. The doll opens the scissor blades wide, positioning a curl between the shiny silver blades.

She snips.

A single ripple tumbles to the linoleum as the woman twists toward the sudden sound, her lips puckered in surprise, eyes wide in shock. Her mouth hinges into a rebuke that turns into fear, into fury, when she sees the doll's face, the hair still caught in the scissors' blades.

Guttural syllables fall upon deaf ears as the doll advances, the woman's angry, foreign words lost in translation. She rears up as the doll shuffles forward, reaching for the scissors, and her sneaker catches on a rigid crate. She topples backward, tripping when the second emptied crate slides between her feet.

The woman twists as she falls. The doll is on top of the woman before her body hits the floor, forcing her onto her stomach. Her cheek to the cold, hard floor.

The woman's hands claw out, but the doll captures her wrists, jerking the arms backward while anchoring a foot in her slender neck. The doll drives her weight between the woman's shoulder blades as she lowers herself to one knee, stroking gloved fingers through the woman's long hair. It's a trick to catch a wave, but her scissors close again.

Another.

Another.

It's not enough, these small cuts. Tears course into the woman's snarling lips as she struggles under the doll's weight. She's a rabid thing, a ragged thing. The doll's gaze falls on the tool crate, on the battery-powered palm sander.

The woman thrashes, but the doll has the tool in her hands now. She racks the object against the woman's head, two hard knocks, and on the third, the woman quiets.

A mercy, the doll thinks. *To stun before shearing.*

The woman goes stiff the moment the sander touches her head. Her sneakers whimper against the linoleum as the doll digs her knee into the woman's back, seizes a fistful of wavy hair, pulls it back. The doll uses the scissors to slash incisions above the temples and around the ears. The woman shrieks with each small cut, each seam loosened.

Her screams still hang in the air when the doll powers the sander on.

Five layers of skin comprise the connective tissue of the human scalp, but it's the fourth, the least substantial, that anchors the scalp to the skull. The doll sands through one layer, then through two, using her weight to press the tool against the woman's skull, to sand through curls, through skin, through nerves. By the time she reaches the third layer, her sander hand is red, and the woman is limp. Tamed, at last.

The dolls yanks the tool away after she sands through the fourth layer, and the bundle in her glove squelches free from the woman's head.

She considers her work, the woman prone at the center of a spreading red circle on the polished linoleum floor, at the glistening orb that lies at the center of the mess. A pure spot buffed clean and ready to regrow.

The doll's socks paint wet splotches on the stark white floor as she makes her way down the church hallway and pushes open the heavy exit door. Copper hangs heavy in the air and the doll stops at the doorway, scenting the night air through her perfect plastic nose as she sloughs off layers of ruined gloves and bootees and socks and listens for the automatic locks behind her.

She pads barefoot across the parking lot and climbs into the quiet warmth of the sedan. She feels around for the fuse on the floorboard, but sets it in the cupholder, still detached, before starting the engine. When the car reaches the edge of the street, the doll takes off her mask, pats dry the moisture beaded along her skin, and heads toward home.

CHAPTER TWENTY

The Dream Bean Killer was wearing a mask.

That's why Kellen screamed when I pulled the costume face from the Boogie Bash storage tub. It's no wonder the police have found no leads on the woman with the pert nose, blond hair to the jawline, beauty mark. That woman doesn't exist. Whoever killed Barb, whoever attacked Maribel and Kellen, may have been a woman, but the face they'd seen wasn't hers.

All this talk about living in a slasher movie, and I'd forgotten one of the most obvious tropes. Of course, the villain would wear a mask.

A mask with an eerie resemblance to my dead mother's face. A Ben Cooper costume doll mask.

She's easy to find online.

Like all Ben Cooper costumes, the doll originally came in two pieces: a molded plastic string mask, and a plastic smock designed to suggest a wedding gown. Unlike the face in the Boogie Bash storage bin, the mask on my screen is intact, with a square of white mesh veil attached.

Rob sets a mug of steaming Sleepytime tea on the coaster beside my desktop monitor and I click out of the internet browser, scuttling back into my email inbox before my darling husband can see what's on my screen.

"If you're not coming to bed, then the least I can do is keep you hydrated," he says, and waits for me to take a sip. We've been married long enough for Rob to know I wasn't just checking email, but he'll play along to avoid another fight.

"Thanks." The tea is hot, but twin cold spots burn on my skin when Rob's eyes break away to the corkboard still strung with the recent attacks.

Parallel lines of Charlene's name rake through the mist of tea fog when I return the cup to its coaster and get back to my screen. My editor's subject lines increase in unread panic as they march up my inbox: **Just wondering when I can expect pages?** the line at the bottom says. **EARTH TO JILLIAN,** screams the most recent message from the top. It's been weeks since Charlene and I brainstormed about dolls in space, and I still have yet to send her a single page. My unfinished manuscript is still more a blank draft than an actual work in progress.

On the other side of the desk, Rob can't read my screen, but he can still see the new wrinkle twist home on my face. "Everything good with Charlene?"

"Yep." I click out of my inbox and into Microsoft Word, resisting the urge to finger the deepening trench on my forehead when my cursor blinks on the untitled title page. Rob's brows lower over narrowed eyes, and guilt sloshes in the pit of my stomach. It's not a lie if I promise to make it true, right? If I get Charlene an outline, she'll be happy—unlike my sister, whose unanswered calls and texts clog my phone like pine needles bunged in a pool drain.

Another day, another missed morning sister chat. My little sister may be closing in on her mid-thirties, but she's never outgrown the need for constant attention.

I get it. We only ever had each other, but between the move, my late book, and the recent slate of brutal attacks on the women in my peer group, I've been a little too distracted for chitchat.

My sister's ear must be burning all the way over on the West Coast because a new message from Kitty flashes on my phone. I flip the cell over and breathe in the quiet comfort of the basic-black protective cover. If I miss FaceTime, she'll activate emergency protocol and call Rob next. At the moment, that's a risk I'm willing to take.

My husband's jaw clenches, but he lets me off the hook. "Lugosi is in bed with Tanner, and I'm going up." He rounds the desk. "Drink your tea."

Rob leans over my chair so that his lips brush the top of my head, then his hand twists my chin so he can kiss my lips. The familiar scents of Resa-Cote and maple cling to his T-shirt, and wet rings my mouth when Rob's lips pull away.

All this time staring at my monitor and never once did I hear the drums from the basement. Soundproofing must be complete.

"I'll keep your side of the bed warm." This isn't an invitation. It's a reminder not to stay up too late, lose myself to the gaze of all those darkened little conservatory windowpanes, staring at me with empty black eyes.

I promise to come up soon, and with another kiss to the top of my head, Rob bids me good night. I hold my breath until his footsteps disappear up the stairs, and when the bedroom door closes, I lift the teacup, swivel my chair, and return to my corkboard.

Just because I was wrong about Patti doesn't mean that I can't still figure this murder mystery out.

Okay, here's where we are:

- The day I arrived in Brunswick, Darla greeted me with a shrink-wrapped welcome basket and invited me to brunch with the Brunswick PTA at the Dream Bean Café, where I met Maribel, Kellen, Beth, and Sasha.
- Maribel said she wouldn't attend Doll's Night because she had a "real" spa appointment, and Barb, the barista with the giant cake-wedge tattoo, body-shamed my sweet new neighbor over a silly croissant order.

I'd kept the sugar-stained pastry sack and Darla's Dollface business card. Both are tacked to the board, and the red pocket PTA folder, which contained all the board's contact info and details for the school year's upcoming events, is on top of my desk.

- Barb was murdered later that night behind the Dream Bean. There'd been no useful security footage, but it'd taken the attacker several attempts to saw through the woman's throat with a serrated blade—a bread knife, maybe.
- Maribel's attack came a few days later, on Doll's Night, when someone broke into her home and stabbed her with a pair of scissors. Unlike the Dream Bean's security cameras, Maribel glimpsed her attacker, but she hadn't realized she'd seen a mask, and her faulty description kicked off a wild-goose chase.
- The cops had already ruled out the rest of the PTA women when Detective Steve gathered us in the principal's office to tell us about Maribel because none of us matched the description she'd given the cops. And law enforcement had still been looking for the wrong suspect when Kellen was mowed down and her eyeball enucleated after the Ice Cream Social.

Which means that it *could* be one of us.

The honeyed sweetness of the tea turns to lukewarm grit against my teeth, and I chew the chalky taste away as I set the cup back on the coaster. The cursor blinks impatiently on the empty page on my monitor, the desktop version of Messenger still lit with Kitty's unread notification. I should answer my sister, my editor. I should make my cursor dance across the empty page, heat life back into my fingers as they tap across the keyboard. Instead, I pull up the search-engine browser.

For the first time since we moved in, I not only want to know more about the woman who used to live in my creaky-not-creepy home. I want to know more about *all* the women on the Brunswick PTA—and their families.

After printing the photo of the Ben Cooper doll mask, I open a fresh tab and type each woman's name into the search engine in turn. Other than their respective social media pages, local news mentions for various Brunswick Elementary–related activities, and a few hits of Rosa's name on book-related sites, it's a dead end.

So, I turn to the spouses. Kellen's wife, Rena, is an attorney at a fancy white-collar firm in the City, and squeaky-clean. Besides a mention in a church newsletter of Sasha's Old Goat, whose name is apparently Rick, there's nothing on him; and Beth's husband is as invisible online as he is in the Brunswick PTA landscape. The only stuff I can find about Maribel's ex is exactly the sort of stuff you'd expect from a divorced, middle-aged dad named Chad, but while the guy is definitely scuzzy, it's nothing criminal. Detective Hudson's page on the Brunswick Police Department site has a list of awards and accomplishments long enough to make any criminal think twice, so that rules him out.

That leaves Dr. Dave Lashett.

His hospital-page medical profile shows that Darla's husband is not just a surgeon. He's a neurosurgeon.

I'm an author, not a medical professional, so I google the specialty just to be sure I know what it is. My sleuthing abilities are already in question after the fail with Patti. The last thing I need is to get too attached to a theory about a man who turns out to be some sort of nerve doctor or toe surgeon or something. My husband and sister would definitely think I'd gone off my rocker then, just like my mother.

But Dr. Dave Lashett is not a nerve doctor or toe surgeon. He's a brain surgeon.

According to WebMD (always a reputable source), neurosurgeons diagnose and treat conditions that affect the nervous system, including the brain, spinal cord, and nerves. Unlike neurologists, who also treat the nervous system, neurosurgeons perform surgery on everything from the skull to the spine—including the eye.

Bitter honey rises in my throat, hoarfrost on my frozen insides. The man operates on the head, and every single one of the attacker's victims have suffered head injuries.

But the attacks don't track for a *surgeon,* do they?

The attacker knew how far to puncture Maribel's skull without harming her brain, and they knew how to enucleate an eyeball, but a man skilled in cranial procedures would have known how to slice a throat. Surgeons, like my editor, pride themselves on precision. If Dave Lashett were the Dream Bean Killer in the Ben Cooper doll mask, then surely he'd have used the right tool for the job instead of hacking away with a serrated blade—wouldn't he?

And the bone shards in Maribel's skull, Kellen's battered eye socket and ruined eyeball. These are not surgical moves.

I could see how the man might want to off a series of women who'd bullied his wife, but Dave Lashett doesn't strike me as the type of character who'd intentionally botch his work just for the sake of covering his tracks. The opposite, actually: Wouldn't he want to make sure he got it right?

I remember the medical textbook that had slipped from under the passenger seat in Dave's nondescript beige town car.

He's constantly studying, Darla had said, when the book bumped my heel.

A lifelong learner like Dr. Lashett would have carried out his attacks by the book, but even if it were experimental, he'd know enough to not make such obvious mistakes.

His wife wouldn't.

But Darla? No way. No way is my sweet, matronly new neighbor a crazed murderous attacker. Sure, she's a horror-movie afficionado, but so am I, and you don't see me running around cutting up people.

Darla had greeted me on my first day in the neighborhood with a gift basket and a brunch invitation, for Frankenstein's sake.

Sure, she'd also known things about me that I hadn't told my Realtor, like what breed of dog Lugosi is, but so does everyone else who's ever checked my social media. The LEGOs, the men's shaving kit, these were spot-on but easy guesses from another married woman with elementary-aged kids. The cosmetic samples . . . Even if she'd gone down a deep internet rabbit hole, maybe Darla could have learned about my mother's suicide, maybe even that Mom peddled beauty products door-to-door, but not how she'd made up her face the day she died.

She hadn't even known I have a sister—or had she?

I pull up Kitty's socials and check her followers. At the bottom of the list: Dollface. No posts, no followers.

Dollface, and a slasher villain in a Ben Cooper doll-faced mask. Holy hell, how did I not see that one a mile away?

The Dollface company website is still a landing page, the familiar delicate script promising a full site soon. The only familiar imagery is Darla's teal-and-pink Caboodles, prominently displayed under the site's main header. *Unleash your true inner beauty,* the site demands, and the lingering cold spots on my skin become frostbite.

When I'd arrived at Number Thirty-Four for Doll's Night, there'd been the distinct, lingering smell of silver polish—even Sasha had commented on the eggy telltale smell. There are dozens of serrated blades in your average suburban kitchen: steak knives, bread knives, cake knives. Had Darla been polishing away evidence from serving ware after she'd cut the slab of pastry inked on Barb's neck? I remember the rusty red on her pruning shears the morning after Maribel's attack, the vintage gelato scooper she'd shown off at the Ice Cream Social. If there are medical texts tucked under the passenger seat of her husband's conveniently fastidious car, then inevitably there are plenty scattered about Darla's household. Some likely even have detailed information on traumatic cranial injuries.

Another notification from Kitty pops across my screen over the fishy MLM site.

Still alive, sister? Kitty's first message says, followed by a link to her latest makeup tutorial. The thumbnail shows my sister dolled up in shades of green and purple, with a bright mass of green hair, a black-and-white-striped suit, and a moldy smile. A streak of silver shines behind her.

The way that poor couple died in *Beetlejuice* wasn't the sad part, Kitty always said. Drowning when their car went off that bridge was horrible, but even more horrible was that they were forced to spend eternity trapped in their former home, watching it be destroyed from the inside out.

Every good horror story starts with a creepy house, indeed.

When Rosa had said that Patti hated Darla back at the Ice Cream Social, I'd assumed either Patti had been a Mean Girl playing nice or a nice girl playing mean. Almost everything we know about the Dream Bean Killer's attacks has come from the detective's wife.

Maybe there's more.

My sister's frozen face preens on-screen while I pull the internet browser back up, click the back button to rewind to Steve's profile on the Brunswick Police Department's home page. I select the Domestic Violence Central Registry from the site's navigation menu, then type Patti's name into the search bar.

A result pops up. Not everything is public record in New Jersey, but Patricia Townsend's restraining order against Darla Lashett is.

The order is for harassment and stalking, and dated only weeks before we put in our offer. My Realtor wasn't eager to get rid of the buyer with skull-print tights. She'd just had a very motivated seller.

Not only was the blonde I'd mistaken in the Brunswick PTA group not a killer, but she was a victim. Patti didn't hate Darla because Patti was a Mean Girl. Patti hated Darla because Darla is crazy.

"Mom?"

Tanner's voice shunts my pulse into my throat, rocking my body so hard that the desk chair's wheels slip beneath my weight. Sock-footed in bootee pj's and with a kaiju clutched to his chest, the kid stands in the office doorway while I choke down my own pulse.

"What are you doing out of bed?"

"I had a nightmare." Tanner rubs a tiny fist against a sleep-puffed eye. "Can you check under my bed for monsters?"

"Of course." Anything to get away from the horror on my monitor—and then I remember the watching windows, the unchanged locks. Suddenly it feels like a really good idea to make sure my son is the only thing tucked safely into his bed. My phone goes into my robe pocket, my son's hand into mine, and we make our way upstairs.

Dozens of plastic ceiling stars beam constellations onto Tanner's twin-size mattress. Cassiopeia and Ursa Major blink down at me, but Orion glares down brightest of all. I try not to think about dolls in space as I check under my son's bed, in his closet, inside his toy chest.

"All clear," I tell him, when we've rooted out no monsters, and Tanner begrudgingly climbs back into bed. He asks me to wait until he falls asleep to leave, and when his breaths turn to snuffles, I shut the bedroom door behind me. Lugosi lopes down the stairs, leading back to my office, where Patti's restraining order waits on my computer screen.

What am I supposed to do now? All roads may lead to Darla, but I was wrong before. Darla is my friend. I don't want her to be the Dream Bean Killer.

The retriever freezes on the landing. Goose bumps march up my arms as the dog stalks into my office, puts his snout to the window glass, and begins to growl.

I can't remember the last time I heard Lugosi bark, let alone growl. Maybe never. Goldens are known for their sunny dispositions, not for their guard-dog abilities.

Which means whatever has his feather-duster tail rigid as he snarls through the windows isn't good.

My bare toes crush against cool wood as I take the stairs one at a time.

Don't invite any crazy, knife-wielding lunatics into your house, Kitty had said last month when we'd just moved into our new creaky-not-creepy home. That morning it had been Darla standing on the porch, my sweet new neighbor with a welcome basket filled with gifts for my family. Darla, with her sugar smiles, mom jeans, sparkly headbands. With her invitation to brunch.

Her Keds.

You could help me end my last year as president with a bang! Darla said then, and now my heart hammers in my chest as I pad down the stairs while my dog's breath fogs the windows.

She's standing on my front lawn.

Pert nose, blond hair to the jawline, beauty mark. Knit together by shadow and moonlight, the doll-faced killer stands in the center of the yard, looking straight through her mask's eye holes, directly at me.

My mouth opens, but no sound falls out. Then the wind blows and the figure in the lawn blows with it and it's not a woman at all.

It's a shrub. A mass of night-blackened branches and leaves. And someone has strung the Ben Cooper costume mask exactly where a woman's face would be.

In my pocket, the phone vibrates with an incoming notification. My eyes still on the mask hung outside my office window, I pull the phone out. It's the middle of the night, but the text isn't from my sister, nagging about our missed daily chat. It's from Rosa.

Sasha was scalped with a hand sander, the cop's wife says. They found her in the church. She'd been returning the tools—alone.

The mask smiles over my reflection in the window glass, and now I'm screaming.

I know who the Dream Bean Killer is.

It's Darla.

CHAPTER TWENTY-ONE

This is a prank. A terrible prank, but a prank nonetheless."

Steve Hudson's baritone slides over my shoulder from where he stands behind me in the master bedroom's threshold while I stare at my reflection in the window overlooking the backyard. The detective's voice sounds weary, but not as weary as my eyes. He might have gone home and gotten a few hours of sleep after Sasha's crime scene, but I was awake all night, staring at my corkboard, at the doll in the trees outside. The second Rob woke up, I told him about Sasha, pointed to the mask on the other side of my office window, and we called the cops.

Then Rob's cell rang, too. Some tanker ran aground on the Gulf Coast, and there's oil sheen for miles. The Coast Guard is being deployed, and Lieutenant Marshall is on the next flight back to Houston.

Right on cue, because in a slasher the only thing standing between the villain and the Final Girl is always suddenly called away by the top of act three.

It's noon by the time Steve shows up, and already Rob's almost late for his flight.

"We never should have released that description." The detective grips the Ben Cooper doll mask while I stare out the window, doing my absolute best not to become a hysterical woman. Outside, in the backyard, Tanner and Lugosi play fetch under a storm-cloud sky. "This close to Halloween, you can find a mask that matches just about anything. People love to make the news."

Apparently, the mask staring through my downstairs windows hadn't been the only face found in the trees last night. A Halloween-season prank, Power Suit said on ABC7, and Kitty helpfully texted me a friendly reminder about the 2016 Scary Clown Trend, when people randomly decided to dress as clowns and stand by the side of the road, because the world isn't frightening enough already, I guess?

Soon, the doll faces hung in New Jersey front-yard trees might get its own hashtag, too.

Prank or not, there'd been reports of all manner of Halloween masks strung in trees after law enforcement released the description of the Dream Bean Killer. Most were facsimiles of a woman's face, some not. But of all the masks leering out from suburban landscaping, none but mine was a Ben Cooper doll-face mask—the very same one that had made Kellen scream.

"One woman is dead, and three others have been mutilated." Behind me, Rob's voice is as close to snapping as I've ever heard it. One caveat to life as a military family is that the needs of the country come before problems at home, which means that oil spill in the Gulf gets first dibs on my husband. His hands are tied; he's leaving. "This is far more serious than just a prank, Detective Hudson," he tells the cop. "I need to know my wife and son are going to be safe while I'm deployed."

Rob says he'll be gone a few days, a week at most, but it'll be longer. It's always longer with oil spills.

When Steve promises my husband that the Brunswick PD will keep a close eye on his family, it's with that official-sounding tone of Men in Charge. We've graduated from warm bedside manner and the buddy system to a police escort and a security detail parked at the front curb, and yet no one will take me seriously because I'm just a suburb mom with a corkboard and a penchant for horror.

Go figure.

"Thanks for coming by, Steve." Rob's voice shows the detective out behind me. "We appreciate everything the Brunswick Police Department is doing."

My phone buzzes with an incoming text while my husband and the other man disappear down the stairs. I wrestle the slick rectangle out of my sweatpants and clear the alert without reading Kitty's message. When she calls, I send her to voicemail, just like I've done to Darla, whose calls this morning rival my sister's.

Tanner and Lugosi keep on with the tennis ball in the backyard while, in another window, Rob and Steve appear in the driveway. After a few words I can't hear and a firm handshake, Rob does that palm-up goodbye that guys do, and the detective slides in the driver's door of the cruiser parked behind my Honda. He situates himself behind the steering wheel and tosses the mask into the passenger seat, says something into his radio, and I return to the backyard view.

The doll's face hanging before my front window wasn't the one from the Boogie Bash costume box, but it had the same pert nose, blond hair to the jawline, beauty mark. At least Hudson called it a prank, and not a coincidence. Fresh out of those by now, I guess.

"Tanner's costume came." Rob reappears in the bedroom with the mail. The all-too-familiar sound of unboxing accompanies his voice, and he shows me the padded suit the same green as our son's lucky lunch box. Tanner requested a kaiju, of course. The plush Godzilla onesie is the best I could find online.

"Have you decided on your costume yet?" Rob's voice tries for perfectly normal, like we hadn't just had a cop in our bedroom, promising to keep me safe from a serial suburban mutilator.

"No." Of course, I haven't decided on my costume. I haven't even thought about Halloween, though my mind's been full of nothing but horror.

I can't believe the Dream Bean Killer is Darla.

I can't believe I'm the *only* one who believes the Dream Bean Killer is Darla. About halfway through my corkboard spiel, Steve told me he appreciated my help, but they had it covered.

That'll play well on the inevitable *Dateline* special.

"She said she found that tennis ball down by her house," I tell my husband, about the yellow orb Lugosi drops at Tanner's feet in the backyard, with its splotchy Coast Guard seal. "I just figured maybe it rolled out of the Honda."

Rob grunts. Him, I'd walked all the way through the revised plot on my office corkboard. He'd played devil's advocate about the silver polish and the pruning shears that might have had dried blood, not rust, on their tips, the medical textbook and gelato scoop, but the restraining order caught his attention. Steve assured us that the matter had been amicably resolved—a misunderstanding, he said.

And yet, Patti still moved.

It's not impossible the fuzzy yellow ball slipped free of the Honda's back seat and rolled down the street toward Number Thirty-Four. It's just about as likely as some merry prankster hanging my dead mother's face at my front door.

"Fucking hurricane season!" Rob's voice booms like a kick drum in the room behind me.

In the window glass, his reflection tosses a carry-on onto the bed. The suitcase hits the mattress like cymbals. If he didn't have to rush, he'd be in the basement, taking out his stress on his drum set. "These weather systems move through fast. We should be able to get things cleaned up quick," Rob mutters, more to himself than to me. "Unless it's another Deepwater Horizon."

I remember. "Spring 2010, sixty days in Louisiana."

"I tried to get them to send somebody else, but I'm the only one with the right qualifications." Rob apologizes over the sound of dresser drawers jerked open, items wrenched out. "The Coast Guard doesn't give me a choice. The phone rings, some bigwig gives an order, and I'm gone."

It's not an excuse, just the reality of the situation. And it sucks.

In my pocket, my phone buzzes. Outside, thunder.

Rob wrenches a zipper closed. "I told Tanner to come in. It's about to rain."

Raindrops splatter across the glass, proving my husband right. Wet lines streak across my forehead in the window, and Tanner and Lugosi pack it in. Downstairs, the kitchen door opens, closes, and a stampede starts up the stairs.

"Hey, Tanner," Rob calls through the double bedroom doors. "Go ahead and get your bathwater going. No bubbles this time, bud. In and out."

Sweat sticks my clothes to my chest when I turn away from the window, but the phone in my pocket won't stop buzzing—about the mask prank, about Sasha. The whole thing is a scene from a horror novel I didn't write: The devout arrive for the midnight liturgy, find a woman lying in a pool of her own scalp blood under the hallway fluorescents by the hand-tool library.

The text thread is kept alive with panic and platitudes, updates from ABC7. Stay safe, use the buddy system, be fierce. It's an ongoing investigation, but they'll catch him. The suspect profile still reads *woman,* but the media keeps slipping on the pronoun. Even when a woman kills someone and mutilates three others, she's still the edit, not the first draft.

But Beth's message bubble says her church friends have added the PTA to their weekly prayer circle, and the cops sent a car to my curb, so that should fix it.

Down the hall, bathwater begins to run.

"Jill." Rob's breath is warm on my neck, and I have no idea when he moved over to my side of the bed. "I would never leave if I had any other choice, but I need you to be here while I'm gone."

"Whoever scalped Sasha didn't use a blade," I tell him for the five hundredth time. My fingers crook into the blinds, pinching down a two-inch wooden slat that hides my second-floor bedroom from the street view outside.

From this vantage point, Number Thirty-Four is in full view: the potted mums, the BRUNSWICK ELEMENTARY sign, the purple minivan, and the pristine beige town car. Bland and slightly out-of-date, in hindsight the sedan is perfect for a neurosurgeon, or someone flying under the radar. Having a germophobe husband that scrubs his car every time the wind blows, even better.

"Steve says she used the hand sander Sasha borrowed from the church's tool library." I crane my head over my shoulder, watch as Rob folds a stack of navy blue T-shirts into the open suitcase on our bed. "She knew Sasha had shirked the buddy system, knew she had a key. Only the people in that cafeteria knew those tools were borrowed and that Sasha would take them back alone."

The sound of running bathwater goes quiet, and I catch the scent of Mr. Bubble when the air-conditioning clicks on.

Tanner didn't listen to his dad about the bubble bath.

"Did I tell you I saw my book on her coffee table?"

Rob harrumphs from the foot of the bed. His toiletry bag lies on the mattress beside the suitcase. The men's toiletry kit from Darla's welcome gift basket glares at me, travel-size products waiting to be stuffed in. Rob pushes the items into the carry-on one by one, lips thinned into a line, jaw clenched so tight it might snap off like that missing arm on Tanner's kaiju.

"I'm sure Darla wanted to read your book," he says. "Considering she lives next door to its author."

"She said she never has time to read."

Movement stirs outside, and I yank my fingers from the blinds, flinching when the slats snap shut. I'm pretty sure Darla couldn't spot me in my upstairs bedroom window if she walked out to her minivan, but I'm never totally sure how reflections in windows work.

Would I be standing in the spotlight or be a silhouette against a dark sky?

She probably can't hear me either way, but it's best to avoid the possibility altogether.

There's a creak on the stairs, a phantom footstep, and I hear Darla's voice again, the day she'd dragged me upstairs to paint my face: *You're going to be such a* doll.

Rob comes around the bed again, fingers curling into my shoulders as he turns me to him. His beard is longer than usual, I notice, his five-o'clock shadow looking more like midnight. Keeping clean-shaven is a job requirement, but tell that to the collection of silvery-black hair lining my darling husband's jaw, his beautiful lips.

"Jill," he says, voice firm, but whatever he's about to say next is cut off by the four peals of the Westminster Chimes.

My insides go slick.

"Don't answer it." Even as I say it, Lugosi's nails tap-dance across the hardwood, followed by a bathwater splash, the pitter-patter of Tanner's small feet, fresh from the tub, and I lunge toward the bedroom doors. Panic swells in my stomach, carbonating on its way up my throat to fizzes on my tongue, and Rob's hands tighten their hold. "It could be her!" I almost scream.

He can either hold me back and leave bruises or let go. I'm halfway to the stairs when the front-door locks click open.

"Aunt Kitty!" Tanner's voice slaps me across the face on the balcony, and I peer out at the foyer below. My son clutches a towel around his waist with one hand. Leftover bubbles cling to his arm, his hair. He didn't bother to wash off the suds before rocketing out of the bath.

The door swings open and suddenly my little sister is in the threshold, and if she's been on a cross-country flight, I can't tell.

I round on my darling husband. "You called my *sister*?" My words come out through gritted teeth because if I open my mouth any wider, I *will* scream.

Rob blanches at the accusation and puts his palms up. "I didn't," he says, innocent. "I swear."

"So, she just showed up?" Even as I say it, the look on my husband's face says he's as surprised by my sister's sudden appearance as I am. Doing the unexpected is Kitty's whole vibe these days, but appearing on my doorstep, now, really? I love her, I *need* her, but I would have preferred to get my head on straight before company.

My bare feet slick in the cool spots Tanner's wet bathtub feet have left on the carpet, on the hardwood, as I take the stairs two at a time and herd Kitty indoors before my neighbor sees. My sister looks the same as always (airbrushed, picture-perfect), but I don't recognize the Barbie-pink duffel she lugs through the door.

It's never a good sign when Kitty shows up with luggage.

Tanner is gushing about the detective with the real badge who'd just left, but I shush him and lock the door behind me.

"What are you doing here?"

Her face blooms into a smile. "Can't a girl just want to see her sister?"

"You could have called."

She flinches, then rolls her eyes and digs through her purse for her phone. "I *have* called, *and* texted." She brandishes a screen crammed with one-sided messages, no responses. "You won't answer. You leave me on read. You don't call back. What am I supposed to do?" Kitty's eyes rage. "Just wait around on the other side of the world, wondering what the hell is going on while you ignore me?"

"Watch your language." It's not so much the swear as it is her tone that's starting to rattle against the back of my teeth. Kitty is a hot-air balloon: Let her off course and she'll burn across the sky.

The wheels of Rob's luggage thunder down the stairs ahead of him, and Tanner hollers up, "Daddy! Aunt Kitty is here!"

"I see that, buddy." When he reaches the landing, Rob hoists Tanner up for a quick hug, and his arm hooks my waist when he returns our son to the floor. His touch is soft, but his voice is too tight when he pulls me against him. "I love you," he whispers into my hair. "Stay home. Be careful. Let your sister help take your mind off things." Then he shoulders a bag and nods at my sister. "Kitty."

"Throb." My sister smirks as she tucks her phone back into her purse.

"Take care of her," Rob tells her, then he shoots me one last look over his shoulder and doesn't look back as she closes the front door behind him. Tanner and Lugosi rebound up the stairs, and I hear the splash when my son jumps back into the tub.

"Trouble in paradise?" my sister asks as Rob's truck grumbles down the driveway. "You guys are usually all *Lady and the Tramp* level in love."

"We're fine." *I'm* not fine. "How's Leaf?"

Kitty flaps her wrist in a way that tells me Leaf has made like a tree. "Okay, what's going on, Jill?" she asks as truck tires peel backward, but I push past her to see the street ahead. Is Darla watching? Did she see Rob leave? Does she think I'm alone?

Where's that security detail, Detective Hudson?

"Jill?" Kitty stomps behind me. "What the hell is going on with you? I'm *right here*!" she shrills.

My sister's attention span requires the short version, but at least she won't think I'm crazy.

"I think I'm living out a slasher movie," I confess. "I think my neighbor is attacking all her frenemies, and I think I might be next."

Kitty sighs, and maybe it *was* a mistake to tell my sister the truth, because her sigh is the long-held kind. The kind that's been waiting forever to come out, like she's always known this day would come, the day I become just like our mother. And it must be so because she puts her arms around my shoulders.

"Don't you remember what we said the day Mom died, Jilly Bean?"

When I don't answer right away, Kitty sighs again and stamps a lipsticky kiss into my check. "You took care of me"—my little sister admires her mark—"and now I'm here to take care of you."

CHAPTER TWENTY-TWO

Kitty twirls polka-dotted blue skirts in the floor-length bedroom mirror. She blows her costumed reflection a kiss through heart-shaped lips, swivels on candy cane–stockinged legs, and rounds on me. I'm sideways at the window, red lines where my fingers are wedged in the blinds, eyes on fire from staring out at the street below.

At the cop car rooted to my curb.

At the purple minivan parked at Number Thirty-Four.

At the house's open garage door, the painted wooden barrels in its driveway.

Cobalt and crimson blur as my sister pirouettes in my peripheral vision. "What do you think?"

Outside, a yellow school bus caterpillars up the street. Its lights flash red, air brakes squeal, and children spill out, scurrying under their beetle backs into houses on either side of the street. My son's green backpack blasts through the bus doors last. Tanner's fuzzy-duckling head charges up our front lawn, and Lugosi bolts out of the master bedroom, zooms down the stairs. Three black rails rake across my vision as the school bus huffs away, and Kitty peers over my shoulder through the window.

"Did you know those black lines down the bus's side are to mark its floor, seat line, and seat tops? The stripes help emergency crews know where to cut in case there's an accident," she says.

Downstairs, the front door swings open, then slams shut, and Tanner's voice carries up the stairs when he yells that he's home.

"Depending on the size of the kids on board, cutting along that top line might lop off someone's head," I tell my sister. "Imagine if some emergency crews went in to save endangered kiddos and ended up slicing their heads clean off?"

"Whoa, Jilly Bean." Kitty feigns scandalized. "That's dark."

"That's why we don't believe everything we read on social media." I tap the side of my head. "Snopes exists for a reason, Kitty Kat."

I track Tanner's movements downstairs as he pitter-patters into the kitchen for an after-school snack. The refrigerator slurps open, followed by the jingle of aluminum cans, the crash of the ice maker spitting cubes into a plastic cup, the rattle of the dog-treat jar on the counter. The fridge door hisses closed half a second before faint cartoon chatter floats upstairs.

School is officially out for the day, which means Boogie Bash is only a couple of hours away.

With another squeal of its brakes, the yellow school bus lets off a couple more beetle-backed kids at Number Thirty-Four. Darla rushes down the driveway from inside the garage, arms waving as she enlists her children to help heave the orange barrels into the minivan's trunk one by one. The barrels are destined for Boogie Bash, but what they're for, I have no idea. Candy bowls, maybe? Some kind of carnival game? Apple bobbing?

Whatever it is, I'll find out soon.

A police babysitter, a husband called away on work at the last minute, and my sister's unexpected arrival were enough to excuse me from final Boogie Bash preparations, but not to dismiss me from tonight's event altogether. Tanner I could buy off with a trip down the Wawa candy aisle, but even my pleas about being behind on my manuscript and Charlene's unanswered emails still lurking in my inbox weren't enough to get me off the Boogie Bash hook. My reflection frowns in the bedroom window as Darla disappears indoors with her children. What good are a Hershey's-soaked third grader, a frustrated editor, and a forever-late haunted-space story when the death of one woman and the mutilations of three others weren't even enough to cancel the night's big event?

Prank or not, after someone hung the mask on my front landscaping, the principal agreed to block off access to everything but the cafeteria and to relocate the parking-lot trunk-or-treat inside. The police department had already assigned a handful of uniforms to patrol the school after the security briefing Darla and I had with Hart. Otherwise, that was that. Some locked doors and bored cops looking to pick up a bit of overtime, and the show would go on.

Our Halloween Boogie Bash would be amazing with a horror author's help, Darla had told me, that first day in my kitchen. *You could help me end my last year as president with a bang!*

Outside, the yellow bus creaks around the corner at the end of the street. I haven't returned a single text, haven't accepted a single call, from my neighbor in a week. Darla is a murderess, a mutilator, but she was—is?—also my friend . . . or is she? Every time her name flashes on my phone screen, I get a pang of guilt somewhere deep in my core, right next to the hole left by my mother's memory.

But right here, I can feel Kitty's pout at the foot of the bed. "Decapitation is for later," she says about the rub rails on the school bus sides, and swishes her petticoats behind me. "More importantly, what do you think about my dress?"

Anybody else, and it'd probably be weird to show up with a costume prepared for a children's school event for a kid that's not even your own, but my sister jumps at any excuse to dress up. So long as she avoids any photos of the actual children, an elementary school Halloween festival is just another opportunity for content creation.

A child's monster roar echoes up from the entryway. Downstairs, Tanner is getting into character for the party, too.

I'm the odd one out, as usual.

"Jill, stop staring out the stupid window and pay attention to me!" In the window's reflection, my sister crooks her joints like a marionette and moves without strings. "Don't you like my dress?"

I cross my arms over my spooky T-shirt as I peel myself away from the window, chewing at my tongue while my sister dances around my bedroom like a demented rag doll. A red choker slashes across her throat. A bright blue bow pins red yarn braids to the top of her head. The red polka-dots on the bow look like blood splatter, and when she twirls, frilly tulle winks into view—the same white collar she'd worn when she'd painted herself into a clown, repurposed into a petticoat.

"You know this is a party for elementary schoolers, right?" The costume is too scary, probably, with the blood splatter, but those bloomers are definitely not G-rated.

"Don't be such a prude, Jilly Bean." Kitty blows me a kiss and twirls on stilted, candy cane–striped legs to where she's left her suitcase flipped open on the middle of the bedroom floor. She bends to pluck out a bundle of luggage-wrinkled fabric, then stands with the cloth held in front of her. She lets the bundle fall into shape and a manic grin spreads across her face.

She's got to be kidding me. "We are not showing up at Boogie Bash dressed up like the Grady twins."

"Jill!" Kitty stomps a black patent Mary Jane hard enough to flatten the carpet. She jostles the identical doll's dress at me. It's not the same as those of the murdered twins from the movie, with their matching white collars and pink sashes, but it's close. "It's got pockets."

"Not a chance," I tell the costume pinched in Kitty's fingertips, with its little red stitches *and* its pockets. "No way."

She drapes the dress meant for me over the comforter and flips a red yarn braid over her shoulder on her way back to her reflection. "Don't be such a stick-in-the-mud, Jilly Bean." Kitty leans toward the mirror to adjust her wig. "It's a great costume."

"I've already got a costume."

I watch Kitty's reflection roll its eyes in the mirror. "That's not a costume. It's a boring old T-shirt you pulled out of a drawer."

It is, in fact, a brand-new T-shirt featuring a trio of seasonally appropriate, monsterfied movie-theater concessions: a soda-fountain paper cup (with a bloody carving knife), a popcorn box (with a bloody hatchet), and a masked hot dog (with a bloody chain saw). All frolic beneath the slogan LET'S GO TO THE MOVIES.

A little on the nose, but the shirt is cute, harmless, and about as far as I'd intended to go toward dressing up for Boogie Bash.

"I thought you'd like the dress." Still fussing with her rag-doll wig, Kitty straightens the braids, then smooths them down like twin red ropes on either side of her face. "The real Annabelle doll is a Raggedy Ann, not that creepy porcelain thing they used in the movies."

Like I don't know. "Since when are you so into horror factoids?"

She bats double-layered falsies and grins at me in the glass. "Just playing to your strengths. Besides, I had to do a lot of research for my Spooky Season makeup tutorials."

Oh, right. *Those.*

"Then you should also know that the real Annabelle is locked behind glass with a little plaque that says WARNING: POSITIVELY DO NOT OPEN." Rob's pillow is cold when I pull it off the bed to strip off the king-size pillowcase for Tanner's trick-or-treat bag. "Or it was until the Warrens died, anyway. And their Occult Museum closed."

Kitty pulls a face. "I didn't know *they* were real." She shrugs. "I thought they were, like, you know, exorcists made up for the movies, or whatever."

My sister's internet sleuthing skills need some work if she managed to get the doll right but not learn about the controversial Warrens, considering the couple were literally the main characters of many films and books, including their own—but I'd gotten the villain of my own life slasher wrong, so I have no room to talk. "They were some of the most famous paranormal investigators for decades,"

I tell Kitty, about the Warrens. "They worked on something like ten thousand cases—not just Annabelle, but Amityville, too."

Ed Warren was a self-professed demonologist and Lorraine was a clairvoyant, but there's not a glimmer of recognition in Kitty's eyes.

"They founded the New England Society for Psychic Research in the fifties?" I try, just in case something rings a bell, but whatever interest my sister had in the Warrens or their cleansed demonic artifacts, it's gone now.

She spins away from the mirror, bounces on her Mary Janes, and fixes me with a sinister smirk. "Let me do your makeup. I want to try out a new tutorial I'm working on for this costume."

Kitty's irises are usually brown like mine. But today, behind layers of false eyelashes, they're as blue as her doll dress, as the oceans around my mother's eyes, that day in the master-bedroom closet. I must have missed when Kitty slipped in contacts.

I don't want to play dress-up with my sister.

"Come on, Jilly Bean." Kitty preens, and the oceans around her eyes deepen, pulling me under, the waves rolling me just like those of my mother's waterbed, so long ago. "It'll be just like when we were kids."

I expect her to sit me on the bed like Darla did, but Kitty drops to the floor, crosses her legs, and pats the space in front of her.

"On the carpet?"

She rolls her eyes as she stabs both hands into her suitcase and pulls out a Caboodles. It's missing the Dollface branding, but otherwise my sister's showcase is just like my neighbor's.

Just like mine, actually, with its cracked plastic and faded logo. "Wait, is that—"

"Look familiar?" Kitty grins, reading my thoughts. "I've held on to it this whole time."

She beams up at me from the floor, all her shiny pink compacts arranged around her feet, and I resist the urge to shudder when she pats the carpet again. Weeks ago, I'd told Rob my life felt like a *Stepford*

Wives meets *Twilight Zone* slasher. Every day, that mash-up gets more and more on the nose.

"Come on, Jill," Kitty whines, voice like helium. "You've had your fun, now it's my turn."

I have no idea what fun she's referring to, exactly, but I give in and sit on the bedroom floor across from my sister.

Kitty strokes the carpet with fingers tipped in cherry red and tells me to close my eyes. "The base for this look is superdrying, so I need to practically drown you in moisturizer first." She waits for me to obey before she pads cool gel over my forehead, across my cheeks, under my jaw. "Okay, tell me everything," her disembodied voice says on the other side of my eyelids. "Why do you think your sweet new neighbor bestie is attacking people?"

"Really?" So far, neither my darling husband nor law enforcement have been interested in my theories on Darla's attacks, but my sister's ear is specially tuned for hot goss, even if she did drench Darla's description in a heavy dose of sarcasm.

"Yes, really. I want to know exactly what's taken all your attention since you moved in." Moisturizer is smoothed along the bridge of my nose. "I mean, it's *totally* crazy, this idea of Carla, like, attacking people or whatever. But that doesn't mean you're wrong."

"Darla." The cool gel turns cold when my sister stops patting. "Her name is Darla. Not Carla."

I open my eyes in time to see Kitty flap her wrist in dismissal, then cap the moisturizer. "Potayto, potahto." She rolls her fingers through a pile of cosmetic compacts in the bottom layer of her Caboodles, selects another small tube of gel and what might be a giant white crayon, and gestures that I should close my eyes again. "Primer will help the color stick"—she waggles first the gel and then the crayon—"and the jumbo pencil will help intensify the color."

When my lids close, Kitty applies a coat of primer lash line to my brow, almost thick enough to seal my eyelids shut. "Go on. About Darla."

"Well, everything is exactly like I had figured it, I just had my attention on the wrong person." My sister grunts, but I ignore it. I've recited my suspicions so many times now, stared at the beats mapped out on my office corkboard, that the whole thing is the world's most masochistic earworm, forever repeating itself on a loop in my head.

"The day we met, Darla brought over a welcome basket, right?" I say, starting from the beginning. "She invited me to the PTA brunch at the Dream Bean, and that's where that barista insulted her over a stupid cream cheese–filled croissant." I'd ordered an extra croissant, said something about feasting on our enemies, and Darla mentioned inspiration. At the time, I'd thought she'd meant about figuring out my new book idea, but in retrospect, was that what set my sweet neighbor off on her rampage? God, I hope not.

"Anyway, that night, someone slit that barista's throat. And then a couple of days later, after her Doll's Night party—"

"I know all this already." Impatience tightens Kitty's voice, and I peel back an eyelid to see her select a pod of blue cream from the Caboodles' belly. Her fingers tweeze out a slim eye-shadow brush. "That's where you met the librarian who doesn't forget a face." Kitty rolls her eyes and uses the brush to signal my eyes closed when she catches me looking.

"Yeah, that's Rosa, but she wasn't the next one attacked." I remind my sister about Maribel—who didn't show up at Doll's Night because she said she had a real spa appointment and would be home getting her beauty rest.

The pod in Kitty's hand pops open and the fluffy tip of a brush traces over the ridge of my eyeball, pushing into the crease of my eyelid. "I started with a pretty light blue." Her brush edges up toward my brow. "I'm going behind and filling in with a deeper shade to make your eyes pop." The brush pulls away, and Kitty's breath slides across my skin as she inspects her work. "Okay, Doll's Night. Maribel." She snaps the pods shut and the noise springs my eyelids open. "Keep going."

Right. "When I got to Darla's that day, I noticed this weird eggy silver-polish smell, right?" I assemble the relevant details. "They said that whoever slit Barb's throat used a serrated blade, like a bread knife. She was cleaning the murder weapon right under our noses. Had to be."

My sister makes a face like she's impressed. "And then what, she stabbed Maribel with silver serving ware?"

"They thought Maribel was stabbed with scissors, but Darla had been gardening that day." I remember the mums on Darla's front lawn, her pristine flower beds. "When I went over for the party, she talked about deadheading—snipping off old blooms to make way for new growth." Maribel had just been through a divorce, and Darla had said all that weird fresh-start stuff when she'd practiced giving me a makeover.

"The security-camera footage from the Dream Bean was a lost cause," I tell Kitty. "But Maribel saw her attacker's reflection before she was stabbed." That's how they knew it was a woman, with short blond hair, pert nose, beauty mark. The description haunts me now when I know she'd been wearing a Ben Cooper costume mask, peddling Dollface, calling me *a* doll. "I saw what I thought was rust on Darla's shears when I went by to tell her what had happened, but I think it was blood. Those short-nosed pruning shears look a lot like scissors."

I watch my sister sweep the remaining blue shadow from the tip of her brush onto a spare piece of tissue, then trade the small brush for a thick white sponge and a tube of cream paint. When she reaches for me with the sponge, my body pulls away on its own. "I'll just give you a little sheer covering—a porcelain finish." Kitty rolls her eyes. "Detective Hudson is married to Rosa the Librarian Who Doesn't Forget a Face, right?"

My nod makes her grunt. This time my eyes stay open, but I hold my head still while my sister paints a new layer of skin across my face for "more coverage."

Kitty's teeth pinch her tongue against her lip. Concentrating, she shades in more white pencil between my eyebrows, along the bridge of my nose, inside the bowl of my chin, then blends the pencil into my cheeks with her fingers. Her fingertip tugs down my lower eyelid and my vision blurs as she glides cold white along the inner edge, corner to tear duct. "To create the illusion of bigger eyes," my sister explains.

She uses an eyeliner brush to edge my new false waterline in blue shadow while I tell her what happened to Kellen.

"Enucleated, that's wild." Kitty rummages through *my* old Caboodles and plucks out a slim tube of liquid black eyeliner. I try not to think of decapitated children as she rakes black lines over my eyes, a thick strip of black along the edge of my eyelashes, and wings cold wet to the outsides of my eyes. "And you think that was Darla, too?"

I tell my sister about Patti's favorite gelato scoop. "We'd just finished the Ice Cream Social." My sister pulls the skin around my eyes upward to trace a thin line under my new fake waterline, the eyeliner wet like old tears. "And Kellen had been drunk at the event."

The white sponge is back in Kitty's hand. She taps where skin shows over the bodice of her blue rag-doll dress, tells me to take off my shirt, and I obey, so she can paint white cream over my heartbeat. "And there was one more victim, right?"

"Sasha, yeah." My sister uses a brush the size of a peony to blot white powder over my face and chest before going back to my eyes with the darker blue eye shadow to shade in the new waterline. "She was scalped with a hand sander."

While Kitty glues on a pair of false eyelashes, I tell her all about Boogie Bash prep, how Sasha borrowed the tools from her church's tool library, the same place she'd been returning them when attacked. While the falsies dry, Kitty brushes red eye shadow through my brows, then instructs me to blink through a mascara wand to fuse my top lashes to the false pair.

She adds demi-lashes to the corners of my eyes for extra lift, then stitches bottom lashes under my new false waterline with the black eyeliner. "So, she slit the barista's throat, stabbed gardening scissors into Maribel's skull, used an ice cream scooper to spoon out Kellen's eye, and scalped Sasha with a hand sander. And what does any of this have to do with the woman who used to live in your house?"

That's the part I haven't figured out. "Darla acts like she and Patti were best friends, right? All that talk about carpooling and PTA and moving my coffeepot around." Kitty makes a face, and maybe I forgot to tell her about the traveling Keurig, or the "found" tennis ball, or all that movement I thought I'd sensed outside my downstairs windows at night.

"I don't really know," I admit. "It's like all the attacks were punishment for bad behavior. Maybe it has nothing to do with Patti at all."

"Everybody has their reasons." Kitty shrugs—a touch blasé, perhaps, but very much on brand for my little sister. "Didn't you say Darla's husband is a neurologist or something?" She moves away from my face and plunges hands back into her Caboodles.

"A neurosurgeon." Oh, right, I almost forgot to tell Kitty about the medical textbook I'd seen the day Darla and I carpooled in Dave's car. "I think that's how she figured out to always go for the head, but do just enough damage to maim, not kill?"

Except for Barb, anyway, but maybe Darla had decided the barista didn't deserve a fresh start.

"Heads *are* fascinating." Kitty uses a dark brown eyeliner to reshape the center of my lips into a heart, then a tube of scarlet-red lipstick to finish the look. "They house four of our five senses." She squints to concentrate on her work as she dots freckles across my cheeks. "We see, smell, hear, and taste with our heads. They contain our brain, the core of our nervous system."

My sister palms my cheeks to make sure the freckles have dried before she smears on bright pink blush. She pulls a mirror from the Caboodles, then scoots to sit next to me on the master-bedroom carpet.

"Our heads are the most precious parts of our bodies." Kitty's reflection slides side by side against mine as she holds up a compact mirror. "Look at us. Twins!"

"You're the only one who doesn't think I'm completely out of my mind," I tell my sister in the tiny mirror. "I know this all sounds completely ridiculous on paper, but I just *know* in my gut that I'm right."

I'd been right this whole time, really. Just had the wrong person. I don't want to believe Darla would be capable of such a heinous, monstrous thing. Of course I would finally make a friend, someone who could even be a *best* friend, and she turns out to be a slasher villain.

Honestly, given my track record—a mentally unstable mother, a sister with a borderline histrionic attention complex, a career spent dreaming up terrors—it sorta tracks.

Kitty snaps the compact closed and squirms until she sits in front of me, hands holding mine, our knees touching.

"Why wouldn't I believe you? You're my sister." Kitty's grin crawls up the sides of her cheeks until her whole face smiles. "Besides, people can be more than one thing," she says with an exaggerated wink. "Ted Bundy killed some people but saved others by working on a suicide hotline. Hitler painted dogs."

Why my little sister knows this, I have no idea, but she's correct. Mostly.

"Hitler painted architecture—bad architecture. But despite the fact that you're comparing my neighbor to a serial killer and to an actual mass murderer, it's still weirdly comforting to have someone tell me that maybe I'm right." I tell her that I was starting to feel like I was going crazy. *Just like mom.*

Kitty rubs her fingers over my knuckles, then cradles my palm in her hand while she traces her index finger down the length of my thumb. "We all need someone to pay attention to us." My skin melts in her hand. "Besides, if you don't see the horror right in front of you, how will you ever survive it?"

"I'm glad you're here to take care of me," I tell my sister.

"Me, too." Kitty says and squeezes back.

CHAPTER TWENTY-THREE

"Two dolls and a kaiju walk into a school—"

It's not the kickoff to a bad joke. It's Boogie Bash.

"Don't start," I tell my sister.

Miniature superheroes and homemade creatures shriek across Brunswick Elementary's pumpkin-littered front lawn. Tanner stomps through a heap of fallen leaves like its Tokyo. Kitty flips a yarn braid over one shoulder, crooks her elbow in mine, and hoists her shiny Mary Janes high to avoid the shrapnel.

The red circles on my sister's cheeks swell into a smile as she hauls me toward the school. "Oh, come on, Jilly Bean," she says. "You need to learn to enjoy yourself. This *is* a party."

"It's *something,* that's for sure." Normally, a Halloween festival, even one meant for children, would totally be my bag. But tonight, my anxiety is amped so high that the only skeleton bones rattling in the evening breeze are mine.

At the school, rows of white cardboard fangs transform the cafeteria's exterior entrance into a giant open maw. Hot, heavy laundry-basket breath burps out from a fog machine, and the stink of candy sugar and buttered popcorn churns in my stomach. The giant black-balloon spider crooked directly over the double doors is very cool, but also very definitely going to give a fair few of the costumed kiddos barreling into the monster's mouth nightmares tonight.

Parents *will* complain. For once, it won't be "my" fault.

Besides, barreling into this monster's mouth is probably going to give me nightmares, too. Somewhere on the other side of the fanged entry waits Darla.

I still can't get my head around the fact that my sweet new neighbor might be the Dream Bean Killer—*is* the Dream Bean Killer. Or at the very least, the woman behind the doll's mask who attacked Maribel, Kellen, Sasha.

They always say it's the ones closest to you, the ones you never expect, but still. Darla, really?

No matter how much my gut, my corkboard, says it's true, I don't want it to be Darla.

Leaves demolished, Tanner realizes Kitty and I dawdle behind him and doubles back.

"Mommm," he whines. "Hurry up!" The high shrills of creaking doors mix with the ghostly moans filtering through the school PA system to muffle his words, but my son's impatience prickles along my forearm. His hand pulls against mine, but the kid lets go and darts ahead toward the school's hungry teeth before I can get a grip on his little kaiju paw. "We're missing *everything,*" he calls over his shoulder, bouncing on his heels behind a line of other costumed kids.

Kitty's flexes her arm inside mine. "Yeah, Mom, you're missing *everything.*"

"Shut up, Katherine." I flex back.

Sharp pain tears into my ankle as a cowboy in a red vinyl ten-gallon pinballs his way toward the doors, his parents nowhere to be seen as his spurs dig into my Achilles. A grim reaper's party-store scythe scratches along the concrete behind her before her harried mom swats it upright. My kid's wearing a plush green monster onesie with padded rubber feet and carrying an empty pillowcase to collect candy. Today is not the day to let my eight-year-old go charging into a monster's maw without me.

My sister makes it into the school's cafeteria just fine, but naturally my skirt snags on a fang the second I shuffle past one hungry white tooth. Some women can frolic through fields of barbed wire with nary a second thought. The rest of us can't manage to get past a row of cardboard dentistry.

"Hang on, kid." The Boogie Bash doors officially opened a mere fourteen minutes ago, but the way my son groans you'd think they'd already run out of candy. Still, who knows how long, how many Amazon boxes, how many paper cuts, it took to create this cardboard cafeteria-door beast. Just because I don't want to let my son out of my sight doesn't mean I'm ready to ruin someone's (probably Beth's) hard work.

"Mom!" Two incisors ahead of me, Tanner begins to summon atomic breath.

Good grief, kid. I'm trying.

My stupid skirt is still stuck in the stupid line of fanged teeth, but at least this gaping jaw is the only way in and out of the school. Beyond the foyer, the corridor doors are shut tight, and the rest of the school is dark. Hart has made good on our agreement to ramp up security measures for the night's event, though the effort seems a little ridiculous now, considering it'd mostly been Darla's plan. Still, I'm pleased to spot a few cops in the room—until I realize the little figures in blue picked up their uniforms at Spirit Halloween.

Tanner squawks again. I'm still caught in the toothy entrance, but the closest thing to a Ben Cooper doll mask in my Boogie Bash field of vision is Kitty, whose tulle petticoat has escaped entrapment completely.

"I got him," she says, and Tanner's plush reptilian tail disappears inside a bubble of giggles and squeals and my sister's arms. Just like that, they're gone.

Sorry, cardboard teeth monster. I yank my skirts free, flinch at the incriminating rip, and spill into the school behind my family members. Tanner groans when I reach for his hand, and I let my fingers drop to my side. My heart burns, but I get it. No self-respecting third grader wants to hold his mommy's hand at a party.

Another hip-high cowboy slinks by, probably the one with my blood on his spurs, followed by an ice-skater and a tall brunette with black shoe polish–ringed eyes and a raccoon tail safety-pinned to a pair of drab gray sweatpants. "Nice doll costume," Raccoon Girl says as she passes, and the smirk on her painted black lips promises she's going to be hell in middle school.

Firsthand experience has taught me that mean girls start young, but dang if my feelings didn't just get hurt by a fifth grader.

I resist the urge to yank the silly red yarn wig off my head and stomp it into the glitter-flecked floor. Another batch of noisy elementary schoolers spirals by, and a future migraine dots my vision. How in the actual hell did I let my sister talk me into wearing this ridiculous outfit?

Other than the fact it's got pockets, zero redeeming qualities.

The things I do for my sister—but then, Kitty's always had a way of getting what she wants.

We're halfway inside the school when a boy roughly Tanner's height breaks away from the kid throng and rushes over. He's got an absurdly large prop spoon clutched in his fist, and maybe a dozen Fun Pac cereal boxes pinned to his chest, accessorized by plastic spoons coated in fake blood. Little globs of hot glue dot colorful loops and toasted-wheat squares across his shirt and pants. A papier-mâché bowl crowns his head.

"I'm a 'cereal killer,' get it?" The kid's eyes wander down Tanner's plush green suit, padded feet, tail. "What are you? A lizard?"

"I'm a kaiju." Tanner adjusts his reptile hood over his fuzzy-duckling hair, raises clawed hands, and roars. "Like Godzilla," he says because the cereal killer looks confused.

"Cool." The boys study each other's costumes while the spooky haunted-house sounds pumping through the PA system turn into music. The first few pungent notes of "Monster Mash" creak through the speakers, and my anxiety ticks down a notch.

Even with an *actual* serial attacker around, it's impossible not to get swept up in the dulcet current of Bobby "Boris" Pickett.

Sugary, shrink-wrapped goods wink in high piles atop the cafeteria tables along the far wall. Tanner's eyes go wide as his gaze trick-or-treats across the room—the serving bowls overfilled with name-brand candies, the piles of iced-sugar cookies. Buffets of decorating supplies are arranged at the edge of the stage, accompanied by mounds of dollar-store party trinkets. Witch-hat ring toss is stationed in one corner of the cafeteria, something that might be candy-corn bowling in another.

And now my eyes are as big as my son's. Even with all those Sterilite totes we'd unpacked from the PTA closet, I still had not expected this level of boogie.

My son's eyes bulge. "Mom, Aunt Kitty—look!"

A gang of costumed kids congregate in the center of the room. The collection of wooden barrels I'd seen in Number Thirty-Four's driveway have been filled to the brim with water, adorned with jack-o'-lantern faces cut from jagged pieces of black construction paper, and planted inside a makeshift plywood cemetery under an orange, purple, and black crepe-paper sky. Beside the tubs, small plastic cauldrons and spoon-rest ladles, surrounded by flimsy wood gravestones and empty Market Basket grocery sacks that probably once carried apples. A caped parent volunteer lifts a little monster up at one barrel, and he spoons out a Honeycrisp as big as a Dream Bean muffin. Raccoon Girl stretches her upper body over another barrel, plunges headfirst into the water, and emerges with a stem clenched between her teeth. Her eyeliner runs down her cheeks when she pulls up, which, annoyingly, just makes her look cooler.

A twinkling moonbeam moves between the barrels, wearing a

coordinated pointy hat and carrying a crooked broom. Just like she'd promised Hart, Darla herself presides over the children bobbing for apples. Clearly, the painted wooden barrels under the PTA president's watchful eye are the solution to last year's bob flood problem.

"That's her," I tell Kitty, who's pressed in so tight against me that I can't tell where her red yarn braids end and mine begin. "My neighbor."

The smile curving Kitty's lips is not one of my favorites.

Her hand slides into mine and tightens to pull me forward, but Tanner whines at my side before my sister can tell me where we're going. "Mom, can I go play with my friends?" my son asks, about the apple barrels. He blinks puppy-dog eyes up at me (the most formidable weapon of the young and beloved), which is totally and completely unfair.

One *please* isn't enough, so when I resist his first attempt to flee, Tanner doubles down on the pout, amps up the whimper, and summons crocodile tears. *"Please,"* he tries again. "It's Boogie Bash."

They tell you a lot about becoming a parent when you have children. It's mostly bad stuff, tallied up in some kind of masochistic math equation: Add up how expensive they are, subtract how much sleep you'll lose, and it equals how sticky they're not only going to get themselves, but every single thing you own—especially the stuff you literally never think about having to clean, like doorknobs and drawer handles. These will be the worst of them all. New mothers are instructed to hover, but not become overprotective. To be bears, not helicopters. To love unconditionally, but not smother. To hold on tight, but be ready to let go.

Probably, I should tell Tanner no. He'll tantrum, sure, but he'll do it tethered to my side. But there's only one way into the school, one way out. All the doors are locked. A handful of full-size uniforms patrol the cafeteria, the front lawn. There are any number of adults that I trust in the room, and only one that I don't—and even in slashers, the kids are always fine.

"Go," I tell him before I lose my nerve, watching as Tanner and his cereal-killer friend are swallowed by the throng in the middle of the room. Of all the wisdom handed down to new parents, what no one tells you is how much you'll need those babies as much as they'll need you. Eight years old, and I still have to remember how to breathe when my son's fuzzy-duckling head disappears past the wooden barrels.

A candy wrapper skitters across the floor on a current of party noise, and I curl my fingers in my dress pockets. Beside me, Kitty loops her elbow back through mine. "He'll be *fine,* Jill," she purrs against my ear.

"He better be."

My sister points to a line of women planted along the far wall of the bustling cafeteria as she leads me to the outskirts of the room. "Those must be your mean-mommy friends," she says, hauling me forward. There's a pirate with a red headscarf fashioned from an athletic band, an eye patch to match, and a casted "peg leg," and a fortune teller swathed in layers of scarves and paisley and topped with a purple velvet turban. Beside them hovers an angel with a pair of gold wings and a gilded halo, beset by a black cat's skintight bodysuit and a pair of fur-trimmed stiletto boots that make Kitty's candy-cane thigh highs practically virginal by comparison. Injuries aside, with those scowls, there is no mistaking who these women are.

"Okay, so Kellen is the pirate and Maribel is the Gypsy," Kitty whispers in my ear, and I cringe. "But who are the angel and the cat?"

"I think the appropriate term is *fortune teller.*" Some Romani are reclaiming the fifteenth-century racial slur, but it's probably best not to tiptoe over the line on someone else's culture. "The angel is Beth, the cat is Rosa. The sweet one and the librarian who never forgets a face," I add, just in case Kitty has forgotten.

Kellen's good eye widens when Kitty and I approach. Without the identical yarn braids, doll's faces, and dresses, my sister and I only resemble each other, but with these costumes, we're practically twins.

I'd mentioned my sister's sudden arrival on the PTA group text, but hadn't included her planned attendance at Boogie Bash, not that I'd known. "She just got into town a few days ago," I say, after we've finished introductions, and the cloud of passive confusion clears off the women's faces.

They all agree it's nice to meet Kitty, but only Rosa is nice enough to say hello.

Kitty's smirk is the one I know means she's up to no good. "I've heard so much about you all, but there's someone missing, isn't there? Aren't there seven women on the PTA?"

Maribel tugs at her turban and Kellen adjusts her eye patch, because we all know that my sister doesn't mean Darla, busy helping kids bob apples out of the orange barrels. She means Sasha. Kitty isn't going to spill my beans on the Brunswick PTA Mean Girls moniker, but that doesn't mean she's above a little needling.

The other women turn away while Rosa smooths flyaway hairs from the kitten-ear headband tucked into her long dark hair and fluffs the curls that fall artfully over her shoulder. The primping seems almost cruel, considering that Sasha is missing from tonight's event because the attacker sheared off her scalp with a hand sander, but then the behavior is a usual part of Rosa's body language.

Still, ouch.

"Sasha is getting some much-needed rest at home," Rosa says, and shoulders a plastic grocery sack of extra apples. "Steve says she's lucky to be alive." Rosa gestures at the cluster of PTA husbands across the cafeteria—Darla's Dave, Maribel's Chad, Sasha's Old Goat. I hadn't paid enough attention to Sasha's husband before to remember the Old Goat's hair, but tonight his bald head is as shiny as the sheen of sweat on Dave Lashett's upper lip. Steve blows a kiss when he catches his wife looking and jerks a thumb at Maribel's ex in the universal gesture for *This guy,* so at least it's not all fun and games in the Dad Clump.

"If the person who attacked Sasha had used a knife or some kind of blade instead of a hand sander," Rosa says, "she'd have bled out right there in the church hallway." Her shudder ripples through the other women, but my sister and I know a thing or two about watching someone bleed out.

Beth flutters her angel wings. "That's too horrible to even think about."

"I read that it can take up to two years to heal from a scalping and the hair will never grow back the same." My sister is like me when it comes to harping on the gory details: Sometimes she doesn't know when to quit. "That's *if* you can stave off infections."

An awkward silence fills the space before a replay of "Monster Mash."

Kitty's pout softens her words' sting. "I hope she gets better soon."

"You hope who gets better soon, dear?" Darla's voice slinks over my shoulder, and her eyebrows jump high enough to almost brush against the underside of her midnight-blue witch's hat when I turn. All those foil stars and glitter to match her costume, but she's wearing her Keds. "Oh, Jill dear. I didn't recognize you in your doll costume."

Well, Darla dear, that makes two of us.

"My sister made it," I tell her, because even though my neighbor is probably a murderous maniac, it should still be noted that the costume was not my idea.

Darla's eyes narrow as she sizes up my sister. Darla clears her throat so roughly that the sound disperses the other women, and when it's just us three, her words come coated in venom: "You must be Kitty."

Beside me, Kitty's arm snakes around my waist, but before she can say anything, Principal Hart gusts in on a gale of khaki and forehead sweat. He peels a baseball cap the same ugly taupe as his shirt off his head and uses the tails of a crimson neckerchief to blot the moisture beaded on his brow. Overhead lights reflect off the colorful patches stitched to his shoulders, breast pockets, collar.

A Boy Scout costume is a strong choice for an elementary school principal.

Hart beams at Darla and squeegees another mass of sweat from his cheeks. "You've put on a fantastic Boogie Bash, Mrs. Lashett." He gives me a double take like he barely recognizes me. "It's good to see you, Mrs. Marshall," he adds at the exact second I've decided he's completely forgotten who I am.

"Thank you for listening to our concerns about safety tonight," I tell him. Not that it's done any good, with Darla standing right next to me, but then her beef is with the PTA women, not their kids.

Hart pats at his forehead again. "That's my job."

A thin line of sweaty dark brown rims the man's Scout cap as he leers at my little sister. He wipes his palm against his slacks before offering it to Kitty along with some line about his fancy title at the top of the elementary school hierarchy. "And you are?" he asks, hand outstretched like he's trick-or-treating.

The blush in Hart's cheeks has nothing to do with the heat. This guy is *not* hitting on my sister right here, right in front of me, in front of Darla, at freakin' Boogie Bash.

"I'm Kitty." My sister straightens her posture and tilts her head back, without even a flicker of falsies toward Hart's outstretched hand. "*Jill's* sister," she says, stressing my first name, because women's identities are more than their marital honorifics.

A bead of sweat trickles nauseatingly down the man's ear. "Mrs. Kitty?" he presses. "I had no idea Mrs. Marshall had such a lovely younger sister."

Barf.

"Just Kitty," Kitty says, like there's not a chance in hell. She begins to vibrate at my side, and I've got to remember to ask her what happened with Leaf. None of my sister's boyfriends last long, but usually there's an amazing breakup story. It's a shame to miss one, but maybe we've all been too preoccupied with the slasher villain in our midst.

Or at least I have, which is, after all, why Kitty jumped on a plane and flew all the way across the country without so much as an itinerary screenshot. My sister can only handle so many missed morning chats and ignored texts, and with the long distance stretched between us, she'd been compelled to take drastic measures.

When no one says anything, Hart's lips turn down. He claps his hands together and turns back to Mrs. Lashett. "I'll be in my office if you need me. Otherwise, I'll leave the party to you girls."

Hours pass in a blur of popcorn stink, loose confetti, and empty candy wrappers, while the Boogie Bash party playlist runs largely to theme songs from animated movies and at least seven repeats of Harry Belafonte's "Jump in the Line." Every time the track clicks over, I check my phone, hoping for a text from Rob, but every time the screen is blank. The lack of reception in the building isn't a surprise: Most schools do what they can to keep students off their devices while at school. Still, technology problems (dead phone batteries, downed cell towers, cut phone lines) are also a slasher trope, so empty bars on my phone screen aren't doing my mental health any favors.

At least the radio silence gives me an excuse not to respond to Charlene.

Finally, Boogie Bash comes to an end without bloodshed. Kellen's wife hauls herself out the fang-toothed doors without a goodbye, and Detective Hudson promises he'll be back as soon as he delivers Maribel home.

"And leave me, and Darla, and Jill?" Rosa asks with a crinkle of her painted-on whiskers.

These people *have* seen a horror movie, right? You're not supposed to separate at the end, yet somehow the one person with a gun always manages to disappear before the climax.

"I guess I could stay until he's back," Beth volunteers, her halo bobbing at Maribel's side. "Four's gotta be safer than three . . . right?"

I don't want to be the Debbie Downer, but putting the entire victim pool in one place feels a little like stocking one of the apple-bobbing barrels with all the fish. Beth staying behind makes it three against one, which is better than two . . . but it's Beth.

A groggy kaiju whimpers at my side, and I ask my sister to take my son home and get him tucked in. If the rest of us are staying behind, at least it's together. The sooner we get this place cleaned up, the sooner we can all get home safe.

"You're sure?" Kitty asks. "We can wait for you."

Maybe I should tell my sister to forget it, that Tanner can hang while we tidy up and we'll all go home at once. But Darla's taken her victims one at a time. She couldn't take all three of us at once. Besides, a sugar coma weighs against my son's eyelids and leftover brown squishes in the corner of his lips.

"Go," I tell Kitty. "I'll be home as soon as I can."

If anything *does* happen tonight, I want my baby as far away from it all as possible. Still, the rationalization doesn't prevent me from hugging Tanner so long that he cries wolf about a stomachache.

Kitty and Tanner wave goodbye as the other women get straight to work pulling apart the cafeteria tables that block the interior doors. Darla unlocks the doors that lead into the school's belly, and her crooked broom slides through, followed by Rosa's long black tail and Beth's golden wings. My sister's skirt disappears alongside my son's plush green tail as they travel back through the row of cardboard teeth in the monster's mouth, which regurgitates them back into the fresh night air.

Suddenly, I'm alone in an empty room littered with fallen confetti and discarded candy wrappers.

The school PA system clicks silent.

The cafeteria lights go black.

Nope.

Come what may, as little interest as I have in being a Final Girl, I'd rather be that than a sitting duck. I push the interior doors open and step into the darkened school.

The classroom doors are shut, their lights off, as I make my way up and down a series of hallways, toward, I think, the PTA closet. Somewhere, echoes of voices bicker over how to best proceed with cleanup, something about starting with the barrels, and the pressure in my chest breaks free—

A figure appears in the shadows at the other end of the hallway. Even in the near dark I see the gleam of the weapon in its hands.

In *her* hands.

"There you are, Jill," my sweet new neighbor's voice says. "I've been looking for you."

CHAPTER TWENTY-FOUR

When the doll emerges through the fanged entry and peels open the doors to the school, she finds the cat-suited woman alone in the center of the abandoned party room.

She's bent at the hips, the motions of her black velour limbs casting the cafeteria in a sea of sparkles as the woman works over the painted wooden barrels. Their construction-paper features smile, scream, scowl, leaking confetti onto the floor as she rocks, forward and back, her hands skimming over the tops of the barrels, collecting apples.

Water drips from the cat-suited woman's fingertips each time she lifts an apple from the water, a shallow puddle forming at her feet. The doll watches as the woman balances her weight as she pushes up onto the tip of one of her stiletto boots, driving the heel of the other into the rubber floor as she feels inside a scowling barrel. The woman's long black tail swings behind her as she spoons an apple from the pool, then drops it into the plastic grocery sack in her other hand.

The woman leans over another barrel, picks up another apple, and drops it into the plastic grocery sack—then another, then another. She sighs when a construction paper nose floats free from a jack-o'-barrel, into the water at her feet.

For the woman, the party is over. But for the doll, it's only just begun.

The doll uses her body to hold open one side of the wide double doors, her fingers gripping the threshold, her knees grinding against the frame. She watches as the woman finishes with another barrel, her heels *click-clack*ing to the next. The doll's breathing begins to rag from the weight of the door, but then the air-conditioning clicks on, covering her sounds as she sucks air in through her nose, exhales through her mouth.

An apple floats out of the woman's reach in the last barrel, and she pushes her velour sleeves to her elbows, adjusts her kitten-ear headband, and stretches forward. The ends of her locks dip into the water, and her long hair clumps together in soggy tangles when she pulls the last fruit free. The woman's profile scowls as she dredges the wet mass from the wooden barrel, holding her soggy locks like hair pulled from a drain.

Cats and water, the doll thinks as the woman flips the mass of wet hair over her shoulder, then readjusts her kitten ears. *Too bad.*

The doll lets go of the door.

She inches her way across the cafeteria floor as the door swings closed after her. Still bent over the apple-bobbing barrels, the woman startles like a bird when the door slams shut. The red fruit in her hand topples back into the water, splashing like wings in a tiny backyard pool.

The cat-suited woman's eyes go wide when she sees the doll's beautiful face.

She jerks upright and her wet palm claps across her chest. A gasp catches in her throat, but her eyes squint over the doll's dress, her blue-limned eyes, her perfect heart-shaped lips.

"You scared me half to death," the woman says.

Only half.

"I didn't realize you were still here." She returns to the task, one hand plunging elbow first, then shoulder, into another barrel, her fingers bumping apples aside to feel deeper. She sucks air between her teeth as her arm lifts out of the water.

"Cereal," the woman hisses as she inspects the soggy bit clenched in her fingers. "How come whenever there are kids around, there's *always* cereal?"

The doll says nothing. She has little interest in children, but she's not here for them.

Confetti and glitter dust up as the doll closes the distance between the doorway and the cluster of wooden barrels. She moves quickly, keeping her steps light as she sidesteps the puddles.

She doesn't want to get herself all wet, too.

The woman drops the mushy cereal bits into the plastic bag with the apples. "You'd think there'd be enough candy at a Halloween carnival that kids wouldn't need snacks from home," she says as the doll arrives beside her. "But not even trick-or-treating can get between an elementary schooler and their Froot Loops."

The doll stands at the edge of the barrels. She stares down into the water.

This close, the barrels seem deeper, the thick wooden walls stronger, the metal trim more reliable. Water ripples atop each three-foot pool, not deep enough to swim in, but deep enough for other things—like kittens—to sink.

The woman finishes with the plastic grocery sack and stoops to add it to the pile at the edge of the barrels. When she stands, the doll reaches out to stroke the long, matted tresses draped over the woman's shoulder.

The woman jerks still, her sculpted eyebrows and carefully penciled whiskers twisting in confusion. "You okay?"

"So soft," the doll says as the woman's hair slips through her fingers. Soft as kitten fur, indeed.

"Thanks?" The woman's smile is fake when she pulls away; she's pretending.

"There's more cereal," the doll says. "At the bottom."

The woman huffs at the colorful circles dredged underwater. When she reaches to fish out the soggy mass, the doll moves behind her, both feet solid on the water-slicked floor. In her stilettos, the cat-suited woman is taller, but she sways unsteadily when the doll presses in against her, pinning her against the wooden barrel.

"Deeper," the doll says as she collects the hair into a long silken rope. "There's more at the bottom."

The cat-suited woman chokes out an uncertain laugh. "I'll get it when we dump the water."

The doll doesn't respond.

"You're freaking me out."

The doll stays quiet. She pulls the silken rope through her palms.

Again.

Again.

The woman clamps her hands against the tub's rim. She leans back, bracing her knees into the barrel as the doll twists the hair rope in her hand, until the cat trembles against her.

"Let me go." The woman's voice is meant to sound hard, commanding, but panic has sharpened the edges. Her shrill tone tingles beneath the doll's skin, the sensation sizzling beneath her fingers, inside her chest.

She licks her lips when a whine builds in the woman's throat.

"Get away from me." Pinned, the woman's heels slip against the wet floor. Her hands grip the barrel's thick wooden rims as she struggles to hold herself up, but the doll presses harder. The doll yanks the rope in her hand, and the other woman's balance falters, the sharp heels beginning to slide beneath her.

The doll yanks again, this time hard to one side, and the woman's apple-picking hand splashes into the water. She hisses as her fingers scramble along the barrel's smooth interior, unable to get purchase. Her long legs begin to buckle as the doll pushes . . . pushes . . . pushes.

The woman slips, tips forward, and the doll uses the momentum to push her underwater.

She bucks.

The doll holds.

The woman thrusts her body backward, but the doll uses her own weight to push her down. Down, as her arms flail, splashing in the water. Down, as she twists and writhes and thrashes, as her kitten-ear headband bobs like an apple to the water's surface.

A sharp stiletto heel catches the doll's tights, ripping them at the knee. She lurches at the sudden pain and the woman almost breaks above water, but the doll recovers, grabs the woman's thighs, and thrusts her headfirst into the barrel, then uses her weight to hold the cat under.

It's been so long since the doll felt warm water rush over her hands while life dissolved beneath her fingertips.

The doll smiles as the woman's movements begin to go still.

She waits until the water is calm, then the doll lifts her hand and plucks at the strands of dark hair twisted between her fingers. She flicks them into the barrel, watching how they collect, like pine needles, cast down from an indifferent sky.

The kitten-ear headband floats atop the still surface, and the doll fishes the band from the barrel. She sets it atop her own head and shivers when water trickles down the sides of her cheeks.

The doll's socks squelch as she crouches beside the barrel. She drops to her hands and knees, then twists her hips and settles, enjoying the sweet splash of spilled water against her back as she plucks strips of construction paper from the rubber floor. When she's chosen eyes, a nose, and a mouth, the doll arranges herself against the wood and smooths the barrel's ruined face over her own.

She waits until the paper dries and flecks off her skin, then the doll climbs to her feet.

The woman has twisted about in the barrel. She faces upward from her shallow grave, her hair an ink cloud around sightless eyes. Her mouth is stretched into a silent scream.

The doll smiles. *It's just like before,* she thinks, *just like the last time.*

And then she heads inside the school.

CHAPTER TWENTY-FIVE

With the children gone and the haunted-house soundtrack off, the only sounds of life left in the dark, empty hallways of Brunswick Elementary belong to me, Beth, and Rosa.

And Darla.

"Jill, dear," my sweet new neighbor's voice calls, tucked somewhere in the dark at the other end of the hall. "We need to talk."

Over my dead body, which might be exactly how I end up if Darla catches me.

Her Keds thud in the hollow spaces between the claps of my Mary Janes as I sprint down the kindergarten corridor, careening through the first-grade hall and into second. Black smudges blot my peripheral vision where the heavy makeup has begun to sweat, and chemical bitterness coats my tongue when I lick my lips. One of my fake eyelashes slides down my cheek, tickling the side of my nose. Fleeing for my life from my sweet new neighbor completely sucks, but having to do it in my sister's ridiculous costume?

Actual bullshit.

The school is a maze, and I have no map, but when I round another corner, a familiar sight comes into view. Miss Frost's apple-tree door waves me toward her classroom. The knob doesn't budge when I twist, but the doorway gives me cover long enough to kick off my shoes and lose the wig. The downed falsie flutters free of my nose, and I peel the other one out of my vision as I use my arm to wipe away the ruined doll-face makeup. After I rub my forearm over my face, it comes back with a long dark smear down the center.

My whole face is probably one giant melted smear—not unlike my mother's the day she died, which might be funny in a twisty, ironic sort of way if it weren't so terribly, terribly sad.

"Is that you, Jill?" Darla's voice calls from the hallway intersection. She isn't sure which direction I've gone in, but neither am I sure what direction she's in. "Why on earth are you hiding down there in the dark?"

Because you're trying to kill me, I want to yell, but the remains of my lipstick seal my mouth shut out of sheer self-preservation. One peep and Darla will know exactly where I am. My sense of irony burns through my fear. Right now, a few minutes away, my sister is tucking my son into his bed under a constellated sky, while I'm here, trapped in a black hole of a school with a woman wearing a dress painted with glow-in-the-dark stars. This cannot be what Charlene had in mind when she suggested I write about dolls in space.

A slow, steady hum vibrates at the back of my throat. How is this happening? Like, *how* is this happening? A sweet suburban mom snapping and going on a full-blown homicidal revenge spree against a group of Mean Girl PTA moms? For sure, yeah. That part at least makes sense. But why kill one and only maim the others? To teach them some kind of lesson? I mean, I *get* it, but I don't get it. What is the endgame here? And even if this *whole* thing is some sort of elaborate disciplinary measure, what the hell does it have to do with me? Patti and Darla might not have been friends, but Darla and I are.

At least, I *thought* we were.

Darla calls out my name again, and I run my fingertips on the apple marked with Tanner's name. I infuse as much love as I can into the strokes, then kick the discarded shoes aside. My neighbor might want to lurk around these dark school hallways playing Nurse Ratched, but I am going home.

Now.

I just have to get out of this locked mousetrap of a school first.

"It's just me, dear," Darla calls, and I'm on the move.

My socks slip against the linoleum, but I manage to scramble upright and get control before I wipe out. The soft swish of skirts in the distance tells me that Darla has figured out what hallway I'm in, followed by a giggle that makes me worry I've chosen wrong. Her voice rambles on like tinnitus, a high-pitched ring over the *thunk* of locked doorknob after locked doorknob. She's talking, but I can't make out a single word.

Locked, locked, locked. Every door to every darkened classroom sticks in my grip. Every padlocked emergency exit and wire-glassed window I pass tightens the vise in my chest.

I take the next turn too hard, and my socks slide out from beneath me. A wall of KinderMats breaks my fall.

Crap.

Fourth graders don't get naptime, which means I've looped myself into a knot. The school is a series of connected squares, each grade level on its own side, offices up front, library in the back. Only the cafeteria with its fanged front doorway had been allocated for Boogie Bash, which means the rest of the school is locked up tight. One way in, one way out, just like Hart promised. To get out, I have to turn around—right back toward Darla.

This *is* a slasher movie, and I've made every single idiotic Final Girl mistake: ignoring failing technology, wearing the ridiculous outfit, walking right into the trap.

"Jill?" Darla's whine is low now, like she's trying not to scare off a frightened animal, which is me. "Wait for me."

Darla's giggle slithers under my skin. "I'm not going to hurt you."

The stitch in my side slows me down long enough to think. Kindergarten is behind me, which means I'm somewhere near the front of the school, which means the administrative offices are somewhere close.

Up ahead, at the corner: the PTA closet.

I run like hell for the door, but the knob sticks in my grip. Why is it locked? Other than the cafeteria, this is *literally* the one door that's supposed to be open.

I press my forehead to the door and palm at the wood. "Beth? Rosa?"

Anyone in the little room—anyone still conscious, anyway—would hear the words spit between my clenched teeth, but there isn't so much as breath on the other side of the locked PTA closet door. I rattle the doorknob for good measure. Hammer my first against the door when it still doesn't give.

My body chose flight, but one wrong turn could lead into a fight. In a one-on-one fight, I could take Darla . . . probably. A million years ago, I had some childhood spats with my little sister, but these days my strongest muscles are in my typing fingers. I've seen Darla hoist her own body weight in storage tubs, not to mention what she's accomplished with gardening tools and kitchen gadgets. If an ice cream scoop can be a weapon in the woman's hands, anything can.

I check my phone, but it's still dead.

"Jill!" Somewhere in the distance, the rustle of Darla's skirts. "Stop running. I need to talk to you."

I don't want to fight with my neighbor.

Trapped between the PTA closet door and a hand-to-hand fight, I remind myself I'm a horror author. I know this story. I can plot my way through this. I just have to think through the scene.

Hiding in a classroom is out; they're all locked. Elementary school windows are reinforced with wire mesh so they don't shatter during a fire, so busting out isn't an option. The emergency exits are padlocked. There's probably a fire alarm somewhere, definitely some sort of security alarm, but who knows where that could be.

And where the crap are Rosa and Beth?

Wait.

Rosa and Beth *and* Hart. I'd forgotten all about the principal, who'd said he'd be in his office. If the women aren't in the PTA closet, then maybe they're in the office with the principal?

The man's not exactly the hero type, but his office will have a landline, which means a way to call for help. A cell-signal blocker is one online shopping cart away, but surely Darla didn't think to cut the phone lines? Nobody even remembers landlines anymore.

"Jill, dear, we need to talk." Darla's voice is too close.

It's so dark I can barely make out her features when she steps around the corner, directly between me and what I *think* might be the right way to the principal's office and that glorious, lifesaving, prehistoric grounded phone line.

The rod in Darla's hand stretches from her elbow to her wrist, round at one end. The heavy hallway shadows obscure the stars glowing on her dress, but the silver in her hand still has some luster in the pale light.

My hands are up, pushing her away from twenty feet. "There's nothing to talk about, Darla."

I imagine she's smiling, because Darla is always smiling. The rod in her hand gleams in some trick of the meager light of the darkened hallway, and it's not a rod, it's that cereal-killer kid's costume spoon.

It might be silly, were it not for that ice cream scooper.

The prop adds a good foot to Darla's reach. I can outrun her—if she doesn't pin me against the wall first.

Fifteen feet and mine are moving backward as I ready to flee.

"Where are Beth and Rosa?" I ask, and if a question slows Darla down, gets her talking, good. If she tells me where the other women are, even better.

We're only ten feet apart now, and my knees quiver when she takes another step forward. "I've taken care of Beth, but that's what I'm trying to tell you. Rosa . . ."

The way she doesn't finish her sentence tells me everything I need to know.

"You killed her like you killed Barb!" The words burst out of me. "I know it was you, Darla."

She shakes her head. "I . . . I overreacted."

No shit she overreacted. "You sawed the woman's throat open with a bread knife!"

Darla shakes her head. Her hands rise, the empty one like that of a little kid caught with her hand in the cookie jar, the other one brandishing silver like a movie villain. "I was inspired by what you'd said at the café."

"When I said to feast on your enemies, I meant the croissants—it was figurative, Darla!" She is *not* about to blame this on me. "And Maribel and Kellen and Sasha, were they overreactions, too?" Eight feet now, and my feet are still inching backward, but Darla's have started to inch forward. If I'm going to pull off this escape, there's not much time.

"I just wanted to help make them better," Darla says, close enough now that I can see her pink smile, her powdered-doughnut cheeks. "I meant what I said on Doll's Night. I wanted to help them get rid of their flaws. Give them fresh starts."

This woman has a real problem with metaphor. "Is that what you're going to do to me, too? Carve me up like Barb? Stab my skull, gouge my eyes, scalp my head?"

Darla inches closer and the distance narrows. "Oh, Jill, I would *never*—you're my friend," she says impatiently, like mine is a completely unreasonable question. "My neighbor!"

A problem with synonyms then, too.

One of my feet slides too fast and trips over my other, but the wall helps keep me upright. "So was Patti! I know about the restraining order, Darla."

Darla's smile breaks into a shaggy sneer. "Patti was just like them!" Darla's voice rises until it's almost a yell. "Just as catty, just as self-centered, just as *ugly*. No matter what I did, she was *never* my friend—always too good, too much better than me. When she left and you moved in, I thought you'd be just like them." Darla shakes her head, and the rough edges of her rictus grin soften into her usual smile, then begin to melt. "But you're not. You're like *me*!"

"I'm *nothing* like you." My little slides have taken me to the end of the hall, but when I peer around the corner, there's a light. A big, beautiful beacon to the administrative offices, and behind a pane of frosted glass are human-shaped shadows. I hadn't been going the wrong way after all. "You're just the same as Patti. You were never *my* friend. You figured out what kind of dog I had, read my books, asked about my sister." Realization is a hurricane in my head. Nothing that had happened since I'd met Darla had been an accident—a *coincidence*—not even being invited to that first PTA brunch. Darla promised no obligation, but she'd had the PTA pocket folder waiting in her minivan.

That Darla is the Dream Bean Killer only stings half as much as the betrayal.

"You stole Lugosi's tennis ball and pretended it rolled down the street!" I scream at her. "*You* moved my Keurig!"

"Jill," Darla says sweetly, "the Keurig was in the wrong place." She keeps going. "After Patti left, I figured out a way to help the rest of the Brunswick PTA get a fresh start, too. I was going to help them shed their flaws, release their inner beauty, and then when I met you, I realized that I could still carry out my plan, but I wouldn't just be helping those other women with their fresh starts, I'd be helping *you*, too!" Darla moves as she speaks, closing what little distance separates us. "Oh, but Jill, dear, don't you see? I didn't do this just for me. I did it for you, too, because I *am* your friend! You were struggling so hard to come up with a concept for your new book, and I wanted to inspire you just like you'd inspired me!"

Holy shit. I've been so worried about moving into Stepford that I didn't realize I'd shacked up next door to Annie Wilkes. One hell of a combo for a slasher villain: a batshit-crazy woman in love with an idea and willing to destroy other people's lives for it—especially if it gives her bestie a new story line.

It's almost an honor, until Darla attempts to sledgehammer my ankle, hobble me with a giant toy cereal spoon.

"So why did you leave your mask outside my window?" The rest I can twist into logic, but not the face hung outside my window. "Kellen screamed that day we found the tub of masks because she recognized it. You must have known I'd figure it out, why else would you hang it outside my front door if not to scare me? It was a threat."

The light behind me illuminates Darla's face as she stops in her tracks, confusion twisting her features. "You're mistaken, dear. I never hung a mask outside your house."

Stalk, threaten, terrorize—and now she's going to gaslight me? "So *that's* the part you didn't do?" Of all the horror, if that stupid mask strung on my lawn is the one thing that's actually a prank . . . "Pert nose, blond hair to the jawline, beauty mark. You expect me to believe some rando hung a copycat mask on *my* house when *my* neighbor is the Dream Bean Killer?"

Bad ending, even for this story.

"My mask *was* at home, but it went missing, and then . . ." Darla cuts herself off with a shake of her head, like she's gotten it wrong, needs to start over. "Jill, I *need* to tell you—"

Whatever she needs to tell me, I don't want to hear it. My foot slides out in front of me when I bolt around the corner, and my leg hits the ground hard enough to shove my kneecap up between my eyes, but I'm back on my feet, running, running, running toward the shadowy figures in the office light.

I think I'm yelling, too, because my mouth is already open when I blast into the principal's office.

One of the shadowed figures is a coatrack. The other used to be the principal. Whatever tool she'd used when she'd gotten to Hart, it wasn't strong enough for Darla to saw through the man's neck.

Not all the way, at least.

She'd started at the back, then worked her way around. The man's head hangs tilted forward and to the side, far enough offset that you know the two halves of the neck won't match up when you try to fix the head upright. Red limns his bulged and bloodshot eyes, drips down his cheeks to join the red gouge that rims his throat, and his tongue spools out between parted lips. A knot of jagged white sticks out from where the man's throat should be—bone, maybe, or spinal cord.

The scream building in my throat clogs my ears. I pinch my nose and squeeze my knees because if I don't, I am going to puke, or pass out, or pee my skirts.

Footsteps are in the hallway now. Darla's voice calls, but I can't hear her over the water in my brain.

I don't look at Hart as I scramble around his desk, not at the way his body sags in his chair, pulled down by fluid and deadweight. *This is Boogie Bash*, I remind myself. *This is Boogie Bash, and it's just a prop in the principal's chair.*

The floor turns slick under my feet, then warm, then wet. Just a prop—and this, all this, it's just like before, just like with Mom.

The footsteps are closer.

The phone is dead when I finally get my hand on the phone receiver on the desk. Darla remembered to cut the landline after all.

"Jill, have you heard anything I said?" She's winded when she slides into the threshold, blocking the doorway. Silver glimmers at her side, tucked in the midnight-blue folds of her skirt. "I'm trying to warn you—"

"Stay back, Darla." This may be a slasher, but the villain already had her monologue. Now it's time for the Final Girl's speech. "You almost had me, back in the hallway. For a second, I'd almost thought that there might be *some* tiny little bit of you that was telling the truth—that's actually my friend—but this?" I motion to the dead man, slumped over, mostly headless, in his desk chair. "This is ugly, Darla." Darla blanches like I've slapped her. "And so are you, and it doesn't have a damn thing to do with your outsides."

The little slate with the apple lettering slides out of the metal holder when I snatch the placard off Hart's desk. One of its sharp square corners catches her forearm when I slash at the woman in front of me.

A long red line swells on her skin and Darla raises her arm, trying to fend me off as my next slash catches her palm. My next opens her cheek. The kid's costume prop hits the floor, and I kick it away, still slashing little red stitches in her arms, her hands, her throat.

Darla crumbles, and I shove past her, bouncing off the door as I run as fast as my socked feet will carry me out of the office. Now I know where I'm going. Up ahead, the lights in the cafeteria are on.

My sights are set on the fang-toothed exit when I remember the lights were off when I left—and those faraway voices bickering, one saying to start with the barrels.

There's a moment in every horror movie when the monster is right behind you: The creature appears full frame for the first time, the villain is revealed in the light. This is that moment.

I close my eyes and turn. When I open them, the first thing I see is a pair of stunning calves crooked over the edge of one of the apple-bobbing barrels. Rosa's stilettos stab upward from the water, the heel of one shoe caught on the rim, her body held under.

Drowned, she floats in the shallow water, her hair splayed out on either side of her.

Just like Norman.

"I wondered when you'd show up," a voice says.

The scream I keep swallowing begins to fizz at the base of my throat. It hits a boil and my knees go soft, crumbling my body to the floor in a puddle of blood-soaked stockings and blue tulle.

Red drips from the long, thin blade clutched in her hand as she emerges from behind a wooden scene flat. Rosa's kitten-ear headband sits atop her red yarn wig, her blue dress is coated in red, and the white cream paint on her cheeks is pink with other people's blood.

My sister grins. "Are you ready for the plot twist, Jilly Bean?"

CHAPTER TWENTY-SIX

Kitty's petticoat claps against her thighs when she steps out from behind the wooden graveyard at the back of the school cafeteria. Deep splotches of dripping crimson stain the blue doll's dress. Red ribbons unfurl down her stockings, bleeding the torn white stripes pink as she pads in her Mary Janes toward the cluster of wooden barrels in the center of the room.

"Hi, Jill from New York!" Acoustics stretch her voice as Kitty stalks toward her sister, frozen like a frightened deer in the room's fanged exit. Kitty trails the blade's tip along the wood as she moves through the barrels, knees locked, steps stiff and mechanical. She comes to a stop, her Mary Janes shoulder width apart, and stares at her sister's dark hair frizzing where red braids should be.

All this, and she didn't even bother to stay in costume.

"I mean *New Jersey*." Kitty adjusts her kitten-ear headband. "Do I *finally* have your attention?"

Her sister has lost the yarn wig and the black Mary Janes, both sets of her falsies, but her dress is still as blue as the eye shadow ringed around her eyes. Kitty watches emotions spill across her sister's face: panic, recognition, relief. Her red-heart lips shape a name, but then her eyes clock the blade's razor-sharp edge, the thin line dripping crimson, and her brows crease, her jaw clenches, but she doesn't step back.

It's so cute that Kitty can't help but laugh. "Oh, Jilly Bean, you look so surprised."

Kitty raises the paper-cutter guillotine blade above her head, clasps her hands together, and spins like a music-box ballerina. Red drops like sequins fly from her skirt, drip when she curtsies, and smear when the curved blade sweeps across the floor. "Don't you like my best villain look of the season?" she screams. "It's the one you can't stop talking about!"

Her sister's gaze darts between the smears, then at the crimson drops, last at the congregation of water-filled barrels, expressionless without their construction-paper faces. She starts to say something about the drowned woman, but then cuts herself off, screaming about her own precious baby doll.

When Kitty twirls instead of answers, the sister asks again. *Offspring, offspring,* her voice flaps like wings, flimsy little bird wings on a hot summer afternoon. All she cares about is what happened to that little crotch goblin, that little attention sponge.

She reminds Kitty that they're *sisters.*

Kitty stops her spin cold and squares her feet in a shallow puddle. "Now, we have to be careful that we don't let our emotional attachment do all the talking." She clicks her tongue. The kitten-ear headband has slipped askew in all her twirling, and she rights it with her blade hand. "You have to let go of the things that you have no control over, Jill. You need to learn to be *present.* Get your nose out of the books, Jillian!"

In her hand, the blade drips as Kitty flings her arms wide, an inspired pose. "I mean, look where we are!" She stabs at the tables of forgotten sweets at one end of the room, the abandoned party games and discarded wooden cutouts at the other.

"All the world's a stage, isn't it? This one is just like a scene from a horror movie." Kitty talks over her shoulder while she totters to the barrels in the center of the room. "My favorite is the one with the girl who fought off vampires at her high school dance. But you probably prefer the one where the kids dump blood all over the prom queen?

I'd love to disagree, but that's OG right there." Kitty makes her fingers into a chef's kiss, then smacks her lips. "Original."

More spilled water pools between the wooden dams, and red from her stockings tinges the little pool pink as she weaves among the barrels. Her sister calls her name again, asks what the hell some movie has to do with tonight, with *this,* as she tiptoes between the puddles.

Kitty pauses so her sister can name that movie, too. Tell her it's based on a book, that both versions end in fire. Her sister likes to be right, but she needs to *pay attention.*

"Do you have any idea how hard it would be to *sneak* five hundred gallons of pigs' blood into an elementary school? Five *hundred* gallons?" Kitty plunges one hand into the only full barrel in the room and fishes out the drowned cat's tail. She cuts it to test the thin blade. The grip seemed much more solid before, its heft so much meatier, when she'd wrested the sharp arm from the paper cutter.

But that was before she'd used it on the principal.

"It's so much easier to work with what's already *inside* the school." Kitty pricks the blade's edge against her fingertip and smiles when a red teardrop beads on her skin. "It's just a shame that guillotine paper-cutter blades are only made to cut a few millimeters at a time."

Kitty drags the blade across her palm, and her sister stumbles at the other end of the room. "Twenty pages, that's it!" she says, about the blade's strength. "Do you have any idea how hard it is to cut off a head with a blade only made to cut through a few sheets of paper?" Kitty hitches one knee against one of the wooden barrels. "You really have to *commit* to—"

A sharp screech on the other side of the cafeteria jerks Kitty's attention away as the witch crashes into the cafeteria.

"*You.*" Kitty swings the blade at the other woman. "You thought you could take my sister away from me!"

The witch narrows her eyes while the sister's face warms from pale to pink. She says something else about her offspring and smears at the tears running down her face.

"Oh, Jilly Bean, *this* is who you've replaced me with?" Kitty points the blade at the witch, then holds it dripping high above her head as she swings one Mary Jane over the barrel's edge. Cool water soaks through her skin as her legs sink into the shallow depths. The red from her tights tints the water pink. "You're always so smart, so perceptive, so focused on the details, and yet you still manage to get things so terribly, *tragically* wrong. It'd be cute if it weren't so *boring*. Two stars."

She spins in the barrel, aiming the blade at a collection of wooden tombstones at the edge of the room, then the witch, then at the drowned cat. Kitty settles herself onto the rim of the barrel, dangles her feet in the blood-tinged water, and glares at her sister.

"Being an influencer comes with a lot of perks, you know. I get to show other women how to live their best, most *fulfilled* lives—but pathetic suburban women are always the same: too busy slogging through their sad suburban existence to even think about how sad and pathetic they are. They waste their beauty and their youth, Jill, just throw it away on husbands who don't even notice their last haircut, much less remember much of anything else. You *mommies* and *wives* try to achieve normal, to achieve better-than-usual, to achieve *perfection,* and for who—your husbands, your *children*?" Kitty rolls her eyes and laughs. "You're always so worried about not fitting in—did you ever actually take two seconds and think about why you even wanted to be one of them?

"Don't you remember Mom, Jilly Bean?" Kitty wraps her arms so tightly around herself that the blade's wet edge kisses her cheek. "That perfect little family was all she ever wanted, and then Dad left, and we weren't *enough* anymore for her. So she left us, too!"

The sister says something, on the other side of the room, but Kitty holds the blade against her own throat. She isn't finished.

"And what did you do when she decided to leave, Jill? I tried to get your attention, tried to make you *see me,* but you'd rather lie there on that stupid waterbed and watch her die!" A lick of salt turns her words bitter while her sister screams back at her from the other side of the room, something about how they were just children, how she was just a child.

"And what did you promise, Jill? What did you tell me the day that Mom left?"

Kitty doesn't wait for an answer.

"You promised to always take care of me—*always*! But you didn't keep your promise, did you, Jilly Bean?" she sneers. "You left me behind. You went and started your own family, with your *own* children. You moved farther and farther away—like I'm nothing!"

Kitty's voice scratches her throat on the way out. "You left me, and I had to find a way to get your attention, so you didn't forget all about me."

The blade in her hands is chipped in some places, but still sharp enough to hold on to the bits of flesh and tendon in its teeth. "I gotta hand it to you, Darla." She taps the blade to her temple. "Head wounds are a *lot* harder than they look."

Red smears like lipstick when she wipes the blade on her skirt. Then she touches its tip to her mouth, her nose, her eyes. "The human head contains twenty bones and up to thirty-two teeth, most of our five sensory organs. The brain, obviously"—Kitty taps the guillotine handle against her head—"and then there's all the muscles and glands and nerves and veins and arteries and ligaments. There's so much to cut through that one blow to the neck does practically nothing." She draws the blade's edge down the side of her face until it rests against her throat. She reflects on the mess in the principal's office, what she'd left in the chair behind the desk. "Two isn't much better. You practically have to saw through."

Kitty flings one leg over the edge of the wooden barrel. Her other catches the rim as she slides to the floor, and a pink tidal wave rushes under her legs when the pool dumps over.

She ignores the water. She marches to another barrel and grabs a floating swatch of matted dark hair. "Water is a much simpler death. No mess."

She wrenches the drowned woman's head out of the water, twisting the face under the low light as she admires the sheen on her wet skin, the way droplets collect in her eyelashes, in the corners of her lips. "Beheading is such a nasty business. Drowning is much prettier."

Her sister is surprised. Kitty can tell.

"Did you know that doctors in the 1700s believed a severed head could retain consciousness, maybe even feel pain, for up to a minute?" She studies the drowned woman's face. "Guess what they suggested as an alternative method of execution?" She points the dead woman's head in her sister's direction, so that its mouth opens as if in answer.

"Drowning!" Kitty lets the head drop back into the water. "Isn't that ironic?"

Her sister says something about the bird, about how finding him drowned and floating in the backyard pool on the day—*that* day—must have done something, broken something—

"*Finding* him? Don't you get it, Jill? Norman didn't drown. *I* drowned him!"

Kitty jumps to her feet, the blade swinging in her grip. "I held that stupid bird underwater until he stopped twitching while you were watching our mother die! How did you *think* he got into the pool, Jill? He was a *bird.* He had *wings*!"

Kitty flings her arms out, not wide enough to touch the sides of the room, just wide enough to fly.

"Mom saw the whole thing, you know. She was supposed to be watching me swim—I *begged* her to come out and watch me—but she just sat there drooling on the porch, so I climbed out of the pool, and I walked right over, right in front of her, and I opened the cage, and I took Norman out." Kitty looks at her palm, at the tiny white line barely there on the end of her index finger. She pricks the scar with the blade's tip. "The little asshole pecked my hand when I wrapped my fingers around him, but you didn't even see the blood, did you, Jill?" Red swells on her skin.

"You know, it's actually kind of sad. That was the *one time* you didn't tell me I'd gotten something wrong."

Kitty uses the blade to prick the tip of her middle finger, then ring, pinkie.

"You named him Norman because of the movie, *Psycho,* the one we watched for Halloween, remember? You didn't tell me that Norman Bates decapitated Marion Crane in the book, but I found out for myself. Just because you're an author doesn't mean you're the only one who knows how to read."

Red streams down Kitty's hand, the stitches at the ends of her fingers cut open. She presses the blade into the soft lump of muscle inside her forearm until color swells underneath as she pulls open a long red stitch on the inside of her arm.

"You promised, but you didn't *take care* of me, did you, Jilly Bean?"

Kitty holds the guillotine blade to her throat, presses the edge into her skin until both turn warm. Until red runs down her fingers. "What do I have to do to get your attention? I had to come all the way here just to get your attention, and you're right: You can see *everything* through all those little eyeball windows, right into your office. I thought I'd make it look like Darla was the next in the string of attacks, but then I saw the police report on your monitor, and an opportunity presented itself when I found the mask on your corkboard in her car's back seat." Kitty points at Darla. "But even with all of that in your face—even when I filmed a makeup tutorial *in your basement*—you still never thought about me, did you? I was right under your nose, down in that stupid soundproofed basement, and you never even knew! You were so preoccupied with Darla, Darla, Darla—did you even notice how much her mask looks like Mom?"

Kitty stares at her sister. She slices again, deeper.

Again.

Again.

"Are you going to take care of me now, Jilly Bean?"

CHAPTER TWENTY-SEVEN

This can't be real.

Back home, the evidence trail pinned on my office corkboard points to Darla. Darla, who murdered Barb. Darla, who stabbed Maribel, who gouged Kellen, who scalped Sasha.

Darla is the Dream Bean Killer, the Doll-Faced Killer. Not my sister. Not Kitty.

And yet . . .

Kitty stands over a woman she's drowned in an apple-bobbing barrel. Kitty stands drenched in someone else's blood. Kitty stands with a bloodied paper-cutter blade pressed to her throat.

That long-ago day in my mother's bedroom rushes back into memory: my mother, surrounded by compacts in the closet. My sister, vibrating at the foot of the bed. The stink of chlorine and lipstick wax fills my nose, while my little sister's screech about the bird in the pool stings my ears. I ride the ripples of Norman's wings, splayed out in the current of pine-needled water while my mother slices at her skin from the bedroom carpet, and then all is silent, and red, and still.

We all go a little mad sometimes, don't we?

There are so many ways for a woman to come unstitched.

The paper-cutter blade draws a thin red stitch across my sister's throat. "Are you going to take care of me now, Jilly Bean?" she asks again, and I'm ripped back into the present.

"Kitty, stop." It had been all I'd managed before.

You're lying. Stop. Please stop.

Because you lie about everything.

Sour fluid fills my mouth, coating the words forming against the back of my teeth. I want to scream about Rosa, floating in a wooden apple-bobbing barrel in the center of the school cafeteria. About Beth, still missing. About Hart, sawed nearly headless in his office.

About Mom, and about Norman.

Tanner. Oh my God. My son.

He'd left Boogie Bash with my sister.

A thin red line drips down Kitty's neck, blotting itself on the frill of her collar. I don't care if my sweet new neighbor is a murderess, if my sister is a monster. All I care about is my son.

"Where is Tanner?" The taste of his name on my tongue makes me gag. "Kitty, what have you done to my son?"

The words louder now, more urgent, scratching my insides raw, tearing my insides open just like the blade at my sister's throat.

Kitty's lower lip puffs out in an exaggerated pout. "You still don't care about me, do you?" She pulls the blade, cutting another stich. "I got him home like you asked because *I'm a good sister*!" The end of her sentence ends in a scream as she points the red blade at me. "*I* don't break *my* promises," she screams again.

Beside me, Darla's skirts swish. Silver from the costume spoon hums along the edge of my peripheral vision as she draws closer, her skin raw and red where the principal's nameplate scratched open her forearms, her chest. "Jill, dear—"

"Get away from my sister!" In the barrel Kitty's hand flexes around the paper cutter.

Not the handle. She's grabbed the blade. Red wells between her fingers, and I motion Darla away. Just because my sister *is* a monster doesn't mean that my neighbor *isn't.* Kitty killed Rosa and Hart, but she had nothing to do with the other women.

"Get away, Darla!" The words rip from my throat. "Stay away from me!"

Kitty presses the blade against her skin again. Crimson ribbons run from the dashes on her arms, her ankles, her neck.

A second line spreads open on one side, and the bright drop on Kitty's throat is as red as the yarn braids on her head—as the streak that runs down her forearm, beads on her elbow, drips to the puddle at her black Mary Janes.

My sister is stark-raving mad. My neighbor is a lunatic.

But my son is fine.

He's fine, he's fine. I can breathe again. Whatever happens next, Tanner is safe.

"Jill, dear. Listen to me." Darla's close enough that one long reach would connect our fingertips, but I'm moving now, tepid tub water trickling over my toes as the school's fanged exit shrinks at my back. "I'm your friend," she says. "I'm here to help you."

"Kitty, don't do this." I ignore the other woman and take another step toward my sister. Whatever else, she's still my sister. I may have failed my mother, may even have failed my sister. Mom's is dead, but Kitty is still here, still alive, and I won't watch someone else I love cut herself apart on the floor.

Not again.

Wet soaks through my stockings. This close, I can see where the freckles Kitty dotted on her cheeks have smudged into bruises. Where the dim overhead lights catch in the whites of her eyes, and the red heart painted on her lips has started to rub away from her licking her lips. She might be paling already from blood loss, or that might just be the cream paint.

"Please, Jilly Bean." Kitty's pout is made for the camera. "Pay attention." She pushes the curved edge deep into her skin and pulls the blade across her throat.

Behind me, Darla's voice is lost in the thunder of my footfalls as I rush across the confetti-soaked floor to my sister, unballing my fists as I reach for her weapon. One hand closes over the end of the blade, the other over Kitty's fist. I catch fire in one hand, a red pigtail in my grip. The yarn does nothing to lessen the pain that radiates through my fingers when the blade bites under my knuckles.

I tug hard enough to jerk Kitty's wig askew, but not enough to wrench the blade away from her throat.

"Let go, Katherine!" I use my Big Sister Voice.

My sister's free hand clamps between mine in the center of the blade. She squeezes, and the red from her cuts soak into mine, turning the metal slick in our hands. "Make me, Jillian."

The blade warms my palm. Kitty's fingers twitch under mine. And pain, so much pain.

This is not the time to fight with my sister.

Darla shouts from the other side of the cafeteria, but Kitty's laugh drowns out the words. Her wig is still caught under my hand, and when she pulls back, her head cocks to the side, stretching the cut in her neck. Her pout twists into a sinister smirk, and a demented doll, not my sister, stares back at me over the dripping red steel.

"Do you ever think about Mom, Jilly?" the Kitty doll asks. "Do you replay that day in your head, over and over and over—what you saw, what you sat there and let happen while you did *nothing*?" She holds tight to the rubber handle, and our eyes lock over the red-slicked blade. "Do you think about how you watched our mother die?"

The hand wrapped around Kitty's fist loosens and slides down onto the blade. This time I feel nothing when the metal slides through my skin.

"No."

Kitty's eyes go dark on the other side of the blade. "You're lying."

I am lying. I remember everything: how Mom padded on creams and foundations but didn't blend the lines at her throat. How she smeared blue eye shadow around her eyes, ringed her lips in shades of pink, scarlet, and fuchsia. I didn't see the lines at first. The stitches.

I didn't know she was making herself up to die.

"We were kids, Kitty." I didn't know what was happening until it was too late. "Just because I'm older than you doesn't mean I wasn't a child, too. She left *both of* us."

My sister tightens her grip on the bloody blade and pulls the sharp edge closer to her, and suddenly my hands are helping to push the sharp metal into soft flesh, to spill red. Puddles squelch under her shoes when she adjusts her stance.

"Maybe it's my fault," she says, the pressure on her neck straining her voice, so it comes out in a childish whine. A tear drips down Kitty's cheek. "Do you think what I did to Norman pushed her over the edge?"

Did it?

Another drop spills from Kitty's eye and slips down her cheek. Red runs from the gash on her neck, staining the top of her doll-dress bodice.

"Did she kill herself because of me?" my sister asks, but she doesn't stop cutting herself until I relax my grip.

"Mom was sick, Kitty." I let one hand fall away so that my fingers can wipe away her tears. "That's all. She was depressed and she needed help, and it wasn't our fault that she didn't get it." I cup my sister's chin in my palm and blood smears her jaw red, just like Mom's, but I blink the memory away and stare into my little sister's eyes. "What happened to Mom had absolutely nothing to do with you."

Kitty smiles.

She smiles harder.

Her grin stretches across her face like ink in water, curling from ear to ear.

She digs her chin into my palm, pushes her throat against the blade, and hacks out a laugh. "That's *your* biggest flaw, sweet sister," she says. A pink triangle darts out to lick the thick blood smeared on the blade, then she tongues the thick stuff around her mouth until her lips shine red. "You can't see what's right in front of you. You never could."

My free hand clamps back down on the blade in my sister's hands. I yank at it, try to wrench the sharp edge from the tender skin of her neck—but it's too late.

Kitty pulls the handle down and back, and her red yarn braids fly off her head when the blade slices through my palm on its journey toward her rib cage. Sudden, searing pain screams up one hand, into my arm, my shoulders, but I keep my other hand wrapped around my sister's on the handle.

Someone's foot slips in the spilled water, and we go down together, tumbling in a bloody heap to the filthy floor, both of us grappling for the blade, carving red stitches across each other's skin. Wind rushes out of my lungs when my back hits the hard floor and metallic water rushes against my scalp. I suck in air and reach for the blade, but Kitty's fist is still clenched around the handle, and when she pulls, it slips through my mangled hands.

Kitty knees me in the ribs and stars blink in the dark spots the pain leaves in my vision. My sister scrambles over me, on top of me, until she's straddling my waist. She grinds her weight into my lungs to keep my breath short. Before I can get my arms up, pull her off me, she scoots her body forward and stamps my elbows down with her knees.

I can't move. I can barely breathe.

My sister twists the curved blade in her hands, slicing off a layer of both of our palms as she leans down and presses the sharp edge into my throat. I feel the blade bite into my neck. Feel warmth spill over my skin.

"Stop," I try to say. "Please," I think I say, but the doll on top of me pushes harder, and the light starts to fade.

Pain sears.

Dark spots bloom.

I think of my darling husband. Of my son. Of my dog.

Stars move behind my sister. Over Kitty's shoulder, Darla raises the silver rod over her head, and her eyes meet mine.

Dolls in space, I have time to think, and over Kitty's shoulder, Darla swings the cereal killer's spoon.

From the way the rod falls, I know the prop is heavier than I'd thought. I flinch when it makes contact, the loud crack whipping through the cafeteria's acoustics. My sister slumps to the side, unconscious in a pool of her own blood and water.

"Jill, dear, I was trying to tell you." Darla still holds the prop weapon as she stands over me. She clamps one hand over her heart and blows a deep exhale, chest bobbing. "Your sister is a bit of a problem."

Darla rolls Kitty's body onto its back. She's unconscious, but breathing, and Darla helps me sit up. She leaves me to breathe while she dumps apples from the plastic grocery sacks left scattered around the faceless barrels, then shakes the bags out.

"What happens now?" I ask. My ruined hands smear bloody trails on the floor when I struggle to push myself up, but Darla's back, standing over me with plastic bags ready in her hands. "Are you going to suffocate me?"

"Of course not, dear." Darla tsks, like it's a silly suggestion.

She twists the bags into ropes.

She'll strangle me, then. Wrap the plastic around my neck and squeeze.

Just because I didn't suspect Kitty doesn't mean I was wrong about Darla.

My palms press against the rubber floor, slip in the spilled water. There's a horrible pain in one of my legs and my wrists won't bend. Nothing's broken, but every part of my body hurts.

Darla titters as she drops to her knees, talking as she ties plastic sacks around Kitty's arms to stanch the bleeding. "I never intended to hurt anyone, Jill, dear. Especially you. Not after we met."

She shuffles to Rosa's body and unclips the tail from her costume. Back over to Kitty, she wraps the tail around my sister's elbows, then works it into a complicated knot. "You were so kind to me, not like those other girls. All I wanted to do was to help them see their flaws, help them *improve*—become more beautiful versions of themselves."

Darla smiles at me, every bit as batshit crazy as my sister.

"You killed Barb."

Darla's smile sinks. "She pushed me so far. She got me so mad." The woman's hands clench into cannonball fists, and her supernova wedding ring sparkles under the cafeteria lights. Pink sparkles, thanks to the red streamers dangling overhead. "Anyway, after that unfortunate . . . event . . . I was more careful. I guess she was a lesson for *me*." Darla casts a sad, sidelong glance at Rosa's barrel. "I'd wanted to teach Rosa next, but I was too late. I knew when I saw her, I was too late."

I don't know if *her* is Rosa or Kitty.

"She meant to kill me. Kitty." My thoughts swim in hectic circles around the bloody doll on the floor. This can't be real. Can't be right. "My sister meant to *kill me*."

Just like she'd killed Norman and Hart and Rosa. *Had* Mom known about Kitty? Had our sister somehow been involved in our mother's death?

Darla shakes her head. "When you found my mask in your yard, I knew something was wrong. Then I saw your furnace in the back of one of Kitty's social posts." Darla doesn't flinch when she tells me she'd been cyber-stalking my sister.

I remember the shiny silver streak in the background of Kitty's *Beetlejuice* photo. Kitty had been so curious about the furnace in my basement.

"I knew something was wrong when she was here tonight," Darla says about Kitty. "I told Beth to run."

Beth. I'd almost forgotten all about Beth. "Where is she?"

"Calling for help. There's a set of spare keys in the front office.

I know where they are. I gave them to her and told her to leave through the side exit, call Steve and nine one one."

"I don't understand." I really, *really* don't. "You saved me—why?"

Darla lowers herself beside me on the wet cafeteria floor. "Because you're my friend. Aren't you?"

"Yes, Darla." My sweet new neighbor hurt other women but saved me from my own sister. And I'd thought my husband would never understand the complexity of female friendships. "We're friends."

What was it Kitty had said, earlier in my bedroom—that a person can be more than one thing? My sister is psychotic, but she's still my sister. Darla brutally mutilated three women, slaughtered another, but she saved my life because she's my friend. Beauty really is in the eye of the beholder, isn't it?

For a few moments we sit in silence side by side, covered in blood and confetti. Then the doors of the school's fanged maw open, and Detective Hudson leads a gang of uniformed officers into the cafeteria.

CHAPTER TWENTY-EIGHT

Detective Steve Hudson's big black police SUV flashes red and blue on Brunswick Elementary's fanged front entry. Cool nighttime air has wilted the balloon archway over the entrance, but the gauzy sheet ghosts still sway from oak branches. Pumpkin litter and fallen leaves still speckle the school's front lawn. It isn't the scent of sugar and chemical popcorn butter that hangs on the breeze now, but it smells like Halloween just the same.

Darla Lashett's last Boogie Bash as PTA president has ended with a bang after all.

A cold current sweeps through my chest when my butt hits the ambulance tailgate. "I need to be taken home," I tell the uniform who wraps a blanket around my shoulders. One of the medics said the thin foil would keep me warm, but my insides won't stop rattling any more than my fingers will stop squeezing the mass of red yarn in my hands. "I need to check on my son."

Blood from my sister's wig stains the bandages wrapped around my hands. Her blood. Mine. Hart's, too, probably.

"We're sending a car to get him now." The too-young officer talks to me like he's afraid I might break.

I might. I might fall apart if I don't get my arms around Tanner.

"Mrs. Marshall," he says, to be sure he has my attention. "I need to get your statement while things are fresh."

While things are fresh? I'm going to remember every second of this night for the rest of my life.

Before I can say anything, another ambulance brakes to a stop behind the row of police cars in the school drop-off lane, lights flashing, sirens off. A gruff older officer shuffles past, gesturing for the young cop to stay with me. Whatever Beth had told Hudson when she'd called for help, he'd brought backup. Hart's body had been loaded into the first ambulance to arrive on scene, but someone had had to peel the detective's dead wife out of his arms before he let her go. I've never before heard a man make the sound that came out of Steve's mouth when they took Rosa away.

Part of me wonders if the principal's head had stayed attached when the paramedics transferred him from chair to gurney. The rest of me doesn't want to know.

The younger officer shifts his weight, but it's nerves, not impatience. "I'm sorry, Mrs. Marshall," he says gently. "But—"

"Leave her alone, Travis." Wrapped in his own foil blanket, Steve sags on the ambulance's tailgate beside me. The man's skin and the foil sheet are nearly the same shade of gray, his hair mussed, his lips thin. "We'll get a statement later."

The younger officer hesitates, but even though the other man is wrapped up like a soggy take-out burrito, his badge still says DETECTIVE across the top, and so the rookie closes his notebook. The officer nods, mutters something that sounds like *Yes, sir,* or maybe an apology, and steps aside.

Steve nods at me but doesn't speak, which is good, because my mouth is full of words that don't go together. What is there to say in this situation, anyway? *I'm sorry my crazy little sister drowned your wife at a school carnival.*

I look away when Hudson blinks.

Nothing. You say absolutely nothing.

The front doors to the school push open. Beside me, a noise like choking forces its way out of Steve's throat. Everything goes silent as paramedics wheel Rosa's body out of the school. Dark splotches mark where her wet costume has soaked through the blue cloth draped over the gurney, and water drips over the tray's metal edges, but otherwise the shape on the rolling aluminum slab is just a shape. Just a lump of lifeless flesh and not a wife and a mother. Not a woman drowned while cleaning up after a school carnival. Not a librarian who never forgets a face.

Rosa wasn't the nicest girl of the Mean Girl PTA, but she didn't deserve to die.

None of them *deserved* it—but hopefully they did learn something from it.

The gurney wheels touch metal as the paramedics slide Rosa's body into the ambulance parked in the drop-off lane, but I don't hear it. I don't hear the double back doors shut. I don't hear Steve stand, or the crinkle of his foil blanket as he walks away. I don't even know he's left the tailgate until I see him alone in the middle of the school's front lawn, watching what used to be his life pull out and silently drive away.

The younger officer is back.

He mutters something under his breath, and the slick black rectangle he slides into my hand lights up when he walks way. Familiar letters shine on the screen, but it takes me a minute to realize they spell out my darling husband's name. A dozen texts from Rob stream across my phone's screen, along with a hearty tally of missed calls.

Video calls, too. He's activated emergency protocol.

Now my cell phone has a signal.

Rob's name flashes an incoming call while I'm still staring at the phone I don't remember losing. Probably it fell out of my dress pocket while Kitty and I rolled around in the blood and the water. It's a wonder the thing didn't get broken, its glass shattered while my sister tried to cut me apart on the Brunswick cafeteria floor.

"What the hell is happening, Jill?" My husband's voice rushes across the line when the call connects. "Are you okay? Tell me you're okay," he says, relief only barely outweighing the panic in his tone.

"I'm okay."

I'm decidedly *not* okay, but I'll live.

"Tanner is fine," Rob says, and a mountain moves inside my chest. My knees rumble. The too-young cop said they were sending a car, but the only headlights approaching the school belong to ambulances. "That sweaty Lashett guy down the road called to say Tanner showed up on his doorstep—"

The phone slips in my hand, but I cram it back against my ear to hear the rest of what Rob has to say.

"Said his aunt made him walk home from Boogie Bash in the middle of the night while she stayed behind to clean up your mess?" Rob's voice beats against the line. "Tanner didn't have any keys and couldn't get in the house, so he walked down to the only neighbors he knew." My husband's tongue licks at his lips on the other end of the phone line.

He doesn't know what to do, this far away. I don't either, and I'm right here.

A pair of uniformed officers emerge from the wreckage of the school's gaping cardboard maw. Between them, Darla walks with her arms locked behind her back. She scans the scene outside: the leftover party decorations, the line of police cars, the small army of cops and medics. When her gaze lands on the one remaining ambulance—on which I sit huddled on the phone at its back—her face breaks into a smile. Her shoulder jerks like she tries to wave.

A goodbye wave, maybe? To match the hello she'd given through my front door when she'd brought over her shrink-wrapped gift basket and welcomed me to the neighborhood?

Don't invite any crazy, knife-wielding lunatics into your house, Kitty had said that morning.

Famous last words.

It's not ironic and absolutely *nothing* is funny, but a smirk twists my lips as the two officers lower Darla into a squad car, then shut the door to seal her in. My new neighbor is a lot of things, but none of them is psychic. Even if she did see things coming quickly enough to save my life in the end.

"Darla is the Dream Bean Killer, just like I said," I tell Rob. "But it turns out she's not nearly as crazy as my sister."

Rob gurgles something that might be my sister's name, might be a mash-up of every swear word he's ever heard. Whatever he says, it ends with "My command has cleared me to leave. I'm on the next flight home."

Now that is something to smile about. "I'll tell you everything when you get here."

Darla's eyes find me again, from the other side of the squad-car window. She smiles harder when an ABC7 news van careens around the corner. She doesn't blink when it pulls into the space Rosa's ambulance left in the drop-off lane.

I'm the first to look away. "Just get here," I say.

"I love you." Rob's voice is warm on the other end of the line. "If anything would have happened to you or Tanner . . ." There's a thickness in my darling husband's tone that means he's holding back tears. "I'm so sorry I didn't believe you."

"It's okay. I probably wouldn't have believed me either." A few clues strung together on an author's corkboard make for good detective fiction, but cracking a case requires a little more bloodshed, apparently. "And I love you, too."

In the drop-off lane, the overdressed reporter slips out of the news van, microphone in hand just like the morning she'd crashed the Dream Bean crime scene. The cameraman behind her sweeps the area: a still shot of the school, a lingering arc over the cops and medics, a quick glimpse of flashing blue and red. When his lens finds me swaddled in foil against the ambulance's back doors, his arm motions Power Suit in my direction, but the officer who gave me the blanket heads them off before they make it halfway across the lawn. Camera Guy keeps the lens fixed on me, though. Come tomorrow morning, my picture will be splashed all over the ABC7 home page.

Tragedy works wonders for book sales. Charlene will eat it up.

So will Darla.

The paramedic that comes back to check on me looks barely tall enough to reach the driver's-seat pedals, but his arms could rescue an entire family out of a burning building all on their own.

"They'll bring her out next," he says, about my sister. "Do you want to ride with her to the hospital?" The medic makes a face that shows this is his first time dealing with a vic who's also the next of kin. "There will be a police escort."

"I have to get to my son." The prospect of walking up Number Thirty-Four's driveway past the deadheaded mums to collect my son from a man whose wife is still smiling at me from the back seat of a cop car makes my gut churn—but probably somebody else will debrief Dave Lashett about Darla.

The medic does the same weight-shifting maneuver the young officer did, then nods at my ruined hands. "You'll still need stitches. We can't do them in the field. It's not sterile."

Headlights cast the medic in shadow as a beige town car glides to a stop alongside the curb. I have to blink away the blindness when the engine quits, and its headlights go dark. "They can wait," I think I say, about the stitches, but my feet are already moving toward the car, toward the opening back-seat door and the fuzzy-duckling head that emerges.

A few hours ago, my eight-year-old was too heavy to carry, but he's weightless against my chest when I scoop him up. The green kaiju costume presses cool against the soggy mess of my doll's dress. Somewhere between the ambulance and my son I lost the silver blanket, the blood-soaked yarn wig, even my cell phone. But who cares. I've got the entire world in my arms.

Tanner's feet kick against my shins. "I don't want Aunt Kitty to take me home anymore." The wiggly tone in his voice proves he's been crying. The brown ring around his lips, evidence that he's tried to self-soothe with chocolate. Puffy pink circles rim his eyes, and he wipes at them. "She left me all alone in the dark."

I bury my face into my son's hair, then cover his cheeks in kisses and whisper into his shoulder, "I've got you now." He'll never have to worry about being along in the dark. Not while I'm alive.

"What in the hell is going on around here?" Darla's husband heaves himself out of the driver's seat of the town car, then stops to catch his breath with his palms planted on the roof of his boring beige sedan. "Somebody have some kind of accident? Where's Darla?"

Dave huffs. The good doctor is going to have a rough night ahead of him.

Plastic scratches over my shoulder when I readjust Tanner on my hip. When I ask him what's in his hand, he holds up a fuse. "What is it?"

"It's a fuse," I tell him, like one from a car. From Dave's car, I realize. Darla must have used his car for her attacks, pulled the fuse to keep the lights off so she could sneak up on her victims. What was it she'd said back at the Dream Bean Café, about finding inspiration? And that day she'd come over to make me over, I'd told her I'd been waiting for the right spark to light the whole idea up. Here it is, right in the palm of my hand.

A sheen of fresh sweat shines on Dave's forehead as he looks from me to the school. When he looks back, his eyes clock the wound on my face. "That's gonna leave a scar."

Yeah, no kidding.

When he asks after his wife again, Steve Hudson's voice slides over my shoulder. I tuck the little plastic tooth into my pocket when Steve tells Dave they need to talk, and I sneak away before I hear more. This is not a conversation I want to be part of, not even as an eavesdropper.

Besides, the school doors have opened again between the construction-paper fangs. Too many bodies crowd around to see the person strapped down atop the metal gurney, but with Rosa's and Hart's bodies taken away, and Darla safely tucked in the back seat of a squad car, there's only one person left inside the school.

"Stay right here, okay?" It's like peeling off my own skin when I set my son on the grass, but Tanner doesn't need to see the bloodied woman on the gurney.

He doesn't, but I do.

Tanner gives me puppy-dog eyes, but I squeeze him and promise I'll be right back.

Kitty is five years, three months, and six days younger than me, but she looks too small under the white sheet when I make my way to the ambulance. A sheen of blood, sweat, and barrel water covers her from head to toe, but her face and arms have been wiped clean, Darla's makeshift tourniquets replaced with proper dressings until her injuries can be treated. Handcuffs pin her to the rails. She twitches when the gurney passes, then stops before being lifted into the waiting ambulance.

"Can I talk to her?" I ask the officer who'd given me my phone. He looks to his superior, and the gruff older man looks hard at me. When I don't turn away, he nods, shoots a meaningful look at the medics, and motions the others to give me some space.

"Make it fast," he says, and I have no idea if that's for my benefit or the paramedics'. Either way, I don't need long.

"Jill?" Kitty's eyes are open when I approach the gurney, but she squints in the glare of the ambulance's bright lights. Her voice is groggy, like she's just woken from a long nap, but that's probably from some sort of sedative, or maybe exhaustion, or simply blood loss, between the blade and the bludgeoning. "Jilly Bean, is that you?"

"I'm right here, Kitty-Kat." Cuffed to the guardrail, my sister's hand reaches for mine, but I stand just out of reach, watching as her fingertips pass a deep breath away from my dress. I don't want to touch her, but I do. I need to feel her warm skin, her beating pulse.

Kitty sighs when my fingers curl around hers. She blinks to adjust to the new light, and her eyes search my face, then drop to take in my ruined hands, the bit of gauze taped over my throat. When she looks at me again, she's no longer the crazed doll who'd pressed a knife into my skin, who'd sawed off one man's head and held a woman's underwater. She's not the beauty influencer, the free-spirited young woman posing for the perfect shot.

The bloody, broken doll strapped to the gurney might be a monster, but she's still my little sister, crying at the edge of our backyard pool while our mother dies, with no one in the world to keep her afloat but me.

A tear curls down Kitty's cheek, and I swallow down salt and fire. "What happens now?" she asks.

"You'll take care of me." I pull my hand away from hers, wipe a mess of tangled brown hair out of her eyes. "And I'll take care of you."

The paramedics clamp the edges of Kitty's gurney, and the officers oversee as she is lifted into the ambulance. By the time the doors shut behind her, Tanner is back in my arms.

It's over.

Stitches can wait. My car, still parked in the elementary school lot beside Darla's purple minivan, can wait. With my son held tight inside my arms, I turn away from the school and begin the short walk home—to the darkened windows of my downstairs office, to Lugosi's long golden tail, and to throw away the corkboard I no longer need.

"Look, Mom." Tanner snuggles into my shoulder and points up at the stars. "There's Orion. Just like on my ceiling."

Kitty's ambulance turns on its lights but keeps its sirens off, and I stare up at the constellations sparkling overhead as it pulls away. Here I am, at the end of my very own slasher story: a Final Girl in a bloody party dress, holding a happy ending in her arms, and staring up at the stars.

I guess Charlene's going to get her novel about dolls in space, after all.

ACKNOWLEDGMENTS

Years ago, when my family transferred to New Jersey, I found myself living in a creaky-not-creepy house much too large for three people, on an uppity suburban street much too posh for me to feel comfortable in, surrounded by elementary PTA wonder moms I was sure that I would *never* fit in with.

Luckily, I was wrong.

Those years became some of the best of my adult life, and those PTA wonder moms, some of my best friends. We pulled and pushed each other through our children's elementary years—through tantrums and milestones and birthday parties and potlucks. We TP'd each other's houses, kept each other's secrets, and helped raise each other's children. We boogied and we bashed, and we survived the jump scares and perils of female friendship.

Those four years might have lasted forever, but the plot twisted as it always does, and life moved on.

This book is for those women—for Rose, Kristin, Pilar, Inga, Caribel, Brooke, Lisa, and Marla—and for all the wonder women I am lucky enough to call friends.

Thank you to my agent, Italia Gandolfo, who sometimes snorts at my ideas, but listens anyway. To Christopher Brooks for making

Dollface come alive. To Joe Veltre and Hannah Vaughn at Gersh for believing in her.

To Alexandra Sehulster, Ashley Quintana, Sarah Melnyk, Allison Ziegler, and the entire team at Minotaur. To Amanda Rutter, Jess Lofton, and the Solaris team. To Dana Kaye, Jordan Brown, Julia Borcherts, Nicole Leimbach, Ellie Imbody, and the entire Kaye Publicity team. It's a special sort of magic to be surrounded by so many wonder women.

To Nat Cassidy, Clay McLeod Chapman, Delilah S. Dawson, Christopher Golden, Christina Henry, James "Murr" Murray, and Darren Wearmouth, for cheering this grisly glitter mess on.

To Nadia Hasan, for being my trusted reader and book wife.

To my mom, who hates Chapter Zero, and to my sister-in-spirit, Lisa, who has never drowned anything (that I'm aware of).

To Wake, who has outgrown his fuzzy duckling hair, but still lets me pinch his cheeks on special occasions.

To *Throb*, for makin' sure the dishes are *done*.

And to Finn, who's learned to answer to any silly name that I call him, because he's the very best boy.

ABOUT THE AUTHOR

Pete Vilotti

Lindy Ryan is an award-winning author and anthologist whose books have received starred reviews from *Publishers Weekly, Booklist,* and *Library Journal.* She also writes seasonal romance as Lindy Miller, with several projects adapted for the screen. Author-in-residence at *Rue Morgue* and a columnist at *BookTrib,* Ryan was a *Publishers Weekly* Star Watch Honoree in 2020 and has been declared a "champion for women's voices in horror" and one of horror's most masterful anthology curators. She is an award-winning professor at Rutgers University, and a guest faculty mentor in Western Connecticut State University's Creative Writing MFA program. Learn more about Lindy at www.LindyRyanWrites.com.